Crossed Reins

by

Graysen Morgen

2021

Crossed Reins © 2021 Graysen Morgen
Triplicity Publishing, LLC

ISBN-13: 978-1-970042-13-9
ISBN-10: 1-970042-13-3

This is a work of fiction. Names, characters, places, and incidents are the product of the author's imagination and are used fictitiously. Any resemblance to actual persons, living or dead, business establishments, events of any kind, or locales is entirely coincidental.

Printed in the United States of America
First Edition – 2021
Cover Design: Triplicity Publishing, LLC
Interior Design: Triplicity Publishing, LLC
Editor: Megan Brady - Triplicity Publishing, LLC

Also by Graysen Morgen

Special thanks to my editor, Megan Brady.
Muchas gracias!

For my wife.
Siempre te quiero.

ONE

Tens of thousands of people were elbow to elbow, packing the grandstands, bars, and club suites of Santa Rosa Race Park. Hundreds more stood in various lines, money and credit cards in one hand and their top picks in the other, each silently hoping he or she had the winning horse or trifecta trio. The grand marshal blew the bugle horn for the ten-minute warning, meaning the betting windows would soon be closing. The jockeyed horses slowly made their way from the stables onto the track, showing off the color and design of their one of a kind silks as they were paraded in a line past the east end of the clubhouse before making a u-turn and heading out to the starting gate for the running of the Chardonnay Derby, a high stakes thoroughbred race.

"Look, Carly Rae! There's Tibby!" a man who looked strikingly similar to George W. Bush said, nudging the young woman next to him.

She grinned and tucked a strand of her short, buttery blonde hair behind her ear. "Daddy, I see him." Her heart pounded a little harder in her chest as her best friend since she could walk, trotted past on a large, plain brown colored colt named *Magic Hat.* Both the jockey and the horse were wearing hot pink and purple silks with the number five on them. *They definitely got his colors right,* she thought, waving despite knowing he couldn't see her in the sea of people.

"Oh, I hope he wins!" her father said. "I put a hundred bucks on him. Don't tell your mama."

She shook her head and laughed. She knew George Tibbetts, Jr. like the back of her hand. They'd grown up together on her parent's cattle ranch up in Wyoming. Tibby, as most everyone called him, was the son of the ranch foreman who had worked for her father for thirty years. He'd already had a handful of mildly successful races as a jockey, but this was only the third race for the horse. So far, neither of them had finished better than fourth together. She hadn't had the heart to tell her father he'd wasted his money. She'd been a little more realistic, betting on him to place or show, and only twenty bucks at that. He was a long shot at 20:1 odds.

Anticipation buzzed all around as the horses were led into the starting gates. Carly Rae and her father jumped to their feet along with everyone else. The pistol pop that started the race was silenced by the roar of the crowd. Everything seemed to happened in slow motion as the gates burst open and the massive horses shot out like rockets. Carly Rae missed Tibby because her eyes were drawn to a horse in blue and white checkered silks, named *Sir Rigsby*. He was dark bay colored with nearly black legs and not a single speck of white. She remembered seeing him trot by with the number seven on his side. He'd seemed completely unfazed by the noise of the crowd, and his handler and jockey both had difficulty directing him.

Now, as she watched the start, she knew something awful had happened. When that horses gate burst open, he didn't take off like the others. He was much more timid and wound up throwing his jockey. Several track employees rushed to help the jockey while a nearby handler grabbed the horse, who was muddling about like he had no clue what was going on.

"He finished third!" her father yelled. "Damn."

"What?" Carly Rae looked up at the screen in the center of the track. The top four finishers were listed. "Sweet!"

"Don't tell me you won money on that," her father chuckled.

"Of course, I did." She grinned. "Did you see that horse throw the jockey? Number seven, I think."

"No. I missed it," he replied as they began exiting with the rest of the crowd.

"I'm going to go see Tibby. He's probably back at the stable by now. I'll catch up with you outside."

"Don't be too long. I'll find George. We need to get to the airport. You know how much I hate flying," he sighed.

"I know, but you're glad you came, right?"

"Sure. I wouldn't have turned down the invite. Tibby and George are family. Besides, I got to see you." He smiled.

She stood on her tip toes to kiss his cheek.

"You have a long drive," he said, checking his watch.

"I'm staying in Reno tonight. Everything is all packed and ready. I'll get Firefly loaded up and head out in the morning."

"It's going to take you two and half days to get home."

"Nah. It's about thirteen hours from there. I'll be home in a day and a half. I've done it many times."

He shook his head at his only child as she walked away.

*

"I don't know what to tell you. That goddamn horse won't listen to anyone!" a man growled.

Carly Rae turned her head to see two men, one in jeans and the other impeccably dressed in a three-piece suit. They were standing outside of the stable door for horse seven, *Sir Rigsby*.

"What's going on?" she asked, giving Tibby a hug.

"I don't know. They've been arguing for a few minutes."

Carly Rae watched the horse with his head poked out of the open upper half of the stall door, completely unaffected by their raised voices. Several other horses were starting to become restless.

"Great race, by the way. I won sixty-five bucks off you."

He laughed. "Magic took off too fast on me and burned out. I think we could've at least finished second."

She felt bad. She'd missed the entire race. "You know that horse threw his jockey, right? It was like he could care less when the gate opened."

"Weird," he mumbled, turning to watch the confrontation.

"You're fired! And take your shitty jockey with you too!" the well-dressed man shouted.

"That piece of shit horse is a joke! Good luck loser!" the other guy yelled back as he walked away.

"You're about to be for sale," the well-dressed man grumbled in the horse's direction.

"Looks like the owner just fired his trainer and jockey," Tibby whispered.

"Yeah. Something isn't right." She kept watching the horse. Suddenly, she grabbed Magic Hat's empty metal oat pail and slammed it against the door of the open stall next to him. All of the horses began to whinny and rustle around...all except Sir Rigsby. Even his owner was startled enough to jump off the ground. "I'll be damned," she whispered and set the bucket down.

"What the hell did you do that for?" the man in the suit said as she stepped closer. He was tall and broad with beady brown eyes and a square jaw. His neatly trimmed hair was dark and thick, but his mustache and goatee were salt and pepper colored.

"I know what to do with that horse," she said.

"Huh?"

"Your horse."

"You want to buy him?" he asked.

"What? No. Train him."

"Train him?" He shook his head. "Young lady, I have no idea what you're getting at. Who are you, anyway?"

"I'm sorry." She stuck her hand out. "Carly Rae Walsh."

He chewed the side of his cheek, wishing he had a cigar as he perused her. She was country girl cute, dressed in Wrangler blue jeans, brown, square-toed boots, and a peach colored, V-neck shirt that hugged her slender frame. Her short blonde hair was parted on the side and barely long enough to tuck behind her ears. The ends sort of flipped up in the back just above her collar. Striking baby blue eyes bore into him and a playful smile spread across her face as she waited with her hand out. She looked young, way too young to buy a race horse.

"Where did you say you were from?" he asked, returning the firm grip of her handshake.

"I didn't. Mister..."

"McKinley. Harris McKinley."

"Mr. McKinley, what I am trying to say to you is, your horse can be trained, and he can be trained to win. I know what to do with him."

"What did you say your name was? Carly something? I've never heard of you. Are you a trainer?"

"Carly Rae Walsh," she repeated. "I've trained many horses. I'm actually a professional barrel racer. I've won a few championships. My point is, I know what to do with your horse."

"What makes you so sure? I wasted a lot of money on the trainer I just fired and he was highly recommended by the man who sold me the horse. The jockey was supposed to be great, too."

"Do you know your horse is hearing impaired?" she said, crossing her arms.

"What?"

"Deaf. He can't hear anything. That's why he is having such a hard time. It's not his fault."

Mr. McKinley's eyebrows rose.

"That's why I slammed the bucket. I watched him move before the race. I could tell he was different. He threw the jockey because he has no idea what is going on around him. I'm sure that fancy trainer you just fired had no idea. He probably spent hours whipping him instead of teaching him to use his other senses."

"You got all of this just by watching him?"

"Yes, sir. I've spent my entire life on a horse. My father…who is probably impatiently waiting on me at the moment, owns a cattle ranch. I've been riding horses and moving cattle since I was big enough to ride a pony. I've been barrel racing for the past twelve years. I'm quite good at it. Anyway, I have three months free in my schedule. The next big race here is the Golden Stakes. I can have your horse ready by then."

"You really think you can train a deaf horse to be a derby winner?"

"Why not?"

He shrugged, knowing at this point he really had no other choice. It was that or sell the horse he'd bought as an investment to hopefully make some money. If he sold it, he'd certainly be losing money.

"Where do you live? My horse was kept with the previous trainer, but I'm moving him to my stable in Sonoma."

"Reno at the moment. I am usually touring with the barrel racing circuit, but like I said, I'm free for the next three months. I was actually heading back to my family's ranch in Wyoming in the morning."

He nodded...sighing lightly as he thought for a moment. "I have a small guest house on the property. You can stay there rent and utility free. I've spent enough money on this damn horse as it is, but I'll pay you $1000 a month. If he wins, you get a ten percent cut. If he doesn't, you're fired and he's out of here."

"I can work with that. I'll need to stable my barrel horse and train with her as well...in my spare time, of course."

"Our stable has plenty of open stalls. We have a covered and open arena. You can use the open arena all you want. We probably have barrels you can use. Just stay away from the covered arena. My daughter is a classically trained, world champion dressage rider and that is her training area."

Carly Rae nodded. "We have a deal." She held her hand out.

"Three months. You promise Sir Rigsby will be ready?"

"He'll be more than ready."

Mr. McKinley shook her hand. "I hope you're right," he mumbled. "I'm putting a lot of trust in you."

"I know that. You should probably know I'm not barrel racing for the next three months because I was suspended by the racing federation."

"What for?"

"Another competitor tried to kill my horse and we got into an altercation. What she did was proven. She was banned for life, but because I got into a physical fight with her and spent the night in jail, I was suspended for six months. I'm halfway through my suspension. I don't regret what I did. My horse is my life. I'd do it all over again."

"I understand. Thank you for telling me." He reached into his pocket and pulled out a business card. "Here is the address to our property and my phone number. How soon can you be there?"

"Tomorrow."

"Great. We'll get you set up in the guest house and put on the payroll. We have a stable hand named Ollie. He feeds the horses, mucks the stalls, and pretty much does everything else as well. I'm sure you have your way of doing things. Just show him what you want and how you want it. He's a good worker. Also, Arthur Wallace is my daughter's trainer. You may see him around. They work together two or three times a week."

"Sounds good. I should be there around lunchtime tomorrow."

He nodded and walked away.

"Um…what the hell was that?" Tibby asked.

"I got a job. Long story. I need to get moving. Our fathers have a flight to catch, and I need to get back to Reno. I'll call you." She hugged him quickly and took off running towards the parking lot.

TWO

"I don't see why you keep wasting your time with that horse," Allison McKinley grumbled, eyeing her father as she dismounted her large dapple grey mare. "And why does this new trainer have to live here? The last trainer kept the horse at his stable."

A young man appeared, taking the reins from her and walking her horse towards the stable. "Give her a couple of treats from the red bag in the feed room, please, Ollie," she said, removing her riding helmet and turning her attention back to her father.

"She doesn't live in the state," he replied, lighting a cigar.

"I thought you were quitting," she scolded.

He shrugged. "There's more. Her horse will be stabled here too, and she has free rein of the property…except the covered arena." He watched his daughter's face distort as her mind raced. "She's a barrel racer, so in her off time, she'll be training in the open arena."

"Great." She gritted her teeth. She and her horse didn't need any distractions. *He hired a country bumpkin rodeo queen to train his thoroughbred. He's lost his damn mind.*

"She's here," he said, seeing his phone ringing to allow someone through the front gate of the property.

"Wonderful," she muttered and walked away. Her horse needed to be brushed and fed.

"Give her a chance, Allison. I need this horse to win," he called to her back.

*

Carly Rae had no idea what to expect. Her father had given her one of his fatherly wisdom speeches on the way back to Reno, mostly telling her she could do anything she put her mind to, while reiterating the fact that training a thoroughbred was going to be the hardest thing she had ever done. He'd never tell her what to do, only offer advice. Her mistakes were hers to make, and she rarely made them.

"Here we go," she said to the empty cab as she put the truck in drive and waited for the gates to swing open. She followed the road that wound around towards what appeared to be the stable and work area, with the opposite way leading towards a large, two-story house.

She turned down the blues song blasting on the stereo and pulled to a stop, killing the engine when she saw Harris McKinley wave. He was walking towards her, dressed in pressed jeans and a black button shirt under a black blazer. Brown leather shoes matched his brown belt. A thin line of smoke rose from the cigar in his right hand.

"Mr. McKinley," she said, getting out the truck and holding her hand out to him. She was dressed in jeans, boots, and a white tank top that hugged her upper body.

"How was the drive?" he asked.

"Fine. I'm sure Firefly is ready to get out, stretch her legs, and eat a little hay, though."

"Take a walk with me first. I'll show you around."

The stench of his cigar wafted in the air, making her stomach roll. Nevertheless, Carly Rae fell in step as he pointed out the white stable building with green trim, in

11

front of them. Next to it on the right were the side by side arenas; one was completely open and the other was covered with a tin roof. Two turnout pastures were on the other side of the covered arena and adjacent to the stable, and a large pond sat about twenty-five yards away on the opposite side of the stable.

"Let's head inside," he said, snubbing out his cigar before ushering her into the stable. "The hay barn is on the back of the building. The tack room and feed rooms are here on the right, the stalls are in the back past the wash and brush area. We have eight of them. Sir Rigsby is on one end and my daughter's horse, Luna Mist, is on the other end and the opposite side. Feel free to choose whatever one you want, but please be courteous to my daughter. She prefers to have the stalls around her horse empty."

"Sure." Carly Rae nodded.

"Speaking of my daughter…" he said as a woman walked out of a stall wearing tan jodhpur riding pants, a black short sleeved shirt, and black knee-high riding boots. A chestnut colored braid hung down past her shoulders. She turned milk chocolate brown eyes in their direction as she closed the gate of the stall. "Allison, I'd like you to meet Carly Rae Walsh."

"Hi," Carly Rae said, extending her hand.

The woman standing in front of Allison looked every bit the part of a country girl with Wrangler jeans, square toed western boots, and a shiny buckle on her leather belt. The only thing missing was a cowboy hat which she probably had somewhere. Her naturally bright blonde hair and grinning smile made her look young…too young to be a horse trainer. Allison avoided the big blue eyes staring back at her.

"Nice to meet you. That's Luna Mist in the stall back there. I'd appreciate it if you would avoid startling her," she said. "Father," she added, kissing his cheek before walking out of the stable.

"She's not as cross as she seems. Her mother, my late wife, was French, but raised in the United Kingdom. Allison attended boarding school there. That's where she learned to ride dressage. She's every bit of her mother from tip to toe." He smiled. "I just wish she'd ease up a little. Dressage is her entire life," he sighed.

"I understand passion for something. Barrel racing is very much my life as well."

"Yes." He nodded in agreement. "Anyhow, the guest house is up a little closer to the main house, just around the corner," he continued as they walked back outside. "Ollie!" he called, relighting his cigar.

A young man came out of the covered arena where he'd been re-grading the dirt with the tractor a few minutes earlier.

"This is Carly Rae. She's Sir Rigsby's new trainer. Anything she says, goes. She has a barrel racing horse that will be stabled here, and the open arena is hers to do as she pleases. Also, she will be staying in the guest house, so please get her the key as soon as possible so she can get settled in."

"Yes, sir," he said, sticking his hand out to her.

Carly Rae smiled and shook back. "I'm sure we'll get to know each other well."

"Yes, ma'am."

"You don't have to call me ma'am. Carly Rae will be fine."

"Got it. Let me go get you that key. It's in the stable office."

"Well, I'll leave you to it. Ollie can go over everything on Sir Rigsby with you. Let me know if you have any questions. I'm usually around or up at the main house."

"Thank you," she said. As soon as he walked away, she turned back towards the barn and Ollie appeared with a key ring that had two keys dangling from it.

"One is for the guest house. The other is for the stable," he informed.

"Great. If you wouldn't mind giving me a hand, I have a mare that I need to get out of that trailer and into a stall. I'm sure she's tired, hungry, and as excited as I am to check out her new home for the next three months."

"Sure." He smiled, walking alongside her. "This is a nice rig you have here."

Carly Rae pulled the back door of the trailer down, revealing the chestnut colored palomino horse. She had a black muzzle and an interrupted white stripe on her face. All four of her legs had white socks, and her mane and tail were as light, buttery blonde as her owner's hair. Seeing Carly Rae made her neigh with excitement.

"Hey girl. It's time to go get settled," Carly Rae soothed, patting her side and her neck as she stepped inside and removed the reins from the bar they were tied to. "Come on," she said, clicking her teeth.

The horse began backing out of the trailer into the sunlight.

"She's gorgeous!" Ollie exclaimed.

"Thank you." Carly Rae smiled a row of perfect, white teeth. "Firefly, this is Ollie. He'll be nice to you, if you're nice to him," she said. "This is my girl, Firefly. We've won two pro rodeo barrel racing championships together."

"Wow. That's amazing," he replied, patting her neck and letting her sniff his hand to get used to him.

"She's very gentle, but will bite if you mistreat her."

"Good to know. And don't worry, Firefly. I'm gentle, too."

"Come on, girl. Let's go pick out a stall," Carly Rae said, tugging her reins slightly to get her moving as she led her inside the stable.

"I'd recommend this one on the end across from Sir Rigsby. Ms. Allison keeps Luna Mist on the other end. She's not too keen on anything being around her."

"So, I've heard. This stall should be fine." Carly Rae opened the door and led the horse inside.

"If you turn that nozzle down there, the trough will fill up with spring water. Does she eat a special diet like Luna Mist and Sir Rigsby?"

"Yes. I have a couple of 50lb bags of her feed mix in the trailer. She also gets alfalfa hay as a treat," she said as she turned on the water and removed her bridle. "Here you go, girl. This is your home…for a few months anyhow."

"I'll go get her food stored in the feed room. Would you like me to give her a pail now? Tomorrow is my order day, so I will add her food to the list. Let me know if there is anything else you need to put on there."

"Ollie, you don't have to do all of that. I can take care of her."

"It's not a problem, Ms. Carly Rae. I'm the stable hand, so it actually *is* my job."

"It's just Carly Rae. There's nothing formal about me." She smiled.

He nodded.

"Well, if you don't mind doing your job, I guess I'll go find this guest house and get settled in."

"You can see the main house from here. The guest house is just off to the left. You can't miss it. You can drop your trailer out where the other trailers are kept. There's a gravel parking space out front of the guest house for your truck. It's one of those tiny houses, so there's no garage or anything, but it's pretty spacious. Mr. Harris had it completely remodeled just last year. Everything is brand new. It has all of the furniture and pots and pans and stuff."

"Sounds good. Let me know if you have any trouble out of her. I'll come out later and check on her."

"I'm sure she will be fine. I'm here from six to five Monday through Friday. I feed the horses breakfast, lunch, and dinner, and turn them out while I muck the stalls. I also wash and brush them. I can tack them up if you need me to as well. I also drag the arenas once they are closed for the day. Let me know if there is anything you need done."

"As a matter of fact, I need three barrels for the open arena. If you tell me where I can find them, I'll get them myself."

"We usually have some. I'll look around for you."

"Thanks. I'm not in any rush, but I'd like to have it set up by the end of the week," she said, patting Firefly's head.

THREE

The guesthouse was unlike anything Carly Rae had ever seen. It was a rust brown colored rectangle with an A-frame roof, similar to a large shed or garage. The front door was blue and the windows had white trim. An open concrete porch ran the length of it, surrounded by a three-foot tall, dog ear picket fence, painted the same color brown as the siding. Two blue Adirondack chairs were together near the door.

The upside-down L-shaped kitchen was the first thing she saw when she stepped inside. White marble countertops had blue cabinets underneath and a matching, small square island was in the middle. Drawers were on one side of the island and two bar stools were adjacent to each other on the opposite side. Brown floating shelves were along the wall above the counter top, over the stove and in the corner, holding the dishes and glassware, and pots and pans hung in the opening in the middle. All of the major appliances were stainless, but a white coffee pot and microwave blended into the corner of the otherwise bare counter. A window above the sink looked out over the property.

To the right of the kitchen, just passed the island, sat a chocolate colored suede couch with a chaise on one end, and a small coffee table. All of the walls in the house were white shiplap and the open beams were the same brown color as the kitchen shelves. Two large horse pictures hung on the wall, flanking the window over the couch.

The tightly-spaced bathroom, just on the other side of the kitchen wall, had a standard tub and shower combo with a glass door, a small cabinet with a ceramic bowl on top for the sink, and a compact toilet. Next to that room was a bi-fold door that hid the apartment style, over/under washer and dryer combo.

The end of the short hallway opened to the bedroom. A full-size bed was in the middle, with floating nightstands in the wall on either side, and a low-profile dresser along the opposite wall. The black furniture and shelving contrasted nicely against the white shiplap walls and bedding set. A flat screen TV hung on the wall next to the door of the small walk-in closet.

Carly Rae spent most of the barrel racing season living out of her horse trailer or the apartment she rented in Reno near the stable where she kept her horse, so she was used to small spaces and had always packed lightly. It had taken her less than thirty minutes to unpack and get situated in her new living space.

*

It was dark by the time Carly Rae made her way back out to the stable. A nightlight system stayed on to keep it from being pitch black inside, and each stall had a switch for its own overhead light as well. She wasn't completely familiar with her surroundings, so she flipped on half of the overhead lights, leaving the lights over the stalls off, before quietly opening the door to Firefly's stall and slipping inside.

"What do you think of your new home, girl? Have you met your neighbors?" she asked, petting the horse's neck in long strokes. "I know it's not permanent, but three months is a lot longer than anywhere else." She reached back, pulling half of a fresh carrot from her back pocket. "Don't tell the others," she whispered, holding it while Firefly chomped down. "I think you're going to like it here," she continued. "I have a big job ahead of me and I'm going to need your help."

When the large mare finished the carrot, Carly Rae shoved that hand into her front pocket and used the other to pet her face as she yawned. "It's been a long day for both of us. I'll see you in the morning," she said before walking out and closing the door.

*

"Half of the lights are on in the stable," Allison said when she walked into her father's home office. The entire room was the color of an aged whiskey barrel, except for the antique crème colored, leather chairs across from the desk, and the black wingback chair her father was sitting in. The upper half of an entire wall had a built-in bookcase full of books, with large drawers filling the bottom half and a marble fireplace situated in the center.

She padded barefoot over the thick area rug and leaned against the corner of one of the floor-to-ceiling windows behind the chairs, crossing her arms as she looked out at the property. Her eyes scanned over the heavy-duty Ford truck parked at the guest house, and focused on the stable a hundred yards away.

"It's probably the new trainer," he replied, chewing on his barely lit cigar as he perused the estate's financials for the month.

"It's nine o'clock at night. What could she possibly be in there doing?" she grumbled.

"Checking on her horse, I assume."

She sighed. "I forgot she had a horse. I hope she didn't put him anywhere near Luna Mist."

"Your precious Luna will be fine," he said as he snubbed out the remainder of his cigar in the nearby ashtray and looked up to see her staring back at him. "I told her the nearby stalls were off limits."

She nodded.

"Give her a chance. She's very nice and seems to know a lot about horses."

"She's a rodeo clown," she muttered.

"You are most definitely your mother's daughter," he sighed, getting up from the desk. "Come on. It's time for me to call it a night."

She met him in the middle of the room and walked out arm in arm at his side. "If I'm so much like her, why I can't I get through to you like she could?"

He stopped walking. "What do you mean?"

"The cigars. I harp on you constantly about quitting, yet you still light up. If it were her nagging, you would've stopped the next day."

"I think she knew I smoked them, or at least had to smell it on me once in a while. I hid it mostly."

"Then, why do it in front of me?"

He shrugged. "You're right. I'll stop smoking in front of you. I apologize."

"Father…that's not the point. I want you to completely quit. I've already lost one parent. Do you think I want to bury you, too? I'm only twenty-four. I'd like to have you around for many more years."

He smiled. "You're right. See, you *are* just like her."

She kissed his cheek. "I'm going up to bed. Goodnight."

"Goodnight, and don't worry about the new trainer. I think you could be friends."

She ignored his last comment as she made her way up the half spiral staircase with wrought iron rails on both sides. She'd been living back at home for just over two years after finishing up at college. It had been a little over a year since her mother passed suddenly from a heart condition she never knew she'd had. Allison and her mother, Colette, were the epitome of twins from their looks down to their stalwart personalities.

FOUR

Carly Rae walked into the stable at five after seven, carrying a steaming cup of coffee. She was dressed in Wrangler jeans, the same brown, square toed boots from the day before, and a white button-down shirt with blue stripes in a plaid pattern. It was neatly tucked into her jeans with a thick, brown leather belt and shiny buckle. The first three buttons were open, revealing the dark blue tank top underneath.

"You've definitely spent some time around the rodeo," Ollie said.

"I grew up on a ranch, roping steer and driving cattle before I was ten."

"Wow. I had no idea you were a real-life cowgirl." He looked at her in awe.

She smiled and walked over to Firefly's open door. "Did she have any loose stool last night?"

"Nope. Everything was fine. She seems pretty comfortable. She trotted around when I turned her out," he replied as he walked down to Luna Mist's door and swung it open.

Carly Rae raised her brow and looked around.

"Ms. Allison is out in the arena. She has Luna Mist training by six a.m., and then again after lunch."

"Every day?"

"Monday through Friday," he called over his shoulder as he began putting down fresh hay for the floor."

She peeked in at Sir Rigsby who was munching alfalfa from the net on the door, oblivious to the woman watching him. "Ollie," she called.

He walked out of Luna Mist's stall with the wheelbarrow and headed towards her to replace Firefly's floor. "Yes, ma'…um, Carly Rae."

"No one is to handle Sir Rigsby except me. I don't mind you turning out Firefly. Like I said, she's a good horse. You can put food in his pail, but don't mess with him otherwise."

"Okay." He nodded suspiciously. Even the prized Luna Mist didn't have guidelines that strict.

"He's deaf. I have to train him to understand my commands, and to do so, he has to rely solely on me. I'm pretty sure the last trainer had no idea and was using force to handle him."

Ollie put both of his hands on top of the hay fork handle and rested his chin on them. "Are you serious? I've near heard of a deaf horse."

"Most of them are overo paint horses. It has something to do with their genetics. Nearly all of them have blue eyes as well. I had a paint pony who was partially deaf when I was a kid. Her name was Matilda. Anyway, that's how I learned about it."

"That's awesome."

"Yeah. So, I just wanted to make sure no one bothered with him. Also, can you give me a list of his food and snacks when you get a chance? I know you said today was your order day. I may need to make some changes to his diet or at least tweak it a little."

"Sure. I'll get it to you after I finish Firefly's stall. I have to have the order in by nine."

Carly Rae nodded, sipping her coffee as she walked out of the stable towards the arenas. She saw movement in the covered arena out the corner of her eye, but her gaze fixated on the three meticulously placed barrels in the open arena. *Holy shit.* She went back inside, but Ollie had disappeared, having finished Firefly's stall. She headed back outside, walking past the arenas to the turn out circles where Firefly was busy grazing.

"Hey, girl," she said, clicking her teeth as she climbed up on the fence to sit on the top rail. Firefly lifted her head and meandered over to her. "Not bad, huh?" Carly Rae smiled, petting her head. "No," she chided, pulling her mug away when the horse tried to take a sniff. "Did you see what Ollie found for us? You need to be super nice to him, you hear me?" she continued, petting her neck in long strokes. "I'll tell him to leave you out here a little longer, but don't eat too much grass. It gives you gas," she added, hopping down off the rail. "We'll go for a ride later, okay?"

Her attention turned to the covered arena again as she walked back by. Allison McKinley was dressed similar to the day before in her tight jodhpurs, form fitting shirt, and knee-high riding boots. The large dapple gray under her spun around in a perfect pirouette. Carly Rae found it mesmerizing watching the rider and the horse worked together as one, performing their routine.

"She's something...isn't she?" Harris McKinley muttered, walking up beside her, impeccably dressed as usual. If it weren't for Ollie and his worn jeans and old boots, she'd feel extremely underdressed around the McKinley's.

"Uh... yeah. Yes. What breed of horse is that?"

"She's a Lusitano. Meaning a very expensive, pure blood sport horse from Portugal," he said with a half smile.

"Well, I don't know much about dressage, but they seem to make it look easy."

He laughed. "If you call long hours of training and serious discipline…easy, I can't wait to see what you do with Sir Rigsby. How is he, by the way?"

She sipped the last of her coffee. "He seems to have settled in okay. I'm going to go introduce myself here in a minute."

He nodded.

"Getting him to trust me is the first step. He has to learn how we communicate with each other. It's not going to happen overnight. It may take a couple of weeks. It all depends on him and how he takes to me. I don't believe in whip training a horse at all, so he will have no reason to fear me."

"It sounds like you have a plan."

"Were you doubting your decision?" she asked.

"Could you blame me?"

"No, sir. You don't know me from Adam. I'd second guess myself too, but I'd give you a chance to prove me wrong."

"Exactly." He smiled. "I like your tenacity."

She laughed. "My dad calls it my stubborn streak and says it's a mile wide."

"I'm pretty sure my daughter has you beat. I'm afraid she's relentlessly persistent, but very reserved. I hope you get to know her while you're here. She could use a friend."

Carly Rae nodded.

"I noticed Ollie found you some barrels," he said, changing the subject.

"Yes, he must have done it this morning."

"He's a very hard worker and a great stable hand. He has worked here for close to ten years. He took care of my wife's horses, as well as Allison's when she was home from boarding school, and then college after that. He and his wife have a four-year old son, Oliver Jr., who has down syndrome. We gave him a pony last year for his birthday. It is trained to work with special needs children and specifically, down syndrome. They live about thirty minutes away and have a couple of acres with an old barn."

"I bet he loves to ride on him."

"Oh, yeah. Ollie takes him out for a ride just about every night." He smiled.

Carly Rae saw Allison break from her training and begin walking the horse in their direction. "I should probably get to work," she said, leaving before she had to speak to his uptight daughter.

*

"That piaffe looked very good," Harris said.

"It's getting better. She's still moving to the left," she replied. "Something didn't sit well with me, so I looked her up last night. Do you know why she's here?" she said, nodding towards the retreating woman.

"Of course. She's training Sir Rigsby."

Allison raised a brow. "I mean—"

"I know what you meant," he said seriously. "Her business is just that...*her* business."

"So, you invited a felon to come live on our property?"

"Allison..." He shook his head. "I'm only going to say this once. You have to stop being so judgmental. It wasn't a great trait of your mother's, and it certainly doesn't look good on you either. Carly Rae and I discussed everything. I'm fine with the person I hired. Maybe if you got to know her, she'd tell you what happened, instead of you believing everything you read online." He walked away before she could say anything else.

*

"Hi," Carly Rae said, walking up to Sir Rigsby's stall. The door was closed, but his long, dark bay colored head was sticking out over the top. She rolled her sleeves to her elbows and stuck her open palm out, allowing him to sniff the strawberries she was offering, as well as her scent. "It's okay," she whispered, looking him in the eyes. *Come on, boy. I won't hurt you.*

The horse neighed, then bent down, sniffing the air around her hand and the bare flesh of her arm several times more before finally taking the fruit from her palm. She petted the side of his neck with a heavy hand as he chewed, showing him her strength and confidence. As soon as he finished, he began sniffing around for more treats. She kept her arms out for him to sniff before reaching into the container she'd brought with her and holding her hand out with strawberries again. Sir Rigsby hesitated for a second, but she pet him once more with her free hand to let him know it was okay. He leaned down and ate the fruit. She continued the same gesture over and over, petting his neck to let him know it was okay each time, while simultaneously letting him associate her scent with kindness. *I hope it doesn't take too long for you to trust me. I can't wait to ride you.*

When Carly Rae had finally run out of strawberries, she pet Sir Rigsby's face, avoiding his ears…as he sniffed as much of her as he could. She was completely unaware of the woman staring from afar while brushing down her horse, until Ollie walked in with Firefly on the lead. Carly Rae's eyes met Allison's. Even with the distance between them she could feel the negative energy from the other woman.

"Just tie her up over there," Carly Rae said. "I'm about to take her out for a ride."

"Sure. Would you like me to tack her up for you?"

"Nah. I've got it. Thanks."

"I'm not sure how much you let her graze, but—"

Carly Rae laughed. "I know, it gives her gas."

"Yeah," he chuckled, making a gesture to fan his nose. "Wow."

"The vet said it was fine, but I limit her to only a couple of hours a day. I ride her every day anyway, so she gets a lot of exercise."

He nodded. "Ms. Allison, would you like me to drag the arena again before your afternoon ride?"

"No. That won't be necessary," she replied, pulling her eyes from the gregarious blond.

"How is Sir Rigsby doing?" Ollie asked when Carly Rae left his stall and walked over to where the tack room was located.

"So far, so good. I'm sure it'll take more than strawberries to gain his trust. I'm hoping to be able to ride him by the end of the week at the latest," she answered, before he left the stable. "I hope you didn't mind me watching this morning. I hadn't intended to, but your father called me over," she said in Allison's direction as she passed by her.

"It's fine. I'm used to large crowds. I've learned to ignore my surroundings," Allison answered as she continued brushing her horse.

"She's stunning," Carly Rae said, referring to the horse.

"Yes, thank you," Allison replied, watching her throw a riding blanket and saddle onto Firefly's back. Then, she replaced the lead halter with a bitless bridle that had a closed rein. *Is her hair and the horse's mane the same shade of blond?* She continued brushing Luna Mist, but kept her eyes on Carly Rae as she tightened everything down before grabbing the rein and walking her out of the stable.

Once she was outside, Carly Rae climbed up onto the horses back, sliding her butt into the saddle in one fluid motion, then she clicked her teeth and squeezed the horse slightly with her legs to get it walking.

*

The ride around the McKinley Estate was beautiful. The ten acres were surrounded by vineyards, with Sugarloaf Mountain in the distance. The few acres around the main house and stable had no trees, except for a cluster of oaks next to the pond. However, the remainder of the property was lush with trees. Carly Rae had ridden Firefly all the way to the far edge and back. She'd needed the exercise after having been pent up for the last few days at the stable in Reno, then in the trailer for the drive over to Sonoma.

Allison had disappeared, more than likely into the main house, and Ollie was busy with work when she'd returned. She brushed Firefly down, and put her back in the stall. There'd been no need to turn her out since they'd stopped a few times to allow her to rest and graze on the tall green grass.

Carly Rae went directly to Sir Rigsby as soon as she'd finished. She wanted him to know her scent, but also Firefly's because she would be using her to help with the training as it progressed. She needed him to be comfortable with both of them.

"I think I'm going to call you Rigs. I hope you don't mind," she mumbled to the deaf horse. He sniffed her arm, then her hand, looking for treats. She shook her head no. "I'm not coming over here with treats every time, mister. You'll be too fat to run to the end of the stable, much less around a large track." She continued petting him over and over until he'd seemingly had enough and pulled away to munch on his hay. She'd spent a good amount of time touching him and letting him get to know her, which was the first step.

*

The afternoon sun brought the temperature up just over eighty. Carly Rae had removed her button-down shirt, opting for just the tank top underneath as she wrestled the three barrels into place in the open arena. She measured and adjusted several times, making sure everything was perfect, before calling it a day.

The hot water from the shower soothed muscles she hadn't used in a while, causing her to stand under the spray until it turned cold. Once she was dressed, she tossed her dinner in the microwave and plopped down on the couch. She'd nearly dozed off when the timer beeped loudly.

Steamed veggies and frozen, precooked chicken didn't taste as bad as it sounded. She'd added a little pepper and light seasoning to give everything extra flavor. She knew how to cook enough not to starve, but after working long hours, the last thing she wanted to do was stand over a stove just to make a simple meal for herself. So, she'd opted for frozen, yet cooked, chicken and various types of seafood. Growing up on a cattle ranch, she was not a beef eater at all, and neither were her parents, nor her best friend Tibby and his family.

She thought about going out to the stable as she washed the couple of dishes she'd used, but Firefly had seemed fine all day. There was no need to go bother her.

FIVE

"You didn't tell me she was setting up a barrel course. Are we doing rodeo stuff here now?" Allison asked as she sipped her tea from the window in her father's office. "There's no way Luna Mist will be able to concentrate with that ruckus."

Harris closed the screen on his computer and looked over at her. "You have to learn to coexist. Give her a try. Who knows, you may actually get along."

Ha! Allison shook her head. "I'm starting to think you've lost your mind, old man."

"Who are you calling old?" he chided with a smile. "Isn't Arthur coming out today?"

"He's probably here. I'm keeping him waiting on purpose," she replied.

He shook his head. "He's a good trainer, Allison."

"Good isn't good enough, Father. Not if I'm going to make a winning comeback after taking nearly a year off to mourn the death of my mother."

He pursed his lips as she sipped her tea and walked over, kissing his cheek before leaving the room.

*

"I'm looking for my best friend. I believe she is moonlighting as the new horse trainer," Tibby said.

"I'll show you moonlighting when my horse kicks your ass," Carly Rae mumbled on her way out the door with the phone between her ear and shoulder and a piece of toast between her teeth as she fiddled with the lock. She'd slept straight through her alarm and woke up late, something completely out of character for her.

He laughed. "Seriously, though. Are you really training the horse who threw that jockey in my race?"

"Yep."

"You've always been a sucker for a good challenge."

"Uh huh," she replied, munching down the last of her breakfast as she walked into the stable. "I need to get to work. I'll talk you later," she added, ending the call. She turned the ringer off and placed the phone on the wall of Firefly's stall when she opened the door. "Good morning, girl. Are you ready to do a little training?"

Firefly whinnied and sniffed her with excitement.

Carly Rae glanced over at Sir Rigsby who was steadily munching on his breakfast. She walked over slowly and he stuck his head out to sniff her. "Hey, sweet boy," she whispered, petting the side of his neck and face. "We're going to turnout together in a little while," she said, moving her hand up to pet his long face.

Firefly neighed, but Sir Rigsby had no idea.

"All right, girl. Let's go," she said, walking back over to her beautiful chestnut palomino. She placed the halter over her head and clipped a lead to it. The horse followed as she walked down to the tack room and tied the lead to the hook on the wall. Firefly stood still, waiting patiently as Carly Rae placed a blanket and then a saddle on her back, strapping it in place. Then, she bent down and began putting black orthopedic sports boots on the horse's legs. She hadn't planned to run her anywhere near full speed, but she always made sure she was protected nonetheless.

"Good morning," Ollie called, bringing in a wheelbarrow load of fresh hay for Luna Mist's stall. "How long will you be out on her?" he asked.

"An hour or so. I'm going to do a little training on the barrels," she replied, climbing up into the saddle. "I'm going to turn her out when I'm done though."

"I'll muck her stall while you're gone then."

"I'm also going to turnout Sir Rigsby in the other pen, so you'll be able to get to his, too."

"Great."

*

"You've got it. That's it," Arthur said in a heavy English accent.

"She keeps missing the flying change," Allison growled.

"She'll get the tempi changes. This is a new routine. You can't expect her to master it in two weeks."

Allison ignored him as she instructed the horse to start over.

"You have to let her get through the routine," he muttered, shaking his head.

"I'm not going to let her learn it the wrong way," she shot back, putting the horse into a piaffe, then an in-place trot, followed by an extended gait at the canter. The large dapple grey mare moved beautifully as she transitioned to the flying changes, a series of lead changes at the canter. The horse did the first two, then faltered on the third.

"Damnit," Allison spat.

"Forget the tempi changes. Let's see the pirouette and half-pass," Arthur instructed.

Allison reluctantly made the horse spin around in place, creating the perfect pirouette. She was about to start the half-pass, when movement out of the corner of her eye nearly caused her to fall out of the saddle. She pulled the reins, stopping the horse in place as she turned her head towards the open arena. Carly Rae was atop her horse, riding around the arena in a trot, seemingly warming her up.

"Great," she mumbled. "This is all I need."

"Who's that?" Arthur called. "And why have you stopped? Let's see the half-pass."

"She's some rodeo clown my father hired to train his race horse," Allison sighed, setting up for the half-pass, which made the horse go on a diagonal line, moving sideways and forward at the same time.

"Not bad. She needs to lean more, though. We'll work on it. One thing at a time," Arthur said.

*

"You're itching to run. I feel it. But, you have to warm up," Carly Rae said to her horse. "The last thing we need is an injury. Come on, let's go slow," she added, clicking her teeth while giving the horse a light squeeze with her legs. She pulled on the left side of the closed rein, directing her around the left barrel, then she released to make her go straight across to the next one. She grabbed the right side, sending her into a right-hand turn coming around the barrel, that set her up for the last barrel at the top of the triangle. She pulled the right side again, forcing the horse to circle the barrel from the right. Then she straightened out and picked up speed slightly as she ran out of the arena.

They were only moving at a quarter of their race speed at most, but it felt invigorating to be circling barrels again. Carly Rae bent forward, rubbing Firefly's neck. "Good girl! I'm pretty sure you've missed it as much as I have."

She focused her eyes on the woman atop the large dapple gray in the closed arena while she waited for her horse to rest for a second. Luna Mist shifted from a piaffe to an extended gait that lengthened her trot as she lurched forward. She saw the man talking and shaking his head, but she couldn't quite hear what he was saying.

"Let's go, Firefly!" she called, squeezing the horse to make her take off around the barrels once again. She kept the same slower speed as she ran her through the course over and over.

*

"You missed the passage," Arthur called out.

"I know that," Allison grumbled, starting the routine over. *I can't concentrate.* She glanced over at the open arena, watching Carly Rae race her horse around.

"Start at the passage, then move through the extended gait and collected gaits," Arthur instructed, pulling her back to her own training session.

Damnit. Allison sighed in frustration and forced the horse through the three skills.

"You need more finesse in your transitions. Each movement is great, but they are all rough around the edges."

"That's because she needs to learn how to fully do each action before we progress to the next," she said sharply, blowing out a breath of frustration. "Let's end the session for the day."

"That's fine. I'll see you in two days."

She nodded as he walked away. Her attention shifted back to the open arena as Carly Rae led her horse around the barrels once more. She missed her riding out of the arena and over to the turnout pen as she forced herself to focus on correcting her horse's subtle mistakes.

*

Carly Rae left Firefly on her own to walk around and graze as she cooled down. Meanwhile, she went inside the stable and grabbed a halter and lead and headed over to Sir Rigsby's stall. He was looking down when she walked closer. She waved her arm to put motion in his peripheral vision. His head popped and he whinnied in her direction as he put his head over the top of the stall door.

"It's okay, boy," she cooed as she pet him. He sniffed her. "You smell the carrots, don't you," she laughed. "Behave, and I'll let you have them." She slipped the halter over his head with no protest from him, and clipped the lead to it. Then, she opened the stall door and gave a little tug. He began walking beside her. She kept the lead loose, then pulled it down, forcing him to tuck his face and stop moving. She pet his neck, reassuring him. Then, she let the lead slack again and gave it a light tug as she began walking out of the stable. He moved alongside her as she directed him towards the open turnout circle and led him inside.

The natural oils in the massive thoroughbred's dark bay coat shined in the sunlight as he grazed. Carly Rae gave him a few minutes to get used to his surroundings before pulling one of the baby carrots from her pocket. She slapped the lead softly, similar to slapping the rein, to get him to walk, then tugged it left or right to control his direction. His gait was slow as he walked beside her in the pen. Each time she pulled back on the lead, forcing his head down, he stopped immediately. She quickly pet him and gave him a carrot. Then, she'd lightly slap the lead again and started all over. She did this several times, making sure he understood when his head was pulled back, that meant stop right there in that spot. The harder or faster she slapped the lead, ordered him to pick up his pace to a trot and almost a canter. Then, she'd pulled it back a little to get him to slow back down to a walk. He quickly understood a light pull was slower and a hard pull was stop, and a single slap was walk, but two or three was faster and faster.

After an hour of lead training, she tied him loosely to the rail of the pen so that he could graze without getting stuck with his back to her. This way, he wouldn't spook when she came back for him.

"Are you almost finished?" I need one of the turnouts for my horse," Allison said from a few feet away.

Carly Rae had no idea how long she'd been standing there watching her. "Yeah. I'm about to take Firefly inside, actually," she replied, walking over to the other pen where her horse was meandering about here and there, chewing on the grass. She clicked her mouth and whistled. Firefly's head shot up and she trotted right over to her. "Come on, girl," she said, giving her a carrot from her pocket as she put the lead back on her halter. She opened the gate and led her back into the stable. "Let's go brush you down," she said, tying her up near the wash station where all of the brushes and coat care supplies were located. She selected a soft bristle brush and began running it around her head, then down her neck and front legs, working her way from the front to the back of the horse. Afterwards, she brushed out her long blonde mane and matching tail. Firefly moved around a little, enjoying the brush down like a massage. When she was completely finished, Carly Rae gave her another carrot and put her back in her stall. She pet her head between her ears, which was her favorite spot, then left her to relax.

By the time she went back out to Sir Rigsby, Luna Mist was alone in the turnout pen next to him with no sign of Allison or her trainer. Carly Rae picked up where she'd left off and the horse knew each command right away as if she'd never left. "You're doing great," she said. "I'll be riding you soon."

"I hope so," Harris McKinley called from the side rail, startling her. The horse kept right on going, completely unaware of his presence.

"We're heading in the right direction. He takes to commands well. He's very smart. It's just a matter of me teaching him each one visually and physically. I have to make sure he knows what stop and go mean before I get on his back," she said.

"I understand. I don't even know how to stop a horse that doesn't understand whoa." He smiled.

"I'm pretty sure that won't work with him," she laughed.

"No...I guess not."

"I'll get up on him in the next day or two, depending on how our session goes in the morning."

"Sounds good. I won't keep you," he said. "I was actually looking for my daughter."

"I haven't seen her since she turned out Luna Mist."

"Hmm…she usually doesn't go far from that horse when she's not stabled. I'll check the arena."

Carly Rae went back to her training of starting, stopping, speeding up, and slowing down. Sir Rigsby seemed to have each movement down pat. When she was down to a single carrot in her pocket, she led him back into the stable and brushed him the same way she'd brushed Firefly earlier, and just like her, he seemed to enjoy it.

"Come on, Rigs. Let's get you back in your stall," she said, mostly to herself as she led him over, ushering him inside before closing the door. Then, she grabbed a brush and went back over to him. The massive thoroughbred stepped back, giving her space when she entered his stall once more. She closed the door and held her arm up again for him to sniff while she looped the lead over the hook on the door to keep him tethered to that area of the stall. She continued letting him sniff her as she brushed his neck and shoulder. This went on for several minutes, and by the time she'd reached his back and then his other side, he'd had enough of sniffing her.

When she was finished, she walked back out and removed his halter and lead when he stuck his head over the door, following her as he sniffed. Then, she pet his head and face and gave him her last carrot. "That's it. You ate them all." She smiled, petting his neck while he chewed.

Allison walked into the stable with Luna Mist and tied her up to brush her as Carly Rae was walking away from Sir Rigsby's stall.

"Your father is looking for you," she said in passing.

"He found me."

"How was training today?" Carly Rae asked, trying to create small talk.

"Peachy," Allison replied without looking at her.

Carly Rae nodded, then hesitated a second before finally walking away.

SIX

"It's impossible," Allison grumbled.

Harris McKinley looked over at his daughter as he took a bite of the juicy steak on his plate. "Impossible is a strong word, don't you think?"

"What would you call it, then?" she sighed, pushing the food around her own plate.

"Distracted."

"Huh? Why would you say that?"

"Allison, I've seen you out there training day in and day out. You're a phenomenal dressage rider. But, you have been out of sorts since Carly Rae arrived. So...yes, distracted."

She ignored him and went back to pushing her food around.

*

"Today's the day," Carly Rae said cheerfully as she walked into the stable. The smell of manure, leather, and hay permeated the air, reminding her of home for a split second.

Ollie popped his head out of the feed room in time to see her walking into the tack room. "Are you riding him?!" he questioned, noticing she was wearing a wide-brimmed, straw Stetson hat, along with her usual jeans, boots, and button-down shirt over a tank top.

"Yep," she replied cheerfully, walking towards Sir Rigsby's stall with a bridle. "We're going for a ride. What do you think?" she said, smiling and petting his head and face before sliding the bridle easily over his head. His mouth opened, fitting the bit perfectly. "Stay in the feed room for a minute, Ollie," she called, opening the door and guiding him out of the stall. She tied his rein to the hook on the wall beside the tack room.

"No problem," he replied.

Sir Rigsby moved around a little, but stilled as she put the blanket on his back. They weren't racing, so she'd chosen a regular riding saddle. She thought about putting on a helmet, but the best way to not get thrown was to not let him sense fear. They needed to be equally comfortable and trust each other. She'd kept her hat on instead.

"Come out slowly so that he sees you," she said.

Sir Rigsby started to back up slightly when Ollie made his appearance, but she kept a hold of him, all the while petting his neck. He easily calmed. She needed him to get used to things happening around him.

"That went well. You can move about to do your work, but stay away from the turnout pens. I don't need anything spooking him. I'll be pissed if he throws me."

More like dead, he thought.

Carly Rae grabbed his rein and she and Sir Rigsby walked out of the stable together, passing by the arenas on the right as they made their way over to the turnout pens. She glanced at the closed arena, noticing Allison was once again atop her horse, practicing vigilantly. Sir Rigsby had kept his eyes straight ahead, following her direction, so he never saw her.

Once they were inside the pen, she closed the gate. "Here we go," she said, petting his head as he sniffed her hat. She exhaled the nerves binding her stomach as she continued petting his neck all the way to the saddle. Then, she grabbed the rein and saddle horn with one hand, stuck her foot in the stirrup and pulled herself up, swinging her other leg over as her butt slid into the saddle. She held the rein up and back, keeping his head pulled slightly so he would know not to move. He'd learned her commands while using a halter and then a bitless bridle, but now she needed to make sure he remembered them while using the bit since he was required to use it for races.

"You're a tall boy!" she said, noticing the whole hand height difference between Sir Rigsby and Firefly. She bent forward, petting the back of his neck before releasing tension on the rein. Sir Rigsby began walking forward. She pet him again to reassure him. This was her way of saying good boy. Then, she pulled up and straight back on the reins. He stopped immediately. She rubbed his neck with one hand while holding the rein without tension in the other. He stood still, awaiting his next command. Then, she slapped the rein softly to get him moving again and squeezed with her left leg slightly while pulling in on that side of the rein. He began a subtle turn in that direction. Once again, she pet his neck. "Good boy!" she cooed, despite knowing he couldn't hear her.

She continued on, making him walk in a full left-hand circle around the pen, then again in the opposite direction. She practiced starting and stopping, as well as following the pen circle in both directions several times before increasing his gait to a trot and starting all over with each instruction.

Beads of sweat rolled from her temples down the sides of her cheeks as the late morning sun beat down. Thankfully, northern California wasn't as humid as the southern part of the state, but the mid eighty-degree temperature was still hot. She unbuttoned her shirt and led him over towards the rail so she could hang it on the first rung, leaving her in a dark blue tank top.

*

Allison pulled the rein back, bringing her large horse to a stop as she watched Carly Rae mount the thoroughbred in the turnout pen. She was about the same height as Allison's 5'5", but she appeared smaller atop the large race horse, and the Stetson had made her look every bit the cowgirl that she was.

Suddenly, the horse under her moved, breaking Allison's stare. "Damnit," she mumbled. "Come on, Luna. We have work to do." She maneuvered her into position and went through her routine once more, concentrating on the first four movements in the skill set. She tried to execute her instructions perfectly, but her attention kept shifting to the turnout pens as Carly Rae rode the horse around the circle over and over. "Do you really have to take your clothes off?" she huffed, noticing Carly Rae removing her outer shirt.

*

Once Carly Rae had finished her training session, she'd climbed down and left Sir Rigsby in the turnout pen to graze a little before taking him back inside the stable and brushing him down. She'd also given him a couple of strawberries as a treat for doing well.

The lunch hour had come and gone by the time she made it back to the tiny house to make herself a sandwich.

She wiped the dirt from her boots and hung her hat on the wall hook by the door when she walked inside. The half hour she'd allotted herself wouldn't be long enough, but the cool air felt great on her skin as she went about preparing her food.

*

Allison twisted her chestnut colored braid up into a bun and went about brushing Luna Mist who was tethered to a hook in her stall. The day had been long and mostly counterproductive on her part. Arthur was due back in the morning for another training session that she wasn't looking forward to.

She never drank during the day, but a glass of wine was quickly making its way to her dinner menu, as was a relaxing soak in her garden tub. Her mind wandered as she ran the rubber curry comb in circles all over the horse to both massage her and shed hair.

She'd switch to the soft bristled brush to remove the loose hair when Ollie and Carly Rae walked into the stable. She quietly listened to their conversation as she brushed her horse.

"What's life like on the rodeo circuit?" Ollie asked.

"Oh…I don't know. It's a lot of fun, but… brutal…mostly. I guess. You live out of a horse trailer or RV and you're on the road constantly. There are several barrel racing circuits. I spent a few years racing a handful at the same time competitively. It wore me out physically and mentally. I was running two different horses back then."

"What happened to them?"

"One is retired to the ranch life back home, and Firefly is the other. She was only a little over a year old back then."

"What do you get when you win?"

"In the Women's Professional Rodeo Association there are sixty qualifying events, five in each of their thirteen circuits. You can race as many as you want, but your top 7 finishes are the only points they use. Each one usually has a $5,000 purse, so it pays well to win. There are also other circuits outside of WPRA schedule that hold big events with cash purses and other prizes throughout the year. If you ride well, have a fast, healthy horse, and don't mind the lifestyle, you can make a good living at it."

"Have you won a lot of races?"

"I started with the junior rodeo when I was ten, so I've won and lost a lot over the years. But yes, I've won the big money races and a few championships along the way."

"That's awesome. So, do you have male fans who dote on you like the women do with the bull riding men?"

She laughed. "Oh yeah, men and women, to be honest. It's not super crazy, but if you want to have a little fun…there's always someone waiting and willing."

"Wow," he said, just as a loud thud rang out. Both he and Carly Rae jumped off the ground and Firefly startled in her stall, whinnying and kicking her back legs out.

"Calm down, girl," Carly Rae said, rushing to her. "It's okay." She looked across at Sir Rigsby who continued munching on hay, completely oblivious. Even Luna Mist, who was a few stalls down, whinnied. "What the hell was that?" she said, looking at Ollie as he checked the empty stalls.

"I dropped the brush," Allison said, walking out of Luna Mist's stall and passing by them like it was nothing.

Carly Rae raised a brow in Ollie's direction. He pursed his lips and shrugged. He was the hired help, so it wasn't his position to get involved. They walked out together, closing up the stable for the night before heading in their opposite directions, Ollie to his truck and Carly Rae to the tiny house.

*

Allison's chestnut hair fell a few inches below her shoulder in natural, loose waves as she brushed it. She was sitting at the vanity sink in her bathroom, having just showered and blown her hair dry. The woman looking back at her in the mirror resembled her mother so much, it was almost startling. If she quieted her mind, she could almost hear her voice. She had an assertive English accent with a French twist. She was very proper and completely un-American having grown up as a French girl in London.

"Oh, how I miss you, Mum," she sighed, setting the brush down as she got up. Her father's laughter resonated through the house as she made her way down the stairs. *Who is he talking to?*

*

Carly Rae knocked lightly on the door with her knuckles instead of ringing the doorbell. The last place she wanted to be was the doorstep of the McKinley's house, but she'd accepted Harris's invitation to dinner. *It's not like I could've said no thanks, your daughter's an ass and the last thing I want to do is spend more time around her,* she thought as she waited patiently.

Suddenly, the lock clicked and the door swung open, revealing glossy parquet hardwood floors. Harris stood in the doorway with a crooked smile on his face. He was dressed in jeans and a black button down with a tan sport coat.

"Come in," he said, swinging the door open. "Allison should be down in a minute," he added, closing it behind her. A wide, spiral staircase with wrought iron rails on both sides, wound up to the second floor. An upright piano was against the wall nearby and the open dining area was visible beyond the staircase.

"Your house is beautiful," she said as they walked over to the table.

"Thanks. My late wife designed and decorated it," he replied. "Would you like a drink?"

"Oh, no. I'm fine." *Although, I might need one to get through this dinner.*

"I've been known to burn macaroni and cheese, and I'm afraid my daughter is blessed with my cooking gene. Thankfully, we use a personal chef delivery service."

"My mother is the cook in our family. Luckily, she taught me a thing or two, so I won't starve." She smiled. "Although, I eat a lot of precooked meals or in restaurants because it's easier than cooking for myself. My dad isn't much of a cook either. His specialty is the lazy man's dinner."

"What's that?"

"Baked beans loaded with chunks of turkey hot dog," she grimaced. "I love my dad, and granted, he makes it over an open fire pit, but I hated it when he was in charge of dinner."

"My daughter would disown me," he laughed.

Carly Rae saw movement out of the corner of her eye and looked up to see Allison coming down the stairs. She was dressed in tight black pants similar to her riding jodhpurs and a maroon blouse with a deep v-neck. Her hair fell in loose waves down her back and in front of her right shoulder. Carly Rae's stomach began to tighten as her mouth watered. She'd never seen a woman so breathtaking.

*

Allison couldn't believe her eyes. Of all the people to be sitting at their dinner table, it was the rodeo queen. However, she looked a lot less rodeo at the moment. She was still wearing jeans and boots, but the button-down shirt and tank top had been replaced by a white flutter sleeve top that hugged her lithe frame and small breasts. Petite diamond stud earrings glistened in her ears. *Is she interested in my father? She's young enough to be his daughter!*

"I didn't know we were having company this evening," she said, kissing him on the cheek as she sat down adjacent to him, putting her across from Carly Rae.

"I invited Carly Rae for dinner so we could get to know her and talk business, of course," he replied. "Dinner is heating and should be ready in a moment."

Allison nodded as her eyes wandered across the table to the woman looking back at her. She hadn't been close enough to see how blue her eyes were until now. *You're cute as hell. I'll give you that. But, my father is off limits, rodeo queen.* She gritted her teeth and looked away.

"I saw you riding Sir Rigsby today. How did that go? I was going to come down, but I didn't want to spook him," Harris said.

"It was fine. He's a smart horse and a fast learner. I'm going slow and being gentle with him, but we'll be ready to stretch his legs soon. I was actually going to talk to you about that. He needs a place to run."

"Like a training track?"

"Yes. Exactly."

"Wonderful. Now, we'll have a horse track, a barrel course, and a dressage arena," Allison grumbled.

Her father ignored her. "That's not a bad idea. We have plenty of acreage out past the stable area."

"I know. I've ridden my horse all the way to the wine grapes growing next door," Carly Rae said. "Your property is very charming. The lush trees that separate everyone are beautiful. Some of them have to be close to a hundred years old."

"Yes, they probably are. Make sure you stay on our land. Horses tend to eat the wine grapes and piss off the neighbors…right, Allison?" He smiled.

"Sure," she replied, getting up. "I'm going to pour a glass of wine. Would anyone like one?" she asked, looking at her father.

"Nah." He shook his head.

"I'll have one," Carly Rae said as she started to walk away. She wasn't a wine drinker at all, but she needed something to get her through dinner.

"So, Allison was about eleven or twelve and had a mare that was a chocolate colored, crossbred pony. At the time, she was learning dressage, but was interested in steeple chase and we bought her this pony-horse to start training on. That's actually why we have both arenas. The open area used to be for steeple chase, but that's another story. Anyhow, she used to ride that damn thing all over, including the neighboring vineyards. One afternoon, I got a call because she and her pony-horse had been eating grapes right off the vine."

"Oh, my God," Carly Rae laughed.

Harris chuckled. "My wife was pissed. She knew all of our neighbors quite well, so of course she was embarrassed that *her* daughter would do such a thing. I found it funny as hell. She's a lot like her mom, but that was definitely something she got from me."

Carly Rae shook her head and smiled.

"Dinner should be heated and ready to go. I hope you like surf and turf. It's crab-stuffed fillets with lobster pasta as the side."

"I actually don't eat beef," Carly Rae said. "Growing up on a cattle ranch tends to do that to you. My family doesn't either, actually."

"Oh…okay. Uh…"

"I'm perfectly fine with the rest of it. Just save the steak for lunch tomorrow." She grinned.

Allison stood behind him, rolling her eyes. *Why does she have to be so playful and easy going?*

*

By the time dinner ended, Carly Rae couldn't wait to get out of that house. Harris was kind and held a great conversation, but his daughter stared at her with daggers through the entire meal. *She genuinely hates me,* she thought as she walked back to the tiny house. The single glass of wine she'd had was from a local winery and had paired nicely with the food. She wasn't sure if it was that or the tension between her and Allison that had given her a splitting headache.

SEVEN

"Good boy," Carly Rae said, petting Sir Rigsby's neck as he slowed his gait from a canter to a walk and entered the turnout pen. They had been out riding around the property most of the morning. He was eager to run, but she was yet to set him free. They'd worked on all of the same commands she'd taught him, but utilizing the open terrain had given him much more room to canter, giving him a faster speed under her control. She no longer had to pet him to reassure him, but she did it anyhow.

"He's looking more like a race horse," Harris called, walking towards the pen.

Carly Rae hopped down from the saddle and climbed up on the fence, sitting on the top rail. She hadn't seen him since the dinner a few nights earlier. "He's definitely ready to run," she said. "Grass will do for now, but he needs to be running."

"Layout a spot and I'll have Ollie scalp it."

"I can drive a tractor," she said, watching Sir Rigsby munch on the grass. "My family's ranch is cattle and hay. I've driven just about every piece of equipment there is. He has other duties to take care of."

"That's fine."

"We'll need a starting gate, too," she added.

He nodded. "I actually came out here to tell you I'm sorry about Allison. She's her mother through and through," he sighed. "Collette, my late wife, was a world champion steeple chase rider. She died a little over a year ago and Allison has had a hard time ever since."

"There's no need to apologize. I understand," she replied.

He nodded. "Just so you know, I don't expect you to work with Sir Rigsby on the weekends. Those are your days off."

"I figured as much, but I wanted to spend time with him as much as possible to build trust between us. Three months is going to go by fast."

"Yes, it will," he said, looking around. Then, he lit a cigar as he walked away.

Carly Rae hopped down and went into the stable to get a lead. Ollie had just finished mucking his stall when she walked in. "Do you know where I can find a few cans of spray paint?"

He pursed his lips in thought for a second. "No, but I'm meeting my wife for lunch today. It's her birthday. I can swing by the hardware store for you."

"I was seeing if there was any around here. I can run out to the store on my own."

"It's fine. The hardware store is close to the restaurant."

"Okay, thanks. I need the kind for marking a yard. They're usually fluorescent orange or yellow. Get four if you can, and tell your wife happy birthday."

"Will do."

*

"What on earth is she doing now?" Allison mumbled, watching Carly Rae off in the distance as she took Luna Mist from the turnout pen. The blonde was out in a meadow area of the property, about forty yards from the arenas, turnout pens, and stable area…sitting on the tractor in her tank top and Stetson hat. It didn't take Allison long to realize Carly Rae was forming the training track she and her father had discussed. She'd seen her just before lunchtime, sitting casually on the fence while talking with him, obviously talking him into allowing the track. She shook her head as she led the horse towards the stable. *Three months can't come soon enough.*

*

As soon as Carly Rae finished painting the track line, she got on the tractor and began scalping the grass down to the roots as she followed the paint lines. She watched the orange line on the inside edge of the oval disappear as she moved along slowly. The track began coming into view behind her. "Rigs, you're going to love this," she whispered to herself.

When she finished, she pulled the lever to raise the blades and drove back over to the shed it was housed in. Then, she backed it in so that the mower attached to the back was next to the grader that was used to drag the arenas. She climbed down and unhooked the mower before hopping back in the seat and hooking the grader back to the tractor so Ollie wouldn't have to do it later.

"You know your way around a tractor," Ollie said, walking over when she parked it and killed the engine. "The track looks great."

"Oh yeah. I spent my life on a working cattle ranch with hay fields. Since I started traveling with the rodeo, I don't get to do as much of this as I used to," she said. "Now, I go home and help with the cattle drive twice a year…and occasionally to run things when my mom forces my dad to take her on vacation." She smiled.

He chuckled. "Sounds like my wife with me."

"I'm going to go run the barrels with Firefly for a little bit. Just let me know when you're ready to drag the arena," she said, wiping the sweat from her brow.

"Sure. No problem. It'll be at least an hour."

Carly Rae nodded and began walking towards the stable.

*

"It looks like the rodeo queen finished her race track," Allison said, looking out over the property from her father's office window. She watched intently as Carly Rae raced around the barrels atop her chestnut palomino. She seemed to go faster and faster with each pass. She had no idea how a horse was able to lean over so far and run so fast at the same time. She found it intriguing to watch, but would never admit it. "Do you think she will really be able to train that deaf race horse to win a derby?"

"I certainly hope so," he sighed. *You better too, if you want to remain a world class dressage rider.* Their family estate financials were open on the screen in front of him. His parents and grandparents were real estate tycoons and had left him a large family trust. When his wife passed, he'd received her life insurance, as well as the family trust that she'd inherited, which included a multigenerational winery in France, that was set aside for Allison. He hadn't had the heart to tell his daughter that her mother's family estate had dwindled much more than he'd realized. Which was why he'd purchased the thoroughbred when he heard he was going for a very good price. He jumped on the opportunity to own a race horse sired by two generations of Kentucky Derby winners. What he hadn't known at the time was the reason the horse wasn't nearly triple the price…because he was deaf.

He closed the window on the computer and looked over at her. She was leaning against the frame of the window with her eyes glued to something outside. Quietly, he got out of his chair and walked over to her. Carly Rae was out in the open arena, racing around the three barrels at breakneck speed. "She's a spitfire, isn't she?" he said softly.

"She's something, alright," she mumbled, pushing off the wall.

"She has an open invitation to dinner, so try to be a little more civil the next time…hmm," he said to her back as she walked away.

Allison held her hand up waving in agreement before leaving the room.

EIGHT

"It's going well. He has the basic commands down," Carly Rae said, holding the phone between her shoulder and ear as she put a thick smear of peanut butter on a piece of whole wheat bread.

"That's good. How's the owner treating you?" her father asked.

"Great. His daughter's a piece of work though," she said, adding a large dollop of strawberry jam to another piece of bread before slapping the two sides together to form the perfect lunch sandwich.

"Oh, really…"

"Yeah, she's a world class dressage rider. I'm pretty sure she has a stick stuck up her butt," she mumbled as she chewed. "How are things there?"

"Everything's fine. George said the owner of Magic Hat offered Tibby a contract for the rest of the race season."

"Yeah, he told me. That's awesome, but I wish he would've told me it was a possibility. We're going to need a jockey, and it has to be someone whom I can trust to listen to everything I tell him." She closed and locked the door to the tiny house before making her way back towards the stable. She held what was left of her bulky sandwich with both hands and kept the phone tucked against her shoulder as she walked and ate.

"I know you'll find the right person. That horse is lucky to have you."

"Thanks, Daddy."

"You're welcome. Your mama sends her love, by the way."

"I love and miss you both."

"We miss you, too. Go take that horse for a run. We'll talk soon."

Carly Rae shoved the rest of her sandwich into her mouth and slid her phone into her back pocket just before walking into the stable. "Rigs, saddle up, boy. We're going for a run!" she said, walking over to pet him. He sniffed her and whinnied with excitement.

"Why do you talk to a horse that can't hear?" Allison muttered, shaking her head as she walked into the tack room.

"He can't hear, yes. But, he can see my enthusiasm and that's huge," Carly Rae replied, stepping into the same room to get the bridle and bit she usually used, along with an endurance saddle that was small, lightweight, hornless, and comfortable for both the horse and the rider. It was made for fast, long distance riding, but would work in place of a racing saddle for now.

Allison shrugged and walked back out of the stable without another word.

A few minutes later, Carly Rae had Sir Rigsby saddled with black polo wraps on his legs for stability and protection. She grabbed the rein and her helmet, and walked him out of the stable. Allison was back in the closed arena with Luna Mist when they passed by, and Firefly was in the turnout pen with Ollie getting ready to take her back inside.

Once she was away from everyone and everything, she stopped him and climbed up into the saddle. She guided him in a slow walk through the grass towards their training track, which was nothing more than an extremely low-cut oval with wide turns and two long straight-a-ways. They made a lap around walking to warm him up a bit, then she picked his gait up to a trot for another two laps. The track was around 3/4 of a mile, so she wanted to make sure he got a few miles in for their first day, but not overwork him.

Finally, she slapped the reins, increasing him to a jog for two more laps. Then, she slowed him all the way back to a walk, petting him a few times before changing directions, and picking him back up to a jog going the opposite way to balance out his muscle strength. Afterwards, he trotted for a lap, then she walked him for two more laps to cool down his muscles, before she stopped him and climbed down.

"Good, boy!" She smiled, petting his face and head over and over while he sniffed her helmet. "I know, it looks ridiculous, but it will keep me safe in case of an accident." She finally took it off before leading him back by everything on their way to the stable. Allison had Luna Mist in one of the turnout pens, but Sir Rigsby walked by with no problem. When they reached the stable, she tied the rein to a hook on the wall and removed the saddle. Then, she put him in his stall so she could switch him from the bridle to a halter and lead. She pet his head once more, then walked away to get him a couple of carrots from the refrigerator in the feed room while he drank some of his water. When she returned, she brought him out to the wash area to give him a bath and help cool his muscles further.

Sir Rigsby liked the water and was quite playful as Carly Rae rinsed him off. She cleaned his mane and tail with mild soapy water and gently wiped his face with a wet mitt. Afterwards, she used the sweat scraper to remove excess water from his body. Then, she used a dry sponge to get the water off his legs, finishing with a towel, before towel drying his head, ears, and neck.

Allison came in with Luna Mist just as Carly Rae began massaging his legs with liniment to keep him from having any muscle or tendon pain from his first big workout. Then, she placed cotton wraps on them. He sniffed the air as they walked past, but he was getting much better at paying attention to his surroundings and wasn't startled as easily when he saw a person or another horse. Carly Rae gave him a couple of strawberries for behaving during their first bath experience together, and allowing her to massage his legs.

Allison was leaning against the wall outside of the tack room with her arms crossed when Carly Rae walked over to the wash basin to clean her hands. "Why are you doing this?"

Carly Rae looked around before realizing she was addressing her. "What?"

"Why are you training this horse? And for pennies, nonetheless, when he may not win a dime."

"It's not about the money. I love these animals, and I enjoy it," Carly Rae said, drying her hands on a paper towel. "You know, if you'd let your horse be a horse once in a while, you'd get a lot more out of her," she added.

Completely appalled at the nerve of this woman, Allison stiffened and clenched her jaw.

"Your horse feels all of the tension you're carrying around. Like right now, you look like you want to slap the hell out of me." She shrugged. "You need to loosen up a little."

"You know nothing about the discipline of dressage. It isn't anywhere near your rodeo barrel racing," she snapped and walked away.

"That went well," Carly Rae sighed, tossing her paper towel in the trash.

*

Carly Rae walked past the covered arena after finishing her morning workout with Sir Rigsby. She couldn't help stopping to watch a little bit of Allison's training session. The precise movements of dressage were alien to her, but it was exciting watching Luna Mist perform each action. She clasped her hands together over the top rail and lifted one boot up onto the lowest one.

Allison noticed the horse miss a step in one section of the routine. She immediately made the horse perform the same bit over and over until it was perfect. Then, she'd start from the beginning again to see how the horse handled the troubled area.

Something didn't sit right with Carly Rae. She bit the corner of her mouth as she watched Allison work on the same issue all over again. The horse seemed to know what to do, but she wasn't doing it perfectly every time as she was instructed to.

"She needs reassurance," she called, slightly startling Allison, who'd had no idea she was there. "I know…" Carly Rae held her hand up. "I'm just a rodeo barrel racer, but I believe she knows what you're trying to teach her, she just isn't sure which steps are correct. Give her some praise when she gets it right. She'll also be more inclined to do what you're asking," she said with a smile and a shrug.

Allison turned the horse so that her back was to Carly Rae, seemingly in defiance as she ignored her.

"Suit yourself," Carly Rae muttered, walking away. She had better things to do…like take Firefly for her training runs.

*

"Who the hell does she think she is?" Allison grumbled. "Come on, Luna! From the top." She got the horse into position and began the routine once more. When she faltered a step, Allison corrected it. Luna Mist did it perfectly and Allison pet her neck. "Good, girl," she said, hoping to prove the know-it-all rode queen wrong, but Luna did the steps perfectly when she started her over once more.

Allison watched the blonde race her horse around the barrels in the arena next to her a handful of times before going back to her own training session. The last thing she wanted was to be seen watching her.

"Come on, Luna. Let's go one more time before calling it a day," she said, ushering the horse back into place. A part of her wanted the horse to miss that step again to prove Carly Rae wrong, but Luna Mist had moved through that section of the routine flawlessly.

*

By the time Carly Rae finished her training runs and subsequent cool down with Firefly, Allison was long gone and Luna Mist was back in her stall. She brushed the horse down, gave her a handful of juicy blueberries, which were her favorite, then put her in the stall for the night. Sir Rigsby was lying down when she looked in on him. "Good, boy. That means you're finally relaxing a little bit." She smiled. Hearing her voice, Luna Mist stuck her head out over the door.

"Hey there," Carly Rae said, walking down to her stall. "I know she's stubborn. You haven't tossed her on her ass by now, so you must be used to it." She reached out, petting her. Luna Mist whinnied when she smelled the fruit. "Do you like blueberries?" she asked, opening the container. The horse began sniffing all around. "Don't tell her. She hates me enough as it is," she said, giving the horse a handful of berries.

Luna Mist was definitely more disciplined than Firefly or Sir Rigsby, but she was still a horse who liked to be petted and eat treats. Carly Rae stayed a few minutes longer, showing her a little extra attention since this was their first encounter. "All right, I better go before you get spoiled," she said with a smile, petting her one last time.

Nightfall was still hours away when Carly Rae walked into her rented house, but she was exhausted nonetheless. Her first full week of riding Sir Rigsby in the training track was quickly coming to an end. They'd worked on commands in the beginning, but by the end they were learning how to maintain a line, which would help with keeping him in his racing lane. So far, he was picking up everything she was teaching him, and more than anything, he loved to run. She still hadn't let him gallop, but every other day she let him jog at about half of his full speed. She was working on his form while teaching him proper commands and behavior, while also keeping him in racing condition.

Thankfully, she'd turned down her latest invitation at the main house. Another dinner with Harris and Allison was something she certainly wasn't looking forward to. Instead, she'd opted for a long, hot shower and a quick meal. By the time the first commercial came on for the TV movie she'd decided to watch, she was fast asleep.

NINE

Saturday wound up being the hottest day of the month so far and with a cloudless sky, there was no end in sight. Carly Rae had spent most of the week working individually with Sir Rigsby on the training track, and also with Firefly racing around barrels. She was supposed to take the weekends off, at least from working with Sir Rigsby, but it was quiet around the property and she wanted to try a few new training techniques. She pulled on an old pair of homemade cutoff jean shorts and a black string bikini top, then added her leather belt, and a white tank top. She finished with her boots and Stetson, then shoved her iPod and ear buds into her pocket and left the tiny house.

"Hey, Firefly," she said, hearing her horse whinny when she entered the stable. She walked over, petting her head and face to show her some attention before stepping across to Sir Rigsby. "Hey, Rigs," she greeted with a smile, petting him as he sniffed her hat. She opened her free hand, giving him the strawberries before taking him out of the stall to tack him up.

She led him out of the stable and glanced around, holding his rein. When she didn't see anyone, she climbed up on him and directed him towards the training track as she put the buds in her ears and hit the play button on her iPod. She'd ridden Firefly and countless other horses around the ranch back home while listening to headphones of some sort over the years. Wearing them while riding Sir Rigsby really wasn't all that different. They communicated through touch to begin with. However, she wouldn't be able to hear surrounding noises, including anything that may spook him. Which was why she'd chosen to do it on a weekend day when no one else was around. Thankfully, Allison didn't mess with her horse at all on the weekends, other than feeding her, and Ollie was off.

Carly Rae started the horse off with a few laps of walking around the track, then a light trot to warm him up before picking up his gait to a jogging run to stretch his legs. A mix of blues rock and roll from her favorite band shuffled around her playlist.

Sir Rigsby responded right away to every command she gave him. It was too hot to run him hard, or for a long time in general, so she concentrated on simply exercising him. He was already in racing condition when she'd begun working with him, but she knew he wasn't at his peak. She'd run him hard twice during the week, but hadn't come anywhere near his top speed. She was used to going fast on Firefly, but it was only in short bursts. Sir Rigsby would be able to run his full speed for well over a mile, and she was looking forward to that ride. Until then, she needed to make sure he was getting regular workouts.

*

"Seriously?" Allison muttered, glancing out the window of her father's office when she brought him a fresh cup of coffee.

"Huh?" he mumbled, half ignoring her as he read an email.

"Nothing," she replied, watching Carly Rae out riding the thoroughbred in her cutoffs, bikini top, boots, and hat. *This isn't Texas, or wherever the hell you're from. Are you really trying that hard to get my father?* She glanced back at the man behind the desk, chewing on the corner of his mustache. She hadn't seen him with a cigar in two weeks. *This rodeo queen has another thing coming if she thinks she's getting a hold of you. Mother would've chewed her up and spit her out by now. Don't think I won't do the same.* She pushed away from the window when she saw the horse and rider leaving the track. "Do you want lunch? I'm having leftover soup and salad from dinner last night. I can bring yours up to you."

"I was thinking of doing the same. Thank you," he said, looking over at her and smiling. "Add a piece of bread to mine on the side."

Allison rolled her eyes. Her father couldn't eat unless there was some form of bread with his meal. She blamed her mother. She always had wine and a French baguette to start lunch or dinner and breakfast always had a side of brioche or croissants. "I'll be back in a bit."

*

Carly Rae finished Sir Rigsby's workout and headed off the makeshift training track. She turned her iPod off and removed her ear buds, but stayed up on his back as she directed him closer to the stable. When they were near, she hopped down and guided him inside to remove his saddle and change his bridle to a bitless halter and lead. She set her iPod and ear buds on the shelf in the tack room before petting his head, face, and neck. Then, she fed him a couple of carrots and strawberries and led him back outside towards the large pond that was located on the opposite side of the stable.

"Let's cool down the fun way," she said, tying his lead to one of the trees in the small cluster near the water's edge so she could remove her boots, socks, and hat. She'd already taken off her tank top.

*

Allison set the tray of food on the side of her father's desk. "I'm going to let Arthur go," she said, walking over to the window.

"What? Really?" her father questioned as he tore his bread in half to dip it in his soup.

"It's not working," she sighed as her eyes searched the training track, then the turnout pens, and finally the open arena.

"I thought you were getting along."

"Yes and no. He's not a bad person, I just don't think he's the right trainer for me."

"Hell, he wasn't really a trainer to begin with …you've been training that horse on your own since we got her."

"You're right. I guess he was more of a coach, but even in that atmosphere we weren't on the same page. I don't know." On a whim, she looked out at the pond. "What in the hell?" she gasped, seeing Carly Rae splashing around in the water in her bikini top and cutoff shorts with Sir Rigsby splashing next to her.

"What?" he said between bites of food. "Don't tell me one of the horses is out."

"Huh…no." She shook her head. "It's nothing." *At least nothing that you need to see.*

"Well, you know how I feel about all of this. It's your horse and your decision. You manage things however you see fit, but make sure it's the right choice."

"Thanks," she said with a smile as she walked over to kiss his cheek. "You have soup in your mustache," she whispered before walking out of his office.

*

Carly Rae was soaked from head to toe, along with Sir Rigsby, as they frolicked in the cool pond water. He splashed and played, then went a little deeper to swim around before coming back to her. She kept a hold of his lead the entire time so he couldn't stray too far. Watching him reminded her of her horse, Firefly, who also loved to frolic in the water.

"All right, boy. Time to get out," she said, tugging the lead to get him to step out of the water. She pulled the sweat scraper from her back pocket and began to squeegee the excess pond water from his coat. When he was no longer soaked, she led him into the stable and tied him to the hook in the shower stall so she could bathe him.

After lathering and rinsing each side of him from front to back, she moved to his mane and noticed Allison across from her, leaning against the outside of the tack room with her arms crossed over her chest. Her hair was down and she was dressed in khaki shorts with a black boat neck shirt tucked into them. A wide black belt cinched her small waist. Their eyes met for a brief second before Carly Rae began washing Sir Rigsby's short black mane.

"Taking that horse into the pond is a little nuts," Allison finally said.

"How so?" Carly Rae asked, rinsing the soap. "Interaction like that is very good for him. Your horse would actually benefit from play time and social interaction."

"My horse is of no concern to you."

"Well…since your father is my employer and this is his horse…I guess what I do with him is of no concern to you either," Carly Rae shot back as she moved to his tail. *Why do you have to be such an ass? You're beautiful and it would be so easy to get lost in my job here.* She finished his tail and began to squeegee him once more. He whinnied and moved around when she accidentally tickled him, causing her to miss whatever it was that Allison had said back to her as she calmed him back down. She shook her head and began toweling him off.

"I'm sure my father went over that with you," Allison continued.

Finally having enough, Carly Rae tossed the towel aside and turned around to face her. "What is your problem with me? Have I done something or said something?"

Surprised at her directness, Allison pushed off the wall and met her eye to eye. They were still six feet apart, but the space between them felt as hot as white coals. "I know you're trying to get my father's attention."

Carly Rae raised a brow and began to chuckle. "You're kidding me, right?"

"He's not interested in you, so you might as well stop," Allison said, clenching her jaw.

Carly Rae looked her up and down and grinned. "If there was anyone's attention here that I'd be trying to get, it would be yours."

Stunned, Allison's mouth parted. She looked as if she were contemplating kissing Carly Rae and slapping her…before she turned and walked away.

"Great," Carly Rae sighed. "I can't believe she thought I was into her father. No wonder she's been such a bitch." She shook her head and went back to the horse. "Come on, Rigs. I need to comb some conditioner through your main and tail so you can go relax in the hay and get dirty all over again," she mumbled.

*

Allison went into the house and flopped down on the couch in the parlor. This was her favorite room because it was where she would always find her mother, sitting and sipping her tea. It hadn't been used since her passing. Allison's father spent his time either in his office, his bedroom, or in the den, which was the one room he'd had full control over in the design and decorating process.

"She makes me crazy," Allison whispered as she ran her hand through her long hair, pushing the loose waves back over her shoulder. She grabbed her phone from the coffee table and Googled: Carly Rae Walsh. The first thing that came up was her racing stats with the WPBR organization. After scrolling a little, she found a very vague story about her being suspended due to an altercation with another racer. The article just below it was from three years earlier and had a headline that read: *Barrel Racer Making Waves Across Rodeo As First Out Lesbian*. She quickly read through the short article that talked about Carly Rae coming out to her fellow riders after competing in the sport for a decade and being in the closet the entire time. It also said several of her competitors praised her, but there were still some with old school beliefs who condemned it by saying there was no place in their sport for someone like her. She was quoted as saying she felt like the timing was right; she'd just won her second championship and felt like she needed to be her true self. When asked what she thought about the negative comments, she laughed and said there wasn't enough time in the day to educate people on equality, but hoped everyone would learn to coexist one day because discrimination of any kind had no place in the world.

Allison closed the webpage and bit the corner of her lower lip as she set the phone down beside her. She'd known she was gay for as long as she could remember. Going to an all-girls boarding school halfway around the world had helped her figure that out quite early on. However, she'd never told a soul other than the classmates she'd remained friends with over the years. She couldn't imagine the reaction she would get from the dressage world…much less her own father. She envied Carly Rae for having the courage to come out, especially within the rodeo community.

"And I accused her of wanting my father," she chuckled softly, shaking her head.

"What was that?" Harris said, passing by. He stopped and peered over the top of his glasses at her.

"Nothing."

He smiled and started walking away.

"Hey, let's go out to dinner," she blurted, feeling the need to get away.

"Uh…sure. Maybe we should invite Carly Rae. I don't think she's left since she arrived."

"I'm sure she does. How else does she eat?"

"That's true. I invited her to dinner again, but she had other plans. I wish you'd try to get along with her."

She stopped herself from rolling her eyes.

"Where do you want to go?" he asked. "The Cellar sounds good."

Allison laughed. "You definitely can't invite her to a steakhouse."

"Yeah…you're right." He smiled. "Come on. I'm suddenly starving."

TEN

A couple of days had passed since Carly Rae and Allison had their awkward confrontation. However, it was still fresh on Allison's mind, and when she looked out her bedroom window and saw a fire burning out by the tiny house, she couldn't help going outside.

The sound of a harmonica wailing and the smell of burning wood floated in the air as Allison walked across the property with only the light of the moon to illuminate her path. Carly Rae was sitting in a chair with one booted foot up on the stones of the fire pit and the other stomping a beat on the ground. Both hands covered the harmonica pressed against her lips. Her head bobbed and her body swayed with the music she was listening to on her iPod with one ear bud while she played along. Allison leaned against the patio railing, a little intrigued, slightly envious, and somewhat angry as she watched her.

"You shouldn't have a fire going. It's been too dry out," she said when Carly Rae stopping playing.

Carly Rae held the harmonica in her hand and paused her iPod as she lulled her head to the side to see the woman a few feet away. She raised a brow, then brought her eyes back to the fire as she pulled the instrument back up to her mouth. "Do you want to sit down?" she asked, ignoring her jab about the fire as she went back to playing.

Allison hesitated for nearly a minute. *Nothing ever goes right when I'm around this woman,* she thought before sitting down in the chair beside her. The fire crackled, sending tiny sparks into the sky as she played the harmonica and stomped her foot to the beat. Curious as to what she was listening to, Allison looked around for the iPod or at least the other ear bud, but didn't see either. "What's it about?" she asked when Carly Rae stopped playing to drink from a rocks glass sitting on the ground between their chairs.

"It's the blues. I'm pretty sure they're all about *someone*."

"They sound sad."

"They remind me of home," Carly sighed. "Have you ever listened to the blues?"

Allison shook her head.

Carly Rae gave her the extra ear bud that had been in her pocket. "This is a blues/rock band. I love their music. It's a combination of old blues and new blues sounds mixed with a classic rock twist."

Allison listened as the song began to play. It wasn't like anything she'd ever listened to, but she could see why Carly Rae was playing along. Her harmonica seemed to fit in naturally. She found her foot lightly tapping along to the beat, much like Carly Rae had been stomping her own foot. "It's different," she said when the song ended.

Carly Rae smiled as she reached for her drink. "Not what you were expecting?"

"Something like that." Allison nodded slowly.

"I might wear boots and a Stetson, but that's about as country as it gets and that's from growing up on the ranch. There's a lot of Native American music around there, along with frontier or bluegrass fiddles, harmonicas, and guitars, as well as the blues and indie rock, which was what caught my ear. Of course, country music is much bigger than everything else." She stared at the fire. "The blues sort of remind me of home. I don't get to see my parents often, but the hardworking values instilled in me came directly from the two of them. We used to be out for two, sometimes three days moving cattle in the spring and fall. My grandfather would build a fire for us to use for heat and to cook on, and we'd sit around making our own blues and folk music. He's the one who taught me how to play the harmonica. My father continued the same traditions when he took over. He's sold off some of the land and cut the cattle count down a bit over the years, but I still go back twice a year to help move the herd."

"Is it just cattle?"

"Cattle and hay. My father is the second-generation owner. He took over after my grandfather passed away and turned it into what it is today. I'll probably wind up the third generation in charge at some point…when I'm finished chasing the rodeo scene, I guess." She held her glass up. "You thirsty?"

Allison studied the glass. It looked like milk poured over ice. "What is it?"

Carly Rae laughed. "Do you ever just take a chance, or do you question everything?"

Allison watched the flames dance in her blue eyes.

Carly Rae took another sip and raised a brow.

Oh, what the hell? Allison held her hand out for the glass. She took a bigger sip than she'd anticipated. The cold liquid sloshed around her mouth and soared down her throat, leaving a warm sensation. She didn't care for it at first, but after a second, smaller sip, she handed it back. "Not bad. Is it milk and whiskey?"

"Creamy bourbon and ice," Carly Rae replied, finishing the remainder of the glass.

"I'm more of a wine girl, but that's surprisingly smooth."

"It'll get a hold of you before you know it," Carly Rae laughed.

"I take it that comes from experience."

"Oh, it definitely goes down easily. I won't lie, but I've seen a few people forget it was bourbon." She smiled. "I don't drink a whole lot, but when I do want something, bourbon is always my preference. I happened upon this creamy version a couple of years ago and can't seem to go back to the original."

"I can see why. That's not bad at all. My father likes scotch. Talk about nasty," she grimaced.

"I agree."

"I get my love of fine wine from my mother. She was French, born in Bordeaux, but moved to the UK when she was eight. She learned to ride horses in boarding school and was a natural at steeple chase. She wound up becoming a multi-time world champion. She was a pistol with the grandeur of an Englishwoman, and the feisty temperament of a Frenchwoman. And, she loved horses. In fact, she rode every day until the day she collapsed while walking through the house after suffering from a heart attack. Apparently, she had lived her entire life with a rare heart condition, unbeknownst to her. Less than twenty-four hours later, she had a second, massive attack that took her life."

"Oh, I'm so sorry."

"Thanks. I was tested to make sure it wasn't hereditary, and thankfully, I don't have it. I think my father wanted that for himself as much as he wanted it for me. I don't think he could handle losing both of us."

"That's good, but still sad. How long has she been gone?"

"Fourteen months."

Carly Rae didn't know what to say. She had no idea what it must be like to lose a parent, or in her father's case, to lose the love of his life.

"How did you get to know so much about horses?" Allison asked, changing the subject.

"My dad taught me everything he knew, which he learned from Shikoba, a Choctaw Native American friend of his whose land bordered ours. When Shikoba passed, he left his land to my father because he trusted him to treat it and it's animals with the same respect that he had."

"Wow. That must've been some friendship."

"He didn't own anywhere near as much as my family. Sadly, the government had taken most of his away from him. My father trusted his word and listened to what he had to say. Shikoba helped him in many ways when he took over the business. He was a great man." Carly Rae stoked the fire and stowed her harmonica in her pocket so she wouldn't drop it on the dirty ground.

"Why did you get suspended from the rodeo?" Allison questioned, changing the subject once more as she met her eyes.

"Going straight for the jugular, I see." Carly Rae stared back at her. "I told your father everything the day we met."

"I was just curious."

"It's not a big story, really," she sighed. "I've won three championships on the circuit. I get along with most people on the tour, but there are a few who would love to see me gone. One of them went as far as trying to kill my horse to make that happen."

"Are you serious?"

Carly Rae nodded. "She was about to feed Firefly a handful of homemade snacks full of elderberries. I caught her and it turned into an altercation. I admitted to throwing the first punch, so I went to jail for three days on an assault charge. WPBR review board analyzed the snacks and the video footage from the stable camera. They saw that she was alone and walked up to my horse's stall, holding her hand out. I came around the corner, catching her. My raised voice startled Firefly and she backed away, thankfully not eating any of them. When the results came back, I was suspended for six months for fighting and she was banned for life from WPBR, but it actually went further, banning her from competing in any professionally sanctioned equestrian competition, pretty much ending her career."

"That's crazy. Why would someone intentionally do that? Elderberry is deadly to a horse."

Carly Rae shrugged. "People are nuts."

Allison shook her head. "What about your charge?"

"I had to pay a fine and do twenty hours of community service because it was my first offense. I took Firefly to a special needs school and gave the children rides, let them pet her and brush her, and so on every day for an entire week. I'm pretty sure she loved it as much as they did."

The sincerity in Allison's eyes when she smiled, caught Carly Rae slightly off guard. She wasn't quite sure who this woman sitting next to her was. Gone was the hard-edged bitch who had harped on her at every turn. This woman was softer. She smiled effortlessly, laughed easily, and held her attention.

"I should call it a night. I didn't mean to come out here and take up your personal time. I saw the fire and—"

"It's fine. I promise not to burn down the family estate." Carly Rae grinned. "I'm about to put it out and go to bed myself."

"Goodnight, then." Allison turned and walked away, all the while, replaying their entire conversation in her head as she made her way back to the main house. She was surprised at how easily she had talked about her mother. It had been months since she'd told the story of her death, and although it hadn't gotten any easier, she'd told it to Carly Rae without her even asking.

*

The following Monday, Allison was putting Luna Mist in the turnout pen when she saw Carly Rae racing into the open arena atop Firefly. She leaned her back against the railing, watching intently as the horse lay over nearly forty-five degrees while going around the first barrel. This was the first time she'd seen Carly Rae take her horse through the course at full speed. The amount of control and trust between the animal and rider was fascinating. Firefly performed unbelievably as she straightened out of the turn and headed across to the next barrel, hitting the same angle again as she circled it in the opposite direction. Her long blonde mane flowed in the wind as she raced towards the final barrel, cutting another extremely tight turn before running at breakneck speed back out of the arena.

Allison turned around, pretending to be busy with Luna Mist when Carly Rae brought Firefly to a stop, and walked her around slowly to cool her down. She continued watching from a distance as Carly Rae and Firefly ran the course a few more times before going into the stable.

"That feels good, doesn't it, girl," Carly Rae murmured, massaging Firefly's legs after her bath. She put liniment and a wrap on each one as she finished, then fed her a couple handfuls of blueberries. Her ears perked up when she heard Allison walk by with Luna Mist. They hadn't seen each other since their conversation by the fire over the weekend. "Get some rest. You're going to have a big day tomorrow," she whispered, petting Firefly's head and face before leaving her stall and walking over to wash her hands.

"How fast does your horse run?" Allison said, walking up beside her.

"She can run a quarter mile in a little over twenty seconds. Quarter horses are bred for running extremely fast in a short distance like the quarter mile, hence the name quarter horse. They can run up to 55mph, but it's not sustained like a thoroughbred. They're made for long distances of a mile or more, and max out around 40mph, which they are able to maintain for the entire race."

"Wow. I had no idea," Allison muttered.

"Have you ever taken Luna Mist out free range running?"

"No." Allison shook her head. "She's not bred for that."

"She's still a horse. You'd be surprised at what she can do…if you'll let her."

Allison raised a brow, but bit back the snide comeback. She shrugged instead and walked away.

Carly Rae sighed and shook her head. "And back to square one," she whispered to herself before walking over to Sir Rigsby to pet him. She'd taken him out earlier to do an easy, long distance workout before training with Firefly. "Here you go," she said, handing him a couple of leftover blueberries. "You probably understand women about as much as I do," she added, petting his face.

ELEVEN

The sun hadn't been up long when Carly Rae poured herself a cup of coffee and headed over to the stable from the tiny house. Ollie was already inside checking off his chore list when she walked in and went over to the tack room.

"I fed Sir Rigsby and Firefly half an hour ago," he said, popping his head in. "I'm ready when you are."

"Great. I want to get on the track before it gets too hot. I'm going to turn them out together for a couple of minutes first so he is used to her being around him."

"Sounds good," he said.

"Morning," she called, seeing Allison walk by behind him.

"Ollie, why hasn't Luna Mist been turned out to warm up?" Allison asked, noticing she'd just finished eating.

"She's all bark and no bite," Carly Rae whispered to him with a smile while walking out of the room with Sir Rigsby's race saddle and bridle. "It's my fault," Carly Rae called from inside Sir Rigsby's stall. "I asked him to take care of Sir Rigsby and Firefly first this morning."

"Great," Allison huffed.

Not wanting to start another war, Carly Rae walked out of the stall. She held her hand up to Ollie, silently telling him she'd diffuse the situation as she walked down to Luna Mist's stall. "I asked him to do me a favor. I didn't change the permanent order of things. I'm running Sir

Rigsby with Firefly this morning and I needed them to eat an hour beforehand. I should have let you know. I'm sorry."

Allison looked at the blonde peering over the closed stall door. Her eyes were the prettiest shade of blue that she'd ever seen, reminding her of pools of water only seen in vacation magazines. She heard herself say, "It's fine," as she turned her attention back to Luna Mist. Carly Rae was gone when she looked back.

*

Sir Rigsby and Firefly had sniffed each other a few times in the turnout pen, but kept to themselves otherwise, indicating they were comfortable around one another. Carly Rae connected Firefly's lead to the saddle on Sir Rigsby's back so she could physically control him and give verbal commands to Firefly at the same time.

"What if this doesn't work?" Ollie questioned.

"Then he'll either have to wear blinders or always be in the lead," she said with a grin as she hopped up into the saddle and guided them towards the grassy area that had finally taken the shape of a real training track. The grass was mowed down to the lowest setting and their daily runs had helped wear it down further.

Ollie stayed behind them in case Sir Rigsby had an issue and he needed to take Firefly away. So far, everything was going as planned. Carly Rae directed Sir Rigsby onto the track and kept him at a light walking pace for the first two laps so that Firefly could get a handle on what they were doing. She clicked her teeth to pick up Firefly's pace when she slapped the rein slightly to propel Sir Rigsby into a trot. Then, she pulled the lead, bringing Firefly slightly closer, while petting Sir Rigsby the entire time to reassure him.

After a couple of laps at a trot, she turned both horses around to go in the opposite direction, before increasing their gait to a canter. Firefly moved to Sir Rigsby's other side and stayed right next to him as they went around the track.

"Looking good!" Ollie yelled as they passed by.

Carly Rae smiled and gave a thumbs up. She kept them cantering for another two laps, then slowed them to a walk to cool down before heading back up to the stable. She dismounted Sir Rigsby outside and led them into the wash area where she tied them to opposite wall hooks.

She removed her button-down shirt, hanging it over the wall before turning the hose on the two horses to cool them down.

*

"That run through looked better than it did last week," Harris said. He was leaning against the rail of the covered arena, watching his daughter.

"Yes. We're getting better with transitions. What do you think about that?" she said, nodding behind him where Carly Rae was coming back from the makeshift track with the horses tethered together.

He turned around and watched her climb down out of the saddle and lead the horses into the stable. "I think she's figured out how to communicate with that horse."

"What do you think about her training methods?"

He shrugged. "Are you still letting her bother you?"

"I actually had a decent conversation with her over the weekend."

"Oh, really," he said in surprise as he pursed his lips.

"Yes. I *am* capable of being human."

He laughed.

"Get out of here. I have training to do," she muttered, shooing him as she squeezed the horse with her legs to get her going.

Harris watched them ride back to the center of the arena to start all over, before walking over to the stable.

*

Carly Rae finished putting the liniment and wraps on Sir Rigsby's legs and put him in the stall. She gave him a handful of carrots and pet his head. "You did good today," she said. "Now, go lay down like lazy bones over there and get some rest," she added, tilting her head towards Firefly's stall across from him. She had her legs wrapped, then lay down after eating her snack.

"I thought he can't hear," Harris said, leaning against the wall by the tack room with his arms crossed, looking very much like his daughter.

"He can't, but I talk anyway out of habit."

"I saw you out on the track with both him and your horse. How did he do?"

"Surprisingly great. I don't think he's going to need blinders. I did notice anytime Firefly got close to even with him, he naturally increased his gait. I actually had to slow him a few times, which is a very good sign. He needs to be sprinting at full speed. He's ready for us to start training with a jockey. It'll take a few weeks for me to teach him how to handle Sir Rigsby, but after that, I think he'll be comfortable."

"I've exhausted just about all of my contacts. I can't find a jockey who fits with what we are looking for. Your friend… George Tibbetts, he would've been great, but he signed a contract to ride with Thompson Equestrian Stables for the rest of the year."

"Yeah, I heard about that."

"Didn't you say you grew up together?"

"Yeah. His father is the foreman for my family's ranch. He and my dad are best friends. Tibby and I used to race all over our property from the time we were able to get up on a pony. To this day we still bet on who can wrangle the most stray cattle during the bi-annual drives moving them from one pasture to another." She smiled.

Harris laughed.

"I should've told you to contact him from the beginning." She shook her head. "He would've been great."

Harris checked his watch. "I have a call in a few minutes, but why don't you come up and have dinner with us tonight? We can talk more about everything."

She reluctantly agreed. It was a business dinner, so there was that. However, another forced meal with Allison was the last thing she was looking forward to. "Damnit," she muttered after he'd walked away. She was about to leave the stable when Allison walked in with Luna Mist and tied her to the hook on the wall in the wash area to cool her down.

"Was my father just in here? I thought I saw him."

"Yes."

Allison nodded.

"There are some fresh blueberries in the feed room refrigerator. I put them in there this morning," Carly Rae said.

Allison furled her brow, giving her an odd look.

"For the horse," she said, pointing to Luna Mist.

"Oh…no thanks."

Carly Rae shook her head. "Treats aren't going to hurt her. Besides…she likes them."

Allison opened her mouth to say something, but Carly Rae had left the stable.

*

"What does one wear to her second dinner at the boss's house?" Carly Rae mumbled to herself as she searched the small closet. Her wardrobe consisted almost entirely of jeans, tank tops, and button-down shirts in everything from solid colors to multi-color plaid. "Hell with it," she grumbled, pulling on a fresh pair of jeans and a turquoise paisley button-down with short sleeves. She finished the look with her wide brown belt and oval buckle, and her cleanest pair of boots. She left the top couple of buttons open allowing the collar to form a V that stopped just above her small cleavage. She sprayed a hint of perfume on one wrist, then rubbed them together before walking out the door.

*

Allison was still seething from learning Carly Rae had given her horse treats without asking her. The last thing she wanted to do was sit across from her and eat dinner. She tried not to stare over the top of her wine glass at the blonde, but every time she lifted her eyes, baby blue ones were looking back at her. "I would appreciate it if you'd ask first before giving any treats to my horse," she said.

Carly Rae raised a brow as her lips formed a sly grin. "I apologize. I won't do it again."

"What's wrong?" Harris asked between bites of food.

"When I first arrived, I was getting to know Sir Rigsby. I had just given him some blueberries, so I offered a couple to Luna Mist when I introduced myself to her."

"Blueberries won't hurt her," he said, glancing at his daughter.

"They're not in her diet," Allison replied.

"Treats…in particular, healthy ones like fresh fruit and vegetables, are quite good for a horse, and they are a positive reinforcement," Carly Rae added.

"Yes…like swimming in the pond," Allison retorted.

Carly Rae shrugged. "Sure. It cools them down and they enjoy it. Horses like to play and have fun. You shouldn't deprive them of simple pleasures, especially when you ask so much of them day in and day out with rigorous training regiments. If you let your horse be a horse, you'll get a lot more out of her."

Allison was about to let her have it when her father intervened.

"I asked you to dinner to discuss business, not argue about blueberries," Harris said sternly, eyeing his daughter before turning his attention to Carly Rae. "I've solved our jockey dilemma."

"Great. When do we get started with training?"

"Actually…I'd like you to jockey him."

The remaining water from the sip Carly Rae had just taken, sloshed in her throat, causing her to choke.

"Are you okay?" he asked, concern spreading across his face as he watched her cough.

"Yeah…fine." She cleared her throat. "I don't know if that's a good idea. I'm not a jockey."

"I'm with her," Allison said.

Carly Rae furrowed her brows at her. *Don't get on my side now after throwing me under the bus for giving your horse a damn blueberry.*

"You and that horse have formed a rare bond. There's nowhere near enough time to teach someone how to handle him or develop that trust. Plus, you're already a racer. It can't be that different. You've been riding him like a jockey on the training track."

"How many women are jockeys?" Allison asked. "I've never seen one."

"It's about one percent, but there are some who have done well and won derby and stakes races." Carly Rae shrugged. "It's not a completely harebrained idea. I mean, we'd have to step up our training and get some practice time at a real track using a gate and pistol. I'd have to get licensed, too."

"I've already looked into that. Your work here with Sir Rigsby and your experience as a barrel racer surpasses the apprenticeship for the license. Therefore, all we have to do is two runs on a sanctioned track for you to demonstrate your knowledge of track rules and riding skills, and you'll be able to get your license."

"That's absurd. You have to do a hell of a lot more to be able to drive a car," Allison butted in.

"A horse is quite different from a car," her father said. "So, what do you think?"

Carly Rae bit her lower lip in thought for a moment, a gesture that didn't go unnoticed by Allison as she stared at her. The wine glass she'd hid behind earlier was long empty, leaving no barrier between them as their eyes met.

"I know I can do it. I'll have to cut ten, maybe fifteen pounds though. I'm five foot five, so I'll be on the tall side, but height isn't the problem. Jockeys are small because they are restricted by their weight."

Allison remembered seeing her in the bikini top and jean shorts when she was in the pond with Sir Rigsby, and she certainly wasn't overweight. "You'll be skin and bones if you lose fifteen pounds. That's crazy," she blurted without thinking.

Harris and Carly Rae both stared at her.

"I'd be the same way if I lost that much weight," she added.

"I'll check the condition book and see what the carry weight is for Santa Rosa. Hopefully, we'll be close."

"I should probably skip dessert," Carly Rae said with a smile, causing Harris to laugh. Allison looked from one to the other like they'd gone mad. "On that note, I'll say goodnight. Thank you again for dinner. I'm sure I'll be eating salad from now on," she joked.

Harris walked her to the door. As soon as it was closed, Allison met him in the foyer. "Are you really going to make her race that horse?"

"I'm not *making* her do anything. I asked if she'd be interested," he replied, slipping past her to go clear the table.

"She's not a race jockey."

He paused, holding the plates in his hands. "What's your problem? I thought you couldn't stand her."

"That's not the point."

He shrugged and went to the kitchen. She followed with the wine glasses. Neither said another word about it as they loaded the dishwasher together. When they were finished, Harris retired to the den and Allison headed up to her room.

She fed my horse treats without my permission. Why should I care if she starves herself to death to race that damn horse? She shook her head and peeked out the window. Part of her hoped to see a fire burning or a light in the stable, but the other part of her was happy it was dark out.

TWELVE

"Rigs is ready to run. He's been training on a race schedule recently and his speed has picked up. I can't run him full on because our training track is smaller than the ones he will race on, but he's strong and very smart," Carly Rae said as she sat down on the couch and put her feet up on the table. It had been a long day of training for both Sir Rigsby and Firefly.

"How's Firefly doing?" her father asked.

"She's good. I'm pretty sure they're friends. I tether her to him for short sprints since she's actually faster off the line. It's giving him the sense of having a horse next to him, and also making him faster in the first couple of furlongs. I won't know his top end speed and taper until we get him on a full-sized race track."

"That's great. Have you spoken with Tibby about jockeying him?"

"Yeah, he's under contract. Harris has someone in mind, so we'll see how it goes. How are things there?" she asked, changing the subject. She felt bad about not being truthful about jockeying the horse herself, but she wanted to make sure she could do it before announcing it to everyone.

"Good. With both you and Tibby gone, I'm going to hire a couple of local cowpokes to help with the upcoming cattle drive."

"Daddy, I told you I'd be there, and I will."

"You don't need to come all the way up here just to help me move some cows. You have a lot going on there."

"I get weekends off. Besides, it's not for six more weeks. I'll be there."

"Alright. I'll hire one cowpoke," he laughed.

"Deal," she chuckled before getting off the call to go make a salad for dinner.

*

The next morning, Allison looked around, but didn't see Carly Rae anywhere. Figuring she was out on the training track, she went into the stable. "Hey, Luna girl," she said, rubbing her face as she put the halter over her head. She clipped the lead to the end and opened the door for her to come out. Allison bypassed the tack room as she led her out of the stable and over to the larger of the turnout pens. Once Luna Mist was inside, Allison removed the lead and closed the door, allowing her free rein. "Alright," she sighed nervously. "Uh…go play."

*

It had been about a year since Carly Rae had last gone for a run, but with the need to cut weight quickly, she'd picked right back up where she'd left off. The training track had been the easiest place to run and softer than jogging on asphalt, but after two miles she was spent. She poured as much water down the front of her tank top as she did into her mouth, trying to cool herself down. "Now I see why Rigs gets so many massages. That was brutal," she mumbled to herself as she started walking back towards her rented tiny house.

As she neared the turnout pens she noticed Allison standing near the larger pen, watching Luna Mist trot around like a giddy farm horse. She raised a brow and gave Allison a sideways glance as she walked up.

"I'm giving it a try," she said bluntly. "Not that I think it will actually work."

"Even the busiest people with the most important jobs in the world need a little down time every now and then."

"Her down time is when she's in the stall or tethered on a lead, so being completely free like this is all new to her," Allison said, eyeing her suspiciously. She was dressed in a tank top and shorts, both of which were soaking wet, and sneakers. "Have you been in the pond?"

Carly Rae laughed. "No. I wish. I was out running the training track."

Allison nodded.

"It's the quickest and healthiest way to cut weight."

"I see. So, you're still doing that, huh?"

"Yep. What's your reservation? I didn't think you gave two shits about me or that race horse."

Allison watched a bead of sweet run down the side of her face and drip from her chin. She swallowed hard and cleared her throat. "I think it's crazy to make yourself sickly skinny in order to race a horse that may not do well at all. I keep wondering why you are here and doing all of this. I know he's barely paying you, so it can't be for the money. And if it's for your cut of the winnings, that's a pretty big gamble...considering."

Carly Rae nodded. "You are so passionate about dressage that you've never let your horse actually be a horse for a hot minute. You wear jodhpurs and blouses whether you're riding or not because you're comfortable in them. That's when you feel like yourself the most. Correct me if any of this is wrong."

"What's your point?"

"When you're passionate about something, it's not a job, and it's not a sacrifice. It's your life, and it's what makes you happy. Riding on the back of Firefly, racing around those barrels, it's a hard living, but it's my passion. I wouldn't trade it. And, training this horse is something I'm doing for him as much as myself. Getting to be the one who jockeys him…well, that's both a challenge and a reward. If I wanted to be on easy street, I would've gone home to the ranch and hung out until my suspension was over. I certainly wouldn't have brought Sir Rigsby's situation to your father's attention. However, I care too much for that."

Allison turned her attention back to her horse.

"Just so you know, running around and playing isn't going to make the horse forget the intricate steps ingrained in her head or the discipline it takes to perform them at the highest level. You'd be surprised at how smart these animals really are," Carly Rae said. She was about to walk away when she stopped. "Where's your trainer? I haven't seen him in a while."

"I fired him," Allison replied without looking at her. She wasn't going to tell her she'd been taking her unwanted advice and it had been working, which was also the reason she was standing at the rail watching her horse play in the turnout pen.

Carly Rae nodded and walked away. *That woman infuriates me and intrigues me all the same.*

*

Carly Rae was just about to her tiny house when Harris caught up to her. The last thing she wanted to do was have a conversation. She wanted a shower and needed to feed her starving belly the salad she wasn't looking forward to eating.

"I just got off the phone with the manager for the track. Sir Rigsby will need an up to date weight. The one from his last race won't work. However, he said if he's around the same weight, the jockey and tack will need to be a max of 126 pounds."

"I need to weigh the tack. How much time do we have?"

"That depends on you."

Carly Rae nodded as the numbers played in her head. "I'll check everything and let you know."

"If you don't want to do this, you know you don't have to," he said.

"I want to." She smiled. "I just don't know if we'll be able to make the weight work in our favor."

"I'll let you get back to it." He gave a half smile and walked away.

*

Allison was on her way back into the stable with Luna Mist when her father caught up to her. "Was she just free in the turnout pen?" he asked.

"Yes."

"I've never seen you do that before."

"Trying something new, I guess."

He nodded. "How did it go?"

"I'll find out tomorrow morning. Either she's forgotten everything, or she'll be relaxed and hopefully ready to work on her pirouettes."

"Fun, fun."

"Yeah." She put her in the stall and closed the door, leaving her father on the outside. "Did you know Carly Rae has been out running around the training track?"

"No, but she looked like she'd just been running when I talked to her. It's good exercise. Your mother use to go jogging a lot before you were born."

"She just started two days ago after you guys decided she should jockey that horse."

"Well…she did say she needed to shave a few pounds."

"She's already super fit," she countered as she began brushing her horse.

"True."

*

The next morning, Carly Rae rose with the sun, beating the alarm clock to the punch. She dressed quickly and slapped a little bit of peanut butter on a banana before rushing out the door with a cup of coffee in one hand and her breakfast in the other.

"Good morning," Ollie said with a smile. "I didn't know you can eat peanut butter on a diet."

"If I ate plain oatmeal with cinnamon one more day for breakfast, I was going to kill someone," she replied. "Besides, this isn't a lot of calories. Speaking of weight though, do we have a scale around here? I need to weigh the tack…and myself."

"I'll look around, but I'm not sure."

"It's no big deal. I can run out later and pick one up," she said. "How's Firefly this morning? I'm going to run the barrels with her before heading out to the training track with Sir Rigsby."

"She seems fine. I turned her out for a few minutes after breakfast."

"Sounds good," she said, walking her over to the tack room to get saddled up.

*

Allison had just finished putting Luna Mist in the turnout pen to cool down for a bit after their early morning training session, when she saw Firefly ride into the open arena with Carly Rae high in the saddle. She turned her attention away from her own horse to watch from a safe distance so she'd go unnoticed as they raced around the barrels at breakneck speed. A small dirt cloud flew up behind Firefly as she cut the corners, hugging the barrels tightly before speeding back out of the arena. Carly Rae let her rest for a minute before doing it all over again.

On the third run, Firefly went around the barrel on the right first, then raced over to the one on the left. She looked slightly off as she leaned to go into the turn. Suddenly, she crashed into the barrel, sending Carly Rae flying off of her. Allison gasped as her body hit the ground, rolling over twice before coming to a stop. She began screaming for Ollie at the top of her lungs as she ran towards the open arena.

Carly Rae was shaken, but seemed okay when she slid to a stop and dropped down next to her. She quickly assessed her for blood. "Don't move," she said.

"Oh, my God!" Ollie squealed, rushing over.

Firefly hobbled around, whinnying loudly on the other side of the arena.

"I'm…okay," Carly Rae whispered.

"Go call 911 from the office phone in the stable," Allison said. "Hurry! Then, call my dad's cell. It's probably sitting next to him on his desk."

"Firefly," Carly Rae mumbled. "Is…she…okay?"

"I don't know. *You* could be bleeding internally, though," Allison said.

"Please," Carly Rae whispered, meeting her eyes.

Allison couldn't take the pain she saw in the baby blue pools staring back at her. Ollie had already run off to call for an ambulance, so she looked around for the horse. Firefly limped as she walked, still whinnying. "She's limping," she said.

"Something…happened. I don't…"

Allison spotted Ollie running in their direction. "Go put her horse back in the stable. Be careful, she's limping on the left side," she said.

Carly Rae tried to sit up to see what was going on with Firefly, but Allison wouldn't let her. She cradled her close instead, making sure she remained completely still with one hand on her shoulder and the other on her hip.

Harris jogged into the arena at the same time the ambulance pulled in. Ollie had walked out of the stable and directed them to drive around to the opposite side.

"What happened?" Harris asked as Allison stepped away to let the paramedics work on Carly Rae.

"One minute they were racing around the barrels and in the next, the horse hit the barrel and she flew through the air," she said, trying to hide the quiver in her voice.

"She'll be okay," he murmured, wrapping his arm around her. "How is she?" he asked as they loaded Carly Rae onto a backboard, then placed it on a stretcher.

"She doesn't think anything is broken, and isn't complaining of any pain other than a headache, but we're talking all the precautions. Did anyone see the accident?" one of the medics asked.

"Yes," Allison said. "She was going about 20MPH, maybe more. The horse had a misstep and she went flying off. I saw her roll side to side at least twice." She swallowed the lump in her throat that made her feel like puking. She'd never seen anything like this in her life.

"Where are you taking her?" Harris asked.

"We had the trauma helicopter on the way, but at her request, we will transport her ourselves to Sonoma County General," the other medic replied as they loaded her in the back and began getting everything hooked up.

"I'm riding with you," Allison called, walking away from her father.

"I'm afraid you can't," the medic said.

"Come on, we'll follow them," Harris reassured.

"Sir, I wouldn't advise you to—"

"You just get her to the hospital. I'll worry about getting us there," he demanded.

The medic nodded and rushed around to drive the vehicle. Harris and Allison were already running towards his truck when the ambulance siren began wailing in the distance, having already left the property. Ollie stayed back to call the vet to come look at the horse. Allison prayed it wasn't bad and they didn't have to put her down. She didn't think she could handle watching Carly Rae nearly die and also breaking her heart in the same day.

Harris sped towards the hospital, watching for police, red lights, and idiot drivers all at the same time. He glanced at his daughter only once. She was staring straight ahead, breathing evenly, almost like she was in a daze. It reminded him of the time he'd seen his wife get thrown from her steeplechase horse in a competition. He thought he was going to be sick. It had felt like an out of body experience. Thankfully, she had been fine and only suffered minor bruises and a sprained wrist.

*

Allison watched the lines in the road as they blurred. *Please, just let her be okay,* she kept praying in her head over and over. She hadn't realized they arrived at the hospital until her father shook her shoulders gently, urging her to get out of the truck. "Sorry," she mumbled, passing by him as she got out. He closed her door and walked up to her.

"It's okay. I know you're shaken. That had to be horrific to witness. I'm sorry," he murmured, wrapping his arm around her. "Come on. Let's go in. I'm sure it will be a while before they know anything."

"We should at least be able to stay with her so she's not alone."

"I don't know. I guess we'll see," he said.

*

Carly Rae stared up at the hazel eyes of the doctor. A few red curls fell over her brow as she shined a penlight into Carly Rae's eyes, blinding her worse than the powerfully bright white lights overhead. She was still strapped down, completely unable to move.

"Let's send her for a head and neck CT. We'll work our way down from there," she said to the other trauma doctor and nurse. "You're in good hands, Ms. Walsh," she added, meeting Carly Rae's stare. "Let us know if anything hurts."

Carly Rae could barely speak with the brace around her neck, which was attached to the padding holding her head still. "Okay," she said without moving her mouth.

In what felt like seconds, but had to have been minutes later, she was whisked down the hall and shoved into a cylindrical machine head first. She kept her eyes closed and her breathing steady. She'd only had one other accident and it wasn't as severe, or at least she wasn't treated like it was. She'd wound up with a couple of hairline rib fractures which healed quickly, and hadn't been required to enter the CT tube.

*

Allison paced the floor while her father got a cup of coffee from the machine. They'd been at the hospital for nearly two hours with no update, when she'd walked over to the reception desk for the third time. "Are you sure there is no information you can give us? We're all she has. Her family is in Wyoming."

"Ma'am, I'm sorry. When she gives permission to the doctor, we can update you. Until then, there's nothing more I can do since you're not immediate family."

Allison stormed back over to the chair and flopped down. "She probably has no idea we are even here."

Her father nodded. "I agree. Otherwise, she would've given the okay for us to see her, or at least know her condition. I'm sure they are running tests right now." He handed her a paper cup. "It's some kind of tea."

Allison took the offering, but set it aside without so much as a sniff. Her mind raced in a hundred directions. What if she was hurt worse than she thought? What if she really had been bleeding internally and was in surgery right now? What if….

"Miss," the nurse at the desk called, waving for Allison to come over.

Allison shook away her train of thought and practically ran the ten or so feet that separated them.

"The doctor said Ms. Walsh has given permission for you to come back to where she is," the nurse said, handing her a sticker with the words: Trauma 2 / Allison McKinley, written on it. "You have to wear this on you at all times. She's in trauma bay two. Go through those doors and take the first left. You will see the sign for the trauma unit."

"Thank you," Allison gasped and turned back towards the people in the waiting area. "What about my father?"

"I'm sorry. Only one visitor at a time in trauma."

"Go on. I'll be right here," he said, waving her on.

Allison waited for the automatic doors to open, then she walked through, immediately seeing the word trauma written in red with an arrow. She followed until she was at a second set of automatic doors. She pushed the button and walked inside once they opened. Doctors and nurses were bustling about, paying no attention to her as she walked around looking for bay number two. Finally, she spotted it just as a woman with curly red hair, wearing dark blue scrubs walked in. Allison stepped inside behind her.

"Okay, we have…" the doctor started, then stopped when she saw the dark-haired beauty rush to Carly Rae's side with a deer in the headlights look on her face. She cleared her throat.

"I'm sorry you were back here alone," Allison said.

"You're just in time for the doctor to tell me I'm fine," Carly Rae said, meeting her eyes. "Go on," she added, looking back at the doctor.

"As I was saying, I have your CT results. Your brain tissue, skull and cervical spine all look fine. The ultrasound of your torso is also clear. It appears you did not sustain any severe injuries. However, you do have a concussion. That's what is causing the headache and probably a little fuzziness as well. You'll need to be cautious for a week. If you were to hit your head again, it could cause a serious brain injury. No horseback riding, driving, or jogging for a week. You will want to follow up with your primary care physician if your headache doesn't go away, or if you start to feel pain in other areas before a week has passed." She looked at Allison. "Do you live with her?"

"Uh…sort of," she answered.

"Not really," Carly Rae interjected.

"I don't need to know your personal business, but whatever is said in this room is safe with me. Anyway, just for tonight and maybe tomorrow, it would be good if someone was with her in case she gets dizzy. She'll be very sore for the next few days, so sleep will be great for her."

"Okay," Allison muttered, biting her lower lip. She didn't dare look in Carly Rae's direction.

"With that said, I'll send the nurse in with your discharge papers. You got very lucky, Ms. Walsh."

"Yeah," she sighed, already thinking about how she was going to train Sir Rigsby and cut weight when she couldn't do anything for a week. "How's Firefly?" she asked as soon as the doctor left the room.

"Ollie had the vet come out immediately. He sent a text to my father, but I don't remember what he said other than she wasn't injured in the accident. How are *you* feeling?"

"I'm fine."

"How bad is your headache?"

"It's nothing I can't handle. Why did you say you lived with me and would be there with me tonight?"

"Someone has to look after you. You were just thrown from a horse and have a concussion."

"I'll be alright."

"You do realize this happened on our property and you are considered an employee, right? There's no way I'm letting you stay alone."

"You're looking out for yourself...so I don't sue, is that it?" Carly Rae clenched her jaw, making her head hurt that much worse.

"Yes and no. Yes, we definitely don't need to get sued, and no, I truly want to make sure you're okay."

"Uh huh." Carly Rae was about to say more, but the nurse came in with the discharge papers.

"Sign these and you'll be good to go."

"Where are my clothes?" Carly Rae asked as she signed the papers. She still had her jeans on, but her shirt had been replaced with a hospital gown.

"Right here in this bag hanging on the bed," the nurse replied, taking the clipboard from her.

"I'm going to go tell my father we are ready to leave so he can pull the truck around. It's a bit of a walk."

"I can manage," Carly Rae said.

Allison left the room anyhow.

Carly Rae removed the gown and put her bra and shirt back on.

"She's very pretty," the doctor said, seeing her step out of the room. She nodded towards the exit doors that Allison had just passed through.

"She's a feisty pain in the ass," Carly Rae muttered with a sigh as she headed off in that same direction.

THIRTEEN

All Carly Rae wanted to do was see Firefly and take a shower, but Allison had insisted she eat something and lie down on the couch. Sure enough, she'd fallen asleep, then awoke slightly disoriented two hours later.

Allison rushed over.

"I'm fine," she said groggily as she sat up.

"How's your headache?" Allison asked, leaving some space between them as she sat down on the couch.

"About the same, I guess. Listen." Carly Rae turned towards her. "I'm fine. Really. You don't have to stay here and do all of this. It's not like we're friends," she said, adding, "although, the doctor thought you were my girlfriend."

Allison spit out the mouthful of water she'd just drank, spraying droplets all over the coffee table. Carly Rae chuckled as she cursed and got up to get a paper towel. She quickly wiped up the mess and tossed it in the trash.

"What did you say to her?" she questioned, choosing to lean against the kitchen island a few feet away instead of sitting by her on the couch again.

"Nothing. I left." Carly Rae shrugged. "She assumed. There was no need to explain anything."

Allison nodded.

"I need to go see Firefly."

"Ollie texted me a bit ago. She's resting. The farrier just left."

"How bad was it?"

Allison walked back over to the couch and sat down next to her. "He couldn't find a reason why the shoe came off, but he went ahead and trimmed her hooves and put new shoes on her and the rest of the horses as well. The vet said to watch that one hoof for a few days and see how she is walking. If she goes lame, call him immediately."

Carly Rae shook her head. "I always check her shoes. I didn't see anything wrong with it."

"It's not your fault. It probably came loose during your training. There was no way to know that would happen." Allison looked at the baby blue eyes staring back at her. "Accidents happen. You're extremely lucky you didn't get seriously injured."

Carly Rae shrugged, still blaming herself. "You can't stand me. So, why are you really here?" she said, her voice softening slightly. "I'm not going to sue your father. I know it was his property, but I was riding my own horse. He has no blame in any of this."

"I know that." Allison bit the side of her lower lip. Her hair had come out of its braid at some point, and was now hanging in loose waves around her shoulders. Her chocolate brown eyes held a touch of innocence that Carly Rae had never seen before. "I'm not here because of my father. I told the doctor I would look after you," she sighed, pulling her gaze away as she got up and walked over to the kitchen. She silently wished for something a little stronger as she refilled her glass with ice and water.

Carly Rae began humming one of her favorite Larkin Poe songs as she lay back down on the couch. Allison had obviously made up her mind, and there was no convincing her otherwise.

"I'm going to run up to my house to get a few things. I'll bring dinner back with me," Allison said, looking at the clock on the wall.

Carly Rae nodded and yawned. Her head was still hurting and all she wanted to do was forget this day even happened.

*

"I wasn't sure I'd see you at all," Harris said as his normally genteel daughter walked into his office and plopped down on one of the chairs in front of him like an exhausted maid at the end of her shift. "Is it that bad?" he laughed.

"That woman is as hard headed as a concrete mannequin," she sighed.

He chuckled. "Have you met yourself?"

She stared at him with the same look her mother used to give him.

"She's always been pretty down to earth every time I've talked to her." He shrugged.

"Uh huh."

"How is she doing?" he questioned, leaning back in his chair.

"She says she's fine, but I think she's holding back." *I'm pretty sure I can see it in her eyes.* "Anyway, I told the doctor I'd stay with her tonight. Someone has to look after her in case she gets dizzy."

He nodded.

"She thinks you are worried she's going to sue you," she said.

"That's the least of my worries. Besides, she's not that kind of person."

"She also thinks that's why I'm looking after her."

"I know why," he replied.

"You do?" she questioned, sitting up a little straighter.

"You're just like your mother. You are tough as nails, but you have a kind, caring heart."

"Yeah," she muttered. "Anyway, I'm going to heat up dinner before I head back."

"Is it that time already?" He shook his head. The entire day had been a blur since the accident that morning.

"Do you want me to bring your plate up to you before I go?"

"Yes, might as well," he sighed, looking at his computer.

*

Carly Rae stood under the hot spray, washing away the gritty dirt from the arena that had managed to get under her clothing and into her hair. When she'd had enough of the steam and heat, she turned the water off and stepped out to dry off. She ran the towel over her body and through her short hair before pulling a light grey, ribbed tank top over her naked torso. She stepped into a pair of dark blue bikini briefs and added an old, worn pair of grey cotton shorts over them.

Suddenly, Allison burst through the door. "What are you doing in the shower? What if you'd had a dizzy spell and fell down?" she blurted, as her eyes raked over the woman in front of her. Leftover steam from the shower heated her skin, causing a bead of sweat on the back of her neck under her hair.

"I needed to take a shower. Was I supposed to wait for you to join me?" Carly Rae said.

Allison's jaw flopped open. She quickly slammed it shut and swallowed hard. "Your dinner is in the kitchen," she muttered as she turned and left the room.

Carly Rae followed her down the hall and sat down adjacent to her at the small kitchen island. A plate of grilled chicken and veggies was in front of each of them. "Thank you," she said.

"You're welcome," Allison replied without looking over at her.

"A glass of wine would be good right about now," Carly Rae added.

"More like a bottle," she muttered.

*

Allison changed into a dark blue, satin tank top and shorts pajama set and settled on the couch after Carly Rae had gone to bed. It had been an exhausting day and she was ready to close her eyes. The small couch was somewhat lumpy and certainly nothing like the pillow top, queen-sized mattress up in her room at the main house, but she was too tired to notice.

She was sure she was dreaming when she heard a thud. She moved to roll over and nearly fell off the couch, waking herself up. She realized it wasn't a dream when she heard Carly Rae moving around. She jumped up and went down the hall. "Are you okay?" she called as she went into the bedroom.

"Yeah, I knocked my water glass over. I'm sorry I woke you," Carly Rae said, putting the towel down on the water beside the nightstand. She stood up too fast, causing her brain to slosh. She immediately became light headed. Allison rushed over, wrapping her arms around her before she fell to the floor. "I'm fine," she whispered, trying not to let herself get lost in the woman holding her.

"Uh huh," Allison mumbled. The feeling of Carly Rae's body pinned against hers was absolutely maddening. The thin material between them did nothing to mask the heat building inside of her. Their faces were inches apart with Carly Rae standing eye to eye with her in their bare feet.

Their bodies finally separated as Carly Rae sat on the edge of the bed. "You're really warm," she said, feeling the cool air tinge her skin where Allison had just been.

"It's hot in here," she grumbled, annoyed with herself.

Carly Rae's body was heating up deep inside and it definitely was not from the temperature in the room. "I'm okay now," she said, needing to put some space between them. "You can go back to bed. I didn't mean to wake you."

"It's fine," Allison said. "How's your headache?"

"Better I guess."

"Are you still lightheaded?"

"No."

"Alright," Allison sighed. "Get some sleep."

Carly Rae laid back, listening to the soft steps as Allison made her way back to the couch.

*

The smell of coffee roused Carly Rae from her slumber the next morning. She moved to get up and instantly felt like she'd been run over by a truck.

Everything was sore. It even hurt to breathe. She winced in pain as she rose from the bed and walked to the bathroom.

Allison was sitting at the small kitchen island, sipping a cup of tea while pushing scrambled eggs around on her plate with her fork when Carly Rae appeared, still dressed in the tank top and shorts she'd slept in. She dropped the fork and set the mug down before rushing around to help her, but Carly Rae refused the assistance. Instead, she clenched her jaw and held her breath as she slid onto the stool.

"How are you feeling?" Allison asked, seeing the agony in her face.

"Like I was thrown from a horse," Carly Rae sighed, noticing Allison had changed from her revealing pajamas to a pair of khaki shorts and a black, ballet neck t-shirt. Her hair hung around her shoulders in loose waves.

"Can I make you something to eat? You barely had anything yesterday."

"Coffee is fine."

"You need to eat something," Allison said softly. "Cream and sugar?"

"Both...easy on the sugar. The cream is fat free."

"You're not still trying to lose weight to race that horse, are you?"

"Yes," Carly Rae replied, taking the mug that Allison set in front of her. "That is if I have enough time," she added.

"Even after what happened yesterday?" Allison left her plate of cold eggs alone as she sipped her tea.

"That wasn't the first time I was thrown from a horse, although I hope it's the last. I'm fine. The sore muscles and achy bones will be back to normal long before these two weeks are up."

"What about your concussion? Aren't you the least bit worried?"

"No. As long as I don't hit my head again anytime soon, it'll be okay. My headache is gone. I guess it was no match for the morning after aches and pains," she said, sipping her coffee.

"I still think you should eat something."

"What about you? You're not dieting, yet your breakfast is sitting there, ice cold."

Allison shrugged. "I wasn't as hungry as I thought I was."

Carly Rae nodded. "You don't have to hang out here all day. I know this is the last place you want to be, and honestly, I'm fine. The dizziness is gone. I'm just going to lie around, and probably soak in the tub, like a beat-up punching bag for the next couple of days. There's no reason for you to miss your training with Luna Mist."

Allison bit the edge of her bottom lip in thought. She was actually hoping to do a light session that morning, but wasn't sure how Carly Rae would be feeling. "If you're sure you'll be okay, and promise not to go mess with the horses…."

"I'm damn sure not going outside of this house. I can barely move. Go do what you want. I don't need to be babysat," she insisted.

"Alright. Get some rest, and be careful getting in and out of the tub. If you think you can make it to the main house and up the stairs, you can use my tub. The jets would probably help massage the soreness."

The idea rolled around in Carly Rae's head for a long minute as she drank her coffee. "Thanks, but I don't think I'd be able to get to it…not today anyway."

Allison nodded as she pulled her eyes away. "I'll come check on you around lunchtime."

*

A little after lunchtime, Allison found Carly Rae sound asleep in her bed, still dressed in her tank top and shorts from the night before. She leaned against the wall, watching her in her slumber. She looked peaceful, which made Allison believe her soreness was easing. That, or she'd taken the prescribed pain medication sitting on the nightstand beside the glass of water. Either way, she was happy to see her resting.

"Didn't your parents tell you it was impolite to stare?" Carly Rae grumbled as her blue eyes fluttered open. Her short blonde hair was in slight disarray as she rolled over and sat up.

"I—I'm sorry. I didn't mean to wake you," Allison stammered. "Uh…I brought you lunch."

"It's fine. I need to get up and move around so I don't get stiff," Carly Rae said, wincing a little as she got out of the bed.

"Did you take your pain meds?"

Carly Rae looked back at the bottle on the nightstand. "I dumped those down the toilet yesterday. There's nothing but ibuprofen in there now."

"Aren't you hurting?"

"Yeah, but I'll be fine. Nothing is broken. It's just bruises, and they will heal in a few days," she replied, sliding past her to exit the room. "What did you bring for lunch? It doesn't smell like diet food," she added, smelling the flavors wafting in the air as she walked to the kitchen.

"Well…it's not. I figured you needed a little more sustenance than lettuce. Your body *is* healing after all," Allison replied, following her.

Carly Rae sat on the stool and opened the steaming container of homemade macaroni and cheese. Her stomach growled and her mouth watered. "Are you trying to sabotage me?"

"What?" Allison chuckled, leaning against the counter in the corner between the sink and stove.

"You don't think I can jockey Sir Rigsby. Or, you don't want me to. I haven't figured out which one yet."

"I don't care what you do."

Carly Rae locked eyes with her across the small island. "Then why are you here?"

"Maybe I should ask why you won't let someone help take care of you?"

"You didn't answer my question."

Allison shrugged and crossed her arms. "You didn't answer me either."

"Fine," Carly Rae huffed. "I'm not used to having someone fuss over me."

"Not even your mother?"

"Sure…when I was ten." Carly Rae smiled. "She learned early on that her pretty little girl was a rough and tough tomboy who wanted nothing more than to be on the back of a horse, rip-roaring across the vast acres of land, chasing cows like her daddy."

"I see." Allison bit the side of her lower lip in thought. "I suppose my need to nurture stems from my mother's death. I wasn't here when it happened. She seemed perfectly healthy when I saw her the weekend before. I had no idea a tiny issue would take her from me in the blink of an eye."

117

Carly Rae's eyes softened. "I'm not going to die. It's a simple concussion," she murmured.

"I know that, but witnessing the accident and aftermath...just brought something back, I guess." After a long second, she cleared her throat and pushed off the counter. "Anyway...eat the food. Toss it in the trash. It's really none of my business what you do or how you do it."

Carly Rae watched her leave before she could say anything. The enticing smell of the food in front of her made her stomach growl once more, reminding her that she was starving. "I don't have to eat the entire bowl. A little goes a long way," she mumbled to herself as she dug the spoon in.

FOURTEEN

The next day, Carly Rae felt a little better and found herself walking towards the stable with a cup of coffee in her hand.

"How are you doing?" Ollie asked, seeing her enter.

"I'm good. Still feel like a horse tossed me on my ass though." She winked with a grin.

"I guess it looked a lot worse than it was. I know it scared Miss Allison pretty good. I didn't see it, but I heard her screaming."

Carly Rae nodded. She hadn't realized how bad it must've been for her. "Where is she?" she asked, looking around.

"Out with Luna Mist. She's been letting her play in the turnout pen after their morning training."

"Really?"

"Yeah. It's the damndest thing. She's always been so strict with that horse. She was even riding her around the property yesterday."

"Huh..." Carly Rae mumbled.

Hearing the familiar voice, Firefly poked her head over her stall door and began whinnying and stomping her hoof.

"I see you, girl!" Carly Rae said, setting her mug down and walking over to show her horse how much she missed her. The horse sniffed every square inch of her from her shoulders to the top of her hair. "I'm okay," she cooed, petting her head and face before wrapping her arms around her neck in a hug.

"Her hoof is fine. I've been checking it every day," Ollie said. "I didn't see any limping when she was in the turnout pen this morning. I kept her on a lead though, just in case."

"Great. Thank you for taking care of her for me."

"It's no problem," he replied on the way to Luna Mist's stall with fresh hay for the floor.

Carly Rae saw Sir Rigsby stick his head up in excitement when he saw her. "I'll be there in a minute, boy," she said, knowing he couldn't hear her. She pet Firefly one more time, then walked over to show him the same attention she'd given to her own horse.

"I'm pretty sure he missed you, too," Ollie said, passing back by her with the empty wheelbarrow. "I've turned him out every day, but it's not the same as the training you do with him."

"Yeah," she sighed. "He needs to run."

"Do you think Miss Allison would ride him for you?"

Carly Rae laughed. "She doesn't even want me riding him, so I doubt it."

"Doubt what?" Allison said, walking into the stable with Luna Mist on the lead.

"Ollie asked if you would ride Sir Rigsby for me to exercise him. I said I doubt it."

"You are correct," she replied matter-of-factly, tying Luna Mist to the hook on the wall so she could brush her down.

Carly Rae glanced over at Ollie and shrugged with a grin before going into the feed room to get some treats out of the refrigerator for both horses. "Did the blueberries go bad?" she asked him when she returned with a few strawberries.

"Not that I know of. I gave them each a couple of blueberries yesterday and there was a handful left, I think."

"Hmm…" Carly Rae looked at Allison, who seemed to be ignoring their conversation. "A ghost horse must've eaten them," she said. "A…dapple gray one."

He snickered and shook his head as he walked away, heading out of the stable.

"If you're implying my horse ate your fruit…I will gladly replace it," Allison said, walking by with Luna Mist to put her in the stall.

"I'm not worried about the fruit. I'd be more inclined to get your horse's IQ tested if she was able to not only open the refrigerator, but the plastic container they were in as well," Carly Rae called.

Allison ignored her as she passed back by.

"That mac n' cheese was good yesterday. Thank you."

Allison turned around to look at her. "You actually ate it?"

"Not *all* of it, but yes, I ate lunch."

"You seem to be doing better today."

"I'm still sore, but moving around and seeing these two definitely helps."

"I'm headed up to the house for lunch. Can I bring you anything? Or would you like to come up and eat with us?"

"Thank you, but I'm sure I've taken up enough of your time. I'm going back to my house to make some lunch and lie down."

Allison nodded. Carly Rae's eyes held hers for an extra second before she turned and walked away.

*

A couple of days later, Carly Rae had Sir Rigsby and Firefly out in the turnout pen getting some exercise. She leaned against the railing as they played together. She glanced in the direction of the covered arena, but Allison and Luna Mist weren't inside.

"Do you need any help?" Ollie called, riding by on the tractor on his way to groom the arena.

"I've got it. Thanks," she called with a wave.

After the horses had been in the pen for an hour, she went in and connected a lead to each halter. "Come on. Let's go swimming," she said, tugging to get them going in her direction.

"You shouldn't be doing that. It's only been four days," Allison called as Carly Rae neared the pond with the two horses. She was wearing a black tank top over her bikini, as well as a pair of cut off shorts and her boots.

Carly Rae spun around, seeing her coming out of the stable behind them. "I'm not riding them. I'm taking them to cool down. Do you want to come along…you know, just in case?"

Allison hesitated for a minute. *She's going to do it whether or not I'm there, so I might as well make sure she's safe.* "Fine, but I disagree with this, just so you know."

"Got it," Carly Rae called over her shoulder as she walked the horses down to the water. Firefly went right in and Sir Rigsby followed, albeit a little more tentatively. Carly Rae pulled off her boots and put her socks inside, then placed her tank top over them.

"You're not going in with them, are you?" Allison cringed.

"Sure. Why not?" Carly Rae smiled as she went into the water. Both horses came right to her. She splashed water, encouraging them to play. Once the cool water hit Sir Rigsby, he remembered what it was like to frolic. He and Firefly began splashing around as they played.

Allison quickly backed up to avoid getting wet, but the splashes got her front anyhow. She grumbled under her breath and pulled the damp clothing that clung to her skin.

Carly Rae moved and pretended to slip down to see what she would do.

Allison rushed into the water and knelt at Carly Rae's side with her arm around her bare back in an embrace similar to when she'd helped her next to the bed when she was dizzy. Her heart raced like a thoroughbred in her chest when their eyes locked. "Are you okay?" she mumbled.

"You're in the pond." Carly Rae grinned.

Realizing she'd slipped down on purpose, Allison backed away and splashed her with water. "You ass! I thought you were hurt!" she spat.

Carly Rae laughed as she got up and splashed her back. Both horses played nearby, kicking the water up around them.

Allison shook her head and tried to stop the smile from forming on her lips, but she failed miserably. "These are brand new jodhpurs and I also have my riding boots on!"

"Oh, they'll dry out. Live a little," Carly Rae said, spraying her again with a fan of water.

Allison laughed and slung water back at her.

*

When they'd had enough of the pond, Allison helped Carly Rae take the horses into the stable. They tied their leads to the hook in the wash area, and Carly Rae grabbed the soap while Allison went for the hose. She waited for Carly Rae to lather both sides of Firefly before spraying both her and the horse with the water.

"Hey!" Carly Rae shrieked.

"You were in the way." She shrugged.

"Uh huh."

Allison set the hose down and helped wash her mane and tail. Carly Rae went to wash the horses head and face and rubbed the sponge right over Allison's back.

"Oh, that's just wrong," Allison grumbled through a smile, pretending to be angry.

By the time they'd finished with the horses, both women had pretty much taken baths as well. Allison put Firefly back in her stall, then walked across to Sir Rigsby's stall when Carly Rae closed the door.

Carly Rae gazed at the chocolate brown eyes staring back at her as she reached up, pulling a leaf from Allison's hair that had obviously come from the pond.

Allison leaned forward, taking her by surprise as she closed the distance between them. Carly Rae's lips were soft and inviting, and her face was still wet from playing with the water while washing the horses.

It took Carly Rae a split second to realize what was happening, but once she did, her lips parted and her tongue snaked out, gliding along Allison's. The delicate kiss quickly intensified into a heated exchange, leaving both women breathless. Allison backed away before Carly Rae could pull her in closer.

Carly Rae licked her bottom lip before biting it between her teeth. The staccato beating of her heart was a telltale sign of the desire building low in her belly. She quickly tamped down her body's excitement when she saw the uncertainty in Allison's eyes.

"I'm sorry," Allison whispered. "I can't do this."

Carly Rae felt rooted to the ground as she watched her walk away. In all honesty, she wasn't surprised Allison had kissed her, then apologized like it had been an accident. She'd seemed like the straight-curious type when they'd first met. "That went well," she sighed, looking over at Firefly who had been watching the entire time. "I know. No more straight girls. I agree," she said, petting her face.

*

"What the hell were you thinking?" Allison mumbled as she made her way up to the main house. "That's the last thing you need," she continued chastising herself as she entered through the back door, hoping to slip up to her room and avoid her father's questioning, but he was standing in the kitchen, having just made a fresh cup of coffee.

"What happened to you?" he asked.

"I went swimming, obviously," she grumbled, removing her wet boots.

"Swimming?" he muttered, his brow furrowing. "In the pond?"

"Where else?" she replied, crossing her arms. "It's a long story. I'd rather just go take a shower and forget about it," she added when he opened his mouth to speak.

"Okay," he said with a nod, pursing his lips.

She quickly headed to her room in her soggy, wet socks, too annoyed to take them off.

FIFTEEN

Luna Mist did a perfect pirouette circle before shifting easily into a half pass that sent her moving forward in a diagonal position. From there, she moved through a series of collected gaits, shortening and elevating her stride as she changed from a trot to a canter and back again.

Allison sat in the saddle in full riding gear, giving all of her attention to the run through of their full routine. The regional championship was coming up soon and they'd begun competition format training. She was about to guide Luna Mist through the final section of their routine when she caught sight of Carly Rae, standing against the far rail talking to her father. She faltered slightly, but recovered quickly and stiffened her back, maintaining perfect positioning and full composure.

*

"How are you feeling?" Harris asked, calling Carly Rae over as she passed by.

"Good," she replied, willing her eyes not to focus on the woman atop the massive dapple gray horse, but they failed her miserably. All she could think of was the feeling of Allison's mouth on hers. "What was that?" she questioned, realizing he was talking again.

"I said she's mesmerizing, isn't she?"

She's beautiful. "Uh…yeah." She cleared her throat. "It's all I can do to get my horse to circle a barrel in

126

opposite directions. I can't imagine the discipline it takes to train a horse to do all of those maneuvers perfectly in a routine."

"She's come a long way with this horse. I'm glad she found a way to get her to relax and focus on her training." He cocked his head to the side. "I'd think training a deaf horse to be a derby racer wouldn't be too easy either."

"Nah. You just teach him the signals for gas and brakes and set him free," she said.

"What about the rider?"

"You better know how to drive and hold on at the same time," she laughed.

He chuckled. "When do you think you'll get back to training?"

"Soon, hopefully. I have a doctor's appointment tomorrow to clear me from the concussion. If all goes well, I'll be back on him before the end of the day."

"That's good news. Let me know how it goes. Your health and safety come first."

"Thank you," she said, watching Allison bring the horse to a stop. "I'd better get back to what I was doing," she added, before heading towards the turnout pen.

*

Allison watched Carly Rae leave as she slowly walked the horse towards where her father was standing. They hadn't spoken since the impromptu kiss in the stable two days earlier, and she wasn't sure what to say to her when they did finally speak. It had been a mistake, one she couldn't stop herself from making, and she'd relived it in her dreams for the past two nights as penance, drawing her back like a moth to a flame all over again.

"That looked flawless," her father said, bringing her head out of the clouds.

"Hmm…yeah, it was close," she muttered, glancing towards the turnout pen as she hopped down. "I think we'll be ready," she added, removing her helmet and grabbing the rein to keep Luna Mist from walking away.

"Aren't you always?" He smiled. "Carly Rae is going to the doctor tomorrow to get released. She said she's feeling good."

Allison nodded. "That's great. I haven't seen her in the past few days. I've been too busy with training to notice anything around me," she lied. She'd spent the last two days constantly wondering where she was and what she was doing, yet avoiding her anytime she was nearby.

Her father's cell phone range, ending their conversation. He smiled, kissing her cheek before walking away to take the call. She was sure she smelled the faint hint of cigar, but he'd quit smoking weeks ago. She shrugged it off and started towards the stable with Luna Mist in tow.

*

Carly Rae bounded into the stable the next afternoon, full of excitement like a puppy waiting for a treat.

"I would assume you're so giddy because you got released from the doctor, am I right?" Ollie asked with a big smile on his face.

"Free and clear!"

"All right!" he cheered.

"I just sent a picture of the paperwork to Harris. I don't have time to hand it to him in person," she said, going into the tack room to get a saddle, bridle, and rein.

"Who are you riding?"

"I need Firefly to know that everything is okay. When I come back, me and Rigs are going to the track," she answered, as she removed Firefly from the stall and began tacking her up.

"I'll have him ready and waiting," he said.

As soon as Firefly was ready, Carly Rae grabbed the rein and horn and climbed up into the saddle. Then, she clicked her teeth and gave the horse a light squeeze with her legs to get her moving. "Come on, girl. Let's ride!" she said, leading her away from the stable and towards the back part of the property that butted up against the sprawling grape vineyards. Firefly was hesitant to go full speed at first, but Carly Rae pet her neck, assuring her that it was okay. There was nothing like the steady bounce of a galloping horse, the leather rein in your hand, and the wind in your hair. *God, I missed this!*

By the time Carly Rae had finished her ride, Ollie had completed his chores for the day, except feeding the horses dinner since none of them were in the stable. Allison had kept Luna Mist in the covered arena longer than usual, fine-tuning their routine, and she was on Sir Rigsby, racing around the homemade track, while Ollie put Firefly in the turnout pen.

She made a few laps around at a canter, then opened him to about half speed for another three laps, before bringing him down to a trot for the last two laps. She didn't want to overwork him, just warm him up, stretch him out a little, and cool him back down. She wasn't off of him long, and as soon as she could, she'd had him out exercising in the pen.

"I put Firefly back in her stall, brushed her, and fed her," Ollie said when she caught up to him near the stable. She was walking while guiding Sir Rigsby by the rein.

"You didn't have to do all of that."

"It's fine."

"Where's Allison?" she asked, looking around. She hadn't seen her the entire time she was out riding both horses.

"In the stable, brushing Luna Mist. She just came in with her about ten minutes ago."

"I'll take care of him. You can head home. You're already almost an hour past the end of your shift."

"Are you sure you don't mind?" he asked.

"Ollie, I'm the reason you're late. Thank you for staying and helping me. Now, go on. I'm sure your wife is waiting. I've got it. I know how to feed a horse." She smiled.

Ollie was long gone by the time Carly Rae finished brushing Sir Rigsby and put him in his stall. Allison went about feeding Luna Mist after brushing her, acting as if Carly Rae wasn't in the same stable, only a few stalls away. When it appeared as if she were done and about to leave, Carly Rae stepped out of the stall, right in front of her.

Allison nearly ran into her.

"What's your deal?" Carly Rae said sternly, locking eyes with her. "You act like you hate me, but demand to take care of me. Then, you kiss me. Now, you're ignoring me."

"That's not true," Allison muttered.

"What part? Care to elaborate?"

"I don't hate you," she answered softly.

"Why did you kiss me?" Carly Rae sighed.

"Because you drive me crazy," Allison whispered, stepping closer.

Carly Rae pulled her into one of the open stalls where bales of hay were stored, backing her up against the wall as their mouths came together in a ferocious kiss. Her hands moved along her waist, feeling her warm skin as she pulled her fitted blouse free from the tight jodhpurs. Allison moaned against her mouth at the feeling of Carly Rae's hands sliding up her bare back. She put her arms around Carly Rae's neck, tangling her hands in her short blond hair.

Without breaking their reckless kissing, they managed to make it down to the hay, tangled together with Allison on her back. Carly Rae was half on top of her with one hand beneath her and the other sliding along her smooth abdomen under her shirt. Allison still had one hand in Carly Rae's hair near the base of her neck and the other was under her shirt at the small of her back, inching upwards.

Allison's hips rocked against her as Carly Rae nipped and sucked her bottom lip. She moved her hand to the button closure of her riding pants and popped it open. Just as she slid the zipper down, she heard a male voice.

Both women froze.

"Carly Rae, are you in here?" Harris called as footsteps grew closer.

She quickly removed herself from Allison and straightened her clothing before popping her head up. "I'm here," she said, walking out of the stall.

"Everything okay?" he asked, noticing she was slightly out of sorts.

"Fine. All good," she replied, walking towards him. "I kept the horses out late because I took them both riding when I came back from the doctor. I told Ollie to head home. He'd already stayed an hour late. I'm just finishing up."

"Do you need help?" he asked.

"I've got it." She shrugged him off. "Did you need something?"

"Oh…yeah. I booked us at the track tomorrow. I know you're just coming back, so we don't need to be aggressive. I figured it would be good to get some laps in."

"I'll just keep him at half speed, but yes, it'll be great to be on a full-size track."

"Wonderful. We are leaving at 7:30 in the morning. Plan to be there all day. I've already called Ollie to come in early." He moved to leave and stopped. "Have you seen my daughter?"

"Uh…no…not since earlier when she was training."

He pursed his lips. "I need her to go with us," he said, mostly to himself. "All right. I'll see you in the morning."

As soon as he was gone, she went back to the stall. Allison was standing in the middle. Her clothes were straightened, but a couple needles of pine straw were sticking out of her hair, the only indication of what had transpired between them only minutes before.

"We can't do this," Allison said.

"Why? I mean, obviously not here…" she replied, pulling the straw out of her hair.

"It'll never work, and we will both get hurt," Allison sighed.

Carly Rae nodded in agreement…long after she was left alone in the stable.

*

Allison wanted nothing more than to take a shower and wash away the hay dust and all of the thoughts running through her head that went with it, but she had a more pressing issue to deal with. She rushed up the stairs and made her way into her father's office only to find it empty. "Damn it," she grumbled and ran slap into him as she turned to leave the room.

"Everything okay?" he said with raised brows.

"Peachy," she muttered, backing up to let him into the room.

"I've been looking for you. I scheduled Carly Rae and Sir Rigsby at the track in Santa Rosa tomorrow. I need you to come along with us."

"Why?"

"I need help with split timing."

"I thought the track could break it all the down to each furlong."

"The track is open for training, not racing. We won't be using their transponder system."

"I have a lot to do with Luna Mist. Our competition is getting closer," she replied. "What about Ollie? Take him with you."

"He has too much to do around here," he said. "I know horse racing is of no interest to you, and I understand you are training, but you know I wouldn't ask if I didn't need your help."

Allison shook her head. She needed to put distance between herself and Carly Rae, not be cooped up with her all day. "Fine," she sighed. "What time are we leaving?"

"Seven-thirty."

"Great," she muttered. "I need to shower. I'll be down for dinner afterwards."

*

Carly Rae lay in her bed, staring at the ceiling fan as it spun around slowly above her head. No matter how many times she tried to change her train of thought, the feeling of being entangled with Allison on top of the hay came flooding back. "I don't have time for this," she whispered to herself, before finally falling asleep.

SIXTEEN

Allison spotted Carly Rae leaning against the trailer with her jean-covered legs crossed at the ankles, sipping coffee from a travel mug, when she walked up. Sir Rigsby and all of the equipment had already been stowed, and her father was on the phone.

"Who's he talking to at this hour?" she muttered.

Carly Rae shrugged as she ran her eyes over the woman standing a few feet away. The riding attire she'd always worn had been replaced by jeans, a white quarter-sleeve top, and a pair of black leather ankle boots. Her chocolate brown hair fell around her shoulders with loose waves at the bottom. *She could wear a potato sack and flip flops and she'd still be beautiful,* she thought as she pulled her eyes away.

"Are we ready?" Harris asked, walking over to them as he checked his watch. "It should take a little less than an hour to get there. I was just talking to the track manager. We'll be assigned a stall and gate number to use when we get there. They are grooming the track right now."

"Are we the only horse training this morning?" Carly Rae asked.

"I'm not sure, but I was told there are usually two or three scheduled together."

She nodded.

"Do you need anything before we go?" he asked, looking at his daughter.

"No, I'm good." She glanced at Carly Rae.

"Alright, let's hit the road," he called, walking up to the driver's side of the truck.

"You can ride up front," Allison said.

"Go ahead. I'll be fine in the back," Carly Rae replied, hopping in behind Harris and leaving her to walk around to the front passenger seat.

*

Not long into the forty-five-minute drive, Carly Rae began dozing off as she stared at the trees through the window. She hadn't gotten as much sleep as she'd needed the night before and the caffeine buzz from her weak coffee was already wearing off. The vibrating cell phone in her pocket was like a jolt with a hot poker. She jumped as much as the seatbelt would allow.

"You okay?" Harris asked, looking at her in the rearview mirror.

"Yeah. All good. I must've fallen asleep." She smiled.

"With his driving?" Allison chuckled. "I wouldn't dare."

"What's wrong with the way I drive?" he questioned, furrowing his brow at his daughter.

She shrugged. "Nothing. I just hope your horse doesn't get car sick."

"Oh…you're funny," he mumbled, shaking his head at her.

Carly Rae lost the conversation as she looked down at the text message that had caused all of the commotion. It was from Allison.

I hate that I want to kiss you right now.

She glanced up for a split second. Part of the reason she'd been so fascinated with the trees passing by was because she'd accidentally chosen the seat that had given her a full view of Allison anytime she'd looked ahead, which definitely had not been planned. She would've rather ridden in the trailer with Sir Rigsby than have to look at her for an hour. A simple glance was all it had taken for everything to come flooding right back to her. The mixed message in the text wasn't helping matters.

I hate that you keep leading me on, she typed, then deleted it and started again. *I don't get involved with curious straight women.* She promptly backspaced through that as well. Finally, after watching the trees for another minute or two, she put an emoji face with a raised brow and typed: *Is that all you want to do?* She quickly hit send before she could erase it.

*

Allison looked back over her shoulder after reading the reply. *You have no idea,* she thought, but was too fainthearted to type. Instead, she sent a winking emoji and went back to watching the road like a worried hen. It wasn't that her father was an aggressive driver or even much of a speeder, he simply pointed it the way he wanted it to go and to hell with whoever was around him. Thankfully, most people got out of the way of the large dually truck hauling a fifth wheel horse trailer. Every time she rode with him, she was grateful her mother had taught her how to drive.

*

Carly Rae hadn't been sure what to do with the emoji, so she'd simply left the conversation alone. There really wasn't anything she *could* do...at least, not right then. Allison was beautiful and classy, the epitome of wine country money and equine dressage, and she was a cattle-ranching, rodeo-chasing, barrel racer. They were about as opposite as it could get in the horse world. *I don't have time for this,* she thought, sighing softly as the sign for Santa Rosa Racetrack appeared through the window.

*

Harris backed the trailer near the barn, making it easy for Carly Rae to unload Sir Rigsby. She kept him on the lead, walking him around so he could take in all of the sights and get somewhat familiar with the surroundings. Carly Rae was completely out of her element, but she wasn't about to let on that she was learning as she went. She listened to everything the track manager explained when he'd assigned them a stall and gate number.

"I'm going to make a few trotting laps with him to get used to the dirt under his feet since he's been running on grass for weeks," she said. "Then, I'll open him up. I want to give him a few good passes before we work with the gate. Is that okay with you?"

"You're the trainer. It's your call," Harris replied. "Just give me some kind of signal when you're ready so I can get the clock on him."

"Got it. I'll give the thumbs up as I come by and the next time around I'll let him go."

Allison stood back, listening to their conversation while looking around. She'd never been to a horse track and was slightly curious. She'd lost track of what they were discussing until she realized Carly Rae was gone and Sir Rigsby was in the stall. "Where'd she go?" she asked.

"To get her riding uniform on and weigh her gear," her father replied.

"What happens if she's over?"

"It won't matter today. This isn't a sanctioned race. However, it will give us a good indication as to where we are. I'll run the stop watch when we get out there. I'm going to need you to keep an eye on her with the binoculars and watch for the hand signals."

"Great," she muttered.

*

Carly Rae was happy no one else was in the locker room. She felt ridiculous in the white polyester jockey pants that had tight, green elastic leggings from the knee down which caused her pants to balloon out slightly around her thighs and hips. The shiny microfiber riding boots she slipped on and pulled up over the leggings were unlike anything she'd ever worn. The green Lycra riding shirt she pulled on over her head was a turtleneck with short sleeves and was skin tight like a surfer's rash guard. She felt naked, almost like the shirt was another layer of skin as she opened the Velcro closure on the pants to tuck it in. She was happy to add the black lightweight riding vest over it, which was a safety measure in case of an accident. Then, she finished her riding attire by adding the green and white checkered silk top over the vest, which she'd also tucked into her pants.

"This is certainly different," she mumbled, looking in the mirror at herself. Simply wearing the outfit and holding her helmet and goggles in her hand made everything become very real. Her stomach began to flutter with nerves. "It's just like riding on the grass track," she told herself.

*

"That's definitely a new look," Harris said, noticing the fully dressed jockey walking towards them in the paddock.

"What?" Allison mumbled, turning around to see what he was talking about. She had to do a double take to believe it was actually Carly Rae. Once she did, she couldn't take her eyes off of her.

"Close your mouth. You'll catch flies," Carly Rae whispered as she passed by her.

"How are we on weight?" Harris asked.

"Three pounds over. I can work with that," she replied as she climbed up the step ladder to help her reach the short stirrups of the saddle. "Someone will need to guide him like the groom does on race day. Just grab the lead attached to his bridle and give a little tug. He'll follow along," she added once she was in the saddle and ready to go.

Allison looked at her father, but he just stood there. *Oh, for crying out loud!* She grabbed the lead and pulled, shaking her head the entire time as she walked the horse out of the barn and through the paddock area. As soon as they were on the track, the lead went limp. She looked back to see Carly Rae had released it and grabbed the rein, directing the horse on her own as they took off around her in a soft trot. "You're welcome," she muttered to her retreating back.

"Keep the binoculars on her. She'll give a thumbs up coming by when she is ready to open him up," Harris said when she stepped up next to him along the outside rail in front of the stands. He was holding a stop watch and a clipboard with a pen.

Allison grabbed the binoculars he was holding and brought them to her eyes. Carly Rae was tucked in tight on the saddle like a professional race jockey as the horse trotted along the backstretch. She held them down when they passed by in front of her, picking up their pace to a light jog.

*

Carly Rae was as comfortable as she was going to get in the saddle and Sir Rigsby felt good under her, stretching out his stride as she increased his speed. "Okay, boy. We're going to haul ass the next time around," she said, despite his being hearing impaired. She rubbed his neck and flashed a thumbs up towards Harris. Allison hadn't gone unnoticed standing beside him, but the last thing Carly Rae had needed was a distraction. She focused her attention straight ahead as they made their way down the front straightaway and into the sweeping clubhouse turn.

By the time Sir Rigsby had made his way back around, he was itching to go faster. Carly Rae could feel the tension building in his every move. She held on tight and lifted her butt a few inches out of the saddle into race position as she slapped the rein when they passed by Harris and Allison once more. Sir Rigsby launched into a full speed gallop that nearly sat her back in the saddle. She was used to Firefly and her rapid take off, but her speed burned off after a half mile or so. By that point, Sir Rigsby seemed to be increasing his speed if that was even possible. Her thighs burned from holding herself in position as they rounded the far turn. "Come on, boy!" she said, slapping the rein a few times. Once they'd made one complete lap at full speed and passed by Harris and Allison, she backed him way off, settling on a jogging pace that gradually decreased to a walk.

*

Allison kept the binoculars trained on Carly Rae as she watched in awe. She felt her chest tighten as the horse ran faster and faster, the animal and rider moving together as one, like they'd been doing this for years, while racing past at breakneck speed. Her heart beat wildly with a mixture of excitement and fear and she wasn't even the one in the saddle. She never took her eyes off the horse and rider. Even when they slowed she was looking right at Carly Rae through the binoculars, watching her every move.

"She looks good in green," she mumbled.

"What?" her father questioned.

"I like the green," she said.

"Our colors were blue and yellow last time."

"New rider, new colors." She shrugged, adding, "Maybe it's good luck."

"We'll see," he muttered, watching the horse round the final turn.

*

When Sir Rigsby had cooled enough, she gave the thumbs up and directed him to gallop at full speed again for another lap before slowing him all the way down once more. This time, she brought him to a stop and got down to stretch her legs and give him some water.

"That was great," Harris said excitedly. "He seemed to be getting faster at every furlong."

"Yeah, I think he had a little more in him. If he were chasing, I believe he'd be able to run another horse down," Carly Rae replied, petting Sir Rigsby's neck and head while she drank from her own water bottle. "Let's switch over to the gate. That's going to be the most difficult."

*

Allison looked towards the far end of the track where Carly Rae was directing Sir Rigsby into the gate.

"Come on, horse," her father muttered to himself as he watched through the binoculars.

"Is everything okay?" she asked.

"The last time he was pushed into a gate, he threw the rider when it opened."

"Oh, my God!" she gasped and pulled the binoculars out of his hand.

He gave her a sideways glance, but kept his focus on the gate.

*

"Alright, Rigs. Settle down," Carly Rae said, mostly to herself as the gate was pushed closed behind them. The horse seemed agitated right away. She pet his neck the same way she'd always done to help calm him down.

Suddenly, a loud pop rang out and the gate burst open. Carly Rae had been watching the trigger puller and had already lifted the rein to give it a hard slap as his hand rose in the air. By the time he'd pulled the trigger and opened the gate, she was bringing the rein down hard.

Sir Rigsby bucked a little as he shot out of the gate. He'd taken off with the start speed he was accustomed to at their home training track. Knowing he had more in him, Carly Rae carefully slowed him to a stop, then turned him around to do it again over and over until he was taking off at his fastest speed, and no longer bucking. She knew there would be a time when she couldn't see the trigger puller and would have to rely on the sound she heard, which would put Sir Rigsby a fraction of a second slower out of the gate than his competitors, but if she taught him to go as fast as possible when that gate opened, he would still have a chance at running them down.

Each time Sir Rigsby came out of the gate, she'd let him go a little further down the front straightaway of the track as a reward for going faster. When she felt like he'd taken off at his fastest speed, she let him go all the way around the track.

*

"What's she doing?" Allison asked.

"Teaching him how to calm down and leave the gate like a rocket instead of a wild mustang," her father said, watching as much as he could since she still had the binoculars.

She nodded, holding her breath every time Sir Rigsby and Carly Rae were loaded into the gate. When the front would pop open, her heart would leap into her throat until she saw the horse and rider heading down the track.

"It looks like he's stopped bucking. I bet she's going to run him all the way around when he leaves at the speed she wants," he said, starting the timer every time the pistol fired and stopping it when Carly Rae slowed the horse to turn around. "They're getting close," he added.

I wish I could see her eyes, Allison thought, adjusting the binoculars, zooming out as far as she could. The pop of the pistol caused her to startle and jump, shifting the binocular position. By the time she found the horse and rider again, they were halfway around the track.

"Go! Go! Go!" Harris yelled, shifting his eyes from the horse to the timer and back again.

*

Carly Rae thought she might pass out because she'd pretty much held her breath from the time she slapped the rein when the gate opened, until they were halfway down the back stretch. Her thighs burned from holding her in the crouched position with her butt a few inches off the saddle, and her heart thumped hard in her chest like a bass drum with the staccato of a snare. *This is it! Come on, boy!* She held the rein tight, slapping it over and over as they neared the finish line.

As soon as they crossed the line she pulled back on the rein a little to begin slowing him down and stood up to stretch out her cramping legs. By the time they reached the back straightaway she'd sat down completely in the saddle and he'd slowed to a trot, then a walk. She pulled her legs from the stirrups and let them dangle along his sides as they continued around for another lap to cool him down.

She pointed to the paddock as she passed by Harris and Allison for the last time to let them know she was coming off the track. Once they started in the final turn, she tugged the rein to the right, leading Sir Rigsby towards the exit, then she brought him to a stop when they were off the track so she could get down and lead him through the paddock area herself. She unbuckled her helmet and let it dangle from her left hand while she kept the rein in her right hand. The horse stayed right beside her, following her every move diligently.

*

"I'm merely stating your times were fast enough to place at the last two races here. I've never seen him run like that. Do you think he will do that on race day?" Harris said.

"Race day is a different ball game altogether," Carly Rae said, avoiding the chocolate brown eyes she knew were boring a hole in her as she ran the brush along Sir Rigsby's side to help cool him down since she didn't have time to bathe him. She'd already given him a fresh bucket of water and a couple handfuls of his favorite treats. "If he comes out of the gate like he did today, I think he will be fine," she continued.

"What if he spooks or comes out sluggish?" he asked.

"Then, he'll have to run down the leaders," Carly Rae said. "Some people like the chase," she added, catching Allison's eyes as she walked around to the other side of the horse.

"Do you think he's fast enough for that?" he questioned.

"He has more in him than he showed today. Once he gets a little more used to the race setting, you'll see it. He's a phenomenal horse," she answered, bending down to put liniment and fresh wraps on his legs. When she finished and walked out of the stall, she glanced at Allison, who was leaning against the wall a few feet away with her arms crossed. Their eyes met briefly before she turned towards Harris. "I'll load him when I come back from the locker room."

Allison kept her eyes on Carly Rae's retreating backside until she was out of sight. Then, she pushed off the wall and walked over to the horse who was watching her and sniffing the air. Her father had gone up to the office to inquire about another training session. She wasn't much of a horse talker, but she'd seen and heard Carly Rae do it a hundred times. "I don't have any snacks. You're begging eyes aren't going to work on me."

*

The stable was quiet when Carly Rae brought Sir Rigsby in from the trailer and got him settled in his stall. She'd fallen asleep for most of the ride back from Santa Rosa due to her lack of sleep the night before, along with the high and low of the adrenaline rush from racing around the track. The trip had taken longer with more traffic on the road than they'd encountered early in the morning. She wasn't sure who was happier they were back, her, Sir Rigsby, or Firefly, who had whinnied and stomped for attention until she went over to pet her.

"I think she might be jealous," she said, stepping back over to Sir Rigsby to make sure he had a full pail of food and plenty of alfalfa hay to munch on.

Me too, Allison thought as she walked over to her. "You looked good out there riding him, like you've been a jockey for years," she said.

"I used to want to be one, but I thought I was too tall, and very few women become derby jockeys to begin with," Carly Rae replied, running her hand down Sir Rigsby's face. "But, he makes it easy."

"Seeing you today, I understand why you have to be the one to ride him."

Carly Rae turned her head, her eyes finding Allison's. "I've known for some time that I may be the only one to ever ride or race him because of our bond."

"Is he really completely deaf?" Allison asked.

Carly Rae nodded.

"I think it's amazing what you've been able to do with him," Allison said, moving closer and petting the horses head. Her hand brushed against Carly Rae's, causing a steady thump in the center of her chest. "I could get lost in your beautiful eyes," she whispered.

Carly Rae's tongue snaked out, licking her lips.

Allison's lips parted in anticipation of the fiery kiss she knew was coming, but suddenly Carly Rae backed up a couple of steps, putting space between them and pulling her gaze away.

"We can't keep doing this," Carly Rae sighed. "As tempting as it is, you're right. It would never work." She stepped around her and kept walking, leaving her standing in front of Sir Rigsby's stall.

Allison stared at the stable door long after it had closed. Her attraction to another woman was certainly nothing new, but her draw to Carly Rae was as bewildering as the ease in which Carly Rae had stirred her. She hadn't dated or slept with anyone since she'd left college a few years earlier. The timing had never seemed right, and she'd been too busy with dressage and the accolades that came with being an Olympian, plus the grief of losing her mother suddenly on top of everything. Now, standing in the smelly, dusty stable all alone, she found herself longing for a woman who was her complete opposite in every way possible. "It's for the best. Losing her would hurt like hell," she sighed.

SEVENTEEN

Carly Rae hadn't seen Allison all weekend and she'd been too busy to look for her after the starting gate they'd borrowed was delivered. She'd spent the first three days of the following week training with Sir Rigsby, getting him as used to the gate as she possibly could, as well as running Firefly around the barrels.

After another long day, she pulled her Stetson off and wiped her brow sweat on the upper arm of her shirt. Then, she hung her hat on a nearby hook in the stable and went to work bathing Firefly. They hadn't had a lot of rain recently and the open arena had turned into a mini dustbowl during their training session. Unlike the closed arena with its own sprinkler system, the open arena relied heavily on mother nature.

"I'm going to tow the water trailer around the open arena in the morning before I grade it," Ollie said.

"That's fine. I'll be with Sir Rigsby first anyway," she answered. "You know I can do it myself. Just show me where you hide the tractor keys."

He laughed. "I take them with me so you don't go joy riding!"

She smiled and shook her head.

"Are you planning on doing any training this weekend? I'll be here to receive the hay order and figured I'd go ahead and mow the track while I'm at it."

"No, I'll be in Wyoming. The cattle drive is this weekend and I always go home to help my dad. I'm leaving tomorrow after I finish training, actually. So, I won't be here Friday either."

"That sounds like fun."

"He's old school, so it's long hours in the saddle, sleeping in a tent under the stars, and eating canned beanie weenies cooked over a fire."

"Yep. Definitely fun," he said as he walked away.

She laughed. "I'll trade you!"

"Don't tease me," he called over his shoulder with a smile.

*

Allison had spent the beginning of the week with Luna Mist, going through their freestyle routine that was set to music. The horse had taken to the steps easily and seemed to enjoy it a little more than their more difficult classical dressage routine. They were still a few weeks away from the competition, but Allison was no longer frustrated and Luna Mist was no longer making habitual mistakes.

Spending so much time in the covered arena had left her very little time to notice Carly Rae out on the training track with Sir Rigsby, and by the time she'd switched over to working with Firefly in the open arena, Allison had moved Luna Mist to the turnout pen and then back into the stable.

She'd just finished their training and was bringing Luna Mist inside for a much-needed bath when she caught the tail end of Carly Rae and Ollie's conversation. "Tease him?" she questioned with a raised brow as Carly Rae walked away from the wash area with Firefly.

"He's mowing the track this weekend and I'm going home to help with the cattle drive. He thinks rustling cattle in the open range is more enjoyable. So, I said I'd trade with him," she replied, walking back over after settling Firefly in her stall with some treats.

"Wait…you're leaving?"

"After I finish tomorrow. I'll be back late Sunday night."

Allison nodded.

"Your father already knows. He told me to take Friday off and technically I have weekends off anyway. I'm just not one to sit around on the couch, so I usually spend it working with the horses."

"I wasn't questioning you," she replied, watching Carly Rae cross her arms and legs and lean against a post as she began spraying Luna Mist with the hose.

"Are you washing the horse or wall?" Carly Rae asked with a grin as the spray completely missed the horse.

Allison shrugged it off like she'd meant to spray everything but the giant animal in front of her.

"What do you know about cattle?"

"Cattle?"

"Yes. Cows. Have you ever been around them?"

"Nope. I've never been to a farm or ranch, so nothing really, other than they produce beef, milk, and cheese."

Carly Rae chuckled.

"They're as dumb as a wooden nickel and stubborn as hell."

"I see," Allison mumbled.

"Would you like to go with me and see how a cattle ranch is run?" she asked, regretting the words after they'd left her mouth. What she needed to do was put distance between herself and Allison, not invite her on a road trip to meet her family.

"Uh…" Allison bit the corner of her lip. *That is a bad idea if I've ever heard one.* "Thanks for the invite, but I have a lot to do here this weekend."

Carly Rae nodded and walked out of the stable.

*

"Everything okay?" Harris asked, noticing Allison sitting in the nook her mother had spent most of her time in.

"Yeah," she said with a slight nod.

"You sure?"

"Yes." She smiled.

"How was training?"

"Good. In fact, I'm pretty sure Luna Mist prefers the freestyle performance over classic dressage."

He laughed. "She's stubborn. I wonder where she gets it from?"

"What's that supposed to mean?" She pretended to furrow her brow in anger.

"She has your good qualities, too." He grinned.

"Uh huh."

"Carly Rae will be gone for the weekend, so you'll have the grounds to yourself."

"I know. She actually invited me to tag along and see how a cattle ranch is run," she replied.

"Really?" He nodded. "You should go."

"What? Why?"

"Why not? It would probably be nice to get away from here for a few days and get some fresh air."

"We're only a few weeks out from competition. I need to be training."

"Allison, if that horse doesn't know what to do by now, you might as well not even go. You know that. Besides, I'm sure she could use a break, too." He patted her knee like she was ten years old again. "Who knows. You might like cattle farming and decide to change careers," he joked. "I can see you teaching cows how to do pirouettes in perfect synchronicity."

She laughed and shook her head. "Come on. I'm hungry," she said, getting up and holding her hand out to him.

*

Sweat soaked sheets were tangled around Carly Rae. Lost in a dream that had her chasing after a brunette on horseback, she had no idea the air conditioner in the tiny house had quit working. She was unable to see the woman's face, only her retreating back as she rode a galloping snow-white mare through the forest, but the aching inside of her made her feel like she would die if she didn't catch up to her. She thrashed around in the bed, mentally slapping the reins to make the large black stallion she was riding go faster and faster, until the woman disappeared like a smoky ghost.

Carly Rae opened her eyes, staring into the darkness as reality came flooding back to her. She rarely had dreams, but when she did they were quite vivid. She wiped the sweat from her forehead onto the sheet. "Why is it so hot in here?" she mumbled, getting out of bed. The air conditioner was running, but it was blowing hot air like the heat was turned on. She quickly turned it off and began opening all of the windows. She'd already had a restless night and needed to get up in a couple of hours. She sat on the couch and fell asleep by the time the night air began to cool the house.

When her cell phone lit up, vibrating and playing the soft tune of her alarm, she fumbled for the nightstand and rolled right off the couch, hitting the floor with a thud. "Son of a bitch," she grumbled, getting up. A shower and a cup of coffee couldn't come fast enough as she went about her usual morning routine. She'd already packed the night before so that she'd be ready to go as soon as she'd finished her training day.

*

A knock on the front door startled Allison as she sat at the kitchen island drinking a cup of tea and pushing her breakfast around on her plate. She got up and walked through the formal living room. She couldn't remember the last time someone had been at their front door, other than Carly Rae when she'd come for dinner.

"How'd I know it was you?" she said, pulling it open and seeing Carly Rae standing there with a cup of coffee in her hand and a half-eaten banana in the other.

"Is it too early to talk to your dad?" she asked.

"No. He's up in his office. Come on," Allison said, ushering her in and closing the door behind her. "Is everything okay?"

"The A/C went out in the house last night. I wanted to let him know so he can hopefully get it working while I'm gone," she said as they walked up the spiral staircase.

"That stinks. Why didn't you come up to the house? We have a spare bedroom."

"I didn't notice until a few hours ago. It's fine. I opened all of the windows, but by the time the afternoon sun comes, it will be hot as hell in there."

"His office is at the end of the hall. Just walk in. He's probably on his computer," Allison said, leaving her to find her way.

"I was just about to come join you," Harris muttered, hearing the door.

"Sorry to bother you," Carly Rae said.

"Good morning!" he said in surprise, expecting his daughter. "And it's not a bother. What can I do for you?"

"The A/C quit in the house. It's just blowing hot air."

"Oh, wow. Why didn't you come here? We have plenty of room."

"I didn't notice until this morning. All of the windows are open, but the sun is going to make it pretty hot in there."

"I'll call the service company. I believe they open at eight. What time are you leaving today?"

"Noon at the latest. I'll be back sometime late Sunday night."

"Okay. It'll be fixed or replaced before you return."

"Thanks," she said before leaving the room and making her way back down stairs. She wasn't sure where Allison had gotten off to, so she went to the door to see herself out.

"When are you leaving?" Allison said, appearing out of nowhere with a mug in her hand that had a teabag string hanging over the side.

"By noon," Carly Rae replied. "Why? Did you change your mind?"

Allison bit her lower lip. *Why not?* "Maybe."

"I need to know because I am flying."

"Oh…"

"It's not a big deal. I fly to Salt Lake City and drive the rest of the way. That's the closest airport to where I'm from. The flights less than two hours."

"How long is the drive?"

"About three hours."

"Wow."

"I'm usually somewhere else in the country because of barrel racing, so I always have to fly there and take a rental the rest of the way. I go back for the cattle drive twice a year, so I'm used to it."

Allison nodded. She hesitated for a second and Carly Rae began to walk away. "I'll go," she blurted. "I don't know if I'd be any help with the cattle drive though."

Carly Rae's jaw dropped as she spun around. She closed it and cleared her throat quickly. "You already know how to ride a horse. There's not much more to it, besides roping the strays who decide to run. That doesn't happen often though."

Allison nodded. "Are you sure you don't mind me tagging along?"

"I wouldn't have asked if I didn't want you to go," Carly Rae said. "You'll probably want to pack jeans and a heavy sweater or jacket. It gets a lot colder at night up there."

"Okay. Is there anything else I might need?"

"We'll be sleeping in a tent. Is that a problem?"

Allison raised her brows, thankful her mug hid her expression as she took a sip of tea. "Um…no. That's fine," she said, swallowing.

"Okay. Be ready by eleven-thirty. I'm going to try and finish up early. The flight leaves at two from Santa Rosa."

"Sounds good," Allison replied, pulling the mug back to her mouth once more before she could say she'd changed her mind. She headed back to the kitchen as Carly Rae showed herself out. "Why in the hell did I say yes?" she whispered, shaking her head.

EIGHTEEN

After a short flight, the plane landed with a thud and a bit of a sway, causing Allison to grab for the armrest, subsequently grabbing Carly Rae's hand. She wasn't afraid of flying. She'd flown all around the world with her horse for international dressage competitions, as well as back and forth to the UK for boarding school when she was younger. It was rough landings like that particular one that always scared her. As soon as the plane was rolling down the runway, slowing at a quick pace before making the turn to the jet way, she let go of Carly Rae's hand. Neither woman said anything as they collected their carryon luggage and exited the plane.

Carly Rae had flown in and out of Salt Lake City so many times over the years, she could navigate the airport in the dark. "This way," she said, leading Allison through the crowd of people who were trying to find and follow the signs for baggage claim.

Allison was used to being the one leading and making all of the decisions, but she found herself easily following along, trusting Carly Rae knew where she was going. Before long, the rental counter came into view. She stayed off to the side with their bags while Carly Rae spoke to the woman behind the counter, who seemed to be fake laughing and smiling a little too much. *Is she flirting?* Carly Rae didn't seem as enthusiastic or animated as the rental clerk. Nonetheless, Allison grabbed the handles for their bags and rolled them beside her as she walked over. "Are we all set?" she asked, smiling at Carly Rae while glaring at the rental car employee.

"Uh…yeah." Carly Rae noticed her demeanor and grinned.

"Here are your keys, Ms. Walsh. The vehicle is parked in space 32," the woman said, avoiding Allison. Her bubbly fake laughter was long gone.

"Great. Let's get out of here," Allison replied, grabbing the keys.

"Everything okay?" Carly Rae asked as they walked away.

"All she was trying to do was get into your pants," she mumbled.

"That doesn't mean I was going to let her."

"It's none of my business," Allison replied as they walked across the parking garage towards a black Ford F150 parked in space 32. It was four-wheel-drive, but smaller than the heavy-duty F350 dually truck that she owned and used for towing her horse trailer all over the country.

"You made it your business when you came over to the counter and cut her in half with your eyes."

"What?" Allison shook her head.

Carly Rae hit the button for the automatic locks and followed her to the passenger side. "Meet me halfway at least," she said, holding her hand on the door so Allison couldn't open it.

"What's that supposed to mean?"

"Admit you were jealous!"

"Jealous?" Allison chuckled. "Of that bimbo?"

Carly Rae's eyebrows shot up. "Bimbo? So now we're calling strangers names?"

Allison drew out a deep breath and crossed her arms. "Fine. I saw that she was too busy with her high school crush fake laughing, to get your rental agreement handled, so I stepped in."

Carly Rae shook her head and backed away, letting her open the door as she walked around to the opposite side. She quickly stowed her suitcase in the backseat and climbed into the front seat to drive. "It'll take about three hours as long as we don't run into any accidents," she said, starting the truck and putting on her seatbelt. She set her cell phone in the cup holder and moved the shifter to D.

*

About an hour into the drive, Allison's cell phone died. She'd brought the charger, but it was packed in her suitcase. She set it in the other cup holder and proceeded watching through the windshield as they drove along the highway. "You must do this often," she said.

"Do what?"

"Make this same trip."

Carly Rae shrugged. "Not often, no. I come home twice a year for the cattle drives and I try to make it back at least one or two more times if my schedule allows it. Every year is different. However, this is the only way to get there if I am flying, so I've done it several times over the years. It's sort of second nature by now." She checked the mirror and changed lanes to go around a slower car.

"Why do you fly? Why not drive?"

"Today?"

"Yeah. I figured you'd be taking Firefly with you."

Carly Rae shook her head. "I usually leave her behind unless the barrel racing season is over and we will be at the ranch for longer than a couple of days. My dad has plenty of horses to ride for the cattle drive."

"What exactly is a cattle drive? I mean…I get the idea, I've just never learned much about it other than what you see on TV."

"My family owns around a thousand acres. It's split into sections or fields. In the warm, summer months, the cows are in the farthest field. In the winter months, the herd is brought to the field closest to the house so that they can go through vet visits and be prepared to be sold. Moving them from field to field is called driving them…hence the word cattle drive. In the spring, we drive them back out to one of the farther fields to let them graze freely, making them free range cattle which is top dollar. Then, do it all over again in the fall."

"What about wild animals?"

"We definitely lose a few a year to coyotes or other predators."

"They're beef cattle, right?"

"Correct."

"Kind of makes you want to be a vegetarian."

Carly Rae laughed. "We tried, but it lasted all of three days. We don't have seafood, chickens, or turkeys, so we figured they were fair game."

Allison shook her head and chuckled.

Dusty Springfield's *Son of a Preacher Man* came on the radio. Carly Rae turned the volume up and tapped her hand on the steering wheel.

"You're like an old soul."

"I get it from my dad and my grandpa. They raised me on their music. I honestly never heard anything else until I started traveling with barrel racing. At that point, it was mostly country on the radio."

"My mother only listened to classical music, so that was heard a lot in our house. My father is more into Bob Seger, Fleetwood Mac and other bands from that era."

"My mom listens to whatever gets my dad up dancing," Carly Rae laughed. "A particular song would come on the radio and he'd spin her around the living room. I used to love watching them. I don't think they do a lot of that anymore."

"My parents used to go to vineyard parties quite a bit when I was younger, but I'm not sure if they were ever big dancers."

"Hey, speaking of parents…." Carly Rae turned the volume completely down. "Mine don't know that I am jockeying Sir Rigsby. They only think I am training him."

"Are you planning on telling them?"

"Yes. I don't keep anything from them. I just haven't told them yet. I kind of wanted to do it in person."

Allison nodded as they suddenly slowed and pulled off on an exit.

"Are you hungry?" Carly Rae asked, looking for the nearest drive thru. "We can eat something small, to hold us over. I'm sure my mother is preparing a feast. I'm actually worried I may gain back the weight I lost while I'm home."

"I'm fine with wherever you stop," Allison said, looking around. There were only a couple of places to choose from and none of them looked appealing.

*

"Is this it?" Allison said a little over an hour later when they pulled off onto a gravel road and put the truck in park.

"Yep," Carly Rae replied before getting out to open the large metal cattle gate. *Walsh Ranch* was scrolled in shiny stainless steel across the front of it.

Allison glanced around at the acres and acres of rolling hills expanding on both sides as they drove towards a dark gray, modern looking house with red cedar trim. The long gravel drive led all the way to the attached two-car garage that had separate single doors instead of a wide double door. A few small bushes and plants with white rocks littered the landscaping around the walkway to the front door. "How many acres did you say your family has?"

"A little over a thousand," she said, pulling up beside a white Ford F350 dually truck that was backed up in front of one of the garage doors. A ratty looking old red truck was on the other side of the dually.

"All of this is for cows?"

"No." Carly Rae smiled. "Half of it is hay fields. We breed, raise, and sell beef cows, but we also farm and sell hay that is shipped all over the country."

"Wow."

"It sounds like a much bigger operation than it really is. My dad runs everything and the foreman, George Tibbetts, is his right-hand man. They have a couple of employees on the hay side and a couple that work with the cattle, but mostly the two of them do it all. My mother handles all of the supply ordering, book keeping, livestock certificates, tractor parts orders, and anything else that goes along with it since she retired from the school board. Me and Tibby, that's George's son, grew up right here and began helping when we were little kids."

"Do you plan to move back one day and take over?"

"Honestly…I don't know," she sighed. "My parents are getting older and I know at one point it will come up. I just don't think I'm ready to answer one way or the other."

"That's understandable."

"Come on. I'm sure they heard us pull up, and I'm starving."

"I'm actually pretty hungry myself," Allison said, getting out and retrieving her bag from the backseat.

"Good because I'm serious about my mother's cooking. You'd think she was feeding the entire county."

Allison laughed and followed her along the path to the front door.

*

A Buddy Guy album was spinning on the record player, filling the house with soft music as Carly Rae opened the front door and stepped inside with Allison coming in behind her.

The house had an open, split floor plan with a short, three-foot wall separating the living area from the kitchen/dining area. Two of the bedrooms were just off the main area with a bathroom between them, and the master was on the opposite side behind the garage. The inside of the home was as modern as the outside and completely opposite of the country log cabin with log furniture and a wood-burning stove that had been in Allison's mind the entire trip. The whiskey colored leather couch and recliner were well worn and looked very comfortable, and the square coffee table had a saddle for a base. Large lush green plants sat on tables on both sides of the TV stand, as well as along the top of cabinets in the kitchen, and along the dining hutch.

"There's my girl," Carly Rae's mother said as she walked up with a big smile and hugged her tightly. She was dressed in a blue short-sleeved sweater and jeans, and had long, wavy blonde hair and stunning baby blue eyes like her daughter. "Your hair is starting to curl up on the ends. Are you finally growing it out?"

"No. I just haven't had time to get it cut." Carly Rae smiled.

"I like it," Allison mumbled, causing Carly Rae to raise a brow.

"Hey, kiddo!" her dad said, coming into the living area from the hallway. He was dressed in a light blue plaid, button down shirt with front pockets and jeans with a leather belt and oval buckle.

Allison glanced from Carly Rae's mother to her father and had to do a double take. First of all, he could pass as former President George W. Bush in a lookalike contest. Their similarities in build and mannerisms was uncanny. He even had the same cocky grin. But, as soon as he stepped close to his daughter, Carly Rae was all she saw in his face. She looked just like him, but had her mother's hair and eyes.

Mama, Daddy…this is Allison McKinley. Her father owns the horse I'm training," Carly Rae said. "Allison, these are my parents, Charles and Irene Walsh."

"It's nice to meet you both," she said, holding her hand out.

Irene pulled her into a soft hug. "We're so glad you came with Carly Rae."

Charles also gave her a light hug. "Welcome, and please make yourself at home."

"Thank you." Allison smiled somewhat shyly.

"I wasn't sure if she was sleeping in your room or the guest room, but both are clean and made up," Irene said.

Allison swallowed the sudden lump that formed in her throat.

"She'll be in the guest room," Carly Rae replied, grabbing her bag and leading Allison to the short hallway that opened into the bathroom with a bedroom on each end. "This is my room," she said, walking in and setting her suitcase down.

"Why did she think I would be sleeping in your room?" Allison whispered, following her.

Carly Rae laughed. "She assumed we were together. I've never brought anyone home with me before."

"Oh."

"Allison, I don't keep secrets from my parents. They've known I was gay since my dad caught me kissing a girl in the barn when I was fourteen."

"Wow. Really?"

"Yep. He looked at me and said, 'no sex until you are old enough to understand the consequences that come with it.' I said, 'yes, sir.' And we left it at that. Mama was surprised. I think they wanted me and Tibby to wind up together and get married one day."

Allison nodded as she looked around Carly Rae's room. The full-sized bed frame was made out of logs and had matching furniture, similar to what she'd expected the entire house to look like. The quilt on the bed had a beautiful pattern with all different shades of blue.

"Come on, I'll show you the spare room," Carly Rae said, leading her down the short hall.

The spare room had a full-sized cherry colored sleigh bed with matching antique furniture. A white quilt with a red flower pattern in the middle covered the bed.

Allison set her suitcase down and ran her hand along the smooth wood of the footboard.

"This was my grandparent's bedroom set, and my grandmother hand-stitched the quilts."

"Oh my." Allison moved her hand to the soft quilt. "This is beautiful."

"Yes…it is," Carly Rae replied, looking at her, not the furniture. She turned to walk out of the room. "I'm sure dinner will be ready soon."

*

"Mrs. Walsh, that chicken pot pie was delicious," Allison said with a smile.

"Mrs. Walsh was my mother-in-law and this was her recipe. She was a wonderful woman, may she rest in peace, but please call me Irene."

"Only if you allow me to do the dishes," Allison replied.

"Come on. We can do them together," Irene said as they finished clearing the table. Carly Rae and her father settled in the living area with a map of their land spread across the square-shaped coffee table.

"It's beautiful here. I'm looking forward to seeing more of the land," Allison said as she began washing the dishes while Irene rinsed them and put them in the rack to dry.

"Carly Rae told us you live in the heart of wine country."

"Yes, ma'am. Our property is surrounded by vineyards. I used to sneak into them and eat the grapes when I was a kid."

Irene laughed. "That sounds like something Carly Rae would do."

Allison smiled. "What was she like as a kid? Was she mischievous?"

Irene shook her head and smiled. "She was a good kid, got good grades and treated people respectfully. She did whatever she put her mind to, and learned a few lessons along the way. When she was about eight or nine, her entire world revolved around her pony, Matilda, until she outgrew her. She would ride that thing all over, racing that poor pony around until she was ready to collapse with exhaustion."

Allison laughed. "I can see that. She rides her barrel racing horse at breakneck speed!"

"Doesn't surprise me. She's all in or not at all with everything. She's definitely never done anything half-assed."

"I can certainly see that."

"When she had that nasty spill, she told me you made her follow every single thing the doctor said. I'm grateful she had you to take care of her."

Unsure of what to say, Allison simply smiled.

"So, what about you? She mentioned you are a world class dressage rider and even have an Olympic medal. That's amazing."

"Thank you. I have been riding since I was a small child as well. However, my mother was European and rode steeple chase at the world class level. She started me in dressage and I never looked back. I went to boarding school in the UK from seventh grade until I graduated high school. I competed for my school in classical dressage, but I'd also started competing at a much higher level. I decided to go to college in the states to be closer to my parents and work my way up to the national level here so I could get on the Olympic team. I made the national team my sophomore year of college and won a silver medal the next year at the Olympic games."

"Your parents must be so proud of you."

"Sadly, my mother has passed since then, but yes, they were always very proud. To this day my father is my biggest fan."

"Aww. I'm so sorry about your mother."

"Thank you. It's been fifteen months, but still feels like yesterday sometimes."

"Oh, I know the feeling. I lost my mom eight years ago and a day doesn't go by when I don't think about her," Irene said, drying her hands on a dish towel. "It looks like we're all done here. If we don't go get them involved in something else, they'll talk cows all night," she added, nodding towards the living area.

"What are they doing?"

"Mapping out the route for the cattle drive, more than likely. They've done it so many times, they could probably both do it blindfolded, but they drag the map out and plot a course every time."

*

"The creek is low. We haven't had much rain this summer. If we cross further north, we'll have an easier time with the flatter terrain," Charles said.

"If you're sure the creek is low enough, then yeah. I agree. There's less chance of losing any of the herd over the higher hills on this side," Carly Rae replied, pointing to another area of the map.

"I was out there about a month ago. I think it'll be fine, but we'll look at it again when we get up there."

"Sounds like a plan."

"So, Allison seems nice. She's very pretty," her father said, changing the subject..

Carly Rae nodded.

"She seems very…"

"Classy? That's the first thing I thought of. I'm pretty sure all dressage riders and enthusiasts are polished and refined," she laughed. "It definitely takes a lot of skill to do what she does, though, and she's very good at it."

He nodded. "How is she at sleeping in a tent, and wrangling cattle?"

"I have no idea. I guess we'll find out."

They both chuckled.

"How's the horse training going?"

"Great, actually…"

"Oh, we're just in time," Irene whispered to Allison.

"I was about to get a fire going," Charles said, seeing his wife walking over. "Here, Carly Rae. Fold this up," he added, referring to the map.

"Anyone want some coffee?" Irene asked.

Charles and Carly Rae both said yes as she walked back into the kitchen.

"Mama, do you have any tea? Allison doesn't drink coffee."

"You know what…Mary gave me some the other day. She's gotten on a tea kick lately. It's driving George mad," she laughed, opening the cabinet. "Here it is. Earl Grey is the flavor. I'm not sure what that is."

"It's quite good actually," Allison said, getting up to help her make it.

A few minutes later, everyone was seated in front of the fire with a mug in their hand. Charles was in his recliner and everyone else was on the couch, with Carly Rae between her mother and Allison.

"So, the horse I am training is doing wonderfully. In fact, he responds to me so well…I'm going to be jockeying him."

"What?" her mother questioned. "You're not a jockey."

"Aren't you too big?" her father asked. "They are usually really little like Tibby."

"I've been training to be a jockey while training him to be a race horse. I have my first license and I'll have the second by the time we go to our first race, which is a medium stakes race. It's a little smaller than the big derbies. And yes, I am a little too big. I've lost some weight and still have a few more pounds to go. My height is fine, but somewhat tall for a jockey."

"I thought you looked like you'd lost weight. I don't think you had any fat on you to begin with," Irene said.

Carly Rae laughed.

"What do you think about all of this?" Irene asked, looking around her daughter to see Allison.

"Uh." She cleared her throat. "To be honest, I was completely against it from the start. I didn't think she should put herself through the hell of trying to lose weight, and she wasn't a trained jockey. I thought she and my father were crazy."

Irene looked at Carly Rae and raised her brows as if to say, *you should listen to her.*

"However," Allison continued. "I was at the track recently when she and Sir Rigsby trained in a race setting for the first time, and I was completely blown away. The way she handled the horse looked like she'd been doing this for years, and the way he responded to her, well…I've been around horses all of my life and I wouldn't have a clue where to start if someone handed me the reins to a deaf horse. They look so natural together. Their bond is…beautiful."

"Wow," Irene murmured, nodding her head slowly.

Carly Rae looked at Allison and mouthed, *thank you.*

"Shikoba," Charles whispered, referring to his best friend who had passed away.

"Yeah," Carly Rae said, sharing a tender moment with her father as their eyes met. "He taught me well."

He nodded and looked over at Allison. "I've seen her race around those barrels with her horse damn near on its side. I'm pretty sure this kid could ride a horse at full speed with her eyes closed and still be able to control it," he said with a smile. "Well…when is the race?" he asked his daughter. "We need to put it on the calendar so we can be there."

"Absolutely," Irene added.

"Like I said, it's only a medium stakes race, so it's not the Kentucky Derby, but it will have all of the traditional pomp and circumstance of horse racing."

"Will we be in one of those fancy boxes?" Charles laughed.

"Of course," Allison replied.

"Count me in," Charles said.

"I don't even know what a fancy box is, but I'll be there, too," Irene added. "Does Tibby know?" she asked, looking at Carly Rae before turning her attention back to Allison. "They grew up together and were attached at the hip. He's a race jockey."

Carly Rae shook her head.

"She's told me a little about him and his family," Allison said.

"They have been a staple around here since long before Tibby and Carly Rae were born. The kids used to race each other on their ponies and pretend the barn was their house. Carly Rae always made him shovel the poop because 'it was the man's job,' she'd tell him, and that poor boy would do it every time. They were something else," Irene said with a smile while softly shaking her head.

"Yeah," Charles agreed. "We were pretty sure they would get married one day…."

"Are you guys going to tell stories on me all night?" Carly Rae muttered.

"I like hearing them," Allison said.

"How about the time you decided to ride your horse to school and tied him to the bicycle rack out front?" Charles said.

"Oh, my God. I'd almost forgotten about that," Irene laughed. "I was the vice principal at the time and she was supposed to be home sick. Little did I know, she just didn't want to ride with me. I get a call at my desk about a horse tied up outside right before the bell rang to start the day. I'm thinking what in the hell as I walk outside. There's my daughter's beloved quarter horse, Colonel Mustard, tied to the damn bike rack. I have never laughed so hard in my life, but boy was I mad at the same time."

"She called ranting and raving for me to come down to the school with the trailer to get the horse," Charles said.

Allison laughed so hard she nearly had tears rolling down her cheeks. "What grade were you in?"

"Seventh," Carly Rae replied, shaking her head. "I wasn't allowed to ride my horse for an entire week."

"I can only imagine how you were in high school." Allison smiled.

"I was already barrel racing by then, so I didn't have much time to do anything."

"She'd also discovered a lot more than horses by then," Irene muttered.

Carly Rae shook her head and stood up with her empty mug in her hand. "Do you feel like taking a ride?" she asked Allison before her mother could spill anymore of her childhood secrets.

NINETEEN

"It's not what you expected, is it?" Carly Rae said as she opened the passenger door to the old red truck. The last few rays of sunshine were slowly slipping behind the mountains in the distance.

"I'll admit, I imagined a log cabin with handmade log furniture and fur rugs. Maybe an animal head or two on the wall," Allison said, pulling on her jacket to ward off the cool air as she climbed in.

Carly Rae laughed. "Oh, I'm sure you could find that if you ventured up into the mountains. My parents built this place about ten years ago when they finally tore down my grandparent's old house. There used to be three homes on the property, but this is the only one now. They tore them down and built other buildings on the sites. The barn used to be one of them," she said as she got in on the driver's side. She pushed the clutch to the floor and turned the key. The old truck sputtered to life. "This used to be my grandfather's truck. He bought it new in 1950. It's a Ford F1. Daddy can't bear to part ways with it, so he keeps fixing it when it breaks down. It's been his ranch truck for years. I learned how to drive in this thing, right here on these dirt paths," she said as she shoved the truck in first gear and took off.

Allison grabbed the handle on the door as the truck bounced down the dirt road towards the buildings in the distance. She watched Carly Rae, grinning from ear to ear while sawing at the wheel as they putted down the path. This was home. It was written all over her face.

"Why didn't you drive this thing to school?"

"I did," Carly Rae laughed. "But, I was in high school and had a license. Daddy still had his first truck, an old Ford 100. He was using it as the ranch truck at that time, so I drove ol' red back and forth to school until I graduated. Daddy sold the Ford 100 not long after that."

Allison chuckled.

Carly Rae pulled to a stop outside of the barn and cut the engine. When they went inside, Allison noticed it was partitioned off in sections. The first section was for vetting, and the birthing stalls were beside it in the next section. The larger area in the back had about ten baby calves lying in the hay.

"Oh my! Look how cute they are!" Allison said, going up to the rail. "Are these babies?"

Carly Rae nodded. "It's hard not to get attached."

"I don't know how you look at them knowing their fate. That's horrible," she said, reaching over to pet one of them.

"Cattle have been raised for food for hundreds of years. I don't believe it will ever change."

"Yeah." Allison nodded. "I see why you don't eat beef now."

"Yep."

"I probably won't ever again either." She shook her head.

"The stable isn't far. Do you want to see the horses?"

"Sure," Allison replied, needing to get away from the calves.

Tiny stars littered the pitch-black sky when they stepped back outside. Carly Rae pulled a flashlight from her pocket and switched it on, lighting their path as they went back to the truck.

"You were right. It's definitely a lot colder here at night than at home," Allison said, zipping her jacket.

"Yeah. I love cold nights though, so it doesn't bother me much. Most of the time, I'm somewhere that is sweltering. You never see a rodeo in the snow." She grinned, starting the truck.

The headlights bounced around in front of them as they drove along the path towards the stable. Allison could barely see anything through the windows because of how dark it was. It reminded her of going out into the country while in the UK. No matter where she was, the world always seemed prettier away from the city lights.

"My old racer is in here," Carly Rae said as they got out of the truck.

"Really?" Allison said, looking around. The tack room and feed rooms were across from each other when you first walked in. Eight stalls were behind them, four on each side. The first five had horses in them.

"Gidget!" Carly Rae called. A light-tan palomino with a stark white-blonde mane popped her head out of the first stall on the left and whinnied loudly, shaking her head around. "Hey, girl!" Carly Rae said, petting her face and head. "How's ranch life?"

"You used to race her?"

"Yes. We won my first national championship together. I used to race both her and Firefly, but she's gotten older and started slowing down. I brought her up here at the beginning of the year to retire. She's a ranch horse now."

"Oh, wow."

"I ride her when I'm here for the cattle drives."

"Do you always choose palominos?"

"She was my first, actually. I guess I'm partial to blondes." She shrugged with a grin.

"Uh huh," Allison muttered, shaking her head. "She's pretty," she said, reaching up and petting the horse.

"Yes, and she will let you know it, too. She's a very girly horse, whereas Firefly is a bit of a tomboy. However, she's as docile as can be. You're actually going to ride her when we do the cattle drive."

"Don't you want to ride her?"

"I usually do, but she will be good to you. I'll probably ride Rowdy. He's one of my dad's horses. He's a stud and can be a pain in the ass sometimes."

Allison nodded. Being used to riding very disciplined horses, she was happy to be riding the docile one.

Carly Rae went into the refrigerator in the feed room and came back with a handful of baby carrots. Allison fed a few of them to Gidget while she gave the rest to the other horses, including Rowdy, who was a strawberry roan with a light reddish tan body and a dark red head, mane, tail, and legs.

"He doesn't look menacing," Allison said, petting him while he ate his treat.

"He's a redhead with a temper."

Allison chuckled and shook her head.

"Come on. I want to show you something," Carly Rae said after they washed their hands and headed out to the truck.

The buildings and lights from the house faded in the distance as the red truck bounced down the path and headed into the open land towards the rolling hills.

"How do you know where you're going? It's pitch-black," Allison said.

Carly Rae pointed up to the sky as she crested the first hill and came to a stop. She pulled the emergency brake and shut the truck off. "Hop out," she said, swinging her door open.

Allison got out of the truck and watched her lower the tailgate.

"This is my favorite place," Carly Rae said as she got up into the truck and lay back.

Allison gave her an odd glance, but got in beside her anyhow. "Wow," she whispered, looking up at nothing but darkness, littered with tiny diamond-like stars.

"Wait until we get further out to the pasture the cows are in. There won't be anything but stars and darkness as far as the eye can see."

"It's definitely spectacular. I don't think I've ever seen so many stars."

"Yeah," Carly Rae mumbled. "I used to spend hours out here."

"Is this where you took all of your girlfriends?" Allison teased.

"I didn't really have a girlfriend in high school. The girl I was caught kissing in the barn was the granddaughter of farmer a few miles away, who was here visiting him for a week over the summer. We met at the supply store." Carly Rae lulled her head to the side. She could barely see the woman lying next to her. "I've never brought anyone home…until now."

Allison was thankful she couldn't see the blue eyes she knew were staring back at her. Everything began making sense from her parents assuming they were sleeping in the same room, to the conversation she had with her mother while washing the dishes, and then the old stories afterwards. "Your parents think I'm your girlfriend, don't they?"

"Yep."

"Did you tell them otherwise?"

"I said I was bringing the horse owner's daughter with me to see how we do a cattle drive and show her around the ranch," Carly Rae replied with a shrug. "For all they knew, you could've been ten."

"Your mother knew I was a dressage rider and an Olympian."

"Junior Olympics?" Carly Rae chuckled.

"Nice," Allison muttered. "I'm sure they're wondering what we're out here doing."

Carly Rae shook her head, although Allison couldn't see her. "They're asleep."

"Asleep? It's barely eight o'clock."

"You and I are already an hour off because of the time difference. Plus, they get up at four every morning...which reminds me, if you want breakfast, you better get up with them."

"Geesh. And I thought starting my training by seven-thirty was early," Allison said. "Have they always been like this?"

"Daddy has always worked here on the ranch, so it's been his schedule for most of his life. Mama was a school teacher when I was little. She worked her way up to principal at the high school, then to a position on the school board before she retired. Everyone wanted her to run for

181

county superintendent, but she was ready to move on. She had no interest in politics. She runs the ranch office now. George's wife joined her when she took over. Anyway, I'm pretty sure she always got up with him just to make breakfast so he would get a good meal before working all day. He usually slaps a bologna and mustard sandwich together and calls it lunch."

"Eww."

"No kidding. I definitely did not get the rise before the rooster and love of bologna genes."

Allison laughed. "Yeah, my parents both have…in my mother's case, had…odd traits I thankfully did not get."

"What are they?" Carly Rae asked.

"Well, for starters, my father's love of cigars, which I know he is still smoking, by the way. No matter how hard he tries to hide it."

Carly Rae chuckled.

"He also loves numbers. He's in charge of our entire family estate, which consists of his family and my mother's family. At some point, it will roll down to me and I absolutely hate math."

"You can hire an accountant."

"I plan on it," she replied. "I definitely got my mother's love of wine, though, but her obsession with liquor sauce and foie gras definitely missed me."

"Neither of those sound appealing," Carly Rae said.

"Exactly."

Carly Rae checked the time on her phone. "We should probably get back."

"Look, a shooting star!" Allison exclaimed, sitting up.

"Make a wish," Carly Rae said, watching her excitement.

"Thank you for bringing me here." Allison grabbed her hand. "Not just this spot, but this place, your home."

"You're welcome," Carly Rae replied softly. She ran her thumb over the back of Allison's hand before letting go and hopping off the tailgate. She'd needed to put some space between them before she pulled her close and kissed her.

*

The house was dark except for a lamp left on in the living area when they returned. Carly Rae locked the front door, hung her jacket on the nearby rack, and kicked her boots off next to her father's. "Do you want something to eat or drink?" she asked, turning to Allison.

"Uh...a glass of water is fine," she whispered.

Carly Rae laughed softly. "They can't hear you. They sleep like the dead."

Allison raised her brows.

"I'm serious. I used to sneak in and out all the time."

"If they are such heavy sleepers, why don't they have an alarm system?"

"No one in their right mind would ever think about breaking into this house way out here to begin with, and if they did...they'd be sorry." Carly Rae handed her the glass of water. "You're safe here. I promise."

"I'm not worried." Allison smiled, grazing Carly Rae's fingers with her own as she took the glass.

"Are you planning on getting up with them for breakfast?"

"Is it really at 4 a.m.?"

"That's when they get up. Breakfast is usually on the table by a quarter to five at the latest."

Allison nodded. "Um…are you getting up to eat with them?"

"No." Carly Rae shook her head. "I love my parents, but I'm perfectly fine reheating my food."

"I agree. Just wake me when you get up," she replied. As soon as she was finished with her water, Carly Rae walked across the living area and turned out the light, leaving the house dark. Allison froze, unsure of where to go without bumping into something. "They need some damn nightlights," she mumbled.

Carly Rae stepped up beside her, taking her hand. "Come on, I know the way," she whispered.

A tingle ran down Allison's spine as the warm hand holding hers tugged, leading her blindly towards the short hallway.

"Directly ahead of you is the bathroom. I'll plug the nightlight in so you can see if you get up during the night. Your room is this way," Carly Rae said, leading her to the room on the left. She fought back the desire to pin her against the wall and kiss her hard. *If I kiss her, I'll never be able to sleep beside her in a tent for a night…a few feet from my father.* She let go of the hand she was holding as she flipped the switch for the light, illuminating the room.

"Thanks," Allison muttered, biting the edge of her lower lip as she glanced from Carly Rae to the bed and back again.

"You can have the bathroom first," Carly Rae said, taking a step back to leave the room.

"I won't be long."

Carly Rae nodded. "If you get cold, there are extra blankets in the closet. Anyway, just let me know when you're finished."

As soon as she was gone, Allison closed the door and began changing into the shorts and tank top she'd brought to sleep in. Then, she went ahead and grabbed the extra blanket because she was already cold. "Geesh, do these people believe in running the heater?" she whispered to herself as she walked out of the room with her bathroom bag.

*

Carly Rae changed into shorts and a tank top, then flopped down on the bed with her ankles crossed and her hands clasped under her head as she stared at the ceiling. This was the same room she had when she'd lived there, but it had changed over the years. Gone were the horse calendars and school girl dreams. Everything had been replaced by barrel racing memorabilia from her career. The only things that were the same were her furniture and her grandmother's hand-sewn quilt that covered the bed.

"You look like you're reminiscing," Allison said from the door way. Her hair cascaded over her bare shoulders in loose waves and her arms were crossed shyly in front of her.

"Yeah, I guess maybe I was. Me and these walls have had our share of conversations. I spent many years lying in this very spot contemplating everything from my college major to kissing a girl for the first time."

"I always had a dorm mate at boarding school…often more than one, depending on what year we were in. I'm sure some of those conversations in our early teen years helped shaped all of us. I actually had my first kiss in one of those dorms. She was a year ahead of me and very pretty, but I was too scared I'd get caught to do anything else. I couldn't let anything jeopardize my dressage riding, and I would've been mortified if my parents had found out." Allison smiled. "I waited until college to see what all of the fuss was about."

Carly Rae raised a brow in confusion. "So…you've dated girls, then?"

"Only girls." Allison smiled. "You look surprised."

Carly Rae opened her mouth to say something, but the words wouldn't come out. She finally just nodded.

"My father doesn't know. I never came out to my parents, and then, my mother passed. I haven't dated anyone since I graduated from college, so it hasn't really come up," she sighed. "Anyway, I should get to bed. I was just coming to tell you the bathroom was free."

"Allison," Carly Rae whispered getting up from the bed as she began to walk away. "I won't say anything to him," she said when she turned around.

"I know," Allison replied with a soft smile. "Goodnight."

"Goodnight," Carly Rae mumbled to her retreating back.

TWENTY

The next morning, Carly Rae was sitting at the dining table, fully dressed in jeans, a light pink and grey flannel shirt with a white t-shirt under it, and her brown boots. The flannel was unbuttoned halfway down and the sleeves were rolled back to just below her elbows. Steam casually rose from the cup of coffee she was sipping.

"Hi," Allison said, walking over.

Carly Rae looked up and smiled. Allison was wearing jeans, and a purple v-neck sweater that hugged her torso, showing all of her subtle curves. "Good morning. We have bacon, eggs, and French toast. Plus, fresh coffee and tea," Carly Rae replied, getting up to reheat their breakfast.

"Wow. That's a lot of food."

"Breakfast is the most important meal of the day, especially when you work on a ranch and have the tendency to miss lunch." She shrugged, making herself a plate with very small portions.

Allison followed her over to the counter and began making a plate with equally small portions. "You weren't kidding about gaining weight while you're here. Luna Mist is going to think someone else is on her back," she laughed.

Carly Rae chuckled.

"So, what's the plan for today? Are we leaving for the cattle drive soon?" Allison asked when they sat down adjacent to each other to eat.

"As soon as I finish here, I am heading over to mow one of the hay fields. When I am finished, I'm going to go rake another. We aren't leaving on the cattle drive until later today. We'll ride out to the cows, set up camp for the night, then leave with them at first light. That will give us the entire day to get them all moved. Sometimes, it goes pretty easily and we're back within four or five hours. Other times, it has literally taken sun up to sun down."

"That makes sense."

"Mama said you can join her in the office if you don't want to ride around in a tractor all day."

"I don't mind." Allison shrugged. "Do you always work when you come home?"

"Yes. Each of the hay fields are harvested three times during the year. This will be the last harvest before winter sets in and everything shuts down. They have cattle workers and hay farmers, but daddy and George try to do most of it themselves to save on the labor and put more money into their pockets and back into the ranch. I grew up harvesting these fields and wrangling the cattle, so it's like second nature. I always jump on whatever needs to be done when I'm here. In fact, I would've done this when I arrived yesterday, but my parents ended their work day early because they had a houseguest coming."

"Really?"

"I told you I've never brought anyone home before. This is sort of a big deal to them."

Allison nodded.

"I did mention we aren't together when I talked to my mother on the phone this morning. However, I'm pretty sure she doesn't believe me because she is thrilled you are here."

Allison smiled. "Not to change the subject, but I've never been on a tractor."

"The swather isn't a regular farm tractor. It has a big cab on the front and a digital self-driving system. It saves countless hours because it can do the job faster and with less passes. We'll head out to the equipment building whenever you're finished," Carly Rae said, as she carried her empty plate over to the sink to wash it. "We'll be gone for a while, so I'll fill these with ice and water and bring them," she added, getting two Yeti style cups from the cabinet. "You can bring your tea if you want."

*

"Where's the old red truck?" Allison asked when they stepped outside in the crisp morning air.

"Daddy has it. Come on, we'll take my rental," she said, getting in and starting the engine.

The short drive along the bumpy path they'd taken the night before wasn't anywhere near as rough as it had been in the old truck. Allison took in the sight of the beautiful, lush green rolling hills separated by flat plains as far as the eye could see, and a massive mountain range off in the distance behind them.

Carly Rae pulled up next to the huge metal building that housed all of the ranch equipment and turned the truck off. Various types of red, Massey Ferguson tractors and tractor attachments were spread around inside behind three huge roll-up, bay doors when they walked inside.

"Carly Rae!" a man wearing a backwards baseball cap yelled as he climbed down from the tractor he was working on. "I thought Charles said you weren't coming home."

"Have I ever missed a cattle drive?" She smiled. "He was talking about Tibby."

"Oh, ok."

"Lance, this is Allison McKinley. Allison, this is Lance Denny. He's the mechanic for all of the machinery."

"It's nice to meet you," she said.

"Likewise," he replied, grinning at Carly Rae.

"Daddy wants me to mow field three. Then, rake field one," Carly Rae said, walking over to the wall to grab one of the walkie talkies and the key to the massive machine known as the swather.

"Yeah, he told me. The swather is fueled up and ready to go. I just greased everything yesterday. Your father is coming behind you in the tedder. I'll have the rotary rake hooked up to the seventy-seven."

"Sounds good," she replied. "Where's George?"

"Out on two with the baler."

"Gotcha." She turned to Allison as he went back to work. "Let's go."

Allison followed her over to the massive tractor. The engine was in the back, as were the swiveling wheels. The cab on the front was a huge bubble that allowed the driver to see everything that was going on with the row of spinning disc blades that spanned nearly sixteen feet.

"This is a swather. It's basically a mower that swaths the hay into rows as it is cut. Then, you go over it later the same day, or the following day in a utility tractor that pulls a thing called a tedder. That spreads the hay back out to help it dry. After a couple of days, you go back over it pulling the rake. This flips it over to dry on the bottom, and puts it back into rows. Finally, you bale it up."

"That sounds like a long process."

"It's definitely time consuming, and a lot of work. We have four high quality hay fields. Three of them are timothy hay, and the fourth one is alfalfa," she said, climbing up the stairs of the tractor.

Allison followed, stepping inside with her when she opened the door. There were two seats, with the driver on the right side of the cab beside all of the controls and electronic screens. She sat in the seat closest to the door, while Carly Rae got behind the wheel and started the engine. The staccato hum of the diesel was surprisingly quieter than Allison had expected, due to the enclosed cab.

Carly Rae turned on the walkie talkie. "Carly Rae to Charles," she radioed. "On my way in the swather to field two, over."

"10-4. Let me know when you've finished," he replied.

"Don't leave me crooked lines to clean up!" George radioed.

"Are you sure you remember how to drive that thing? It doesn't have reins," another employee radioed, chuckling the entire time.

"Keep on me and I'll mow crop circles in this field!" she replied with a laugh.

"You boys better leave her alone. You know she'll do it and leave you both to fix it!" her father said.

Carly Rae laughed as she clipped the walkie talkie to the cup holder on the dash. Then, she pressed the clutch in to engage the transmission and let her foot off the brake slowly. The big machine eased out of the building through the open bay door like Carly Rae could do this with her eyes closed.

Allison watched out of the corner of her eye as Carly Rae maneuvered the tractor towards the field off in the distance. She was about as far out of her element as she could possibly get, but somehow it felt comfortable.

Once they arrived at the field, Carly Rae mowed all the way around the outside, then she pressed different buttons to select the settings she wanted and let the tractor take over. She watched the monitor, taking over manual steering as the turns got tighter, but other than that, she left the machine in control as rows and rows of green, five-foot tall hay shoots disappeared.

"Is this thing really driving itself?" Allison asked.

Carly Rae put her hands in the air and the tractor kept chugging along.

"That's crazy!"

"Do you want to drive? I'll take it off auto pilot."

"Uh…" Allison shook her head. "No. I'd probably mess something up."

"Maybe if you mowed your name into the field," Carly Rae laughed.

"Don't tell me you did that."

Carly Rae grinned.

"Oh, my God!" she chuckled. "What happened?"

"You needed to be in a plane or helicopter to really see it, but Daddy was still pissed. My friends and I mowed crop circles in the alfalfa field one time. Daddy had no idea until the local news showed up. We damn near had the FBI out here. He laughed about that one, but I still got in trouble."

"Who knew you were such a bad girl as a kid?" Allison smiled and shook her head.

"I wasn't really bad to be honest. I just did whatever I felt like doing sometimes. I think all kids do that. What about you? Did you ever get in trouble?"

"No. There was no time to even think about doing something foolish in boarding school, and the rules were very strict. My mother had attended the same academies.

192

The last thing I would've wanted to do was embarrass her, or get kicked out."

"I gave my pony a cup of coffee one time to see if it would make her go faster," Carly Rae said.

"Did it work?"

"No. It gave her the shits!"

Allison laughed.

Carly Rae took the controls back over as they were nearing the last row. "Are you sure you don't want to drive?"

"Okay, fine. But, I'm blaming you if something goes wrong."

Carly Rae shrugged and stopped the tractor so they could switch seats. "Okay, so you just let out the clutch and mash the accelerator like you're driving a stick shift and hold the wheel straight. It'll max out at about ten miles per hour. The play in the wheel is set in the middle, so it will react a little more slowly to every little move you make."

Allison took a deep breath and did as she was instructed. She'd only driven a stick shift a couple of times, so she was a little rough on the take off, but the big, heavy tractor barely lurched as it began rolling. She held the steering wheel like her life depended on it as they mowed down the last long line of the field. When she came to the end, she followed Carly Rae's instruction on how to bring it to a stop, raise the blades, and turn them off. Then, they switched seats again so Carly Rae could drive them back to the equipment building.

"Carly Rae to Charles. Field two is ready to be teddered."

"10-4," her father replied.

Carly Rae pulled up at the equipment building and Lance came outside. She told Allison to swing the cab door open when he climbed up on the side of the machine.

"Back it in. I'll guide you," he said.

"Okay."

"The seventy-seven is ready to go with the rotary rake," he added before climbing down.

Carly Rae turned a wide U and switched the swather tractor into reverse. Lance used hand motions to guide her back into the space he wanted it parked in. As soon as they were in position, she killed the engine. "Ready to switch gears?" she asked.

"Sure," Allison said, checking her watch. "Wow. That took three hours!"

"Time flies when you're in the field," Carly Rae replied as they got out of the swather. The other tractor was a traditional large, row crop tractor. It was already sitting outside and had the rotary rake attached to the back with the wide arms pulled up in a V shape. "This one only has one full seat, but there is a padded jump seat you can sit on."

Allison nodded.

"If you need to refill your water there is a cooler around the corner right there and the bathroom is down the hall."

"I'm good," Allison replied.

Carly Rae smiled and headed out of the building. Allison fell in step beside her as they made their way over to the tractor. Carly Rae climbed up first and settled into the driver's seat. Allison followed, sitting in the small jump seat to her left where the cab door was located. It was definitely a much smaller enclosure than the one they'd been in with the other tractor.

"This thing's like a giant version of the tractor Ollie rides around on," Allison laughed.

"Yeah." Carly Rae smiled. "I tried to tell him I know how to drive a tractor and don't need him to do everything for me," she said as she started the engine and pulled away from the building.

"I'll have to bring some pictures back for him. My phone's in the rental truck."

"Do you want to go get it?"

"Nah, we're already going. It's not a big deal. I'll just take a couple when we're done."

Carly Rae nodded and continued down the path that led to field two.

"What do you normally do when you're out here all day by yourself?"

"I usually listen to my iPod," Carly Rae replied as she pulled into the field. The hay was mowed down and separated into perfect rows as far as the eye could see. She locked the brake on the tractor and shut it off.

"I see why you brought me along now," Allison teased.

Carly Rae grinned. "I hate to kick you out, but I have to go put the rake arms down," she said, nodding towards the back of the tractor.

"You move out of that nice, comfortable seat and I'm liable to take over."

Carly Rae shrugged. "Go right ahead. You can't mess this up, literally. We are riding over the rows and spreading the hay back out while flipping it over to dry the other side. This tractor isn't self-driven though." She winked as she climbed down.

Allison watched her walk to the large piece of equipment being pulled behind them. Carly Rae unhooked the latch on each side, lowered the arms down, and latched them back in place. Then, she got back in the tractor…and into the driver's seat.

"What's the matter? You can't steer in a straight line?" Carly Rae teased.

"I figured I'd let you go first. You know…make sure you know what you're doing and everything before I take over and show you how it's done." Allison raised a brow and bit back the smile creeping up on her lips.

Carly Rae laughed and shook her head as she started up the tractor. "Carly Rae to Charles. You copy?" she radioed, pulling the walkie-talkie from her belt.

"Go ahead," he replied.

"I'm raking field two."

"Head back to the house when you're done. Your mama will have lunch ready. We're going to saddle up and head out afterwards."

"10-4."

*

Carly Rae pulled the rake around the outside edge of the entire field before turning down each row one at a time. The tractor was by no means fast, despite her having it in high gear. The rotary rakes did their job, flipping and spreading the hay as they passed over it. Thankfully, Lance had kept all of their equipment in perfect working order, so they rarely had issues to fix while in the field.

She drank from her cup, then set it back in the holder without wavering at all on the line she was raking. "Are you ready to show me how to drive this thing yet?"

Allison shrugged. "You seem to be doing a pretty good job."

Carly Rae stepped on the brake, causing the tractor to lurch to a sudden stop. There were only three rows left to rake, so she killed the engine and looked at Allison, who was literally right next to her with only the armrest separating them. "Your turn."

"What happens if I do it perfectly?" Allison asked, standing so that Carly Rae could raise the arm rest and slide over to the jump seat.

"You get to share my tent tonight."

"And if I mess up?"

"You're on your own with the wildebeests. I hear they are partial to brunettes, so I'd drive carefully."

"Oh, you're funny. First of all, they are in Africa, not Wyoming."

"True. But, seriously though, the coyotes out here are as big as Great Danes. They've been known to eat cows and sheep right in the middle of the pasture."

"That's good to know," Allison grimaced as she started the tractor and headed down the row in front of them. She barely had to touch the wheel at all to keep them in a straight line.

"When you get to the end, make the turn slowly, but don't come to a stop," Carly Rae said, watching her line, while also watching the woman beside her. Allison was smiling slightly as she concentrated on what she was doing.

*

By the time Carly Rae and Allison arrived back at the house, it was one o'clock. Carly Rae's mother had set out a smorgasbord of sandwich making materials for lunch over the entire kitchen island, including ham, turkey, salami, and a handful of different types of cheese, a couple bread choices, and all of the condiments you could think of.

Carly Rae and Allison cleaned up and quickly went to work making their own sandwiches for lunch. "Make sure you eat because dinner will literally be baked beans and hot dogs cooked over the fire tonight," Carly Rae whispered.

Allison nodded. "We should make one to go," she muttered.

"I'm going to send some of this with you guys for tonight. I know daddy likes to make his specialty over the fire, but just in case you want something else," Irene said, smiling at Allison, who mouthed 'thank you' to her.

"What's wrong with franks and beans?" Charles asked.

"Nothing, honey." Irene winked at Allison and Carly Rae hid her laughter while shaking her head.

TWENTY-ONE

Charles was in the stable readying the horses when Carly Rae walked in with Allison. "I thought you would put her on Gidget," he said, nodding towards Allison. "So, I saddled Rowdy for you."

I figured," she replied, smiling at Allison before walking over to Rowdy. "Don't you give me any trouble and we'll get along fine," she whispered, petting his head.

Allison heard someone enter the barn and turned around to see a man about the same age as Charles walk in, wearing jeans, a long-sleeved denim shirt, boots, and a straw cowboy hat similar to the Stetson Carly Rae was wearing. A young, similarly dressed man came in with him.

"The hired hand will be here in a minute. Someone just let him in the gate," the younger guy said.

"Allison, this is George Tibbetts. He's daddy's right-hand man and my best friend's father, and that's Dean, he's one of the ranch hands. Guys, this is Allison McKinley. Her father owns the horse I am training."

Dean nodded.

George smiled. "It's nice to meet you. So, your daddy tells me you're going to jockey that horse, too," he said, looking at Carly Rae.

"I am," she replied with a smile. "Tibby doesn't know yet."

"Oh, boy!" he laughed. "You two will run everyone else off the track just to race each other!"

She chuckled and shook her head.

"Here comes the hand now," Charles said, seeing the stable door open. "You must be Joe Connor."

"Yes, sir," the young man answered, walking up to them. He was dressed similarly in jeans, boots, a long-sleeved shirt and a brown cowboy hat. He stepped close to Allison and tipped his hat in her direction.

"Joe, I'm Charles Walsh. We spoke on the phone," he said, shaking his hand. "This is George, my ranch foreman, and Dean, one of our ranch hands. That's my daughter, Carly Rae and her friend Allison. Anyway, now that we're all here, let's get down to business. The cows are in the north pasture about five miles away, but the terrain is all rolling hills and we have to cross a creek. Our goal is to get out to the cattle quickly, round them up, and set up camp for the night. We'll get up at first light, eat a quick meal, break down the camp and head out. It will take the entire day to get all of the cattle down into the south pasture. We'll work in a V-formation with one, possibly two riders hanging back to chase stragglers. Any questions?"

Everyone shook their heads.

"George will run the left wing, I'll run the right. Dean, you'll be on the left and Joe, you'll be on the right with me. You both have the responsibility of keeping the herd moving while we control the direction. Allison, you'll be at the back, sort of zigzagging back and forth to keep the slower cows moving with the herd. Carly Rae, you'll chase the stragglers."

He stepped over to the horses.

"There is a sleeping bag attached to the saddlebags on each horse. Everyone has carrots and a small sack of feed for their horse in one side of the bag, along with a canteen full of fresh water, and camping supplies for the group. The other side is for your personal items. There are three tents. One on my horse, one with Carly Rae, and one with Dean. The weather is clear with zero percent chance of rain."

"Sounds good," George said. "Here are the walkie talkies for everyone. We will be on channel three. You each have a fresh battery and an extra one in your saddlebag with the camping supplies."

"On the ride out, I'll lead," Charles said. "Carly Rae, can you bring up the rear?"

"Yes, sir."

"Allison, you two stay together. Dean and Joe, you ride behind me and George. If there are no questions, let's get moving. We're burning daylight," Charles said.

Everyone put a few personal items into their saddlebags: extra shirts and socks and toiletries. Then, they grabbed the reins of the horses and filed out of the stable, one behind the other.

"Are you sure you don't want a hat?" Carly Rae asked. "It doesn't have to be a Stetson. I have an old ball cap around here."

Allison bit the edge of her lip. "Okay, fine."

"Daddy, give us a second. I need to grab a hat for Allison."

"There's one in the feed room," Charles said.

She gave him a thumbs up sign and ran back into the stable.

"You can wear my Stetson. It'll be a little big, but I don't mind," Joe said with a smile.

"Thanks, but she's getting the one I want," Allison replied politely as she stared at the stable door.

Sure enough, Carly Rae returned with her worn, red trucker-style Massey Ferguson hat. "Here, I used to wear this old thing all the time while working the hay fields."

"Thanks," Allison said, pulling her ponytail through the hole in the back as she slid it on her head.

*

Carly Rae was the last in line as they crossed one hill after the other. They jogged the horses at a light pace for a bit, then slowed them to a walk to cool down, before sparsely picking up the pace again. "What do you think, so far?" she asked, riding up next to Allison.

"Your family's land is beautiful. I see why you come home to help out."

"Yeah," Carly Rae nodded. "It's not easy, but it's not really work. At least, to me it isn't. I cherish the time I get to spend here."

"I would, too."

"Carly Rae," Charles radioed.

"Go ahead," she replied.

"Ride ahead towards the pass and check the water level. If we can, I want to cross there like we talked about. Otherwise, we'll have to go around to that spot I showed you on the map. George is dropping back to bring up the rear."

"10-4," she said, then clipped the radio to her belt. "I'll see you in a bit. Stay with George. He won't let you get lost."

"Got it," Allison said.

Carly Rae slapped the reins and Rowdy whinnied. "Come on, you pain in the ass!" she growled, slapping them again as she yelled, "Yah!"

The red horse took off at a full gallop, leaving the group behind as his wild red mane blew in the wind. Carly Rae wasn't a fan of the temperamental horse, but she knew how to control him, nonetheless. She squinted her eyes, searching for the stream as they raced down one hill and back up another. Finally, she spotted the waterline. "Whoa!" she yelled. The horse skidded to a stop, nearly sending her flying into the creek. "Damn you," she grumbled, getting down off of him. He meandered over, taking a drink while she checked the measuring sticks at the deepest section. "Charles, you copy?"

"Go ahead," he replied.

"Sixteen inches," she said.

"It's gone down another inch since I last checked it. Great. Stay put. We'll be there shortly."

*

Allison watched Carly Rae ride off at breakneck speed, disappearing within the rolling hills. She adjusted her weight in the saddle and pet Gidget's neck. "I wish you could talk. I bet you'd tell me all about her."

"You're not from around here," Joe said, slowing so that he was next to her with his smug grin. He had a thin mustache and soul patch of hair just below his bottom lip that made him look like a little boy who was trying to be a man. She guessed he was her age, perhaps a couple of years younger.

"No," she replied.

"Tell me, what's a city girl like you doing out here slumming it as a ranch hand? You certainly don't look like you need the money."

She drew in a deep breath to keep from telling him off. The French blood in her always heated quickly. "I wasn't hired. I'm a friend of Carly Rae's. She brought me along to meet her family and see how their ranch was run."

"So…basically, you're free labor. Who the hell would want to drive cattle to see what it was all about?" He shook his head.

"I guess you wouldn't understand," she said.

"Well, you look like you know how to handle a horse, but I'd be happy to give you some pointers." He smiled, wiggling his brows. "There will be a lot more involved than just riding a horse once we get into the thick of it tomorrow."

"Thank you, but I'm sure I will be fine."

He shrugged and increased his pace as Carly Rae and the creek came into view.

*

Carly Rae walked around, stretching her legs while the horse drank. Then, she gave him half of a carrot. "I shouldn't give you this. You damn near tossed me in there," she grumbled.

The horse whinnied and ate the snack as if he didn't care. A few minutes later, she saw her father leading the group about fifty yards away. She got back on Rowdy and waited for them to come up.

"It's shallow enough. The horses' legs should dry in plenty of time before the sun goes down," she said when her father rode up next to her

"I agree," he said, then spun around on his horse to address the group. "We're going to cross here in a single file line."

Carly Rae waited for everyone to go across, then got back in her place at the rear. Allison was the last to cross before her, and she'd passed by with her lips curling into a smile.

She followed behind Allison, but Rowdy hesitated for a second. She gave him a light squeeze to let him know she was in charge and he was crossing the creek. He finally meandered through the water.

Once she was on the other side, she caught up to Allison. "How's it going?"

"Good. That guy Joe just about got the best of me a little bit ago."

Carly Rae furrowed her brow. "What happened?"

"Nothing happened. He's cocky and thinks I'm a big city girl who might need some pointers for tomorrow's ride."

Carly Rae shook her head. "You could ride circles around that idiot."

"Yeah, I know. That's why I didn't bother. He's not worth my time."

Carly Rae smiled at her.

"What?"

"Nothing," she said, shaking her head slowly as she dropped back behind her.

*

Dusk was closing in on them by the time the group found the cattle, who were spread all around the open pasture at the base of two hills. A fire circle with creek stones surrounding it was nearby. A few large tree logs were strategically placed for seating. Everyone dismounted. Charles, George, and Joe began setting up the portable corral with electric fencing about twenty feet from the fire pit to allow the horses a safe place to graze and lie down for the night without running off. Carly Rae, Allison, and Dean fed the horses carrots and handfuls of oats while they waited.

A few minutes later, the fence was up and running with all of the horses inside. Charles began arranging the wood and kindling from their supplies so he could go ahead and get the fire going.

George put one of the tents up, while Joe worked on a second one a few feet away. Carly Rae and Allison took their tent to the other side of the fire pit, creating an isosceles triangle, leaving the fire in the middle.

"This is smaller than I imagined," Allison muttered, crawling inside once they'd finished.

"We can't carry much weight, so they have to be small," Carly Rae replied, unrolling her sleeping bag next to Allison's. "I don't snore."

"Good to know," she replied, backing her way out. *There's no way I can sleep with only a few inches of space between us.* She removed the ball cap she'd been wearing, tossing it inside before walking over to the log closest to their tent. The chill of the night air was starting to creep through the jeans and cable-knit sweater she was wearing. She freed her hair from the ponytail and shook it out. The chocolate locks fell in loose waves around her shoulders. A low whistle caught her attention and she looked over to see Joe watching her. She faked a thin smile and turned back towards the fire.

"You know…there's room in my tent, if you need someone to keep you warm," Joe said, sitting down next to her.

"I'm fine where I am sleeping, thanks." *Heat definitely won't be my problem.*

"I'm sure the other guy in my tent wouldn't mind shacking up with the blonde," he added, trying again.

"Her name is Carly Rae," she said sternly. "Did you pay attention to anything that was said to you before we left?"

He shrugged. "I'm a ranch hand. I know what I'm doing."

Allison shook her head and got up.

*

The sun slid behind the mountain, casting everything in a soft orange glow that slowly faded to black. The blazing fire had burned down to red and orange embers by the time Charles had finished cooking the hotdog and baked bean concoction he was so proud of.

Carly Rae sat on the log beside Allison, who had moved back to her original spot outside of their tent after Joe had slithered away, and purposely bumped shoulders with her.

Allison turned to see her wiggling the soft cooler she'd brought with the extra sandwiches her mother had packed from lunch earlier in the day.

"I could kiss you," she whispered, thankful she didn't have to eat the hot dogs and beans being slopped into bowls for the rest of the group.

"Well…we *are* sleeping together tonight," Carly Rae teased, handing her a sandwich.

"Funny," Allison laughed, shaking her head before taking her first bite.

"How did they wind up with sandwiches?" George said, eyeing the two of them.

"Mama couldn't let Allison eat Daddy's camp specialty on her first trip," Carly Rae said between bites.

"Uh huh, and she just happened to pack one for you, too?"

"Yep." Carly Rae gave him a cheeky grin.

George shook his head and loaded his bowl full of salt and pepper.

*

"Carly Rae, I know you have that harp with you," George said as soon as dinner was finished.

She grinned like a Cheshire cat and said, "Maybe."

"Maybe…Hell. Whip that thing out, girl," he replied with a big smile.

She laughed and went into the tent to retrieve her harmonica.

"Have you heard her play?" he asked Allison.

"Yeah."

"There's blues in that girl's blood. I'm telling you," he said, shaking his head.

Allison nodded. She'd only heard her play once, and had never heard blues music until Carly Rae had introduced her to it. She'd grown up with the likes of Beethoven, Bach, and Chopin.

Carly Rae returned, sitting back down beside Allison. She held the blues harp in her left hand. "What do you want to hear?" she asked, looking at George.

"How about a little Muddy Waters?" he said.

She nodded and pulled her hands together, bringing the harmonica to her mouth. The distinct beginning riff of

Hoochie Coochie Man began playing as she slid her lips along the smooth metal, sucking and blowing air in and out while she tapped her boot on the ground. Everyone's head was bobbing along by the time the song ended. She quickly went into a few more before finally putting the harmonica away.

"I could listen to you play all night long," George said, shaking his head. "But, these old bones need their sleep."

Most everyone began turning in for the night, including Allison, but Carly Rae stayed out by the fire with her father.

"What do you know about this hired hand?" she asked, once everyone had disappeared.

"Not much. He isn't tied to any particular farm or ranch around here, but he's worked on most of them a time or two. Why?"

"He's interested in Allison."

"Well, she's a pretty girl."

"Yeah, but he's pouring it on a little too thick."

"For you, or for her?" he asked. "Listen, I'm not getting into your business, and if he's being disrespectful, I'll send his ass out of here right now, but what's really going on? You told your mama you're not dating her."

"I'm not," she sighed. "It's…complicated."

"You might want to figure it out. You're only there for another five or six weeks."

"Yeah, I know."

"I've seen the way she looks at you. That cocky ranch hand doesn't stand a chance," he said.

She laughed.

"I'm calling it a night. I'll see you in the morning, kiddo." He gave her a quick hug and headed over to his tent.

Carly Rae watched the last of the fire embers burn out, then she unzipped the tent and carefully crawled inside. Allison was sound asleep. She tried not to disturb her as she kicked off her boots, slipped out of her jeans and into a pair of soft cotton sweatpants, and eased into her sleeping bag as quietly as possibly. Thankfully, she'd already brushed her teeth earlier in the evening. She was so tired, her eyes slammed shut before she could give much thought to the woman lying beside her. For all she knew, Allison could've been naked in her sleeping bag, but Carly Rae would've still fallen fast asleep.

*

In the middle of the night, Carly Rae felt something bump her. She knew without fully waking that Allison had snuggled up against her, most likely for the extra warmth. The floral scent of her shampoo and conditioner wafted in the air as she moved, tickling Carly Rae's senses.

The faint sound of an animal howling in the distance woke Allison with a frightening start. She realized she was up against Carly Rae when she tried to adjust her position. The animal howled again, sending chills down her spine. *Is it getting closer? It sounds like it's getting closer.* She mentally panicked.

"What's wrong?" Carly Rae whispered after being woken with an elbow to her ribs.

"Something's out there," Allison whispered back. "It sounds like a wolf, and it's getting closer."

Carly Rae laughed softly. "First of all, it's not a wolf, it's a coyote. Second, I guarantee you it is nowhere near us. It's probably lost and trying to find it's pack somewhere up on the mountain. This is a nightly occurrence out here, especially this far out on our property."

"I thought they eat livestock."

"Not generally. They like cows who are about to give birth, but any of our cows that are pregnant are kept in a pen up close to the barn or even in the barn. We have workers whose job it is to literally ride around our property and hunt for coyotes. If you kill one or two and leave the carcass, they will associate cows with death and not come around."

The animal howled again. It was a long, crying sound almost. Allison turned to face Carly Rae, but couldn't see her face in the pitch black. "Are you sure that's not a wolf?"

"Yes. It's definitely a lost coyote crying for his pack. You're fine. I promise, nothing is going to get you. Go back to sleep. It'll be time to get up soon."

Allison stared around in the darkness until she fell asleep once more. She never heard the eerie animal sound again.

TWENTY-TWO

Just before the sun rose, Carly Rae heard her father starting the fire so he could heat up the water for their instant coffee and oatmeal. She moved to get out of her sleeping bag and noticed Allison had cuddled up against her again. She gently shook her, causing Allison to stir before her eyes fluttered open.

"Good morning," Carly Rae said. "I want to show you something."

"Now? Out there?" Allison yawned. Her body was stiff from lying on the hard ground all night.

"Yes, out there. If we don't go now, we'll miss it," Carly Rae said, slithering out of her blanket.

Allison watched her change from the sweatpants she didn't even know she had on, to her jeans that were neatly folded in the corner beside her boots, which she also pulled on. Shrugging, she finally unzipped her sleeping bag.

"Oh, my God, it's freezing!"

"Ssshhh, you'll wake everyone," Carly Rae hissed. "You'll warm up once you get moving."

Allison hoped she was right as she pulled her jeans on and slipped her calf high boots on over them. "Can I at least brush my hair?"

"It looks fine. Come on," Carly Rae said, opening the tent.

Allison stepped out after her and quickly put her jacket on. Charles was over by the fire. The same pot hung over it from the night before where the beans and hot dogs had been cooked.

"Please tell me hot dogs and beans are not our breakfast," she muttered.

"No," Carly Rae laughed. "He's probably heating water," she said as she grabbed her hand and tugged her along. "We're not going far."

Allison was surprised at the softness of the hand in hers despite the calluses, but the warmth was welcoming against her cool skin, making her reluctant to let go when Carly Rae pulled away and shoved her hands in her pockets.

"Watch," Carly Rae whispered.

Allison turned her eyes towards the black sky. Suddenly, a slice of light tore through the darkness above the mountain peaks in the distance. Slowly, it became wider and brighter. She'd never seen anything so beautiful. "It looks like the heavens are literally opening," she mumbled.

"I've always thought the same thing."

Both women watched as the light began spreading further, revealing the land little by little. The sky looked as if someone had painted orange and yellow hues directly over the mountains and brushed pink wisps of clouds above that.

The colors shifted once the giant ball of light rose from behind the mountain, shining a light so bright, they had to shade their eyes. Allison felt like she was only a few miles from the sun instead of nearly 100 million.

Finally, the bright sun dimmed slightly as it rose a little higher in the sky, casting everything in the bright white light of the day. The lush green grass of the rolling hills glimmered with morning dew.

"We should probably get back. We'll be heading out soon," Carly Rae said, turning to look at her.

Without thinking, Allison reached up and placed her hand on the side of Carly Rae's face. Their lips met naturally in a soft kiss before Carly Rae pulled back slightly, ending the kiss as she covered Allison's hand with her own. "Your hands are freezing!" she exclaimed, pulling it from her face as she gathered her other hand and rubbed them both with her warm hands. "Are you cold?"

"A little, but I'll warm up," Allison said shyly. "Thank you for this. I've never seen anything more beautiful in my life. That was truly amazing. I'll never forget it."

"You're welcome. I've seen the sun rise and set all over this country, but to me, nothing compares to the way it paints this land, as if heaven truly is right above it."

"It really is breathtaking." Allison nodded. "I wish I'd videoed it with my phone."

"I've done that a half dozen times. It's much better live. The video doesn't capture the essence of it."

"I'll just have to come back so I can see it again," Allison teased.

"I'm pretty sure my parents would welcome you with open arms. I'm beginning to think my mother likes you more than me and you just met!"

Allison laughed.

"Breakfast should be ready," Carly Rae said, nodding towards the camp as she let go of Allison's hands which were now warmed up by her own. "I carry an extra set of gloves in case mine get wet. I'll get them for you when we get back," she added as they began walking side by side.

"Fresh hot water just came off the fire," Charles said as Allison and Carly Rae walked up. He handed each a packet of instant coffee and instant oatmeal.

"I'm a long way from wine country," Allison murmured, causing Carly Rae to chuckle.

"It's not as bad as it sounds, and it could definitely be worse. Trust me, I've had worse," she said as she began mixing water into her oatmeal bowl and coffee mug. "When I first started out barrel racing on the rodeo circuit, I needed all of the money I made for gas and horse supplies. My first trailer only had a small sink and a camping toilet. I used a folding cot and a camping stove. I also ate off the dollar menu and drank dollar cups of coffee from the gas station. That first year was nothing but cholesterol and muddy water."

"Yuck!" Allison grimaced as she mixed her own food. Thankfully, she'd brought a teabag from the house since she didn't drink coffee.

Carly Rae laughed and shrugged. "I felt bad for leaving, but they'd insisted I follow my dreams. I wasn't about to let them pay for it, too." She hadn't been born with a silver spoon in her mouth and had watched two generations work their fingers to the bone to provide for their family. She'd also seen how much hard work paid off.

"This isn't bad," Allison said, eating her apple cinnamon oatmeal. "It's all clumped up though."

"The trick is to mix it in slowly."

"Good to know...after the fact."

Carly Rae grinned. "Didn't you say you were coming back? You'll remember for next time."

"I guess you'll see, won't you?"

"Daddy, Allison is signing up now to help with the spring drive," Carly Rae called.

"Great!" he said with the same grinning smile his daughter had.

Allison smiled and shook her head.

"I'm going to get those gloves for you and start packing up the tent," Carly Rae said after she'd finished her breakfast.

"I'll be over to help you in a minute," Allison replied.

"You two certainly are chummy this morning. Who knew you were a vagitarian," Joe said, slithering up next to her.

Allison raised a brow and leaned in close, wrinkling her nose. "You smell like you and Dean spent the night playing hide the sausage."

"What? I ain't no faggot!" he growled.

"Excuse me?" Charles called from the other side of the camp as he turned around to see Joe glaring angrily at Allison. "Come here, boy."

Joe turned and looked at him as Carly Rae crawled out of her tent.

"I didn't stutter," Charles said sternly.

Carly Rae was surprised at her father's raised voice. "What's going on?" she asked, walking back over to Allison.

"Joe and his stupidity. He thinks we slept together last night."

"We did."

"Sex. He thinks we had sex," she muttered, trying not to let anyone hear her.

Carly Rae raised a brow in surprise. "What gave him that idea?"

"He's a man. They think with their pecker." She shrugged. "I may have made things worse though," she sighed.

"How so?"

"I implied that he and Dean were the ones having sex all night."

Carly Rae laughed. "Not likely. Dean's married to his high school sweetheart."

"Good for him."

Carly Rae could hear her father chewing up one side of Joe and down the other about respecting people. "His ass is going to be sore and no one's laid a hand on him," she muttered.

"He deserves it."

"Oh, I agree. This is where me and Daddy are different. He can cut you to the bone with words and guilt trip you for a lifetime. I know. I've been on the blunt end of those conversations. I, on the other hand, will knock you out and get it over with. Hence why I got in the scuffle with the woman who tried to kill my horse. I kicked her ass first and asked questions later."

"Did you learn your lesson?"

"Which time?"

"Either." Allison shrugged.

"I never make the same mistake twice, so yeah...I guess I did."

*

Cattle driving was pretty much just what it had sounded like. Charles and George rode their horses out to the edge of the cattle herd, keeping them headed in the right direction as they slowly meandered towards the southern pasture, which was much closer to the ranch operations buildings and hay fields than the northern pasture, making it easier to care for them during the upcoming winter months. Dean and Joe flanked the pack, making sure the cows continued moving in the direction of the front of the herd. Allison simply rode back and forth behind the herd, keeping all of them moving forward. Carly Rae rode all around, redirecting cattle that had wandered away, while safely guiding them back to the herd. If she found herself not chasing an elusive cow, she was riding with Allison, helping her keep the herd moving.

"How's it going?" Carly Rae asked, allowing Rowdy to walk beside Gidget so he could cool down after just having to run after a stray.

"I'm pretty sure I have the easy job." Allison smiled.

"Yeah, but I have the fun one," Carly Rae said with a grin before taking off after another stray when someone called the position over the radio.

Allison felt a twinge of loneliness as she watched her ride away.

*

Carly Rae scanned the hills for the white cow. "There you are," she said, spotting her off to the side, eating some grass. She kept her distance for a minute or two, then rode up on the large animal. "Let's go!" she yelled, spooking her so she'd take off in the direction of the herd. She had a rope with her, but seldom had to use it. Most of the time, the cows moved along. Occasionally, she'd have to dust off her roping skills and chase after one of the younger, more stubborn ones.

Not long after she wrangled the stray, the group stopped for their third and final break to allow the cattle to graze and rest. Carly Rae got down from Rowdy's back and fed him a couple of long, thick carrots. "Good, boy," she said, petting his neck.

"It seems like you two are getting along," her father said, walking over to her.

"He's behaving."

"That's because Gidget is out here. I'm pretty sure he has a thing for her," he replied.

"Are you thinking of mating them?"

"No. I don't have a need for another horse around here right now. Unless, you're looking to raise another racer."

"No. Not anytime soon. I'm fine with one at the moment. I don't know what will happen with training, and now jockeying, this thoroughbred. I sort of have my hands full."

"Do you think this will be a onetime thing? You jockeying him, I mean."

"I don't know. I'd never give up barrel racing. That's my passion, but working with this horse has been very special. I almost wish he was mine."

"Maybe he'll still suck and you can buy him cheap," he chuckled. "But knowing you, he's going to be a winner."

She smiled.

"We should be in the south pasture in another hour," he said. "Let's get moving so we can get this over with and I can send that bastard down the road."

"He needs a boot in his butt."

Charles laughed. "I'm surprised you haven't done that already."

"I'm supposed to be working on anger management, remember?" she said with a grin, quoting the barrel racing federation who had suspended her, as she got back up on Rowdy.

He chuckled and shook his head as he walked back over to his horse and rounded everyone up to start out once again.

*

When the group arrived at their destination in the south pasture, which was a fenced area close to the barn, they worked together to usher all of the cows into their new home for the next six months. Once they'd finished, Allison, Carly Rae, and Dean led the horses to the stable to feed and brush them down. George went to check on the hay field operations, and Charles went to the front gate with Joe.

"What do you think is being said at the gate?" Allison asked.

"Daddy already gave him a good chewing this morning at the campsite, but he is an upstanding man. Right now, he is paying him the full agreed upon amount while also cutting him to the bone with his words."

"I don't even know what happened, but I guarantee you Joe 'what's-his-name' definitely won't be able find work around this town anymore," Dean added, shaking his head as he brushed one of the horses.

"He was extremely disrespectful," Carly Rae said, leaving it at that. "What do you think, Rowdy? Do you want a braid in your pretty red hair?"

The horse whinnied and tried to back away, but his reins were tied to a hook on the wall to keep him still.

"Looks like his answer is no," Allison laughed.

Carly Rae shrugged and brushed out his long mane. "I would do it anyway, but he was pretty good out there. Usually, he and I fight like a cat on a dog's back."

"True," Dean muttered, moving onto his second horse.

Allison finished with Gidget and put her in the stall at the same time Carly Rae was putting Rowdy in his. "Do you want to tackle the last one together?" she asked, looking at Carly Rae.

"Sure."

Dean was finishing up when they came back over to the horse Charles had ridden. "If I don't see you before you leave, have a safe trip," he said, half hugging Carly Rae. "Allison, it was nice to meet you. Maybe we'll see you back again sometime."

"Thank you. It was nice to meet you as well."

Carly Rae went to work brushing her side of the horse with the rubber brush to get the loose hairs and dirt off him before going back over him with the bristled brush. Once she'd finished, she brushed his tail while Allison worked on his mane. "I don't know about you, but I'm hungry."

"Yes. I'd probably eat your father's hot dogs and beans right now if they were in front of me," Allison replied, closing the gate after they put the horse in the stall.

Carly Rae laughed.

"What's so funny?" Charles said, walking into the stable.

"Allison wants beans and franks for dinner."

Allison gasped and glared at her.

Charles chuckled when he saw the look she gave his daughter. "I just talked to your mama. She's cooking now. I

221

can call her back and tell her to add some beans and hot dogs."

"That won't be necessary. I'm sure whatever she's making is fine," Allison said politely, following them out of the stable.

"You know he knew I was kidding, right?" Carly Rae said when she got into the rental truck.

"Seriously?"

"Yes," Carly Rae laughed as she started the truck.

"Damn you." Allison shook her head and tried not to smile. "I thought he was really about to call her."

"He probably would have, just to mess with you."

"If I'd had to eat beans and franks for dinner, you would have, too."

Carly Rae shrugged. "I usually do. Mama made sandwiches because of you. I don't get special treatment."

Allison nodded.

*

I've Got a Woman by Ray Charles was playing on the turn table when Carly Rae and Allison walked in. Irene was in the kitchen, bobbing along as she prepared dinner. Charles walked out of the kitchen where he'd been taste testing the spaghetti sauce.

"It'll be ready in just a minute," Irene said.

Carly Rae and Allison removed their boots. Then, Carly Rae snuck into the kitchen to say hello to her mother, and simultaneously snatched a piece of garlic bread on her way out.

"I know how many pieces of bread were on that plate, young lady!" her mother called.

Carly Ray shoved one side of it in her mouth and handed Allison the other side. She quickly ate her half of the evidence. All the while, Charles watched the playful banter between the two of them. He and Irene had never seen Carly Rae with anyone, except for the time he caught her in the barn, kissing another girl when they were just teens. She'd never talked about anyone she'd dated and had certainly never brought them home with her. The fact that Allison was there was puzzling, especially since Carly Rae had said they weren't dating.

*

Once everyone had finished with their dinner, Irene got up to start clearing the table. Allison jumped up to help her.

"You're a wonderful cook," she said, carrying her plate to the kitchen.

Irene smiled. "Thank you. What about you? Do you cook?"

"My mother taught me, but it didn't really sink in. My father isn't much of a cook either, so we use a chef service. They deliver our meals once a week. Each night, we go into the freezer and thaw whichever one we want."

Irene nodded. "It's good to know you have a plan. If you relied on my daughter, you'd get bored to death."

Allison laughed.

"Don't get me wrong, she knows the basics, but I tried to teach her a lot more than that. She was too exhausted when she came in at night to do much of anything. If she wasn't racing that horse all over creation, she was working the hay fields or tending to cattle. But, those were all her choices. She was never forced to work on the ranch, she did it without ever being asked and still does it to this day. Her father has told her time and again, he can hire hands to do the cattle drive, but she makes the trip back twice a year to help out. I know it's an excuse to see us and come back here. This will always be her home."

Allison nodded. "She's certainly different from anyone I have ever met," she said, looking out at the dining table where Carly Rae was sitting, talking with her father.

"Anyhow, you don't need to waste your last night here inside busing tables and doing dishes. Go tell my daughter to take you out to see the sunset."

"We watched it rise this morning. It was the most beautiful sight I'd ever seen. Almost like the heavens opened up right in front of us."

"There is so much beauty to be seen in the world, if people would just take a second to stop and look around," Irene sighed. "Anyway, go on. I've got this," she said, starting the dish water.

Allison walked over to the table. "Your mother said for you to take me to see the sunset."

"Did she now?" Carly Rae grinned.

"You'd better do what she says," Charles muttered, handing her the keys to ol' red as he got up. "There's a box of bourbon chocolates in the fridge," he whispered, walking past her.

"We should get going," Carly Rae said, getting up from the table. She walked into the kitchen before meeting Allison in the living area to put her boots back on.

"You don't have to if you don't want to. I know you're tired and probably want a hot shower as badly as I do."

"It's fine. She's right. We missed it the other night. It was almost completely gone before we'd even left the house."

They walked out to ol' red together and climbed in. Carly Rae pushed in the clutch and started the engine. Otis Redding's *Love Man* was blaring on the radio. "Damn, Daddy," Carly Rae mumbled, reaching for the volume.

Allison laughed. "You don't have to turn it off, but definitely bring the volume down a bit."

Carly Rae nodded and jammed the shifter into first gear. The old truck took off down the dirt road that led to the business buildings. They meandered along at about fifteen miles per hour as she passed by them and headed out over the rolling hills to her favorite spot.

"Did you have a good time?"

"Ask me in the morning," Allison laughed. "Seriously though, I did. It certainly hasn't been what I'd expected, but then again, I didn't really know what to expect. I definitely learned a lot. It's really beautiful here."

"I'm sorry about that guy Joe."

"There's no need to be sorry. Some people are assholes. It sounds like your father gave him what he deserved."

"I'm sure he did. It still should've never happened."

Allison reached over, grabbing her forearm. "It's the last night here. I don't want to ruin it talking about him."

Carly Rae smiled at her.

When they reached the flat top of Carly Rae's favorite hill, they came to a stop. She cut the engine and moved to get out.

"Can we leave the radio on?"

Carly Rae shrugged. "Sure. It's going to play this CD. Is that okay?"

"It's fine."

They both left their doors open and Carly Rae turned the volume up before getting out. She put the tailgate down and set the box on it.

"What's that?"

"Bourbon chocolates. Courtesy of Daddy." Carly Rae grinned, opening the lid.

"Oh, lord." Allison smiled and shook her head as she took the one Carly Rae was offering to her. The dark chocolate was good, but the liquor inside was strong and burned slightly as it slid down her throat. "Those pack a punch," she muttered.

Carly Rae laughed and tossed two in her mouth.

Satisfaction came on the radio and Allison held her hand out. "Dance with me," she said.

Carly Rae raised a brow. The look in Allison's eyes was playful. She stepped a little closer and began twirling around with her. They laughed as they danced awkwardly for the rest of that song, followed by the next one.

When *These Arms of Mine* came on, Carly Rae paused. Allison's eyes locked on hers. She moved closer, wrapping her arms around Allison's waist as her arms went up around Carly Rae's neck. They swayed together, pressed against one another like lovers as the sky changed from bright orange to red, then finally purple before fading to black. The radio had switched to *I've Been Loving You Too Long*, but neither woman noticed as they kept moving slowly. Carly Rae couldn't remember ever slow dancing with another woman and the last thing she'd wanted to do in that moment was stop, but the song finally came to an end, and subsequently, so had the CD.

Carly Rae kissed her cheek softly before pulling away. The heavy-lidded eyes looking back at her made her heart pound in her chest. Allison's slightly parted lips were so close…She quickly stopped herself and backed up, putting more space between them. The cool air tinged her warm body where Allison had just been against her. "If I kiss you right now, I won't be able to stop," she whispered.

"I know," Allison sighed as the desire that had been coursing through her veins mere seconds ago was replaced by a dull ache in the pit of her stomach.

"We should probably head back. We both need to shower, and I'm sure you're as exhausted as I am."

Allison pulled her into a hug. "Thank you for inviting me here. I'll never forget it."

"You're welcome."

TWENTY-THREE

The drive back to Salt Lake City seemed to take twice as long. Allison had pretty much left her phone alone for the weekend, other than taking pictures. So, she'd had a few emails to read regarding the upcoming competition, and she'd perused social media, but an hour into the drive all she could think about was watching Carly Rae say goodbye to her parents. It wasn't any longer than a regular goodbye, really, despite knowing they would see each other again in a few weeks at the stakes race. Yet, it seemed more heartfelt than anything she'd ever seen. Her own goodbyes with her parents when she would head back to the other side of the world for boarding school were sentimental, but they had failed in comparison. Her mother had loved her dearly, there was no question about that, but everything with her had always been short, sweet, and to the point. Her father was always just along for the ride and he was genuinely happy in that role. Carly Rae and her parents, on the other hand, hugged each other while wiping away tears. She hated leaving them, but loved the life she'd built for herself. They loved having her home, but were proud of the woman she'd become. It truly was a double-edged sword that glistened with tears as they all said their goodbyes.

"You've been pretty quiet. Are you working on a plan to secretly become a hay farmer or cattle rancher?" Carly Rae teased.

"No," Allison laughed. "I was actually thinking about watching you and your parents say goodbye to each other."

Carly Rae nodded. "Yeah, it gets a little more emotional every time. I think they're afraid I will finally settle down somewhere and rarely visit."

"What about you?"

"You know what it's like when your last goodbye literally becomes your last. They're not old by any means and both of them are in great health, but anything can happen at any time. I'm on the road quite a bit and serious, or even fatal accidents can happen with my job. I guess every time I say goodbye to them, I am reminded how much I love them."

Carly Rae looked over to see Allison wipe a tear from her cheek. "I'm sorry. I didn't mean to upset you. I just meant—"

"You didn't," Allison replied. "My goodbyes with my parents were always quite a bit different, but there was always love shared between us. Listening to you, made me think about my last goodbye with my mother. I haven't thought about it in some time. It was a happy memory. Tears stopped accompanying my memories of her several months ago, so this must have been happy tears."

"Well, I'm glad...I think," Carly Rae mumbled, unsure of what to say.

"I know. It's confusing," Allison chuckled softly. "Let's talk about something else. What time will we be home, or back in Sonoma, I should say?"

"We should get in around five, and technically, it *is* home, at least for right now, anyway."

"What will you do after this? Where will home be?"

"I usually rent a place in Reno. I'm able to stable my horse at a nearby rodeo barn. They have an arena for barrel racing and bull riding training, and it's sort of in the middle of everywhere that we go with the pro tour, so it makes the traveling a little easier on me and Firefly."

"That makes sense. Will you go back there?"

"Probably." She shrugged. "The tour will be just about over by the time my suspension is lifted, so I'll probably hit some of the smaller circuits and special events to make a little extra money. That's what I usually do when it ends. I guess it all depends on how I do with Sir Rigsby."

Allison nodded.

"What about you?"

"I have the regional competition coming up. Nationals will be after the holidays. If I make team USA again, I'll go to world nationals and hopefully, another Olympics."

"Wow. That's incredible. I couldn't imagine being an Olympian, let alone doing it twice."

"It was surreal. My parents were both there with me, but I was extremely focused and missed out on a lot of things. Dressage wasn't starting until the second week, so we missed the opening ceremony. If I get the chance to compete again, I will definitely go early so I can get the full experience."

"I think I'd do that, too. It's a once, maybe twice, in a lifetime opportunity for a lot of the athletes. I wouldn't want to miss a thing. Knowing me, I'd be going to all of the other events."

Allison chuckled.

"We finally made it," Carly Rae said, pulling off the exit that would take them to the airport from the highway.

Allison watched the clouds disappear through the small window as the plane rose above them. She and Carly Rae were on a smaller plane with only four seats per row, two on either side of the center aisle. They'd barely been in the air twenty minutes when she realized Carly Rae was asleep next to her. Perturbed at how easy it was for her fall asleep, Allison found she couldn't pull her eyes away, just as she couldn't back when she was taking care of her after the concussion. Carly Rae looked so peaceful when she slept, almost like she was smiling. *She has to be exhausted.*

"Would you like a drink or snack?" the flight attendant asked, slightly startling her.

"No, thank you," she whispered. They'd just eaten in the airport right before boarding.

Allison turned her attention back to the blue sky as her mind drifted over the last few days. At no point in her lifetime had she ever wanted to participate in a cattle drive or ride around a field all day in a tractor, but she'd truly had a wonderful time. The entire trip had been fast paced with long hours, but it had felt so peaceful. She thought about the last night when they'd slow danced while the sunset painted the sky in the most beautiful colors behind them. If she closed her eyes, she could still feel Carly Rae's warm body pressed against hers and taste the sweetness of her velvety tongue as her lips parted. *We've both agreed it would never work,* she mentally chastised herself, sighing heavily as she looked at the slumbering woman. Suddenly, the plane hit a turbulent spot in the air, causing it to bounce around.

Carly Rae startled awake. Her baby blue eyes studied Allison's face as she stretched. "Are you okay?"

"Yeah. How was your nap?" Allison asked. "You've been asleep for close to an hour."

"Wow. I'm sorry."

"It's fine. Although, I'm envious of your ability to sleep literally anywhere."

Carly Rae shrugged. "In the beginning of my career, I pretty much had to. Gidget and I barely had any space in the trailer, especially after I turned a portion of it into the makeshift living quarters. I'm pretty sure it all started when I was younger. I learned how to sleep in the tractor when I'd have to mow hay fields early in the morning before school, and on a hay bed in the barn when we had a cow or baby calf who'd needed around the clock care."

"The other night, that was the first time I'd slept anywhere but in a bed…indoors."

"Really?"

"Yes. My mother was about as far from camping and the outdoors as you could get, and it's not exactly my father's thing either. I'm pretty sure if he went camping, it would be in an RV with WiFi."

Carly Rae laughed.

"Ladies and gentlemen, we have begun our decent into Santa Rosa. We expect to be on the ground within the next ten minutes. Our gate is open and awaiting our arrival," the pilot said across the speakers.

*

"I'm sure you're ready to be home," Carly Rae said once they were in her truck and on the highway, heading towards the McKinley Estate.

"Yes…and no," Allison sighed. "I'd nearly forgotten about the competition and training schedule. I'm not sure I'm ready to go back, to be honest. It's been nice."

"Where do you want to go?" Carly Rae asked, looking over at her.

"We'll be going to the morgue if you don't watch the road."

Carly Rae flashed a toothy grin as she turned her eyes back to the windshield. "I'm serious. I'll take you anywhere you want to go."

"Why are you so nice to me? I'm sure I haven't been so forthcoming with you."

"I don't know, honestly." Carly Rae shrugged. "Why did you change your mind and go with me to Wyoming?"

"Truthfully, it was my father. He pushed me. I think he thinks I'm getting burned out with dressage," she sighed. "Plus, you intrigue me. I guess I wanted to know more about you."

"Did you learn anything?"

"A lot, actually. I really did have a great time."

"I had a feeling you would." She smiled. "So…where do you want to go? You never answered me. We're getting close to the exit for Sonoma."

"Have you ever been to a winery?"

"No."

"Let's go," Allison said cheerily.

"Alright."

*

"Welcome to H.J. Black Vineyard and Winery. Unfortunately, we're only open for tours by appointment on Sundays," a bubbly woman with dark red hair said.

Allison looked at Carly Rae. "Sorry. You'd think I'd know that, living next door all of my life."

"It's okay. Maybe another time. The horses probably miss us anyway."

"Wait," the woman said. "Allison...McKinley?"

"Yes...." Allison answered, thinking the woman looked familiar.

"Hannah Black. We went to school together," she said with a smile. "At least, until you started going overseas. Wow. It's been at least ten years."

Allison smiled. "Yeah, probably closer to twelve or thirteen. I thought you got married and moved away."

"Divorce happened," she sighed. "Plus, my grandfather retired and finally handed this place over to my dad. I'm the head winemaker, now."

"Didn't you have a brother?"

"Yes, Harold. He's two years older than us. Anyway, he lives in Canada with his wife. She's from Vancouver and he prefers living up there near her family. He's not interested in the family business at all. I guess, all of this will be mine someday."

"That's pretty cool."

"Yeah. By the way, I was so sorry to hear about your mother. She was a nice lady. I remember your tenth birthday party. That was the first and last time I rode a horse."

"Thanks," Allison replied somberly, then smiled when she remembered the party she was referring to. Her mother had invited the entire class to come out for a horse-riding lesson.

"I'm sure you're still riding competitively."

"Yes." She nodded with a smile.

Carly Rae adjusted her feet nervously beside her.

Allison noticed her movement. "Pardon my manners. Hannah, this is Carly Rae Walsh."

"Hi," Carly Rae said.

"She's the trainer and jockey for my father's race horse," Allison blurted.

Carly Rae felt the sting of the verbal slap in the face. She shoved her hands into her front pockets and side stepped, putting plenty of space between herself and Allison.

"It's nice to meet you," Hannah said. "Listen, I was just about to call it a day. I'd love to give you two a private tour…on the house of course."

"Oh, you don't have to do that. We'll book one for another day. It's not like we're far away."

"Nonsense. I have plenty of time. Besides, the regular tours are done by our guide. Don't get me wrong, he knows this winery front and back, but he can't show you what I can."

Allison looked at Carly Rae, who simply shrugged.

"Sounds like we're going on the tour," Allison said cheerfully.

"Let me just lock this door, and we'll be on our way," Hannah replied, locking the tasting room so no one else wandered in wanting a tour. "We're going to end up back here. But first, some brief history on the vineyard and my family. Allison, you may already know this," she said, turning to Carly Rae. "My great-grandfather was Herbert Joseph Black. He planted the first acre of grapevines with his bare hands in 1927 when he was just twenty-two years old. Now, nearly 100 years later, we have grown to over 40 hectares, or 100 acres, and are one of the most productive vineyards in Sonoma County. We only use our grapes, and do not sell our overstock. If we have a particularly good haul, we try new things. We actually have an underground cellar where we store bottles that need to age before they go to market. Most of these are what's called private stock. This is particularly important for some of our cabernet sauvignons, but I'm getting ahead of myself. Come on, let's go see the grapes."

Allison and Carly Rae followed her out of the tasting room to a golf cart that was parked out back. This was obviously her mode of transportation around the large vineyard. As soon as everyone was situated, Hannah mashed the accelerator and the gas-powered golf cart took off down the path that led to the rows and rows of grapevines as far as the eye could see.

"These are our whites. They make everything from chardonnay to sauvignon blanc, and pinot grigio." She pulled to a stop and hopped off the cart. Allison and Carly Rae followed. "Here," she said, plucking a couple from the vine.

"It's very sweet," Allison said. "I don't know why I expected it to taste different."

"They all start out sweet, but the longer they are on the vine, the more the taste changes. These won't be harvested until next year. At this age right now, they'd be a moscato, which is very sweet. That's one of the wines we actually do not produce."

Everyone got back on the cart and she took them out to taste a few more whites that had been on the vine different amounts of time so they could taste the difference. Then, she headed over to the reds.

"These are our pride and joy. Our reds have been compared directly to reds grown in Burgundy and Bordeaux. Perhaps our great-grandfather stole some seeds when he was there during the war," she laughed. "Anyhow, we make merlot, pinot noir, cabernet sauvignon, and some very unique red blends with these grapes. I'll take you around to try a few different ones like we did with the whites."

Again, both Allison and Carly Rae ate the grapes, but Carly Rae kept her comments to herself as she hung back from the conversation.

Once they were finished in the vineyard, they headed over to the fermenting room where thousands of grapes were literally turned into alcohol every day. Hannah went over the process briefly, leaving out the highly scientific points that bored most people. After that, she took them to see where the wine was bottled, and then down to the cellar where the high dollar reds were being aged.

"This is amazing, Hannah. I never realized it was such a massive operation. I mean, I used to sneak over the fence and eat the grapes when I was kid."

Hannah laughed. "You know, your mother actually owned pre-purchased bottles from our private stock. There might still be a few down here aging."

"Seriously?"

"I'll check the records, but I'm sure McKinley has come up. Every month we update everything in our system and take inventory. We have to let our customers know when their wines are ready to be picked up and consumed."

"Wow. I'm sure my father has no idea. Wine is most definitely not his thing. It's not Carly Rae's either," she said with a smile.

Carly Rae simply nodded.

"She's more of a bourbon drinker and my father enjoys a good scotch, most of the time with a cigar, but that's another story. Anyhow, I'd love to find out. How neat would that be?"

"I can check tomorrow and give you a call. I'm sure the number we have on file was for her."

Allison wrote her cell number on a piece of paper and Hannah put it in her pocket.

"Shall we head over to the tasting room?"

"Sure," Allison replied, smiling again at Carly Rae, but got nothing in return.

*

The tasting room was more intimate and could only hold about twenty-five or thirty people max, but was most comfortable with about fifteen. However, there was a 5-star restaurant on the property as well that had two massive ballrooms where numerous people were married every year.

"Have a seat. Everything that I will be pouring is from this year. We'll start with our pinot grigio. It has hints of lime, white pear, and a touch of spice," Hannah said, pouring two glasses.

Allison swooshed the liquid around in the glass, then took a sip. She let it sit on her tongue for a few seconds, swallowing a tiny bit, before spitting it into the discard barrel. Carly Rae didn't know she was supposed to spit it out and simply swallowed it.

"It's light. I almost got a little bit of a floral note," Allison said.

"Good palate," Hannah replied with a smile.

"My mother taught me well," she said somberly.

"Let's move onto the sauvignon blanc. This one has a little bit of citrus and apple, with a touch of vanilla."

Allison did the same as before, sipping, savoring, then spitting. Carly Rae felt weird spitting it out, but she did it anyway.

"I definitely get grapefruit. It ends with the vanilla. I definitely like this," Allison said.

"Thank you. I'm pretty fond of this one myself. If you let it age for a little bit, you'll get even more of the vanilla, as well as the apple," Hannah replied.

"Good to know."

"The last of our whites is the chardonnay. Our chard is pretty much the same every year. It's bold, with caramel and spicy oak flavors. However, this one was a Summer Chardonnay that we made for the first time this year. It has hints of lemon, peach, and honeysuckle."

Allison swooshed it around in her mouth, enjoying the acidity on her tongue before spitting it out. "It's light and elegant. Sort of refreshing."

"Exactly. It was a huge hit for the summer wedding season."

"I can see why. Carly Rae, what do you think? You've been so quiet," Allison said.

"They're fine. I can't pick out the differences between them, but they're all good," she answered, looking at Hannah.

"Shall we move onto the reds?"

"Sure," Allison said, glancing at Carly Rae. "Everything okay?" she whispered.

"Yep. Fine," Carly Rae answered.

"This first red is our pinot noir. It's rich, but light bodied. You'll get hints of dark cherry and black raspberry, as well as spicy oak notes."

"This is smooth, almost silky. I like it," Allison said after swirling it around in her mouth and spitting it out.

"This one is quite popular. It pairs well with a lot of different foods," Hannah replied.

"Next is our merlot. This one is a bit different. It also has cherry notes, but there's also spice and tobacco leaf as well. It finishes with a very subtle hint of chocolate."

Allison looked at Carly Rae who was watching the dark red wine get poured into the glasses. "Thank you," she said, taking the glass from Hannah. She took a sip and let her palate savor the flavors. At first, she hated it, but the finish she got after spitting it out was better than expected. "I've never been a fan of merlot, but that wasn't bad. I definitely got the chocolate, but only after I spit it out."

"Yes, it sort of comes in after the fact. My father loves this one. It took me a little while to get the pairing right. I believe this has been one of our better years with the merlot. Anyway, onto our last wine, the cabernet sauvignon. This one only gets better with age, so unlike the others, this one is from the cellar. It's five years old now, and will keep for another twenty. The flavor palate will continue to blossom as the years go by. You should get hints of boysenberry, black currant, cedar and toasted oak."

Carly Rae immediately spit hers out, but Allison savored the sip, trying to get all of the flavors before discarding it.

"I thought I got licorice," Allison said.

"You did. It's very faint. The long, full body pairs nicely with a juicy cut of fatty rib eye."

Allison nodded.

"That concludes our tasting. We usually offer cheese and fruit at these, but with the room already being closed for the day, there was nothing available."

"It's not a big deal. Thank you so much for giving us the private tour and doing the tasting. I'm really looking forward to seeing if my mother had anything reserved."

"You're very welcome. I'm so glad you came by. Carly Rae, it was nice meeting you. Hopefully, we've opened you up to wine...even if it's just a little bit."

"Thank you," Carly Rae replied.

"Do you have plans to eat at the restaurant? I can call over and have them hold a table for you."

Allison looked at Carly Rae like she was going to say yes, but Carly Rae spoke first.

"Thank you, but we should probably get back to the estate. I have work to do with the race horse."

"Sure. Maybe another time. Allison, I'll be in touch about the reserve list."

*

As soon as they got into the truck Allison turned half in the seat to face Carly Rae. "We didn't have to come here if you didn't want to. You looked miserable the entire time."

"Well, I'm just your father's employee, so..." Carly Rae shrugged. "I wasn't sure if I should do anything other than tag along."

"What? Is that what this is about?"

Carly Rae stared at her.

Allison's blood began to boil. "I was just your boss's daughter when we were in Wyoming!"

"Well... you are! My parents think you're a hell of a lot more than that! You knew it and seemed fine with it...until we got back here!"

"What was I supposed to say to her? I don't know what we are. Are we friends? Are we more than that? I don't know what this thing is between us! I'll probably never see her again anyway, so who cares! It's none of her business who you are to me!"

Carly Rae started the truck and drove towards the McKinley estate without another word being spoken between them.

TWENTY-FOUR

Carly Rae awoke to the sound of pouring rain pelting the windows of the tiny house. Rain in California was rare as it was, but especially in wine country. She'd been away from both horses for three days and had a ton of work to do. The stakes race she was competing in with Sir Rigsby was only three weeks away, and her suspension was scheduled to be lifted two weeks later. She needed to have Sir Rigsby ready to not only race, but win, or at least come damn close to it. Plus, she needed Firefly in top shape to go win some big money races since the pro barrel racing tour would be almost over by the time her suspension was lifted. She'd been leading the points up until her suspension, and there was no way she would be able to win at this point. She usually traveled around anyway to various big money events in the south after the pro season was over. The extra cash paid for her travel and horse care as well her expenses during the off season.

"Damn the rain. This will be a wasted day," she grumbled. A little bit of rain wasn't a big deal with training a race horse, or even a barrel horse, but at the rate it was coming down outside, the grounds were sure to be a soupy, muddy mess and that only led to injuries.

She'd tried to go back to sleep, but she'd barely slept as it was during the night. With nothing else to do, she finally got out of bed and scrambled a cup of egg whites for breakfast while the coffee maker brewed, filling the tiny house with the smell of hazelnut. She hadn't stepped on the scale, but was sure she'd gained at least a pound while being back home. With the derby so close, she needed to keep her weight low and consistent.

*

Ollie walked out of Luna Mist's stall surprised to see Carly Rae. He watched her shake off the rain jacket and hang her straw Stetson hat on a hook to dry. "I figured I wouldn't see you today. I know for sure I won't see Miss Allison. She never brings Luna Mist out if it's raining or wet out here."

"That doesn't surprise me," Carly Rae muttered. "I'm not taking the horses out. I figured I'd come check on them and give them some much needed attention. I have nothing else to do." She shrugged, walking over to pet Firefly who had whinnied and stomped as soon as she'd heard her voice. Sir Rigsby was still lying down, obviously sleeping. "Hey, girl," she whispered, petting her face.

"How was the cattle drive?" he asked, pouring food into Firefly's feed bucket.

"Good. We actually had a nice weekend." Allison hadn't been far from her thoughts. In fact, she was the reason Carly Rae had barely slept. The idea that everything could go so wrong so fast, blew her mind. She chided herself for getting so upset about being called the help, but at the same time, she felt she had every right. Ending their trip in silence, without even so much as a goodbye when they went their separate ways, made her chest ache.

"Yes, we did," Allison said from a few feet away. Neither of them had heard her enter the stable.

A shiver ran down Carly Rae's spine at the sound of her voice. She didn't dare turn her head.

"Ollie, take the rest of the day off," Allison continued. "I'm sure we can manage whatever else needs to be done." She glanced at Carly Rae, wishing she would turn around so she could see her eyes as she walked into the empty stall next to Firefly.

"Are you sure?" he stammered.

"Yes." She nodded.

"Alright. Thank you, Miss Allison," he said before quickly leaving.

"Are we going to talk?" she said as soon as the door closed behind him. The click of her riding boots echoed as she walked over to the stall.

"Some things are better left unsaid," Carly Rae muttered as she moved to side-step around her. Allison reached out, grabbing her wrist. Carly Rae's chest ached when she saw the desire burning in Allison's eyes. She was tired. Tired of fighting. Tired of fleeing. And too damn tired to stop herself. She put her other hand on the back of Allison's head and slammed their lips together.

Allison let go of Carly Rae's wrist and ran her hand up her arm as Carly Rae's hand moved to her waist, resting just above her jeans. Their bodies pressed together like magnets as their passionate kiss deepened.

Carly Rae was lost in the hunger coursing through her body. She no longer cared where she was or what she was doing. Nothing mattered in that moment as she backed Allison up against the wall of the stall and began pulling her shirt free. She ran her hand up under the blouse, over the smooth skin of her torso to cup one breast before sliding it back down to loosen the button and lower the zipper of her jeans. Her other hand was pressed in the center of Allison's back, steadying them both.

Allison's arms were around Carly Rae's neck with one hand tangled in the curled-up hair touching her collar. She sighed into Carly Rae's mouth and spread her legs as Carly Rae's fingers slipped inside her jeans and under her panties, finding the warm wet folds begging to be caressed. Carly Rae barely had any room to maneuver her hand inside the clothing, but it didn't matter. She'd found what she was looking for. She alternated between strokes and circles around the hard, wet center.

After several titillating passes of Carly Rae's fingers over her clit, Allison gasped for air and pulled free of their lustful kiss, burying her head against Carly Rae's neck. Everything inside of her was exploding, turning her brain to mush. She tugged at the short curls at the base of Carly Rae's neck and dug the fingers of her other hand into her upper back as her hips arched, opening herself even further in the confines of the tight pants. Carly Rae took notice, pressing harder with every pass of her fingers, urging them closer to the opening she desperately wished she could reach. It had been a while since she'd touched another woman so intimately, and feeling Allison's body writhing against her in reply had easily sent her over the edge, causing the wetness between her legs to soak her underwear.

Allison panted heavily against Carly Rae's neck, tickling the tiny hairs on her skin as her body neared the release it was desperately pleading for. The darkness behind her closed eyelids turned into specks of white as she finally let go, trembling between Carly Rae and the wall of the stall until her body went limp.

Carly Rae gently pulled her hand free from Allison's clothing and backed up, giving her some space. Before Allison could say or do anything, her cell phone began ringing. A picture of her father filled the screen when she checked it.

"Hi," she quickly answered, wondering where he was as she closed her jeans. The rain was still pouring down outside, so she was fairly certain he hadn't ventured out of the house.

"I can't find Ollie. Have you seen him?"

"I sent him home. There wasn't much to do with this weather. I can take care of Luna Mist and I'm sure Carly Rae will handle the other two horses. There was no need for him to be here for the full day."

"Uh…ok," he mumbled. In all of her years around horses, he'd never seen her do the dirty work of mucking stalls. She would brush her horse and bathe her if Ollie was busy, but she usually relied on him to take care of things…at least until Carly Rae had arrived. "I guess spending time up at that cattle ranch was good for you."

"What's that supposed to mean?" she grumbled, tucking her shirt back into her pants.

"Nothing," he muttered. "I'm looking for the feed order for the month. I need to balance the books. I can't find my copy."

"I'll check the feed office. Carly Rae might know where it is," she said, turning around and finding the stall empty behind her.

"I just saw her truck leave on the gate monitor."

"Damn it," she whispered.

"What was that?"

"I didn't say anything. Anyway, I'll look for it." She ended the call and sighed as she leaned against a stack of hay bales.

*

The McKinley estate disappeared in the rearview, drowned out by the down pouring rain before Carly Rae could put much distance between herself and the gates. There was no destination in mind. She just drove…until the thoughts of Allison were out of her head; until the feeling of touching Allison was gone from her senses; until…she nearly ran out of fuel and had to pull over. The rain had finally stopped, allowing her to see her surroundings a little clearer as she pulled into a gas station and rode around looking for the lone diesel pump. "It should never have happened," she sighed as she got out and began filling her truck up. She had no idea how much fuel she'd had to begin with and no clue where she even was. She hadn't been driving long, certainly less than an hour. For all she knew, she'd been going in circles. She wasn't sure what bothered her more, what had actually taken place, or where it had taken place. Neither were right. It wasn't the right time and definitely not the right place.

"You look lost," an older man said. He was on the other side of the pump, leaning against an old pick up as it filled with fuel. At first glance he reminded her of her father, although he'd looked nothing like him.

"I guess I am…a little bit," she replied. "Where are we?"

"Cordelia," he said. "Did you come up from Vallejo?"

"No, Sonoma," she said, shaking her head. "I don't have my phone. Do you happen to know how I get back? I thought I was on 12," she added, staring at the interstate across the road.

"This out here is 12. Just get back on going west. You'll run into Sonoma in about twenty miles."

"Thanks," she said as the pump clicked, indicating her tank was full. After the receipt printed, she got in the truck and stared at the bottom where *Cordelia, Ca.* was printed. Then, she started it up and headed west.

*

Hot water flowed over Allison's head, covering her face as it ran down the subtle curves of her body before dripping to the floor and swirling down the drain. The more she tried to wash away Carly Rae's touch, the more she felt it. Angry at Carly Rae for leaving and angry at herself for allowing anything to happen between them, she slammed her hand against the cold tile wall and turned the shower off.

As she toweled dry, she thought about looking out the window for Carly Rae's truck, but what was the point? She was the one who'd left her standing in the stable, raw, vulnerable, and questioning. "Damn you," she whispered, burying her face in her hands as she sat down on her bed. She was as much to blame as Carly Rae had been, but she hadn't walked away. That's what bothered her the most.

*

Carly Rae walked into the tiny house and tossed her keys on the counter. The drive had helped, but she wasn't able to clear her head. She wished more than anything that she could saddle up Firefly and ride until they were both exhausted, but the heavy rain hadn't let up. She knew the stable chores hadn't been finished when Ollie left and something told her Allison hadn't completed them either. The last place she wanted to be was inside that stable, but she sighed and headed over there anyhow…all the while, hoping she didn't run into Allison.

The first thing she noticed when she entered the feed room was Allison's loopy handwriting on the feed log. She felt like a rock landed in the empty pit of her stomach. She hadn't meant to leave her to do everything herself, but at the same time, she wasn't the one who had purposely sent Ollie home.

With nothing left to do, she pet both Firefly and Sir Rigsby, then grabbed her hat from the hook she'd left it on and headed towards the tiny house. The heavy downpour had finally subsided, leaving the grounds of the estate covered with puddles. The sun was just starting to peek through the lingering gray sky when she stepped outside.

Allison was leaning against the railing of the short wooden fence that surrounded the front patio of the tiny house. Her arms were crossed over her chest and her legs were crossed at the ankle. Her attire had changed completely from that morning. "Why did you leave?" she said as Carly Rae walked up.

"Surely, you didn't expect me to stay. You got what you wanted."

"What's that supposed to mean?" Allison growled.

"You came into the stable this morning with one thing on your mind. I could see it burning in your eyes. Sending Ollie home like you did…acting like you wanted to talk. That wasn't what you wanted. You and I both know it."

"Wow!" Allison shook her head. "I'm glad you think so little of me," she spat before storming off angrily.

"Damn it," Carly Rae sighed as she flopped down in one of the wet Adirondack chairs and put her head in her hands. *Just bide your time. You'll be gone soon. Free and*

*clear of the heartache Allison McKinley is sure to leave you
with if you let her.*

*

Sometime later, Carly Rae wasn't sure if twenty
minutes or two hours had passed as she sat in the chair,
staring up at the sun's rays streaming through the grey
clouds when Harris called her name. She looked over to see
him riding towards her in a golf cart, splashing through the
water on the ground. "Hop in," he said, pulling up next to
the low fence.

She sighed and did as instructed. The last thing she
wanted to do was have a conversation with him. For all she
knew, Allison had told him everything. "Beautiful day, isn't
it?" she joked, sliding her butt onto the seat and grabbing
the handrail as he mashed the pedal to the floor, sending the
cart careening across the property.

"I'm sure the vineyards are losing their minds at the
moment. We get rain, but nothing like this…at least not in a
year, maybe more. Anyway, that's not my problem. My
worry is my daughter."

Carly Rae's throat squeezed closed. Why was he
driving them away from the stable…and the main house,
for that matter? *He's taking me to the other side of the
property to kill me.*

"This last year has been so hard on her. She's been
working harder than ever before for this upcoming
competition. I know her goal isn't just winning another
world championship. She wants Olympic Gold. I was afraid
she would stop at nothing and burn herself out…until you
came along. How you got my daughter to go to a cattle
ranch and rustle cows a week before one of the biggest

competitions of her life, I'll never know." He shook his head. "I know I suggested it, but I never thought she'd actually go, and enjoy it nonetheless. She looked happier than I have seen her in a long time in every picture she sent me. You got my kid to drive a tractor and plow a field for crying out loud." He shook his head. "And to top it all off, she walked out of the house this morning in a pair of jeans! I've never seen her wear jeans. I never even knew she owned a pair! You have to understand…her mother was a very classy European lady and she raised her daughter to be the same. My wife never wore jeans in her entire life. She lived in jodhpurs and riding boots, and if she was doing something unrelated to horses, she was in a dress or dress slacks. She and Allison were like twins a generation apart. Since we lost her, I've watched my daughter flounder…almost like she's been trying to find herself because she'd lived her life in her mother's shoes all the way into her adult life. I think spending time with you has helped with that tremendously."

Carly Rae was unsure what to say. She sat in the seat beside him, gripping the handrail and staring straight ahead. She too had seen a change in Allison.

"Anyway, what I'm getting at is…I want you to go with us to the dressage competition. I can't make you go. This has nothing to do with your employment here. However, I was hoping you would go for Allison. Seeing you there might help quell the nerves. This is the first competition since her mother passed. I didn't know if you knew that or not. She hasn't competed at all in a year."

"I had no idea. No wonder she's training so hard."

He nodded and brought the cart to a screeching halt in the grass near the training track. "I'm her father. She's going to give me the same stoic manner she'd give her mother, but you're her friend. She's different with you, and when she needs someone to lean on, I want you to be there to support her. Can you do you that…for me?"

"Uh…." A thousand thoughts ran through Carly Rae's mind. Most of them being: *She's not going to want me there.* "Sure. Yeah." She cleared her throat as it began to open back up. "Yes, of course. I wouldn't miss it."

"Great. Now that that's settled…."

Carly Rae knew he wasn't about to kill her and bury her body if he wanted her to go to the competition. "Why did we ride all the way out here?" she asked.

"Allison sent Ollie home for whatever reason. Again, part of the changes I've seen in her. She's never mucked stalls and only feeds her own horse on the weekends. In fact, Ollie took care of bathing and a lot of the brushing for Luna Mist until you came along. Now, she seems to be doing everything on her own. Although, sending him home on a day that he'd barely be able to do anything anyway was a good business decision, I'm pretty sure she did it out of benevolence. She knows he is salaried so it's not saving me any money, and plus he doesn't get a lot of time with his family. With you both gone for three days, he was the sole caretaker of all of the horses, so he basically worked all weekend."

Carly Rae nodded. She knew that wasn't the answer, but she didn't dare correct him.

"Anyhow, because he's not here, I get to show what we did while you were gone. Come on," he said, getting off the golf cart.

Carly Rae followed him over to the track that had been freshly cut before the rain.

He bent down where the track edge meets the infield area and pointed to a small black stake in the ground. "Ollie installed an electronic timing system. There is a start/stop point right here, plus several points along the track. It works with a small transponder that you can attach to yourself or the racing saddle and all of the information is sent directly to an app. You can also move the points around to other areas." He stood and pulled his phone from his pocket, opening the app. "Obviously, you'll want to put this on your phone, but I downloaded it so I could show it to you. I figured more accurate timing might help with your training. Plus, if this horse does as well as we all hope he does, we'll need to make this a bigger, more permanent training track with all of the bells and whistles so we don't have to go to Santa Rosa. We'll be able to manage all of his training right here on the property."

"Wow," she mumbled, looking at all of the app features. "This is amazing."

"I figured you'd like it." He smiled. "You can program it to do all kinds of things. I believe you can also put in our track measurements and it will give you a digital print out of how the horse is running the track."

"I've never seen anything like this. I can't wait to try it out as soon as all of this rain dries up."

"It's not supposed to rain again for a while, so I'm sure it'll dry quickly," he replied as they walked back to the cart.

Carly Rae held on with one hand while downloading the app on her phone with the other as they raced back across the grounds. "When did you get this golf cart?" she asked.

"I've had it for a few years. The batteries were bad. I had them replaced while you were gone."

"Geesh, maybe I need to go away more often."

"No. I spend too much money when you're not here," he laughed.

*

Allison slammed her bedroom door as tears rolled down her face. Carly Rae's words stung like a slap across the face. How had everything gone so awry so quickly? She hadn't meant for things to go as far as they had with Carly Rae, from kissing her initially to traveling to Wyoming with her, both of which were way out of character for Allison. Then, the encounter in the stable... "What was I thinking?" she sighed. Carly Rae had been right about one thing, Allison had sent Ollie home so she could be alone with her. However, she'd never imagined they'd be intimate. She'd figured their encounter would be another heated argument, but had hoped it would be more like their conversations in Wyoming when neither of them had anything weighing heavily on their shoulders for those brief few days.

TWENTY-FIVE

Carly Rae spent the rest of the week working with Sir Rigsby on the training track. The new timing system had proven to be a huge help with monitoring his speed at different furlongs and different paces. No matter how much slower he was out of the gate, he was near his top speed before they'd made a full lap around the track and seemed to still have more gas in the tank. "You love to run, don't you, boy?" she said, petting him as they walked back to the stable together to cool down. She couldn't help looking over at the covered arena where Allison trotted around atop Luna Mist in her full dressage gear. They'd be leaving in less than twenty-four hours for her competition and the two of them still hadn't spoken. "Where the hell did it all go wrong?" she muttered to herself as she pulled her eyes away and continued walking. Sir Rigsby meandered beside her, following along as she guided him with the rein she held in her hand. When they reached the turnout pen, she fed him a carrot, then set him free to roam around and eat grass.

"Firefly is tacked up and ready to go," Ollie said, walking over to her as she closed the pen gate. "I can bring him back in if you need me to."

"I've got it. I appreciate everything you've done for me."

"It's no problem. Having you around has been great for this place...and for her," he said, looking over his shoulder at Allison.

"Yeah," she mumbled, patting him on the arm as she walked away.

*

Allison brought Luna Mist out of the piaffe, where she trotted in place, and spun her around in a beautiful pirouette, before directing her to perform a half pass, which sent her on a diagonal path, moving sideways and forward at the same time. She had the horse finish with a passage, where Luna Mist trotted with pristine elevation, seemingly pausing between strides, as they passed by what would be the judges table. She'd kept her head straight, focusing on each movement she instructed the horse to perform. However, her eyes were glued to Carly Rae as she walked by with Sir Rigsby and put him in the turnout pen. A month ago, she would've lost concentration, causing a misstep with the horse and an angry outburst. She'd not only learned to deal with Carly Rae's presence, but she'd come to embrace it. Now, seeing her just made Allison sad.

"Come on, Luna girl. We're as ready as we're going to get," she sighed, hopping down from the saddle. She'd only given the horse a light run-through of their performance, but had decided to take her over to the open turnout pen beside Sir Rigsby anyway. However, she stopped in place when she saw Firefly galloping around the barrels with Carly Rae deep in the saddle, directing her rein like a madwoman on a mission as they raced by. "I guess we can watch for a minute," she mumbled, holding tightly to Luna Mist's reins, keeping her close as Carly Rae lined her horse up to make another pass over the course. Both horse and rider were nearly on a forty-five-degree angle as they cut a sharp turn around the first barrel, then followed through with the exact opposite stance as they circled the second and third barrels before dashing to the finish line. "They defy gravity, don't they," she said, petting Luna Mist.

When Carly Rae trotted Firefly around to cool her down, she turned her head towards the closed arena. Allison quickly looked away, but not before their eyes met. She tugged Luna Mist's reins and headed towards the turnout pen.

Carly Rae pulled the rein to the side and gave Firefly a light squeeze, sending her trotting off in Allison's direction. "Can we talk?" she asked, getting down from the saddle while Allison put Luna Mist inside the open pen.

"What's there to talk about?" Allison muttered, watching her put Firefly in the pen with Sir Rigsby and grab his rein to pull him out. "I know you're going tomorrow. I don't think you should."

"I don't have a choice. Besides—"

"He's wrong, you know."

"What? Who?" Carly Rae questioned, stepping closer while keeping her hold on Sir Rigsby.

"My father. He thinks you have a lot to do with the changes I've made in my life. He's wrong."

"I was sort of…hoping he wasn't," Carly Rae replied, biting her lower lip.

"Yeah, well you shouldn't think so highly of yourself," Allison spat.

"You're right." She nodded. "But, I'll be there anyway, whether he's right or not."

"Why?"

"Because I want to see you succeed after watching all of the hard work you've put in preparing for this." Carly Rae shoved her free hand into her front pocket to keep from doing something stupid, like touching her. "I'm sorry, Allison."

"Why did you ask me to go with you to Wyoming?"

Carly Rae shrugged. "You looked like you were burning out. I figured it might do you some good to get away."

"Is that all?"

"Yes."

Allison nodded.

"I never intended for anything to happen between us, but I'm not sorry it did."

"You just said you *were* sorry." Allison crossed her arms.

"I'm sorry you don't want me there tomorrow. That I made you feel like that. I never meant to hurt you."

Allison wiped a tear from her cheek. "I'm sorry I made you feel like you were nothing to me, when you were clearly so much more than that. We've both been so crossed up, I don't think either of us expected any of this, or knew what to do with it all. But, I'm also not sorry it happened."

Carly Rae choked back a tear as she cleared her throat.

"I've been looking for you," Harris said, riding up on the golf cart. "I thought you were only doing a light session?"

"I was…did." Allison shook her head. "That cart's going to scare the horses."

Carly Rae allowed Sir Rigsby to sniff it. "He's the only one who will spook because he can't get used to the sound. I think he'll be fine though once he is used to seeing it," she said. "Anyway, I need to go put him away. I'm sure you have a ton of things to do to get prepared for tomorrow," she added, looking at Allison's eyes. A small tear threatened to spill over, tugging at her heartstrings before she pulled her gaze away.

"We're leaving at five in the morning," Harris said as she moved to walk away.

"About that…" she replied, turning towards him.

"It's fine," Allison interjected, nodding her head when Carly Rae looked at her with an odd expression.

"Everything okay?" he asked.

"Uh…yeah." She smiled thinly at him, then tugged Sir Rigsby's rein to get him moving.

"Are you ready?" Harris asked, looking back at his daughter.

"As ready as I'm going to be," she said.

"Hop in, you can ride back to the house with me. Ollie can take care of Luna Mist."

"I've got it."

"I know you do, but humor your old man," he said with a wink.

Allison smiled and got in on the passenger side. "I can't believe you fixed this thing," she muttered as they drove off. "I remember how mom hated it."

He laughed. "Yeah, she did. She used to say, 'an equestrian estate is no place for a golf cart.' That's probably why I let the batteries go bad."

"Why change things now?"

"Why not? Change can be a good thing."

She nodded.

"I know tomorrow is going to be hard on you. But, honestly, I'm so happy to see you competing again. That's what she would've wanted." He reached over, squeezing her hand.

"I know," she agreed with a smile before turning her head and glancing back over her shoulder, but Carly Rae had already gone in the stable.

*

Carly Rae's fingers played with the stitching of the leather seat as she stared mindlessly out the window. She'd barely said two words to Harris or Allison during the two-hour drive, and had mostly ignored their conversation about the competition. She didn't know the first thing about dressage and her thoughts were on Sir Rigsby and the upcoming horse race anyway. She felt ready, but still had some trepidations. The one thing she had going for her was she had a horse who generally loved to run and he was fast. She was more concerned about how he would react to the other horses around him. She hoped they'd done enough training to not have to put him in blinders. If they took the early lead, he'd definitely have no issues with their surroundings.

Her attention shifted drastically when the truck drove through Cordelia, the town she'd driven to just a week earlier. If she closed her eyes, she swore she could feel Allison against her. She sighed audibly as she rolled the window down.

"You don't get car sick, do you?" Harris asked, checking on her in the rearview mirror.

"No," she said, shaking her head as the window rolled back up. "I think I fell asleep and hit the button."

He laughed and kept driving, but Allison looked back at her suspiciously.

*

A half hour later, they pulled through the gates of the large, indoor equestrian center. One lot of the massive complex was full of motor homes and expensive coach buses with horse trailers attached to them. Seeing all of the horse trailers made Carly Rae miss the barrel racing circuit even more. She wondered what it must be like to travel in that kind of style. Some of her competitors had motor homes, but most just had pickup trucks. Many of their competitions had stables on sight, so the racers and bull riders could stay in hotels or motels, but a number of them didn't, leaving them to either sleep in their horse trailer, or if they were lucky, a motor home with a lot more space.

Harris and Allison had been there several times and knew where to go to get to the paddock where the horses were kept.

"We're in stall thirteen," Allison muttered, looking at the paperwork packet.

"Are you superstitious?" Carly Rae asked as they got out.

Allison shook her head. "My mother's birthday was the thirteenth."

Harris put his arm around her shoulders and kissed the side of her head. "I'm sure she's here and will be with you every step of the way."

Allison smiled, then stepped away to unload her horse and get her to the stall so she could stretch her legs and relax.

"I'm going to walk around for a bit, if you don't mind," Carly Rae said, wanting to give Allison some space, and also see what all the fuss was about.

"No, not at all. We'll be right here until she rides at 9:45AM. You'll need this to get back in the stable," Harris replied, handing her the pass with her name on it.

The first thing Carly Rae noticed as soon as she walked away was all of the uppity people milling about. It reminded her of being at the high stakes horse derby when she'd first met Harris, but it was also quite a bit different. Many of the women were wearing breeches, jodhpurs, or jeans and riding boots with blouses. She stood out a little in her Wrangler jeans and dark purple, long-sleeved, button down shirt that was tucked into them. She also wore her leather belt with a shiny oval buckle, and her boots.

She felt a little hungry but it was way too early to eat. Plus, she was strictly watching her weight. She still had another pound to lose from what she'd gained in Wyoming, so she simply walked around checking everything out. She knew if Allison was anything like her, she needed time to herself before the ride to get her thoughts together. The last thing she wanted to do was crowd her space. After perusing all of the other horses in the stalls, she made her way to the grandstands and picked out a seat. She wasn't sure if people had assigned seats with their tickets or not, but she was in the center, about halfway up and figured that was a good place to watch the performances.

As she stared at the dirt-filled arena floor, she thought back to her life five months earlier. Her dating life had been a complete disaster, but racing was going well. She was leading the points in the pro rodeo barrel racing circuit and had won some cash hustling in money races outside of the circuit. It was shaping up to be a great year, then she walked into the stable to get Firefly ready for the race. An hour later, she was sitting in a police station with her world turned upside. Even in that moment of defeat, she'd never imagined she'd be sitting in a dressage arena five months later, or better yet, a couple weeks away from jockeying a thoroughbred in a stakes race with a two-hundred-thousand-dollar purse.

"I was wondering where you'd gone off to," Harris said, sitting down next to her.

"I figured if she was anything like me, she needed some air. Besides, I wanted to see what all the fuss was about."

He nodded. "There's definitely a lot of pomp and circumstance at these events."

"Yeah," she laughed. "I'm sure the stakes race won't be any different."

"That's true. I've been pretty caught up in making sure she was ready for this. I haven't checked in with you. How are *you* doing with that inching closer?"

"I'm good, and so is Sir Rigsby. We'll be fine."

"I know I put a lot on you…"

"Harris, I asked you to. I think I needed this as much as you need a winning horse."

He nodded in agreement. "I know someone who needs you right now. Go talk to her. It'll ease some of the nerves eating away at her."

"I'm not so sure about that," she sighed, getting up from her seat.

"Here's a ten. Bring us a couple of hotdogs on your way back. Mustard and ketchup on mine."

"It's only 9:30!" Carly Rae laughed, shaking her head as she shoved the bill into her back pocket. "I'll bring *you* one. You don't have to jockey a race horse in two weeks!"

*

264

"This is what we've worked so hard for," Allison whispered, petting her horse. "We've done this a thousand times. Just concentrate on the movements," she told herself as much as the horse. "I know we won't be alone out there, Mom," she murmured, kissing the platinum fleur de lis charm that had been her mother's and now hung on the necklace she never took off. A few tears began to fall. She buried her head in the horse's neck until she regained her composure. "Alright. Time to get it together," she muttered, pulling the stall door closed and heading to the locker room to put on her riding attire.

She ignored her fellow riders as much as she could, but several had given their condolences and welcomed her back. Two new riders even came up and asked to take a picture with her. She was liked by most of her competitors, but definitely respected by all. Having won five World Cups, plus two Continental Championships and one World Championship on top of the Olympic Silver Medal, had made her name known throughout the dressage community.

Allison stood in front of her locker wearing pristine white jodhpur pants with a thin black shiny leather belt, as well as a matching white shirt with dark green sleeve cuffs, and black shiny Italian leather dress boots. Her hair was already pulled into a tight bun with a black hairnet bun cover that had a bow and sparkling rhinestones on it. She was surprised at how steady her hands were as she put the white, stock tie around her neck, fastening the hook and loop closure. It was tastefully embellished with a line of green, sparkling stones sewn on in place of a stock pin. Next, she slipped her traditional Shadbelly show coat on over her shoulders and closed the four buttons across the front. The trim on the collar and vest points was dark green, matching the stones on the stock tie. She grabbed the top hat style helmet sitting on the bench and placed it carefully onto her head, positioning it perfectly. She left the chin straps unbuckled and dangling.

"Here we go," Allison said to herself as she exited the locker room and headed towards her horse's stall in the stable. Her ride time was in ten minutes, giving her plenty of time to walk her horse up to the staging area to await their turn.

*

Carly Rae's breath was taken away when her eyes landed on the woman walking her way. Allison looked like she was part of the queen's court. Her international upbringing was clearly evident in the way she carried herself with her shoulders squared and her chin held high. She expected her to start talking in a British accent at any moment.

"Where's my father?" Allison asked.

"In the stands. He said I was the one who needed to come see you. I'm pretty sure he thinks we're best friends."

"I have no idea what gave him that idea," Allison replied, petting her horse with one hand while gather the reins in the other. Their eyes met for a long moment before she said, "I should get going. My time is close."

Carly Rae nodded and stepped aside. "Best of luck to you," she said as Allison led the horse out of the stall.

Allison turned around and murmured, "Thank you," as her lips curled into a soft smile.

Carly Rae watched until the rider and horse were out of sight. Then, she headed up to the stands to join Harris.

TWENTY-SIX

Harris sat on the edge of his seat when the large clock shifted to 9:43AM and the announcer spoke into the microphone.

"Please welcome our next rider, Allison Rousseau McKinley, and her horse, Luna Mist."

Carly Rae watched in awe as the horse and rider entered the arena, trotted to the center of the oval, and came to a stop. Allison bowed her head and held her hand out in salute. Then, they continued moving into position to begin the series of skills tests.

"The Grand Prix Skills Test is always in the morning, or on the first day if the event is spread over two days. This evening, they will perform their freestyle routine," Harris whispered.

Carly Rae nodded as she watched the horse perform a series of movements, starting and stopping after each one. She didn't realize she was holding her breath until she felt like she was going to pass out. She'd never experienced anything so intense in her life. The entire arena was silent as if all eyes were on the rider and horse in the center.

*

Allison went through her mental checklist, ticking off each skill as it was performed. She kept her shoulders squared and her chin up, careful not to move anything except the reins in her hands and use tiny, unseen

267

adjustments with her legs, which directed Luna Mist on where to go and what to do next. *Breathe,* she reminded herself as she fought to remain focused. Her heart thumped like a drum in her chest, sending blood coursing through her veins. Her stomach was a ball of nerves tied into a knot, threatening to cause her to wretch all over the place at any moment.

Finally, Luna Mist trotted back to the center and stopped. Allison bowed her head and held her hand out in salute once more. The crowd erupted in cheer and Allison patted Luna Mist on her shoulder.

"And it's 89% for Allison Rousseau McKinley and Luna Mist. The former world champion is back!" the announcer exclaimed.

Everyone continued cheering as Allison touch her chest where her mother's charm lie against her skin, then she waved and instructed Luna Mist to walk out of the arena. As soon as they were off the floor, Allison hopped down out of the saddle and immediately unclipped the strap under her chin and opened the buttons of her coat so she could take a full, deep breath. Their performance had taken nearly seven minutes and it had been the longest seven minutes of her life. Many riders and spectators who were milling about in the stable gave her thumbs up and smiles as she walked Luna Mist back to her stall.

"You did great, Luna girl!" she praised, petting the horse's face while giving her a handful of blueberries. "I feel like throwing up and you're over here sniffing for more goodies like it was nothing," she laughed, petting her again before checking her hay bag and sliding the stall door closed. She'd already removed her helmet and clipped it on the rail of the stall. She wasn't about to remove the bun and hair net that had taken forever to get put into place.

*

Carly Rae's breath caught in her throat and her feet simply stopped moving when she saw Allison removing her show jacket. A playful smile spread across her lips as Allison caught sight of her.

"Beautiful," Carly Rae muttered as she got her feet moving again. It was the only word that came to mind. That and *kiss her, you fool.* "Your performance was amazing. I'm completely in awe of what you do."

"Thank you," Allison smiled shyly. Her nerves were starting to finally unravel, but the adrenaline began coursing through her veins once more at the sight of Carly Rae walking towards her.

"Eighty-nine. That's how you make a comeback!" Harris said, wrapping his daughter up in a big hug. "I'm so proud of you, and you know she is, too," he whispered.

"Thanks," she murmured, wiping a tear from her cheek as they parted. "I need to go get my time for the freestyle and sign for my official scores before changing clothes. I'll be back in a bit. I left Luna Mist with a hay bag. She'll be fine until later."

"We'll be right here," Harris said.

Carly Rae watched her as she walked away. *How am I going to get through another two weeks?* She sighed inwardly.

"Everything okay?" Harris asked, looking up from his phone.

"Yeah. I'm good." She smiled thinly.

*

Everyone who performed dressage at the grand prix level had worked most of their lives for that achievement alone, not to mention the accolades that came with winning a competition. They were always cordial with each other, but some were stiffer than others and remained stoic, even in the locker room. Allison had always leaned more on the latter side, choosing to smile politely, and speak when spoken to, but she'd mostly kept to herself…until now. She found it surprisingly easy to talk to her competitors who congratulated her on her performance or gave their condolences for her late mother. She was genuinely surprised to see how many of them had welcomed her back.

Once she'd changed from her riding gear to a pair of tan jodhpurs and a black, short sleeved blouse, she hung her show jacket on the hanger next to her clean white shirt and jodhpur pants for the second performance, and placed her stock tie in the shelf to keep it from wrinkling. After that, she wiped down her boots, making them shiny. Then, she closed and locked the door.

*

It was after twelve by the time everyone was ready to go get some lunch. National Dressage Federation officials were posted all around the arena and stable, and several more walked around in plain clothes to make sure no one was cheating or sabotaging other competitors. Allison had been to several competitions with multiple day events where her horse had to be left overnight in event arena stables. She'd always felt safe and comfortable leaving her there, which was why she'd been so shocked to hear about what had happened with Carly Rae and Firefly at a single day event in broad daylight.

"Where are we going to eat?" Allison said. "I'm famished."

"You should've had a hot dog," Harris laughed.

Carly Rae shook her head.

"What?" Allison questioned. She'd been on her phone and had missed what he'd said.

"There's not a lot to choose from. I think they have food trucks outside though. Carly Rae needs to find a salad," Harris replied.

Allison glanced over her shoulder as they walked. "I thought you were done losing weight?"

"I was…until I went home to Wyoming." Carly Rae shook her head.

"She gained two pounds," Harris stated.

"Can we talk about something else, please?" Carly Rae muttered, looking around at the row of food trucks. At this point, she'd literally kill someone for a strawberry shake and a basket of sweet potato fries.

*

After what had turned out to be a not-so-quick lunch because of long lines at the three different trucks they'd chosen to eat from, and a massive search for a place to sit, they wound up back inside the stable.

"Do you know what they need?" Harris said, pondering out loud. "A bar."

"They have beer and wine. I saw it when I was walking around this morning," Carly Rae replied.

"That's not a bar." He shook his head.

"He means a place where he can get a glass of single malt scotch and smoke a cigar…which you're not supposed to do," Allison scolded.

Harris rolled his eyes and grinned at Carly Rae. "I quit."

"Uh huh," Allison grumbled.

"A glass of anything golden brown sounds good right about now," Carly Rae muttered.

"Don't tell me you stopped that, too?" Harris questioned.

"Have you ever had to lose ten pounds?"

"The two of you are driving me crazy. Go find something to do," Allison growled.

Harris raised his brows and nodded his head for Carly Rae to follow him, leaving Allison alone as she walked towards stall number thirteen. Luna Mist was resting quietly when she slid the door open and walked inside.

"Hey, girl," she said, petting the horse's neck as she neighed with delight at seeing her. "We have about an hour to go."

"Excuse me, do you mind pulling her out really quick so we can freshen up her stall?" two young men asked.

"Sure." Allison grabbed Luna Mist's rein and pulled her out. "If you wouldn't mind, close the door on your way out. I'm going to walk her around a little bit."

One guy scooped up the soiled hay from the floor while the other laid a fresh bed down. Allison and Luna Mist were out of sight when they closed the door and went on to the next occupied stall.

*

"Collette used to handle everything behind the scenes," he sighed. "Well, her and whatever trainer we were paying, including Arthur, whom Allison fired a month ago." He shook his head. "My job was to praise her when she had a great ride or dry her tears when she didn't do so well." After a long pause he said, "I guess they're all my jobs now."

Carly Rae nodded. "You know, she's a lot like you, whether you see it or not."

"You think so?" He shrugged and smiled. "Come on, we have less than an hour. We might as well go back to the stands," he said, walking away with her falling in step beside him.

The freestyle to music part of the competition had already started by the time they began looking for good seats that were high enough up and centered. However, many more spectators had taken to their seats for this, the horse dancing and most favorable part of the event, leaving them with little to choose from. After finally settling on a pair a little lower than Harris would've liked, they sat down.

The first thing Carly Rae noticed was each rider had a different style of music. Some performed to pop and other types of music heard on the radio, minus the words. Others performed to hit movie scores. The more traditional riders used prominent classical music as their backdrop. She found it interesting to see the different techniques of each horse and rider combo. Some were fierce and stoic in the way they presented themselves, dancing like they were performing a Paso Doble, while others were precise with the beautiful lines of a Foxtrot. Each pair seemed better than the last.

By the time Allison's name was announced, Carly Rae was completely enthralled. She was perched on the edge of her seat, the same as everyone around her. Luna

Mist moved into the center of the arena, in a similar position to what she'd done earlier in the day, allowing her rider to bow her head and present them to the judges. Then, the music began. Allison had worked with a composer to take Vivaldi's: *The Four Seasons*, a forty-two-minute violin concerti, and arrange it into a seven-minute melody with varying tempo that seemingly still maintained four separate parts. Allison looked regal atop Luna Mist as they performed as classically as their music, never faltering a single movement. Luna Mist's ears were up, not back and skittish. She looked like she was enjoying what she was doing as much as the crowd who cheered for the entire seven minutes.

When their performance ended, Allison and Luna Mist were scored 90%, giving them the win for grand prix freestyle. They left the arena to a roar of applause and a full standing ovation. Carly Rae was blown away by the incredible show they'd put on. She'd only seen bits and pieces of the freestyle because they were usually working on it while she was out at the training track with Sir Rigsby. She'd seen a lot of their grand prix tests because they often saved that for last, mastering those movements while she was in the open arena with Firefly.

"That was phenomenal! I've never seen anything like it," she said as they waited for the awards presentation to be set up in the center of the arena in front of the judges' stand.

"Yeah," Harris muttered, trying to hold back tears.

*

Allison hopped down from the saddle and kissed Luna Mist on the side of her face while petting her over and over. "That was amazing! We did it!" she exclaimed, reaching up to wipe away tears. Her fellow riders came over, shaking her hand and patting her on the shoulder as they congratulated her.

It still truly hadn't sunken in that she'd won the competition until she rode Luna Mist back out in front of the roaring crowd to receive their winners' medals. She was handed the microphone after being asked if she wanted to say a few words.

"This is all so surreal right now. Most of you know I lost my mother suddenly a little over a year ago. I wasn't sure when I would be ready to return to the sport I love so dearly, and the community I've given most of my life to. But, this horse is extraordinary and she deserved to come back. And to win on our return…words cannot describe how happy I am. I know she's proudly looking down at me right now." Everyone applauded loudly. "Thank you," she added, handing back the microphone. She bowed her head and waved to the crowd one more time before climbing back into the saddle and riding out of the arena.

"I'm so damn proud of you!" Harris said, practically pulling her out of the saddle and into a hug as Carly Rae grabbed Luna Mist's reins and pet her neck.

"I think I'm still in shock," Allison laughed.

"Congratulations."

Allison turned to see Carly Rae standing beside her, holding onto her horse. "Thank you," she replied as her mouth curled into a soft smile. Her brown eyes glistened with happy tears mixed with sad ones in the bright overhead lights.

"I'll go cool her down. I know you have a lot going on."

"Are you sure?"

"Yes. I don't mind." Carly Rae smiled before taking the horse for a nice parade walk around the outdoor paddock to cool her legs down. Several people stopped her, asking if that was Luna Mist and could they pet her. She knew the horse deserved the same attention, so she obliged. Luna Mist whinnied with enjoyment several times. After enough time had passed, Carly Rae brought her back inside the stable and over to the stall where treats and fresh hay awaited her. She'd removed her saddle and blanket, but left her in the halter. She was almost finished brushing her by the time Allison and Harris appeared.

"I forgot what it was like to get hounded by the equine media," Allison laughed, removing her show jacket. Then, she pulled her hair free from the net and bun, allowing it to fall freely in loose waves around her shoulders.

Carly Rae bit her lower lip and turned back to the horse. "You should've seen the crowd gathered around Luna Mist. I think just about everyone here wanted to pet her," she said.

"Aww, Luna girl. Did you meet your fans?" Allison cooed, petting her face. "You didn't have to do all of this. I could've taken care of her. I thought you were just walking her back here."

"You were busy. It's fine."

"Thank you," Allison said, still petting her prized possession, but her eyes were locked onto Carly Rae's.

"Are we about ready to hit the road?" Harris asked.

"Uh…yeah." Allison cleared her throat and stepped away from the horse. "Give me a few minutes to change clothes."

"That's fine. We'll get her loaded up," he replied.

The ride back to Sonoma was uneventful. Carly Rae found herself falling asleep against the door for most of it, while Allison and her father talked about the competition. They'd basically taken it apart, breaking down each piece of each performance and had lost her early on.

It was almost ten o'clock at night by the time they got back to the estate. They'd stopped for a quick dinner with the promise to celebrate the win correctly over the next couple of days with a nice dinner and the wine they found out about that her mother had reserved at the vineyard. Harris pulled the trailer to a stop beside the stable.

"I'll put the trailer away tomorrow. There's no sense in messing with that tonight," he said. "Do you need any help out here?"

"No. I can manage. I just need to put all of the tack away and get Luna Mist into her stall. Then, I'll be inside."

"Alright. Carly Rae, thank you for coming with us."

"I wouldn't have missed it." Carly Rae smiled.

"You amaze me, kid," he said, smiling at Allison before walking away.

Carly Rae had already started removing the tack from the trailer when Allison walked over. "I can get this. I'm sure you're tired. It's been a long day."

"I've got it. You deal with her," she replied, nodding towards the horse.

Allison shrugged and went into the back of the trailer to get Luna Mist and go put her in her stall while Carly Rae put everything away. As soon as she finished giving the horse a fresh pail of food in case she was hungry for dinner, Allison walked into the tack room. She grabbed

Carly Rae's hand. "Thank you for helping me…with everything."

"You're welcome. I'm glad it worked out. You and Luna Mist deserve all of the credit, though. You were captivating out there today. I'm glad I was able to see it. What you can do with her…it's absolutely beautiful," she said softly as her hand slipped from Allison's. She took a step back and locked eyes with her before turning and walking out of the stable.

Allison watched her go, unsure of what to say. She was riding the high of winning the competition, laced with the sadness of missing her mother more than ever. The last thing she needed to do was make an impulsive decision, but all she wanted was to feel Carly Rae's hands on her again.

TWENTY-SEVEN

Carly Rae removed her boots at the door and stuffed her socks down inside them. Then, she grabbed the creamy bourbon from the fridge, filled a rocks glass halfway, and emptied it in one long swallow. A heavy sigh escaped her lips as she rinsed out the glass and headed to the bathroom to start the shower. She couldn't get Allison off her mind no matter how hard she'd tried, and feared it would be impossible until she left for good in a few weeks.

She was about to turn the water on when she heard a noise. On instinct, her back stiffened and she paused, waiting to hear it again. If someone was trying to break in, they were about to get a very bad welcome. After a couple of silent seconds, she leaned over once more to turn the shower knob. That's when she heard it again. It wasn't an intruder. Someone was knocking on the door. "What the hell?" she muttered to herself as she walked down the short hallway. The nearly full moon filled the room with a soft glow through the sheer curtains, but it was too dark outside to see who it was through the peephole, so she took a chance and pulled the door open.

Allison was standing in front of her, still dressed in the black V-neck blouse, tan jodhpurs, and black riding boots that she'd worn home from the competition, meaning she more than likely hadn't gone up to the main house and instead, came straight from the stable.

"Is everything okay?" Carly Rae asked, stepping back so she could enter.

"No." Allison shook her head, closing and locking the door.

Carly Rae's mouth watered.

"I can't go on like this," Allison whispered, moving closer. "I'm tired of skirting around the truth every time we see each other."

"Allison—"

"Look at me and tell me you don't have feelings for me."

Carly Rae bit her lower lip.

"Damn it," Allison growled. "Tell me you don't want me as badly as I want you."

"I can't," Carly Rae sighed. "I'd be lying to you."

"Then, why are we spending so much time pushing each other away?"

"What do you want us to do? Spend the night in each other's arms and pretend I'm not leaving after the race in a couple of weeks?"

"I don't want you to go. At least, not without knowing the truth. I was attracted to you the first time I saw you, but I fought it as hard as I could. Your mere presence literally drove me mad. It wasn't until we were in Wyoming that I realized I'd fallen for you."

Carly Rae's head tilted to the side in confusion at hearing those words. "Then, why did you act like I was nothing to you when we were at the winery?"

"Because I haven't felt like this in a long time. I'd forgotten what it was like. I was scared, but mostly stupid. I'm twenty-four years old and my own family has no idea that I'm a lesbian. I've hidden that side of me my entire life. Everyone I've dated, or loved…I kept at arm's length so my family would never know about them. But, I can't hide you. You're right here on the same piece of property, surrounding me day in and day out. I can't escape, and I'm tired of trying to."

Carly Rae stayed silent as a hundred thoughts raced through her head.

"Say something," Allison pleaded softly, her heart fluttering in her chest as she stared into the baby blue eyes looking back at her.

Carly Rae closed the distance between them and put her hands on either side of Allison's face. Her thumb slid gently over Allison's lips before she leaned in, kissing her softly. Allison's mouth opened to her, tasting the lingering bourbon on her lips. Carly Rae's mouth moved with hers, opening and closing together with her lower lip sliding over Allison's seductively slow. When Allison's mouth opened once more, Carly Rae's tongue snaked out, licking her open lips before their mouths closed together again.

Allison reached up, unbuttoning Carly Rae's shirt, careful not to interrupt their delicate, arousing kiss. She unbuckled her belt and opened her jeans, pulling her shirt tail free, before running her hands back up the smooth skin of Carly Rae's lithe torso. Her fingers caressed her bra covered breasts then traced their own path slowly down her stomach once more, landing under the open waistband of her jeans before sliding around to her back. She'd waited so long to get her hands on the body that alluded her dreams, she took her time, savoring the sensation of Carly Rae's bare skin under her fingers as their sensual kissing continued. She opened her mouth against Carly Rae's and their tongues touched, licking each other lazily before their lips closed together once more.

Allison's caresses sent shivers through Carly Rae's nerves, making her move her hands to the wall behind Allison's head to steady herself. She stared into the chocolate brown eyes gazing back at her with intoxicatingly heavy lids, and drew in a deep breath. Their slow, sensual kiss had finally come to an end. Without a word she reached down, grabbing Allison's hand and began walking down the short hallway, stopping at the foot of her bed. Allison let go of her hand and bent down, unzipping her riding boots before taking them off. Carly Rae moved closer, pulling her blouse free from her pants and tugging it up over her head. Allison ran her hands along Carly Rae's mostly bare torso from her belly button up and over her bra to the top of her chest, before pushing her shirt off of her shoulders. The soft material slid down her arms and fell to the floor.

Neither woman was in a hurry as they slowly removed the rest of their clothing piece by piece until there was nothing between them but air. The moonlight coming in through the sheer curtains filled the room in a faint blue hue and cast their figures as shadows on the wall. Carly Rae hesitated for a second as the hunger in Allison's eyes resonated through her body. She inched closer, bringing their breasts together at the same time her hands went to Allison's waist, easing her back towards the bed. Once she was on her back, Carly Rae crawled over her, bringing her mouth right back to Allison's. Just as before, their kissing was deliberately slow and passionate.

Allison casually ran her hands up and down Carly Rae's back as her legs parted naturally, allowing her to sink down between them. She bit back a moan when their hips met. Carly Rae pulled her lips away from Allison's and grazed them along her neck, casually making her way down her chest to her breast. She pulled one brown nipple into her mouth while her finger swirled around the other. Allison's lower body unknowingly thrust upward, searching for more contact. Moving her hand lower, Carly Rae skimmed her fingers over Allison's flat stomach, reveling in the softness of her skin before sliding lower. At the first touch of Carly Rae's fingers, Allison gasped. Carly Rae began inching her lips back up to claim the mouth she couldn't get enough of as her fingers slipped through the wet folds, circling Allison's clit in tranquil, smooth strokes that matched their amorous kissing.

Carly Rae moved to straddle one of Allison's thighs and give herself more room. Allison's hand slid down her back, over her ass and slipped between her legs. Her fingers easily matched Carly Rae's, circling her with the same delicate strokes. Carly Rae pulled Allison's lower lip into her mouth, biting it tenderly before licking it as she ended the kiss and grazed her lips along her neck once more. Allison's hitched breaths against her ear sent shivers down Carly Rae's spine. She slowly pushed two fingers inside of Allison, causing her to cry out with pleasure. Carly Rae ignored the hand that had stilled against her and focused on the gradual, teasing rhythm of her fingers sliding in and out of Allison.

Suddenly, Allison reached down and stilled her hand before pushing it away. As much as she'd wanted to reach the finish, she wanted to touch Carly Rae even more. She'd wanted to feel her body inside and out since the first day she saw her in the bikini and cutoff shorts at the pond.

"Are you okay?" Carly Rae whispered, concerned that maybe she'd hurt her, despite the slow, tenderness of their lovemaking.

Allison moved slightly, then rolled Carly Rae onto her back with her on top. "More than okay," she said with a smile.

Confused, Carly Rae opened her mouth to say something and Allison silenced her with a kiss much like all of the others, before sliding her hand back down between her legs. Carly Rae's hips rose up to meet her fingers when they picked up where they'd left off. She ran her hands over Allison's back as her long hair fanned out over Carly Rae's shoulder.

Allison broke the kiss and took her time running her mouth along Carly Rae's neck, tasting as much of her soft skin as she could while her fingers slipped inside of her. Carly Rae's hips thrust up and a soft moan escaped her mouth. Allison moved back to her lips, kissing her tenderly. The feeling of Carly Rae's velvety tongue against hers made her body ache to be touched again. She ignored the sensation and concentrated on the feeling of Carly Rae's hot, wet muscles quivering around her fingers.

Carly Rae's back arched as her body opened like a flower. She moaned into the mouth covering hers before pulling away and gasping for air as the orgasm ripped through her body like a wild animal tearing at its prey. A kaleidoscope of colors swirled behind her closed lids until what felt like her soul, floated back down to her body like a fluffy cloud. She opened her eyes to chocolate brown ones staring back at her. Allison hovered over her with her fingers mere inches from where they'd just been as her hand rested on her thigh. Carly Rae's lips parted and she bent her head, softly claiming them once more.

Allison went willingly when Carly Rae rolled her to her back without breaking their kiss and settled between her open legs. Her hand slid down Allison's thigh, causing her fully aroused body to throb with need. Every motion Carly Rae made was agonizingly slow. Her mouth opened and closed against Allison's with her tongue enticing her lips in a luring kiss while her fingers grazed her wet folds and teased her opening in the same manner. Carly Rae repeated the same motion with her fingers and mouth until she'd deepened the kiss and slid fully inside of her. Allison moaned against her mouth and bit her lower lip. Her chest burned and her thighs pulsated with electricity as the adrenaline rush of blood raced through her veins. Carly Rae's fingers slid in and out of her only a few times before she tightened, drawing them deeper inside. A murmured cry escaped her mouth as her body peaked. Her breath was ragged against Carly Rae's cheek and her arms were tightly wrapped around her while wave after wave of pleasure washed over like a baptismal fountain.

Carly Rae moved to her side moments after she'd calmed and Allison curled into her. No words were spoken as they each closed their eyes.

TWENTY-EIGHT

Thin rays of sunlight shone through the slit in the curtains and directly onto Carly Rae's face. Sensing the brightness, she rolled over and stretched out. Suddenly, her eyes opened widely. Memories of the night came flooding back to her when she saw the clothing strewn about the floor. However, the sting of waking up alone with cold sheets beside her quelled any excitement she was beginning to feel. She'd been the one to sleep with someone and leave before they woke more times than she cared to admit, but she'd rarely been on the receiving end. The ache in the center of her chest hurt like hell. "How could I let myself make such a huge mistake?" she sighed, flinging the comforter off. Thankfully, it was Sunday, so no one would be wondering where she was considering it was almost nine o'clock. When she swung her legs over the side and stood up a white piece of paper stuck to the bottom of her foot. She sat back down, noticing something written on it as she removed it.

I didn't want to leave you, but I had to get back before my father woke. Come up to the main house for breakfast when you get up.

-XO

Carly Rae studied the loopy handwriting, which was the exact opposite of her own and another reminder of their differences. Sharing a meal with Harris after she'd spent the night with his daughter wasn't exactly on her to-do list, but her growling stomach said otherwise. The thought of seeing Allison made her nervous, but she rushed to take a quick shower and go to breakfast anyhow.

*

If Harris had been surprised to see Carly Rae at his door, he didn't say so. Instead, he pushed the door open and nodded for her to come inside. "We're just sitting down for breakfast."

"Allison invited me. I apologize for being so late. I'm always up with the sun, but I must've slept in," she said, walking with him to the dining room.

"Allison did the same." He smiled. "We all had a pretty long day yesterday."

"Yes," she mumbled, avoiding Allison's questioning eyes, but she still felt them boring into her soul from across the table as she sat down. "This looks and smells delicious."

"I woke up starving and wound up making a feast," Allison laughed softly.

"Please, help yourself," Harris said. "There's enough here to feed the neighbors," he joked.

"I wouldn't go that far," Allison corrected with a smile.

Carly Rae put a small portion of scrambled eggs, a piece of bacon, and a small pancake on her plate.

"Are you still losing weight?" Allison asked.

"I'm still trying to work off what I gained in Wyoming, but I'm almost back to where I need to be." She glanced at Harris. "I'll be ready by race day."

"I hope you don't plan on making this a permanent thing. It's unhealthy," Allison muttered.

"Have you ever heard of Seabiscuit?" Harris questioned as he wiped food from his thick mustache.

"No. What is a sea biscuit?" Allison asked.

Carly Rae laughed.

"It was a famous horse. He was a little too small, had knobby knees and a limp. His rider, Red Pollard, was a little too big and blind in one eye. However, they went on to win several major races together and are both in the horse racing hall of fame."

Allison nodded.

"Carly Rae and Sir Rigsby remind me of Seabiscuit and Red Pollard. Neither is really ideal for horse racing, but together…well, I think they can be great," he said.

Carly Rae paused chewing her food for a second. She was familiar with the horse and his jockey through books and movies, but had never likened her and Sir Rigsby to the pair…until now.

"What does this have to do with her being unhealthy?"

"If I may…" Carly Rae said, butting into their conversation. "First, to be half as good as Seabiscuit and Red Pollard would be amazing. There's a reason people still talk about them over 80 years later. Second, I'm certainly not unhealthy or starving myself. I only had to lose ten pounds. I'm still in great shape and able to control the horse with no problem."

Allison thought back to the hours they'd spent in each other's arms. Carly Rae's body had certainly felt like she was still in great shape. She simply nodded her head and went back to eating her breakfast, which was about the same amount that Carly Rae had on her plate.

*

After breakfast, Carly Rae wound up in the stable. She had weekends off, but the morning had sent her on a whirlwind and she felt like she needed to go for a ride to clear her head. She slipped a bridle over Firefly's head and brought her out to tack her up. Sir Rigsby watched from the stall across from hers. "We'll make some laps around the track in a little bit," she said, petting his head.

"Are you working today?" Allison asked from the doorway.

Carly Rae shook her head. "Just going for a ride. Would you like to join us?"

"Sure." She smiled as she walked past her to get Luna Mist tacked up and ready to go.

Carly Rae waited outside with Firefly, who was eating blueberries from her hand. "We should probably talk about the inevitable. The race is two weeks from yesterday. I'm pretty sure we'll be leaving soon after. I know you've gotten comfortable here."

"Does she ever talk back?" Allison asked, walking up behind her with Luna Mist.

"No, but she's a damn good listener. It's hard to find one of those these days," Carly Rae replied as she grabbed the saddle horn and swung her leg up and over the horse's back.

Allison smiled and shook her head before doing the same.

Firefly was itching to run, but Carly Rae kept her at a half gallop until she was warmed up. Allison never ran Luna Mist. She was classically trained in the dressage arena, so running around free spirited wasn't really in her vocabulary. However, she *was* a horse, and when Firefly took off, Luna Mist found a gear neither she nor Allison knew she'd had. Allison held on tightly, praying she didn't fall off and Luna Mist didn't hurt herself on her joyride, but she had to admit it was thrilling sprinting across the property with the wind blowing through her hair.

After a few minutes, Allison brought Luna Mist back to a walk so she could cool down. They easily fell in step next to Carly Rae and Firefly, who had done the same. "That was crazy! No wonder you race around here all the time."

Carly Rae laughed. "It's addicting. Watch out, Luna, she might trade you in," she teased.

"Highly unlikely," Allison chuckled.

"We should probably rest them for a bit," Carly Rae said as she brought Firefly to a stop and climbed down.

Allison agreed and followed her to a nearby tree where they tied them up to graze on the grass. "I wasn't sure you'd show up for breakfast," she murmured when they walked away side by side.

"I almost didn't."

Allison nodded, but stayed silent.

"I slept well past the sunrise, which is completely out of the ordinary, but it was waking up alone that really caught me off guard. If I hadn't stepped on a handwritten note on my way to the shower, I would've gone on believing it had all been a dream."

"I didn't want to leave, but I had to be back in the house before my father woke up."

"Yeah, the walk of shame probably wouldn't have been a good look," Carly Rae muttered.

Allison grabbed her hand and stopped her. "I'm not ashamed of anything. I just didn't feel like explaining to my father how I'd spent the entire night in your arms." Her eyes squinted in the sunlight, but found Carly Rae's easily. "He may not understand, and I'm not ready for that. Call it cowardice, but he's all I have left."

"I don't like hiding this from him. It doesn't feel right," Carly Rae sighed. "It took everything I had to sit adjacent to him at that table and eat breakfast."

"I understand. But, this is the way I live my life…at least for now."

"I've been someone's little secret. It didn't end well, and I swore I'd never do it again."

"I'd never ask you to do that. You mean so much to me, Carly Rae. The last thing I'd ever want to do is hurt you. I'm merely saying last night was amazing and I didn't want to tarnish it by sashaying through the front door a disheveled mess, wearing the same clothes he'd last seen me in the day before, coming from the only other place I could've slept all night, only to have *the* conversation I've been dreading my whole life. I told you, I can't hide you. You literally live a hundred yards away. However, I *can* hide my personal life until *I'm* ready to have that conversation."

Carly Rae tugged her closer and placed her free hand on her waist. "I don't know how I'm going to leave here in a couple of weeks."

"I wish we hadn't spent so much time avoiding what was right in front of us."

"I know," Carly Rae whispered. "I could've had a lot more awkward breakfasts."

"Funny," Allison said while playfully pressing the center of her chest to push her away.

Instead, Carly Rae moved her hand from Allison's waist to her back and pulled her closer, softly touching their lips together in a delicate kiss that turned very passionate, very quickly.

Allison draped her arms loosely around Carly Rae's neck and leaned back, breaking the sultry kiss. "If we keep this up, we're going to return covered in grass," she laughed.

"Is that so?" Carly Rae grinned.

Allison smiled and shook her head, but she couldn't pull her gaze from those gorgeous baby blue eyes staring back at her. "You make me weak in the knees," she whispered.

The air between them was thick with desire. Carly Rae bit her lower lip to stop herself from kissing her again, knowing if she did, they would end up making love right there on the ground. She swallowed the lump in her throat and sighed as she stepped back, putting some distance between them.

"We should probably get back," Allison said softly, thankful Carly Rae pulled away before they'd completely lost control.

"Yeah…before everything around us goes up in flames." Carly Rae nodded.

Allison smiled. "What do you have planned for the day?"

"I need to ride Sir Rigsby. We don't have a lot of training time left. I'm pushing him hard, so he definitely needs his rest days in between," Carly Rae answered, gathering Allison's hand in hers as they walked towards the horses. The simple act of holding hands with someone felt so foreign to her. Most of the women she'd dated were interested in sex and not much else. The effortless affection she shared with Allison made her chest ache with a yearning that cut straight to her core.

"I may come out and watch, if I can. I usually keep a low profile after a competition to let my mind decompress."

"So, breakfast this morning, and this ride with me…."

"Yeah, completely out of character for me." Allison pursed her lips.

Carly Rae nodded. "Well, he thinks we've become best friends, so…." She shrugged.

"If he only knew," Allison chuckled as she climbed up into the saddle on the back of Luna Mist.

"He'd probably skin me alive," Carly Rae stated seriously, getting onto her horse.

"Nah, he's not as big and scary as he looks."

"Says his little girl," Carly Rae laughed, squeezing Firefly lightly with her legs to get her walking. "After everything that happened in the stable stall, and then he came and got me in the golf cart, I thought he was going to kill me."

Allison guffawed. "What? Why?"

"There was a shovel in the back of it and he drove like a bat out of hell across the property! He wouldn't say anything to me. He looked like a madman on a mission." She shook her head remembering that day all too clearly. "I've never been more scared in my life, and I've had a few run-ins."

"Let me guess…husbands?" Allison chided.

"Boyfriends, and yes…one husband."

Allison shook her head. "No wonder you thought I was straight and playing games."

"There aren't many lesbians in my circle."

"Mine either, to be honest. At least, not since college and my boarding school days. Anyway, what was my father so excited about that made you think you were being murdered?"

"He wanted me to go to the dressage competition with you guys because he thought our friendship was good for you, and he wanted to show me the new timing system he'd had installed while we were gone!"

Allison laughed hysterically. "Oh my God. He acts like a little kid sometimes, I swear."

"Or a crazed father about to kill the person who'd…"

"Fucked his daughter?"

"Uh…yeah, something like that," Carly Rae said, cringing at the vulgar way it sounded.

Allison smiled at her sheepishness. "You know, you had one thing right about me that day. I definitely wanted you, which was why I was so pissed that you just left me. I wanted my hands on *you*, Carly Rae. Don't get me wrong, it was great…right up until the moment you hauled ass."

"I should've stayed and talked to you, but honestly, I figured you just wanted the same thing everyone else did," she sighed.

"I would never use you."

"I was wrong. I'm sorry."

"No need to apologize. I'm pretty sure we're on the same page now."

"Are we?" Carly Rae teased.

"Do I need to come over tonight and remind you?"

"You know where I live." Carly Rae shrugged with a playful grin.

"Great, now I'm sneaking out like I'm sixteen," Allison chuckled.

"I'd sneak in, but…"

"His room is on the same side of the house as mine, so that's definitely not happening."

"I could always fall off my horse again. Then, you'd have to live with me for a couple of days." Carly Rae smiled brightly.

"No! Definitely not. You scared me to death."

"All joking aside, thank you for taking care of me. I know I didn't make it easy for you."

"No, especially not in the thin tank top and shorts you slept in. I thought I was going to die of hunger, and it had nothing to do with food."

"Uh…have you seen what you sleep in? Why do you think I kept trying to get rid of you?"

Allison laughed. "If we'd only been on the same damn page six weeks ago!"

"No kidding," Carly Rae replied as they passed the arenas.

"Hey! Looks like you two are having fun," Harris said, hearing them laughing together as he stepped out of the nearby stable.

"Nothing like a morning ride to get your blood flowing," Carly Rae said cheerily.

"Yeah. Thanks for the invite. This was nice," Allison said, looking at Carly Rae endearingly before turning to her father. "I should do it more often. Luna Mist doesn't get to stretch her legs much."

"Good idea. Anyway, I was looking for you, Carly Rae. You got a letter in the mail while we were gone. I just now found it when I checked the box," he said, handing her a white envelope.

Carly Rae's head cocked to the side like a curious dog. She'd never received mail the entire time she'd lived there. Only her parents and Tibby actually knew where she was. As for everyone else, she'd fallen off the grid. She didn't have social media accounts and her only email account received nothing but spam, so she rarely looked at it. "Oh…thanks," she replied, getting down from the saddle. She took the envelope, noticing her parents address before folding it in half and slipping it into her back pocket. She remembered her father telling her she'd received a letter from the WPBRA when they'd talked on the phone a few days earlier.

"Are you going to open it?" Allison asked as Harris began walking back towards the house. She'd already gotten off her horse and was leading her into the stable.

"It's from my parents," Carly Rae muttered, tying Firefly's rein around a hook so she could brush her down. "They sent me a letter that came there from the Women's Pro Barrel Racing Association. It's probably something to do with my suspension. It's supposed to end right after the stakes race."

Allison tied Luna Mist beside Firefly and grabbed the rubber brush to remove loose hairs. "Are you not opening it because I'm here?" she asked casually.

"What? No. Of course not." Carly Rae paused and set the brush down before pulling the envelope from her pocket. "I didn't think it was a big deal."

Allison watched her face contort as she read it. She desperately wanted to know what it said, but it wasn't her place. She continued brushing Luna Mist, all the while, keeping an eye on her.

"They lifted my suspension and reinstated me, effective immediately. It's dated a week ago," Carly Rae mumbled, stuffing the letter back into the envelope.

"Oh, wow!" Allison put her brush down and rushed around the horse to be closer to her. "That's great news!"

"Yeah." Carly Rae nodded. "I think I'm in shock," she laughed.

"Weren't you getting reinstated at the end of your suspension anyway?"

"Yes. I guess I just wasn't expecting it for another three and a half weeks." She shook her head and grabbed the brush. "We're going racing again!" she exclaimed as she pet Firefly with her free hand. "I have so much to do. I need to check the calendar and see where the next events are, and get us registered. Wow, this is crazy."

Allison loved seeing the excitement on her face, but wondered where that left them. She knew she was still committed to Sir Rigsby and the stakes race, which was a little less than two weeks away. She kept her thoughts to herself while she finished brushing Luna Mist.

Carly Rae hadn't noticed how quiet Allison had gotten, until after she'd checked the calendar for the nearest upcoming race on her phone, and registered herself and Firefly. "Is everything okay?" she asked, putting the device back in her pocket.

"Yeah." Allison smiled. "I'm happy for you."

Carly Rae moved closer. "This doesn't change things. I'm still here until the stakes race."

"I know." She smiled again. *It's just a reminder that you're leaving.*

"I registered Firefly and I for a rodeo event next weekend in Fresno. We have to race slack on Friday night and again Saturday morning. If we make it into the final, we race Saturday night, and then leave after that. Will you come with me?" She reached out, grabbing her hand as her eyes searched the chocolate brown ones looking back at her.

"Yes, I'd love to," Allison replied with a smile. She couldn't imagine having dressage taken away from her, and completely understood what this meant to Carly Rae. There was nowhere else she'd rather be.

"Great!" Carly Rae exclaimed. "I should probably get out to the training track with Sir Rigsby. Are you going to come watch?"

"Yeah, maybe in a little bit. I have a few things to do first," she replied, squeezing the hand that was holding hers.

*

Allison stood off to the side, watching the large thoroughbred stretch out as he rounded the turn and hit the straightaway. The rider on his back was folded nearly in half with her booted feet in the short stirrups and her butt an inch off the seat, all the while guiding the horse to make the perfect lap.

"They look good, don't they?" Harris said, pulling up next to her in the golf cart.

"Yeah," she replied, nodding her head.

"In all of my years, I've never met anyone like her. She's a gift to the equine world and we're probably part of only a handful of people who actually know it."

"I hated her when you first brought her here."

"I know." He smiled.

"I thought she was after you."

"Me?" he laughed. "Why would you think that?"

"Some beautiful, young, hotshot horse whisperer shows up saying she can train your hearing-impaired horse to win big…." She raised a brow and shot him a look. "I was skeptical as hell."

"Yeah, I was pretty sure I was going to find the two of you fighting like cats in the middle of the arena," he chuckled before changing to a more serious tone. "I'm glad you let her into your life. It's good to have friends, especially one like her."

We're so much more than friends, she wanted to say, but the words carried no sound. "Yeah," she sighed.

"I want you to know something, your mother was my world. I don't think there will ever be anyone good enough to fill her shoes, and I'm certainly not interested in finding out," he said, patting her hand.

She leaned over and put her head on his shoulder like she used to do as a little girl. "She would've flipped out over you owning a race horse and building a track out here."

"Yeah," he laughed softly. "Which is why you flipped out. You're so much like her," he paused. "But lately, I've seen a little me in you, too."

"I'm okay with that, as long as I don't start smoking cigars, which I smell on you, by the way."

"I haven't worn this jacket in a while. It must need to go to the dry cleaner," he said, focusing his attention on the horse making another lap around the track.

"Uh huh," Allison grumbled, lifting her head to watch Carly Rae race by.

TWENTY-NINE

Carly Rae had run Firefly hard around the barrels in the open arena Monday, then a light workout Tuesday and another hard run on Wednesday. Thursday was her rest day with no training at all. They were ready, or at least as ready as they were going to get. She was a good horse who followed direction well and ran like she was on a rail with her tail on fire. In all of the years that she'd been racing, Carly Rae had never been nervous…until now.

She secured Firefly in the trailer and fed her a carrot through the open window on the side. "We haven't done this in a hot minute, huh, girl?" The horse crunched away on the carrot without a care in the world.

"I'm starting to get a little jealous of this relationship," Allison teased as she walked up.

Carly Rae grinned and moved closer. Allison quickly looked around to see if Ollie was about. She knew her father was in his office because she'd just said goodbye to him, and the house was on the other side of the trailer.

"He's out on the tractor," Carly Rae said, sensing her unease.

Allison smiled and wrapped her arms around Carly Rae's neck. "You smell good," she murmured, kissing her softly.

"As opposed to?" Carly Rae leaned back with a raised brow and her baby blue eyes squinted in the morning sun.

"Hay and...horse." Allison shrugged. "Not that there's anything wrong with that. I'm sure that's my daily scent, too," she laughed. "I remember the first night you came to dinner at the house. I smelled the same combination of cedar and lavender with a hint of vanilla and thought it was the sexiest thing I'd ever inhaled."

"Then, you saw me," Carly Rae laughed.

"Yeah," Allison chuckled. "Completely blew my mind. I couldn't stand you. I thought you were some rodeo clown trying to get with my newly widowed father, and there I was, salivating over you, myself."

"I still don't get how you thought that. My eyes were only on you from the first time we met. I thought you were a beautiful...snooty bitch." She shrugged with a grin.

"I've been called worse." Allison smiled.

Carly Rae kissed her with just enough intensity to stoke the embers still burning in her belly from the night they'd made love. They hadn't been able to see each other the entire week, other than stolen kisses here and there. "We need to get on the road," Carly Rae said, breaking the kiss.

"Are you sure we don't have five more minutes?" Allison pouted.

Carly Rae grinned and shook her head.

"This is going to be a long weekend," Allison murmured.

*

The three-hour ride down to Fresno was uneventful. They'd stopped once to refuel the truck and check on Firefly, but otherwise made good timing. Several trucks and RVs with horse trailers were scattered about when they pulled into the grounds of the Golden State Equestrian Center.

"Does everyone sleep in their trailer or RV?" Allison asked.

"Yes. Some get hotel or motel rooms and stable their horses for the night. I used to have a smaller trailer with very cramped, homemade living quarters, so I stabled Firefly and Gidget when I could afford it, before I retired her. Anyway, when everything happened with Firefly earlier this year, I traded my trailer in for this newer one and swore I'd never stable any of my horses at an event ever again."

"I don't blame you."

"Good, because the living quarters in the trailer is our home for the next 24 hours," Carly Rae replied as she pulled into the space she'd paid for. She glanced at Allison when she turned the truck off. "You look nervous."

"No, just curious. I've never been camping, other than when we were in Wyoming."

"This will be much better. It's more like staying in a tiny RV. It has a couch, stove, sink, microwave, refrigerator, TV, bed, closet, a/c and heat, and an all-in-one bathroom. The overall space is just much smaller."

Allison nodded. "What exactly is an all-in-one bathroom?"

"The toilet, sink, and shower are all together in one closest-sized space," Carly Rae replied with a smile.

"Oh."

"I probably should've shown you the trailer before we left. You don't get claustrophobic, do you?"

"Uh…not that I know of. I'm sure it'll be fine. I'll be alone with you and a bed. That's all that matters."

"Spoken like a true lesbian," Carly Rae laughed. "Come on, I need to get the trailer plugged in so we have power, then go check in."

*

Allison accompanied Carly Rae to go check in and get her transponder. The race times for the Friday slack were electronically drawn ahead of time and posted twenty-four hours in advance, so she already knew she was in the middle of the group. Several women and a few of the men came up, welcoming Carly Rae back, while the others simply stared in their direction while they waited in line.

"Fancy meeting you here," a woman said as she walked up.

Carly Rae turned around and smiled as she hugged the woman. "Tammy, it's good to see you."

"You too, honey. It's been a hot minute," Tammy said with a thick southern accent. "Anyway, I just wanted to say hi really quick. I need to get back and get ready. I'm second out in the slack."

"Good luck. I'm sitting in the nineties," Carly Rae replied, just before she walked away.

"She seemed nice."

"Yes, most of them are."

"Some of them look like they are salivating over you and others are staring like they want to cut my head off."

Carly Rae laughed.

"It's not funny."

"I'm sorry." Carly Rae's eyes met hers. "No one has ever been with me before…well, except my parents if I'm at an event close to them. I'm sure they're wondering what, or who, I've been doing for the past five and a half months. Then, I show up with a beautiful woman who is clearly not a rodeo girl." She smiled. "They're going to stare at you. However, none of them have the balls to say anything to you, so don't worry about it."

"You think I'm beautiful?"

Carly Rae grinned and shook her head. "Is that all you got out of what I just said? And, yes. The first time I saw you, that's the first word that came to mind. Then, of course, you opened your mouth and bitch became the second word."

Allison guffawed.

"Next," the lady at the registration window called, breaking their conversation. Carly Rae stepped up and slid her pro sanction card under the glass. The woman punched a few keys into the computer, then handed her a paper to sign. "Good luck," she said in monotone before calling up the next person.

"We have about two hours to kill. Let's go get Firefly out so she can relax and have a snack, then I'll give you a tour of the trailer," Carly Rae said as they walked back to the huge lot of horse trailers. "After my slack race, we can have dinner, and I'll show you around, if you want."

*

"This is the smallest living space I've ever been in, and I lived in a dorm in England," Allison said. "But, it definitely looks cozier."

"It's twice the size of my last one," Carly Rae replied. "I actually haven't spent the night in here yet."

"Hmm…" Allison murmured, raising a brow as she stepped closer, draping her arms around her neck. "So, we'll be christening it together then. I like the sound of that."

"Oh, really?" Carly Rae wrapped her arms loosely around Allison's waist and she kissed her softly before leaning back slightly. "If your father didn't have the tiny house, this is where I'd be sleeping. It's pretty much my home for most of the year."

"Wow. I never thought of it like that."

"Yep. Welcome to my home."

Allison smiled at the pretty eyes looking back at her. "You could live in a shoebox and I'd still want to be right here with you."

"Thank you," Carly Rae whispered, kissing her again.

*

A few minutes before her run time, Carly Rae trotted Firefly around to warm her up in the staging area of the paddock. She was dressed in western wear like all of the other riders, which was generally her daily attire anyhow. She'd settled on the solid pink shirt she'd brought with her, saving the dark purple and turquoise ones for the next day. Riders had a choice between a traditional cowboy hat or a helmet, and she wore her straw-white Stetson as usual.

"Here we go, girl," she said to Firefly as she leaned forward to pet her. The man running the start gate counted down with his hand from five as the horse in front of her came running out of the arena. *Five…*she walked Firefly back about twenty feet and turned her around to face the open gate where the invisible electronic start/finish line was located. *Four…*she kept Firefly on a tight rein and walked her around again as her excitement began to build.

Three…as Firefly straightened back out, Carly rein slapped the rein and squeezed her legs in, kicking the horse just enough to let her know it was go time. *Two*…she held onto the rein tightly as Firefly took off at a fast trot, gaining more and more speed with every foot. *One*…Firefly crossed the start line, entering the arena at full speed.

The clock began counting up as Carly directed Firefly to her right, circling the first barrel perfectly before going directly across and around the second barrel. The horse quickly straightened out of the turn and headed to the far barrel, creating a clover leaf pattern as she circled that one and raced back across the finish line, all in a matter of seconds.

*

Allison stood on the side of the spectator area and away from the arena gate, watching in awe as Carly Rae put up one of the fastest times so far. She'd seen her race Firefly around the barrels in the open arena at home, but that failed in comparison to watching her in a competition. Carly Rae barely moved a muscle, other than slapping the rein up and down with her arms, encouraging her horse to go faster and faster. Firefly had taken the turns sharply, nearly defying gravity at a forty-five-degree angle, while avoiding touching a single barrel as dirt flew up behind her hooves. Her long blonde main flowed in the wind like a shampoo commercial for horses.

"They sure are something, aren't they?" a woman beside her said with a sigh before walking away as soon as the run had ended.

Allison hurried over to greet Carly Rae when she climbed down after a brief walk to cool Firefly. "That was amazing!"

"Thanks." Carly Rae smiled. "Hopefully, our time holds up. There's still another twenty-five or thirty riders left to go."

"I noticed a lot of people are riding multiple horses."

"Yeah. Some ride up to four different ones. It gives them a better chance. Only the top thirty from today go on to ride in the slack tomorrow morning. Then, the top twenty from that get split into four divisions based on their time, and move on to ride in the final tomorrow night in front of the crowd and TV cameras. It's sort of like playing roulette. You can put your one-hundred-dollar chip on one particular number, or you can cash it in for five-dollar chips and play several numbers at the same time. Each division is defined by a time split. It looks like this. If the fastest horse has a time of 20 seconds, 20:00 to 20:30 seconds would be the time for 1D, or division one. Then, 20:31 to 21:00 would be for 2D, or division 2, and so on. So, with four divisions, you have more chances of placing in the top three or winning multiple divisions and that's more money in your pocket," Carly Rae explained as they walked back out to the trailers. "The ropers, wranglers, and bull riders also have slacks that take them down to their top ten for the final, but they aren't split into divisions like we are with barrel racing."

"That makes sense. I know you said you used to race Gidget. Have you thought of getting another horse?"

"Firefly has been a 1D horse since I first started racing her. Gidget was a 2D winner most of the time, but sometimes she wound up being a 1D loser at the back of the pack. I learned quickly to count in my head and slow her down just a hair sometimes. She was a great horse, and I won a 2D circuit championship and a 2D national championship with her, along with several other big money races. Firefly is great, too. When she's on her game, she's on a rail and there's no slowing her no matter what. We've won a lot together in the 1D, including a circuit and national championship." She sighed, "I hated retiring Gidget, but she'd gone down to the middle of the pack in 3D. It was time. She loves the ranch and has a great life now, though. Firefly is still young. She's only three, so we have a lot of years left. As horses get older and slow down, their division changes, but they are still winners. Obviously, the money changes as well, but there are big prizes in all divisions. Anyway, when we were in Wyoming my dad asked me if I was going to start looking for another horse anytime soon. He wants to breed Gidget and Rowdy. I think he's nuts, but if it worked, that would be one hell of a horse." She shrugged.

"Poor Gidget," Allison said, scrunching her face.

"He would use artificial insemination," Carly Rae laughed as they continued walking around. She had Firefly's rein in her hand, allowing her to continue cooling down before going back in the trailer to eat and call it a day. "Anyway, the horse would need a year of breaking and training to even start racing. Add in the pregnancy and I'm looking at two years. I just retired her at the beginning of this season. Then, all hell broke loose in May. I hadn't thought much about another horse until he brought it up. I haven't been racing until now, so I haven't really been in the market. It would be nice to have another. Before the start of next season would be ideal, but if he bred them, I'd wait and train the foal."

Allison nodded. "Some dressage riders also have multiple horses. I've thought about it, but I have so much time and a lot of money devoted to Luna Mist. I feel like to have a second, I'd have to take away from what I have invested in her."

"That's understandable. You certainly know what you're doing. I could never do what you do."

"Likewise. I teach horses to prance around like ballet dancers and you teach them to move like their tails are on fire." Allison smiled.

"We're just about back to the trailer. I'm going to load her up and get her dinner ready. After that, we can go back and check out the numbers. The slack should be ending soon."

"Sounds good. What are we doing for dinner later?"

"We can cook in the trailer. I grocery shopped yesterday. Or, if you prefer the concession stand, we can do that too."

"Yuck. No thanks."

Carly Rae laughed. "I lived off concession stand food. My last trailer didn't have a stove or microwave. I had a small camping stove, but rarely ever used it."

"I thought the old trailer had living quarters. It sounds like it just had a bed."

"Pretty much. That and a very tight all-in-one bathroom. It did have heat and A/C though."

"It sounds like you've definitely upgraded."

"Yep. This things a Mercedes compared to the Pinto I used to have," Carly Rae laughed. "Now, go walk through some of those really large horse trailers or big RV's. Those are like a Rolls Royce compared to this," she added as she opened the back door to load Firefly inside.

THIRTY

Carly Rae stood at the booth, reading the names of the top thirty barrel racers who would move on to the Saturday morning slack. Her chest tightened as her eyes moved further and further down the list. She hadn't been lower than the top five in the first slack in years. She bit her lower lip hard, nearly drawing blood when she passed number ten. *I knew she had more in the tank, but she was fast. Damnit, come on!*

A deep sigh escaped her as her eyes finally landed on her name. They were number thirteen. It wasn't the best place to be by any means, but at least they'd made the cut.

"Not used to being that low in the slack, are you?" a familiar female voice uttered.

Carly Rae turned to see a woman wearing tight jeans and a paisley western shirt that showed off the nicely rounded curves of her slim figure. Her straight, dirty blonde hair fell to the top of her shoulders. Her green eyes ran up and down Carly Rae like a searchlight scanning the sea as her pink lips curled into a smile.

"Where's your husband?" Carly Rae muttered.

Ignoring her, the woman went on. "I talked to Shelly Reinhart recently. She said she's suing you, but her lawyer hasn't been able to find you to serve the papers."

"Here I am," Carly Rae sighed, spreading her hands out in front of her. Half a second later, she turned and started walking away. That's when her eyes caught sight of Allison standing to the side, watching the exchange.

"What was that about?" Allison asked as she stepped closer.

Carly Rae shook her head. "Nothing. Just a bunch of bullshit, as usual," she said.

Allison nodded as they headed towards the trailer. "She spoke to me earlier when you were riding."

"What did she say?" Carly Rae questioned, stopping in her tracks.

"I don't remember. Something about you and Firefly being good together."

Carly Rae turned around, briefly catching the woman looking directly at her, before continuing on with Allison at her side. As soon as they entered the trailer, she pulled the door closed, kicked off her boots, and tossed her hat onto the two-person couch. "That woman is Hannah Crosby. We uh…were together for a little bit, before I found out she was married to one of the bull riders. Let's just say it didn't end well."

Allison nodded. "Did you know she was married?"

"No, of course not," Carly Rae answered, meeting her eyes. "I found out about him after he found out about me."

"You don't have to tell me about it if you don't want to."

"There's not much to say, really. We were hooking up for about three months behind closed doors. She kept saying she was worried about everyone else finding out about us, so we kept it hidden. Then, one afternoon while the bull riders were going through slack, we were in my trailer together. He came up, beating on the door. I had no idea who Billy Nash was. I'd never been interested in bull riding. She begged me not to open it. That's when she told me he was her husband. Long story short, we had a huge argument loud enough for the entire facility to hear. I explained that I had no idea she was married. She'd never worn a ring and I'd never seen her with him. I was honestly clueless. At first, I thought she was a curious straight girl, that's about all you ever see around the rodeo. There are definitely no other lesbians. She convinced me she was a lesbian, but very closeted and wasn't sure how people would take to us being together. It made sense at the time. Looking back on it now, I was extremely stupid. Anyway, he didn't believe me, but I didn't care nonetheless. Two months later, Shelly Reinhart, a woman who happened to be a friend of Hannah's, tried to kill my horse." Carly Rae shrugged. "You know the story from there."

"Wow," Allison mumbled. She was standing across from her, leaning against the door to the bathroom with her arms crossed over her chest. The past few months were starting to make a lot more sense. *No wonder you kept thinking I was a straight woman playing games with you, and why you thought I'd just wanted you for sex, and why you aren't comfortable hiding us.* "I'm so sorry."

"It's okay."

"No, it's not. I've done the same thing to you. I feel awful." Allison shook her head.

"The circumstances have similarities, but I assure you, they're quite different."

"I promise you, I am definitely not married to a man, nor am I straight. In fact, I've only ever had sex with women," Allison stated.

"I know, me too." Carly Rae smiled softly. "Anyway, when you saw us talking, Hannah was informing me that Shelly is trying to sue me, but hasn't been able to locate me to have the papers served."

"Seriously?"

Carly Rae nodded. "We both went in front of the review board a week after everything happened. That was the first time I'd seen her since that day. She had a nasty black eye, a bruised cheek and a cut on her lip. I'd beaten her up pretty good."

"Good God," Allison whispered, taken aback. She knew there had been an altercation, but had no idea of the severity.

"I'm not a violent person. I've never been in another fight other than schoolyard pushing and shoving when I was maybe ten. I just…My horse is everything to me. I lost control when I realized she was trying to kill her," she sighed. "In hindsight, I should've let the police handle it."

"I don't fault you," Allison said, reaching out, grabbing her hand. "I'm a little shocked that it was that bad. I won't lie. But, I probably would've done the same thing in your position."

Carly Rae ran her thumb over the back of Allison's hand. "Thank you."

"We can call my father's attorney when we get back."

"I'm sure it's not a big deal," Carly Rae replied, letting go of her hand to start unbuttoning her shirt in preparation to take a shower.

"Carly Rae, she could try to take everything from you, including your horse. She sounds nuts. You need to be prepared. Even if she just wants her doctor bill paid, she doesn't deserve anything."

"It'll be a cold day in hell before that bitch ever steps foot near my horse again!" Carly Rae grumbled as she unbuckled her belt and opened her jeans.

"Good. We'll call the attorney on Monday." Allison smiled, stepping closer. "Have I mentioned how much I like you like this," she murmured, running her fingers down Carly Rae's torso from the bottom of her bra to the top of her panty line while her eyes followed along. Carly Rae's shirt was completely unbuttoned and spread wide and her jeans were loosely hanging onto her hips, with her open belt dangling to the sides.

"No." Carly Rae grinned.

"Don't get me wrong, I like it…a lot. But, why are you undressing?"

"I need a shower."

Allison nodded.

"Care to join me?"

"I like where this is going," Allison replied, leaning in for a searing kiss. "But, that shower is the size of a postage stamp!"

"I guess we'll have to get creative," Carly Rae whispered, pulling Allison's tucked blouse free from her pants.

*

Allison had no idea how warm the water cascading over them was and she didn't care. Her flesh was heated from the inside out as their naked, wet bodies melded together. Her hands slid around Carly Rae's shoulders, tugging the short blonde hair at the back of her neck. Carly Rae's mouth opened, claiming hers as if their kiss was the breath filling her lungs. Her hands cupped Allison's breasts while her thumbs circled her hard nipples. Allison's hips grinded against hers automatically.

Driven by the carnal lust coursing through her veins, Carly Rae pulled out of the seductive kiss and dragged her tongue down Allison's wet torso, taking her into her mouth as she lowered to her knees. Allison cried out like a wild animal in heat as her thighs spread wider, allowing Carly Rae to devour her. She kept one hand tangled in Carly Rae's hair while the other reached for the hands that were on her hips, holding her still against the wall of the shower. She peeled one hand free and ran it up her body, taking one of Carly Rae's fingers into her mouth.

The sensation of Allison's hot, wet mouth sucking on her finger while she sucked on her clit, fanned the flames of her salacious hunger. Warm wetness ran down her thighs, mixing with the spray from the shower.

Allison felt the impending orgasm circling in the distance, but she wanted more. She *needed* more. Suddenly, she tightened her grip in Carly Rae's hair and pulled her to her feet. Carly Rae ran her tongue up Allison's torso before ravishing her mouth with a sultry kiss while her finger slipped inside of her. Tasting herself on Carly Rae's tongue while Carly Rae's finger thrust harder, made her wild with lascivious passion. She reached down between them, lazily rubbing Carly Rae's swollen clit before sliding easily inside of her.

Carly Rae broke the kiss and leaned in, placing her forehead on the wall behind Allison as her mind raced in a thousand different directions. She concentrated on matching her thrust for thrust, holding off the storm of pleasure building inside.

Allison lost control first, roaring like a lioness as her body swallowed Carly Rae's fingers, squeezing and pulling them deeper. Carly Rae let go a fraction of a second later, panting like a savage beast against the sensitive skin of Allison's neck as wave after wave washed over her until there was nothing left.

Seconds turned into a full minute before they were relaxed enough to ease out of each other and peel themselves apart. Freezing water pelted them like icicles piercing their heated skin as they rushed to get out of the tiny enclosure.

"How long were we in there?" Allison asked as she wrapped her hair in a towel and grabbed another to dry off.

"I don't know." Carly Rae shrugged, drying herself. She studied Allison as she went about searching through her suitcase for something to wear, all the while looking quite disordered with the towel falling halfway off her head as she fought to pull her panties up her damp legs. *I'm in love with you.*

THIRTY-ONE

"You know, you never told me where you placed in the run yesterday," Allison said between bites of banana while she waited for her tea water to boil.

Carly Rae heard what she'd said, but wasn't quite listening. Her mind was trying to burn to memory the feeling of waking up with Allison in her arms. She glanced over at her while preparing her coffee. Questioning chocolate brown eyes stared back at her. "Oh…uh, thirteenth. Certainly not our best performance," she sighed, adding, "in fact, it's been years since I was higher than fifth in a slack." She sat down on the couch beside Allison with her cup of coffee. "We'll be fine. She hasn't done this in a while, so she wasn't ready to come out of the trailer and run. She'll look like a different horse today."

Allison nodded. "Are you going to eat something?"

"Yeah. I was waiting for my coffee," she replied, tearing open a low-calorie breakfast bar, which she dipped into her mug before taking a bite.

"That can't be healthy," Allison grimaced, scrunching her face.

"The box says they are." Carly Rae shrugged. "They taste like cardboard, but the coffee helps."

"Do you still have weight to lose?"

"No. I'm just maintaining now. The new saddle is almost four pounds lighter, so I have a little breathing room."

"Is there such a thing as too light?"

"Yes. In that case, they make you put weights in the saddle pockets."

Allison shook her head and got up to toss her banana peel in the garbage.

"There are no weight restrictions with barrel racing, so I never had a particular number I needed to uphold."

Allison was leaning against the counter a couple of feet away in the small space. Her hair fell in loose waves over one shoulder. She was already dressed for the day in a pair of dark blue skinny jeans with a white V-neck blouse tucked neatly into them. The thin tan belt that cinched her waist, matched the riding boots on her feet. She was beautiful in every form of the word, and Carly Rae found it nearly impossible not to stare at her. She wanted her again, and by the look in Allison's eyes, their thoughts weren't far off.

"I need to go check my ride time for this morning," Carly Rae said, pulling her boots on. She was already dressed in her jeans and a teal, short sleeved western shirt. As soon as she was finished, she stood and adjusted her oval belt buckle. "Feel like taking a walk?"

"Sure." Allison smiled.

Carly Rae slid her Stetson onto her head and opened the door.

*

Allison got a better look at all of the cowboys and cowgirls meandering about in the daytime. She couldn't tell the bull riders from the cattle ropers, but it didn't matter, everyone smiled politely and tipped their hats. A few men and several women watched Carly Rae's every move, making her think the blonde barrel racer was a little more popular than she'd let on.

"Come on," Carly Rae said. "I want to introduce you to someone."

Allison smiled and followed along as they walked over to one of the trailers. A solid white palomino was tethered to the side while a woman with shoulder length auburn hair brushed her. A black Stetson hat hung on a hook inside the open trailer door.

"I thought I heard them call your name," the woman said, walking around the horse to wrap Carly Rae in a hug. "Why didn't you tell me you were back? I mean, I've barely heard from you in the last three months since you decided to play with the rich folks and their race horses."

Carly Rae cleared her throat. That's when the woman noticed Allison, who's skinny jeans and riding boots stood out in the sea of Wranglers, Stetsons and shit kickers. She raised a brow and gave Carly Rae a questioning gaze.

"I'm sorry I haven't kept in touch much. I've been busier than I ever thought I'd be. I'm actually jockeying the thoroughbred I've been training in a stakes race next weekend. I wasn't supposed to be reinstated until the week after that, but apparently the board decided to let me back a month early. It took their letter a little bit to catch up to me."

"Wait. You're actually racing the horse?"

"Yep."

"Holy shit."

Carly Rae laughed and turned to Allison. "This is Lacey Sheppard, my friend since the day I joined the rodeo circuit. She's also my roommate in Reno in the off season. Lace, this is Allison McKinley, the horse owner's daughter and…my friend." She hated saying the word friend, but she knew Allison was more comfortable in the closet.

Lacey eyed Allison up and down. She'd known Carly Rae for years, and despite her being fairly private and quiet, she'd always known when someone was more than a friend and this time was no different.

"It's nice to meet you," Allison said.

"Likewise," Lacy replied with a smile.

"Allison is a world class dressage rider," Carly Rae added. "She has an Olympic medal."

"Seriously?" Lacey exclaimed. "That's awesome!"

"Thanks," Allison replied, smiling shyly.

"I need to get back to Firefly. I drew fifteenth for this morning," Carly Rae said. "Good luck, and kick Shelly's ass for me."

"Oh, my pleasure. You know I can't stand that bitch," Lacey grumbled. "You go kick their ass in 1D."

"Don't I always?" Carly Rae grinned before walking away with Allison at her side. "I'm sorry about that. She's a little brash sometimes," she said, as they made their way back to Carly Rae's trailer.

"It's fine. I didn't take offense to it. She seems nice."

"Tibby's my best friend, but she's probably a close second. She's actually the one who bailed me out of jail. We've spent more nights drunk around a campfire than I'll ever remember. We sort of watch out for each other. Most of us get along and have a great competitive camaraderie, but there are some who can be quite spiteful."

"I think that's in every aspect of equine sports. Believe it or not, I have a few nemeses myself."

"Really?"

"Absolutely. I don't think anyone would go as far as hurting someone else's horse, that's beyond extreme. However, some people get their feelings hurt when you beat them over and over. Most of them are from other countries, so to get beat by an American is an insult, especially on their home soil."

"Geesh." Carly Rae shook her head. As soon as they reached her trailer, she opened the side door and stepped into the living quarters. When Allison came in behind her and shut the door, Carly Rae took her hat off and pulled her into her arms. "I hate calling you my friend," she whispered, leaning back to look at her eyes.

"I know," Allison sighed.

"At some point, people are going to catch on. I'm pretty sure Lacey figured it out right away. She knows me well enough, but she's respectful and won't say anything aloud. However, she'll be blowing my phone up with text messages as soon as she gets a chance."

"I have a feeling our circles don't overlap." Allison smiled.

"Uh...that's definitely a no," Carly Rae chuckled.

"I trust you, so if you trust her, I'm fine with you being honest. She's your friend," Allison said, trailing off as she began to get lost in the clear blue eyes gazing back at her.

"If I kiss you right now, we'll be going home because I won't be able to stop and I'll miss my ride time," Carly Rae whispered.

Allison bit her lower lip between her teeth before smiling playfully.

"I need to let Firefly out and warm her up," Carly Rae said, putting some space between them.

"I need to call my father, anyway. I'll be up there before you ride," Allison said, stepping forward and kissing her softly. "For good luck," she whispered.

Carly Rae grinned and shook her head as she walked out of the trailer and headed around to the back door. Firefly was in a completely different mood than she'd been in the night before. Her years of traveling and hanging out in the trailer at rodeo events had come back to her. Carly Rae tethered her to the trailer while she tacked her up with their custom-made saddle. Then, she gave her a treat before climbing up.

They started with a walk through the grassy parking area to stretch her legs and get her blood flowing. As soon as they were away from everyone, Carly Rae let her trot around with a mild gait. "That's it, girl. Warm up and get ready to haul ass," she said, petting her before bringing her back to a walk.

*

Allison saw Carly Rae look her way just before she turned Firefly around and gave her a squeezing kick to send her flying into the arena at full speed. She held her breath as a cloud of dirt flew up when the horse raced around the barrel on the right. It felt like slow motion as she watched Carly Rae lead her across to the left barrel where they changed direction and circled it perfectly. Then, they straightened and raced towards the far barrel before laying nearly on their side as they rounded it. Carly Rae whipped the rein hard and kicked her legs in and out, enticing Firefly to gallop at her top speed back across the arena and through the timing light. Several people who were gathered nearby, watching and awaiting their turns, cheered loudly. Allison glanced around as she clapped and cheered with them. She didn't have to see Shelly staring at her from afar, she could feel the uneasiness. Her eyes paused on her briefly, standing along the rail on the other side of the arena. Allison raised a brow and grinned like a Cheshire cat before walking away.

Carly Rae was returning from the walk they'd taken to cool Firefly down when she arrived back at the trailer. "That was impressive!" Allison said, watching her climb down from the saddle.

"Thanks." Carly Rae smiled and tethered the horse so she could get some water and munch on her hay bag while the tack was removed. "We were definitely faster than last night. She bobbled a little with the first barrel, but I'm pretty sure running with Sir Rigsby has increased her top end speed because she lit up coming out the turn at the far barrel."

"The entire ride looked great from my vantage point. You did great, sweet girl!" she said, petting the horse. "So, what happens now?"

"We wait and see if we made it into the 1D final. Then, we sit back and watch the rodeo until our division final."

"I've never seen a rodeo before, so I'm kind of looking forward to it."

"It's actually a lot of fun. I definitely wouldn't strap myself to a bull and let him fling me to hell and back."

"Yeah, me neither. Hell, I'd be scared to death doing what you just did. It's amazing how you can cut those crazy angles around the barrels on a horse."

"It's pretty intense, that's for sure. It's an adrenaline high like no other, but riding Sir Rigsby around the track is right up there with it. He's such a gentle giant, but when he runs, it's like driving a Ferrari, but in slow motion. Almost like it's so fast, it feels slow. Does that make sense?"

Allison nodded. She knew nothing about racing a horse, or even riding one at full gallop, for that matter. Luna Mist was most definitely not a racer. She had a good speed when they ran around the property, but it didn't hold a candle to Firefly's take off or Sir Rigsby's top end.

"Do the other rodeo events do their slack now, too?" she asked, changing the subject.

"No. They have theirs two days before us. Otherwise, it would be a jumbled mess."

"That makes sense," Allison replied, watching her brush Firefly while she munched on hay as if no one was touching her. "Do you want me to help you?"

Carly Rae shrugged. "I'm used to doing it alone, but if you want to, then sure. There's another brush in the trailer."

Allison began brushing Firefly's long, blonde mane, and then her tail while Carly Rae finished the rest of her.

*

A couple of hours later, Allison stood off to the side while Carly Rae shuffled through the small crowd to read the morning slack results. Those who made the top 20 would be split into the four divisions for the final rodeo later that night. As she watched her from a distance through a pair of dark Versace sunglasses, all she could think of was Carly Rae's clear blue eyes boring into her while they'd made love. She'd never been so connected to another person. It was both terrifying and exhilarating. She'd known weeks ago when they were back in Wyoming, that she was falling for the captivating blonde. But, standing there watching Carly Rae glance back and smile in her direction like she was the only other person around, she knew she was very much in love with her.

"She's in love with you," a female voice muttered.

Allison turned to see Hannah Crosby standing nearby with her arms crossed and her hip cocked to the side. "Excuse me?" she questioned.

"She never looked at me the way she looks at you," Hannah said. "Don't let her go."

Before Allison could say anything, the woman had disappeared into the small crowd.

"Everything okay?" Carly Rae asked as she walked up.

"Yeah." Allison smiled. "How did you do?"

"We're in third, so not too bad." She shrugged.

"Wow. That's great!" Allison exclaimed.

"It looks like this rodeo clown knows what she's doing," Carly Rae teased.

"Oh, for crying out loud," Allison laughed playfully, rolling her eyes behind the dark glasses. "First impressions aren't everything," she added, shaking her head.

Carly Rae shrugged and grinned.

"Looks like I'm going to give you a run for your money tonight," Lacey said, walking up to them.

"Yeah, I saw your name. That's great," Carly Rae said. "When did you start riding Whiskey?"

"A couple of months ago. He's temperamental as hell, but he's fast." She shrugged. "So far, we'd only been in 2D."

"Good luck and welcome to 1D!"

"Thanks!" Lacey started to walk away, then called over her shoulder, "Hey, did you see Hannah got pushed to 3D? I'm sure she's pissed."

"I couldn't care less, to be honest," Carly Rae replied with a shrug as she and Allison headed in the opposite direction towards her trailer.

THIRTY-TWO

As soon as they entered the trailer, Carly Rae put her hat on the counter and pulled Allison into her arms. "Do you know how stunningly beautiful you are?" she whispered. "No matter what I'm doing, when my eyes land on you, it takes my breath away."

Allison ran her fingers through her short hair and smiled at the clear blue eyes looking back at her. "You have no idea, do you?"

Carly Rae raised a brow. "Idea about what?"

"How captivating you are?" Allison studied her for a second as their eyes remained locked. "You may not know everyone here, but they definitely know who you are. I've seen you turn the heads of most women and a lot of men since we arrived."

"That's probably because of the suspension. I'm sure word got around," she sighed as she pulled her eyes away.

"Give yourself more credit than that. You can charm the skin off a rattlesnake." Allison smiled and shook her head. "I thought you were sexy as hell when we first met. Your gorgeous eyes and adorable grin are intoxicating. When you got into the pond in cutoffs and a bikini top, it nearly brought me to my knees." She shook her head. "So, I'm sure these people are engrossed in you because of a lot more than the fight you were in."

Carly Rae thought about her words for a moment. She'd never paid much attention to those around her, mostly because she hadn't cared. Rodeo life was hard enough as it was, add in the fact that she was an out lesbian and it became ten times harder, so she'd chosen to focus on herself and her career early on. "I've honestly never noticed. I don't pay much attention to what's going on around me at these events. I'm here to do my job and move on. My livelihood depends on it." She shrugged. "If anyone was interested in me for friendship or otherwise, they came to me. I never sought anyone out."

"It seems like a lot of them certainly want your attention. I'm wondering how many have actually had it."

"If you're asking how many of these rodeo women I have slept with, the answer is going to surprise you."

"You don't have to tell me. That's none—"

"It is your business, if we're together," Carly Rae stated. "I'm clean, just so you know. There's been no one but you since Hannah, and before her, I guess you could call it a string of three or four one-night-stands over the course of maybe six or eight years. So, definitely not some long laundry list of partners."

"I honestly don't care how many women you've slept with. I went to an all-girls boarding school, so I've definitely had my fair share of hookups, or whatever you call teenagers who are experimenting. I had two short, closeted relationships in college, but there's been no one since I graduated…until now."

Carly Rae brushed a strand of Allison's long hair off her face. "I'd rather be making love with you than thinking about all of the other people either of us has slept with."

Allison closed the distance between them, pressing their lips together in a slow, sultry kiss that left them both wanting more as they parted. "How much time do we have?" she whispered.

"More than enough." Carly Rae grinned.

*

Two hours later, Carly Rae was freshly showered and dressed in her riding attire for the finals. She'd chosen a long-sleeved, dark purple western shirt, and added a layer of shine to her oval belt buckle before she and Allison headed up to the arena to watch the start of the rodeo and await her event.

The pomp and circumstance of dressage riding failed in comparison to the rodeo. Six cowboys rode around the arena waving American flags while the anthem played to start the event. Allison and Carly Rae were squished in the stands with people all around them, mostly dressed in western attire, chugging beers and eating popcorn or peanuts.

The first event was breakaway roping, in which a handful of men and women competed. They rode on horseback, one a time, chasing after a small calf while trying to throw a lariat rope around its neck. Once he or she succeeded, the clock stopped. Whoever had the fastest time at the end of the night won the event.

"Why don't you compete in this? I've seen you rope a grown cow like it was nothing," Allison said.

"I actually used to, but barrel racing was more important, so I gave it up," Carly Rae replied. "Here come the saddle bronc riders," she said, nodding towards the first of the wild horses being loaded into the chute with a rider on his back.

"Is this like bull riding, but on a horse?" Allison asked.

"Yes. The bucking horse tries to throw the rider while he holds on for the allotted time. Then, they are both scored points."

"It seems a little barbaric."

"PETA has tried to get it stopped on several occasions. The rodeo federation is always battling with them." Carly Rae shrugged.

"I'm sure there are rules and regulations that must be followed."

"Oh, absolutely. Each event has its own rule book."

Allison cringed each time a horse bucked its rider. She'd thankfully never been thrown from a horse and seeing Carly Rae get tossed by Firefly in the accident had scared the hell out of her.

"The 4D riders are next," Carly Rae said, seeing the event staff readying the barrels.

"Are the bull riders last?"

Carly Rae nodded. "They have slack just like all of the other events. The best riders will be at the end, as will the best ropers and broncos, plus the fast barrel racers. The final event is the one that is televised."

"So, you'll be on TV?"

"Yeah." Carly Rae smiled. "My parents used to record it every time they saw me on TV. Now, they're just happy to see me doing what I love."

"Do they know about tonight?"

She nodded. "It'll be delayed by an hour, but they'll get to see it."

"That's good." Allison smiled at her before turning her attention to the first of the 4D racers as she sprinted around the barrels on a brown mare. She noticed Carly Rae studying each rider as they raced one after another. Anything she said would fall to silent ears, so she sat back and watched instead. She'd never been interested in watching her competitors, but she knew of others who swore by studying their peers.

After the last barrel racer, the event staff quickly removed the barrels and the chute was loaded with the first bull. A rider carefully lowered himself down onto the animal's back and wrapped his gloved hand tightly with the rope before nodding that he was ready. The gate swung open and the massive white and brown animal began jumping and kicking all around. The cowboy on his back lasted all of four seconds before getting flung off haphazardly. Allison grabbed Carly Rae's forearm as the bull spun around, nearly pounding him with his hoofs before the event staff got him to his feet and out of the way of the animal. The crowd erupted in cheers.

"Oh, my God!"

Carly Rae looked at her and smiled as the bull was ushered out of the arena while another was put into the chute. "Those guys are either adrenaline junkies or have a death wish. I haven't figured it out yet."

"They're crazy! But, I can't stop watching!"

Carly Rae laughed. The excitement and amazement in her voice made Allison sound like a giddy child. Opening her eyes up to something new reminded Carly Rae of their time together in Wyoming.

"After it starts over and bull riders come back around, there will be a ten-minute intermission. I'll be leaving to go get Firefly ready. Are you going to stay here or come with me?"

"Are you sure it won't break your concentration if I'm down there with you?"

Carly Rae smiled. "You're into the bull riding, aren't you?" she teased.

"Funny." Allison smiled and shook her head. "I'm serious."

"No, I'll be fine. You have a much better seat here, though. Down there, you'll just be on the sideline like you were during the slack. Also, they stop and give out the awards after each event in the final group."

"I'll come with you," Allison said.

Carly Rae nodded and grabbed her hand as she stood, leading them through the crowd that was heading down to the concession stand and bathroom area during the short break.

*

Carly Rae walked Firefly around to loosen her up before walking over to the arena to prepare for their ride. The broncos were finishing up, then it would take a minute to get the barrels placed before their final event began. Just as before, there was an electronic drawing to set the riding order. Carly Rae was number three, so she'd be riding in the middle of the group of five. She tilted her head from one side to the other and shook out her shoulders, hoping to relieve some of the tension that was starting to build. She knew all eyes in the barrel racing community would be on her.

"Listen, girl. We have to go out there and show them who's boss," she said, petting Firefly's face before climbing into the saddle.

"Kick ass out there," Lacey said, patting her leg as she walked by with her horse. She'd been the first one out and had finished with a much better time than she'd had earlier that morning.

"It looks like you just did," Carly Rae called. She glanced at Allison, who was standing off to the side of the arena gate. Their eyes locked for a split second and they both smiled. Carly Rae's heart pounded in her chest. She took a deep breath and began walking Firefly around to get her revved up.

*

Allison held her breath as Firefly tore through the arena opening at breakneck speed. A cloud of dirt flew up behind her as she laid out in a forty-five-degree angle, narrowly circling the first barrel before rounding the second one in the same fashion. Then, she galloped around the final barrel in only two strides before racing out of the arena at top speed. It was over in the blink of an eye, but it felt like time had stood still.

Carly Rae brought Firefly to a stop and spun around to see the time posted on the big screen. "Yes!" she cheered, pumping her fist in the air before petting the horse. "Way to go, girl!" She climbed down and pet her some more before walking her around to cool her down.

"You have the best time so far!" Allison exclaimed, hugging her when she caught up to her. "That was an amazing run!"

"Thanks," Carly Rae replied with a big smile as she pulled some treats out of her pocket and fed them to Firefly.

They waited together while the last couple of riders raced around the barrels. One of the horses knocked down a barrel, which disqualified them, but she'd been sluggish out of the gate, so her time wasn't going to beat Firefly anyhow. However, the last rider to go had a fast horse. Carly Rae held her breath and clenched her jaw as she watched the numbers tick on the clock. As the horse raced across the finish line, the number climbed to a tenth of a second above Firefly's.

Carly Rae dropped to her knees. With everything she'd been through, coming back and winning the event was bigger than she'd ever imagined it could be, not to mention she'd started with one of the slowest times she'd ever posted with Firefly. She composed herself quickly and stood back up, shaking her head slightly in disbelief.

"I'm so proud to be standing right here by your side!" Allison said, pulling her into a quick hug. "You're amazing," she whispered before backing away.

"Way to go, girl!" Lacey cheered, patting her on the back. "I'd say you were back, but it almost feels like you never left."

Carly Rae blew out a heavy breath and smiled. "Oh, I definitely left…but, damn it feels good to be back." She grinned. "Come on, Firefly, let's go collect our bounty," she said, tugging her rein as they headed into the arena.

The announcer was down on the floor with the microphone while the event administrator handed out the gold belt buckles, and subsequent medals, before handing over the winnings in the form of checks made out to the top three riders in each division in order from 4D all the way up to 1D. When Carly Rae was handed the medal, she placed it around Firefly's neck.

Allison stood along the arena wall, watching in awe as they were given their awards. She smiled when Carly Rae was handed the microphone and all she said was, 'It's good to be back.'

As soon as the short ceremony was over, the barrel racers walked their horses back out of the arena and the event staff went to work preparing for the final bull riders.

Allison fell in step next to Carly Rae as she walked Firefly back to the trailer.

"Did you want to stay for the last of the bull riding?" she asked.

"No. I'm good. I saw what I came to see." Allison smiled.

"Is that so?"

"Absolutely," she replied, bumping shoulders with her. "I can't wait to kiss you."

"Is that all you want to do?" Carly Rae grinned.

"Don't we have to get on the road?"

"Have you ever heard of rest stops?"

"Oh...I like the way you think." Allison smiled, biting her lower lip between her teeth.

*

Carly Rae punched the number code for the gate and waited for it to swing open. It was a few minutes passed one a.m. when she backed her trailer up near the stable and cut off the truck's engine. Allison was sound asleep beside her with her seat leaned back slightly. She smiled and carefully closed the door when she got out. The moon was barely a sliver in the sky with a few stars spread around it.

"Come on, girl. I know you're as tired as I am," she said, petting Firefly as she got her out of the trailer and walked her into the stable stall full of fresh hay. Luna Mist hung her head over the door of her stall, neighing when she heard Carly Rae talking. She stepped over, taking a peak over the door of Sir Rigsby's stall. He was passed out on the hay bed covering his floor.

Allison was leaning against the truck, yawning like a sleepy child when Carly Rae closed the stable door and turned around.

"I thought we were stopping at a rest area."

"You were already asleep, so I kept driving."

Allison nodded.

"Stay with me tonight, or what's left of it," Carly Rae said, walking closer.

Allison looked up at the dark house. There certainly was no need in waking her father in the middle of the night. Her lips curled into a smile. "There's nowhere I'd rather be."

Carly Rae left her truck and trailer over by the stable and led the way to the tiny house using her phone's flashlight. She kicked her boots off and loosened her belt as soon as she walked in the door.

"I could literally fall back asleep standing up. I have no idea how you drove us home," Allison said as she unzipped her boots and pulled them off.

"I'm used to it. I spent countless hours driving through the night when I was on the tour. I also spent many nights in rest areas. We were only three hours away from here, so that wasn't bad at all," she said, pulling Allison into her arms. She leaned forward, claiming her lips in a tender kiss.

"Is this our last night together?" Allison whispered when they parted.

"Do you want it to be?"

"No, of course not. But, I don't know how we're going to make this work," she sighed.

Carly Rae reached up, running her hand over her cheek. "Do we have to figure it all out right now? I'd rather go sleep with you in my arms."

"I'd rather do that, too," Allison murmured, kissing her softly. Their lips lingered together, teasing and tasting one another until Carly Rae put space between them. She smiled in the dimly lit room and grabbed Allison's hand, tugging her down the hall towards the bedroom.

THIRTY-THREE

"How was the rodeo?" Harris asked, eyeing his daughter over the top of the newspaper he was perusing as she leaned against the wall, staring out the window of his second story office like a little girl lost in a dream.

"Hmm…" she mumbled.

"The rodeo. How was it?" he questioned, raising a brow.

"Uh huh," she mumbled.

Harris lay the paper down on his desk and folded his hands together in the center. "Are you ready to quit dressage and start bull riding?"

"Yeah," she muttered.

He raised a brow and reached for the pen lying beside his computer. Figuring he might accidentally hurt her, he aimed for the window and sent it flying. It bounced off the window with a loud thud.

Allison jumped a foot off the ground. "What the hell!" she grumbled.

"What's got your attention out there?" he asked.

"Nothing," she said, bending to pick up the pen. He didn't need to know Carly Rae was out on the track with Sir Rigsby because if he did, he'd see right through her. "I was just lost in thought, I guess," she lied. "What's going on?" she asked, setting the pen down on the desk as she took a seat across from him.

"I barely saw you yesterday."

"I was with Luna Mist. I took her out riding to stretch her legs a bit. Then, I ran a bunch of errands."

He nodded. "How was the rodeo?"

"Interesting to say the least."

"I assume it's quite a bit different from a dressage competition."

She laughed. "Day and night, but it was fun. Carly Rae won the barrel racing event."

"Wow. That's great. So, are you ready to go ride a bull?" he teased.

"Not likely." She smiled.

*

Carly Rae slowed Sir Rigsby to a trot and then a walk for a couple of laps to cool him before hopping down from the saddle. She adjusted her riding attire, unsure if she'd ever get used to wearing it. "It's only for one race," she told herself as she pet his head to let him know he'd done a good job. They'd come out of the gate slightly behind his usual time, but he'd kept his speed up and held his position on the inside line for the entire two laps that it took to make the size of the actual race track. "Come on, boy. I need to go check the computer and see what our times look like," she said, tugging the rein a little to get him walking beside her. "No grass this week, sorry," she muttered as they passed by the turnout pens. He was on a strict race week diet that would keep him in optimal form. They needed all the help they could get.

Once she had him stowed away in his stall with a fresh bag of alfalfa hay, she headed into the feed room that doubled as the stable office. A laptop computer with a hard, waterproof case was sitting on the desk. She opened it up and powered it on when she plopped down in the chair. It only took a few seconds for the home screen to load. She quickly logged in and waited. The computerized image of their training track came up right away, along with their overall time, start time, and a list of split times. She clicked on the file that contained all of their times since the installment of the system and went to work analyzing their training session before comparing it to the previous times. When she was finished, she shut it down and closed it back up. There was no need to let Harris know how the numbers looked because he had direct access to the program's app from his laptop. However, he wasn't able to see all of the data or the log from all of the other training runs. The app only allowed the most recently recorded times. The other files were stored on the laptop.

"How'd you do?" Ollie asked, walking into the stable as she came out of the feed room.

"Not bad."

"Do you think you'll have a shot at winning?"

Carly Rae bit the corner of her mouth and shrugged. "I think every horse has a shot, if all of the variables fall into place."

"That doesn't help my gambling odds," he laughed.

"Ah…the truth comes out." She smiled.

"Either way, it should be fun. My wife and I are excited. It's our first time going to a horse race."

"Are you bringing your son?"

"He wants to go see the race horses, but it might be a bit much for him."

"Bring him here on your lunch break tomorrow. He can meet a real race horse and a jockey. If it's okay with you, I'll take him for a couple of laps around the track. We won't be running tomorrow, just trotting and jogging to keep Sir Rigsby's legs stretched out."

"Oh, wow. You'd do that for him?"

"Sure." She smiled.

"He's going to be so excited. I better let it be a surprise, or he's not going to let us sleep tonight," he laughed.

"I'm going to go shower and get changed. Can you turnout Firefly for me?"

"Sure thing. I'll do it now and bring her back in when I finish unloading the feed order that just arrived."

"Sounds good," she said before walking out of the stable.

*

The hot spray felt good on the back of Carly Rae's neck as she leaned forward and hung her head under the water. Carnal images flickered behind her closed eyelids of Allison's naked, wet body begging for release when they were in the shower together. She ran her hand through her hair and shook the thoughts away as she stood up straight. There was no time to let her mind wander. She had no idea when she'd even see her again, and she needed to concentrate on the job she was there to do. They were only five days away from the stakes race.

When the water finally ran cold, she turned it off and dressed in an old pair of jeans and a threadbare t-shirt. Then, she padded into the living area and sat down on the couch with her feet crossed at the ankles on the coffee table in front of her. She'd contemplated pouring herself a glass of the creamy bourbon she loved, but it was the middle of the afternoon and the extra calories were definitely not needed. Instead, she grabbed her phone, scrolled through the contacts, and waited for the line to answer on the other end as she leaned her head back against the cushions.

"Well…look who finally found time for her best friend," a male voice chided.

"Since when do you have jokes?" she replied with a laugh.

"Since you became a thoroughbred trainer," he chuckled. "Wait…change that to jockey."

"Funny. Too bad you're not racing with me this weekend. I'd love to kick your ass like I used to do when we were kids riding ponies!"

"Yeah, yeah," he mumbled. "Seriously, though. How are you doing?"

"I'm as nervous as a pregnant heifer when the vet comes to the ranch," she sighed.

"It'll be alright. Just grit your teeth and let it happen. It's over as soon as it begins."

"Great advice," she laughed.

"Get out of the gate and get to the rail. Let the horse do the rest," he said. "How does he handle? Is he fast out of the gate or a late burst of speed?"

"Neither. He's probably going to be middle of the pack out of the gate, but his pace is fast and his top end is strong. He's a chaser."

"Don't let him hit it early then. Keep him on the rail in second or third and open him up coming out of the last turn just before it straightens out. They will pull a lead on him, but if he's fast on the top end, you have a shot at running right by them."

"Thanks."

"You're going to do great. I know it. Dad said both of your parents are going."

"Yeah. Can you imagine being on that flight?" she laughed.

"Are they staying overnight?"

"Yes. The horse owner called and offered them a room in his house. Your dad agreed to watch the ranch, so they're flying in Saturday and leaving on Sunday."

"Wow. That's surprising. My horse owner is a bit of an ass."

"It's definitely not like that here."

"How are things with his daughter? Isn't she an ass, though?"

"She was…in the beginning."

"What changed?"

"Don't know," she mumbled.

"You slept with her!"

She laughed. "It's a little more complicated than that. We're actually together, but she's so far in the closet, her clothes think she's straight."

"Oh, God. Not one of them."

"I thought she was another straight girl playing games at first, until I got to know her."

"Dad said you brought her to the ranch."

"Yeah," she chuckled. "That was sort of spur of the moment, and I honestly thought she wouldn't go."

"He also said she was very pretty and you were very smitten."

"Oh, please," she laughed. "She *is* beautiful though."

"Why is she in the closet?"

"It's a long story, but she's part of the prim and proper dressage world, if that tells you anything. She went to boarding school in the UK and is literally a world champion and Olympic medalist."

343

"Yes. We certainly cannot have the measly barrel racer turned thoroughbred trainer having relations with the prestigious dressage rider. Can you imagine the scandal? My word!" he said in a fake British accent.

Carly Rae guffawed. "You're a mess. Hey, did you hear my suspension was lifted?"

"No! That's great, but wasn't it supposed to be over at the end of this month anyway?"

"Yes, but they actually lifted it over a month ago. The letter went to mom and dad's before finding me here. Anyway, I raced last weekend down in Fresno and won the 1D."

"That's awesome!"

"It felt great to be back. Allison was with me, too."

"Is that *her* name?"

"Yes," she laughed.

"I like it. Tell me those rodeo whores didn't eat her for lunch."

"She's pretty feisty. They didn't stand a chance."

"Good for her. Now, I *really* have to meet this Allison who has you smitten."

Carly Rae laughed. "Maybe one day. I should probably go. Wish me luck," she said before hanging up.

*

Allison had just pulled Luna Mist out of her stall when Carly Rae walked into the barn. She turned, smiling when she saw the blonde walking towards her. "Good morning."

"It is now," Carly Rae said, stopping a few feet away to keep herself from touching her.

"I miss you," Allison whispered.

Carly Rae bit her lower lip and glanced around. When she didn't see Ollie, she pulled Allison into her arms and kissed her like a long-lost lover. After what felt like a minute in Heaven, they parted breathlessly. Carly Rae's clear blue eyes locked onto Allison's.

"Come riding with me," Allison whispered.

Carly Rae didn't think it was a wise idea, but she couldn't say no to her. "Okay," she murmured, turning to get Firefly ready to go. She'd already taken Sir Rigsby out for a long walk, which was his only exercise for the day.

Sensing her hesitation, Allison reached out, grabbing her arm. "Is everything alright? If you have things you need to do, it's fine. I have to take Luna Mist out for some exercise and thought it would be nice to spend time with you. I've barely seen you since we've been back from Fresno."

"I actually have nothing to do right now, so a ride sounds like a great idea." Carly Rae smiled. "Firefly needs some exercise, too."

"You would tell me if something were bothering you, right?"

"Yes." Carly Rae nodded. "I'd be lying if I said I wasn't a little nervous about the stakes race, but it's to be expected. I'll be fine. Come on. Let's get out of here before Ollie comes in and catches us doing a lot more than kissing."

Allison laughed and pushed her away.

*

Under the cover of a dark, moonless night, the slow whine of the steel guitar echoed in Carly Rae's ear bud from the blues song playing on the iPod in her pocket. She blew into the harmonica against her mouth, easily trading licks with the guitar. Her booted foot tapped against the stone of the fire pit as embers rose into the night sky from the wood burning in front of her.

This was her *me* time, a few stolen moments when she lost sight of her surroundings while her ears filled her head with music that made her thoughts drift away. The lyrics never mattered. She identified with them in one way or another, but it was the sound that calmed her restless soul.

A few sips into a glass of bourbon and deeply lost in another song, she realized she wasn't alone. She pulled the harmonica from her lips.

"Don't stop on my account," Allison said, sliding into the seat next to her.

Carly Rae raised a brow as Allison took a long sip from her glass. Her face only distorted slightly as the brown liquor coated her throat all the way to her stomach. She grinned and pulled the harp back to her mouth before easily going right into the song playing in her ear as if she'd never left. The moan and whine of the tiny instrument echoed in the stillness of the night.

Allison had no idea what song she was playing along to and she didn't care. She'd found this side of Carly Rae sexy as hell the first time she'd found her like this, lost in the blues with whiskey on her lips and the low flames of a fire swaying to the music she was playing. That night she'd honestly thought she'd lost her mind. It even scared her a little. She'd never met anyone like Carly Rae and had certainly never been attracted to anyone so much her opposite. But now, as she sat there listening to her play and feeling the heat warm her skin, she welcomed every amorous thought that came to mind.

Carly Rae bent some notes and lengthened others with each draw and blow as she passionately played along to the slow, sultry songs in the same give and take manner as two lovers behind closed doors. However, the song playing in her ear and the harp in her hand were long forgotten when Allison stood up and straddled her legs, sitting back down in her lap. The fire behind her had burned down to a flameless crumble of orange embers. Carly Rae set the harp down and slowly ran her hands up the back of Allison's shirt against her soft skin.

Allison leaned in, teasing Carly Rae's lips with a playful kiss as her hands slid along her collar bone up to the top of her shoulders.

"Do you want to take this inside?" Carly Rae mumbled between kisses.

Allison shrugged. "It's pitch black out here tonight. Who's going to see us?"

"Who are you? And, what have you done to Allison McKinley?" Carly Rae grinned.

"I know something you can do to her," Allison purred as she kissed her again.

Carly Rae swallowed hard as wetness seeped between her legs. "Yeah," she muttered, clearing her throat. "We should definitely take this inside."

THIRTY-FOUR

Carly Rae slowed Sir Rigsby after two laps of walking around the track to stretch his legs. Ollie was off the side of the track, squatting with a young boy beside him, pointing at her and the horse as he spoke to him. She pulled the rein up, bringing the horse to a stop right in front of them and climbed down from the saddle. "Hi there," she said with a smile. "I'm Carly Rae."

"Tell her your name, son," Ollie said to his boy.

"Oliver!" he exclaimed with a big smile.

"It's nice to meet you, Oliver." Carly Rae handed the horse's rein to Ollie and nodded to him as she knelt down in front of the child. "Do you like horses?"

"Uh huh," he replied shyly, still sporting a big smile.

"This is Sir Rigsby. Would you like to pet him?"

Oliver's eyes grew as large as his smile. She held her arms out and he stepped into them. She stood, bringing the child up to pet Sir Rigsby's shoulder and the side of his neck. "He's a very nice horse, and he runs fast!"

Oliver's huge smile never faded as he pet the horse over and over. "Brown horse," he said.

"Yes. He is brown." Carly Rae smiled.

Ollie beamed, watching his son interact with her. He was a very shy boy, but horses had truly brought him out of his shell.

"Oliver, do you want to go for a ride on Sir Rigsby with me?"

The boy nodded and giggled.

"Okay. Stay with your daddy for a minute," she said, handing him to Ollie so she could climb up in the saddle. Once she was situated, she reached out for the boy. Ollie helped her get him in place, basically sitting in her lap with his hands tightly around the horn of the saddle she'd chosen to use. "Here we go," she said, giving the rein a light slap to get Sir Rigsby walking. "Do you want to go fast?" she asked after they'd made a full lap.

"Yeah," he squealed.

"Hold on tight," she said, picking the horse's pace up to a trot.

Oliver giggled and squealed with joy.

When she heard him say, 'go horse, go', she adjusted the rein and sent the horse into a steady jog around the track. He was nowhere near the galloping speed he raced with, but it was plenty fast enough for the excited little boy in her lap. After a couple of laps, Carly Rae brought Sir Rigsby back to a gentle walk to let him cool down.

"Was that fun?" Ollie asked when they stopped in front of him.

"Yeah," Oliver replied, giddily.

"He can ride back to the stable with me, if it's okay with you," Carly Rae said.

"Sure. He's having a blast. I don't know how to thank you for this," Ollie said, holding back tears.

"No thanks needed. He's precious and this is absolutely my pleasure," she replied.

Ollie walked beside them all the way to the stable. Carly Rae handed Oliver down to him before getting out of the saddle. "We have to brush his hair," she said, tying his rein to the hook in his stall. As soon as she removed the saddle, Ollie took it over to the tack room. Oliver watched in awe as Carly Rae brushed his coat until it was nice and shiny. "I'll be right back," she said, leaving Ollie with his father. She returned a minute later with a container. "Do you like blueberries, Oliver?"

The boy squirmed against his father's leg and smiled from ear to ear.

"Sir Rigsby likes them, too. Can you help me feed him?"

He nodded excitedly.

"He knows how to hold his hand out to feed his pony at home," Ollie said.

She nodded and picked him up. Ollie opened the container, holding it close to her. She grabbed a few and held out her hand to the horse. He quickly ate the berries. Then, she put a few berries in Oliver's hand and kept her hand flat under his. He giggled when Sir Rigsby ate the berries from his palm. Together, they fed him about a dozen. Then, she helped Oliver pet his face before putting him back on the ground.

"Thank you for coming to visit me and Sir Rigsby today," she said, squatting down next to him.

Oliver quickly threw his arms around her neck and kissed her cheek.

"What do we say?" Ollie asked.

"Thank you."

"You're welcome, sweet boy!"

"Alright, let's get you home. I have work to do and momma will have your lunch ready soon," Ollie said, grabbing his hand. He turned to leave and saw Allison leaning against the wall near the tack room. "Miss Allison," he said with a nod.

"Is this Oliver?" she questioned, pushing off the wall.

"Yes, ma'am," Ollie replied.

"Oh, my! You're getting so big," she said with a smile.

"I ride a horse," he said to her.

"I saw you. Was it fun?"

"Uh huh! Him run fast."

She smiled and looked past him to where Carly Rae was standing outside of Sir Rigsby's stall.

"You know he's welcome anytime," Allison said, patting Ollie on the shoulder.

"Thank you, ma'am."

Oliver waved bye as Ollie picked him up and carried him out of the stable.

"It looks like I might have some competition," Allison said, walking over to Carly Rae.

"Yeah, he pretty much wrapped me around his little finger. It might be the end of us," Carly Rae teased with a grin.

"You're incredible," Allison said softly. "I saw you riding him around the track."

"He's a sweet child."

"Yeah. He was still in diapers and just learning to walk the last time I saw him," Allison said, walking with her to put the berry container back in the feed room fridge. "You know, he's somewhat of a miracle. They'd tried for years to get pregnant and nothing happened. They finally went to the doctor for help, but nothing he did worked either. Then, out of the blue, she became pregnant."

"Wow. I had no idea."

"You're very good with kids. Didn't you say you took Firefly to do stuff with kids?"

"Yeah, I did that for my community service. We went to a camp for kids with special needs and did riding lessons and showed them how to groom and feed her. We spent the entire week there."

Allison smiled. "Do you want children...one day?"

Carly Rae had never really thought about it and had certainly never been asked that question. "My parents would love grandkids. But, I don't know. It's not something that has crossed my mind. Rodeo life is pretty rough as it is. I couldn't imagine dragging a family along, or worse, leaving them at home for months on end." She shrugged. "I guess if it's in the cards, it'll happen. What about you?"

"Oh, my father would be over the moon if I had a child. I'm pretty sure he or she would replace me overnight," she laughed.

"Yeah, definitely the same with my parents." Carly Rae smiled.

"Speaking of, I need to get going. I'm having lunch with my father. Would you like to join us?"

"Thank you, but I have a ton of things to do."

Allison was about to lean in and kiss her when Harris walked into the stable. "I was looking all over for you," he said to his daughter. "I just ran into Ollie outside with little Oliver. He's getting so big. Anyway, are we still on for lunch?"

"Yes. I was about to head your way," Allison said, smiling at Carly Rae before walking towards him.

"Carly Rae, you're welcome to join us."

"She already invited me, and thank you. I have a lot to do to get ready for this weekend."

"Alright. Another time then." He smiled and walked out of the barn with his daughter. "Ollie said Carly Rae took the boy for a ride on Sir Rigsby and he loved it."

"Yeah, I watched most of it. Then, she helped him feed the horse some treats and brush him down. He took right to her."

"She's the most genuine person I've ever met," he said.

"Wait until you meet her parents," she replied.

*

"I need to tell you something," Harris said, pushing his half-eaten salad to the side.

"Okay," she answered, setting her fork down. Usually when her father said those words it would go one of two ways. It was either something to benefit him, which had been the case when he'd hired Carly Rae and invited her and her horse to live at the estate, or he was meddling where he didn't belong, which happened quite often where dressage was concerned. She waited patiently.

"You know my family's estate was left for me to run when my father passed not long after you were born."

"Yes."

"When your grandparents in Bordeaux passed away five years ago, the family winery was passed to your mother. Her cousin Pierre has been running the daily operation ever since. Anyway, when she died, it passed to me to manage until you inherited it when you turned thirty or were married."

"I know all of this."

"Yes, but what you don't know is it's upside down and has been since before she took over. Neither of us realized it because my family's estate was worth much more and covered all of the expenses. However, that's no longer the case."

353

"What are you saying?"

"I bought Sir Rigsby to try and make some quick cash and perhaps keep things afloat," he sighed. "I'm afraid if he doesn't win this weekend, we are going to have to sell the winery. It's that, or you stop competing in dressage."

Allison stared blankly at him.

"We'll be completely out of money within two years if something doesn't happen soon."

"She loved that winery. It paid for boarding school and steeple chase and…" she paused, trying not to let herself get emotional. "It's starting to make sense now."

"What is?"

"Why you decided to get into horse racing."

He nodded.

"Does Carly Rae know all of this is riding on her shoulders?"

"No," he said, shaking his head.

"I can't ask you to give up your dreams, but selling the winery your mother's grandparents started with their bare hands breaks my heart."

"Why have you waited so long to tell me?"

"You were grieving your mother's death. I couldn't lay this all on you, and honestly, it didn't come to light until a few months afterwards when I took over everything and began forming a trust for you for both estates." When she didn't say anything, he continued. "I didn't fly to New York like I told you. I went to Bordeaux. I had to see for myself. Pierre was hanging on by the skin of his teeth, running the entire operation with only five people, including himself. I met a man on the plane on the way back who was big into horse racing. He set me up with someone he knew who was selling a top bloodline thoroughbred for a good price. I thought if I could get a winning horse, I could use the money for a few years to pad the account for the winery."

"I don't understand. I thought it was doing well."

"It was for a long time, but people are now growing Bordeaux grapes right here in Sonoma and Napa Valley. They're not sourcing them anymore. That was a huge chunk of the budget, and a lot of new, corporate wineries have come to town and bought up the other small operations."

"All this time I thought you were lonely without her and bought that horse as a hobby," she said, shaking her head.

"I'm sorry. I never wanted to tell you any of this, but…one day it will all be yours. You have a right to know what's going on, and you deserve a chance to give your opinion on how we proceed."

"Thank you." She nodded. "Can I think about it?"

"Absolutely. I know I just sprung all of this on you. No decisions will be made until after this weekend, and even then, nothing is in writing as of yet."

"Okay." She stood from her chair and instead of grabbing her plate to take it to the kitchen, she stepped around the side of the table and kissed his cheek. "I love you. I know losing her hasn't been easy on you either." She picked up her plate and walked away. Her brain was still trying to download and sort everything he'd just said to her, but in the back of her mind, she thought about telling him she was a lesbian. He'd just dumped a whole load on her, why not turn the tide and do it right back to him? But, at the same time, she wasn't sure she was ready for his reaction. Together, they had enough on their apparently cracked family plate. Her coming out would only add more weight to the pile.

Once she was finished clearing the table, she headed up to her room. She thought about telling Carly Rae, not because the fate lay in her hands, but because they were together and when she needed someone to talk to, Carly Rae was that person. However, she didn't need this on her shoulders. She was under enough pressure as it was.

THIRTY-FIVE

Carly Rae was nearly finished packing the few personal things she needed for the weekend trip. Her silks and riding gear were already in the trailer. The nerves she'd been feeling days earlier had slowly disappeared. Seeing her parents would be great, and getting the chance to jockey a horse in a stakes race…was a dream she never knew she had.

A soft knock at the door drew her attention as she tossed an extra pair of socks and underwear into the bag before answering it. Her father had always told her that was good luck, for if you were stranded somewhere your feet and butt would be clean.

"Good morning," Allison said, stepping inside and wrapping her arms around Carly Rae's neck.

Carly Rae slid her arms around her waist and pushed her back against the door, closing it at the same time. "Does your father know where you are?" she asked, pressing her lips to Allison's.

"Nope. He's still in the house."

"Aren't we leaving soon?"

"Yes. He had some last-minute stuff to do. He sent me to tell you to go ahead and get Sir Rigsby loaded. Ollie went over your checklist. Everything is in the trailer," she replied with a smile as her hands locked loosely together behind Carly Rae's head.

"I see."

"I also have some good news," she added, softly biting her bottom lip as she kissed her.

Carly Rae's mouth chased when she pulled away. "And," she mumbled, stealing a kiss and making Allison giggle.

"There are two rooms booked at the hotel tonight. Your parents are flying in tomorrow and driving to the track and Ollie's wife is driving over tomorrow. We're all driving back here tomorrow night after the race."

"Go on."

"You and I are sharing a room tonight. My father and Ollie are in the other one."

"Are you sure that's wise? I need my rest, tomorrow is a long…very big day," Carly Rae said seriously.

"I'm sorry. You're right. You should be in your own room. I'll go tell him. Hopefully, he can make arrangements." Allison pulled her arms back and moved to step away, but Carly Rae grabbed her and wrapped her arms tightly around her, bringing Allison fully against her.

"I was kidding. Yes…it's a huge day and it's going to be tiresome, but I want nothing more than to have you in my arms all night tonight."

Allison smiled. "Are you sure?"

"How much time do we have? I'll show you how sure," Carly Rae replied with a grin.

Banging on the door behind them stopped Allison from saying anything.

Carly Rae kissed her passionately, then pulled away to open the door. Ollie was standing in front of her.

"We need to load Sir Rigsby. Mr. Harris is ready to go. Have you seen Allison?"

"I'm right here," she said over Carly Rae's shoulder.

"Let me grab my bag. I'll meet you in the stable," Carly Rae said before shutting the door. "Are you riding in the backseat with me?"

"You actually think that's a good idea?" Allison raised a brow.

Carly Rae grinned like a Cheshire cat.

Allison laughed and shook her head. "Ollie is great company. You'll be fine."

*

Carly Rae wanted to put her ear buds in her ears and disappear for the hour long drive, but Ollie wouldn't allow it. He had a million and one questions about his duties as the groom, which is the person in charge of the horse.

"All you really have to do is parade Rigs around, then take him back to the stall in the paddock. I'll be there as the trainer when the vet checks him. After the jockey introduction, you'll have to saddle him, which we've been over several times. Then, you walk us out to the starting gate when it's time. After the race, if we don't win, you take him back to the stall and unsaddle him."

Are you sure you don't want me to do it? He sounds nervous, Allison texted.

He'll be fine. You should be with your father, she answered. *Besides, you'd be a distraction.*

Allison sent back a kiss emoji and left it at that. She knew nothing about horse racing, other than what she'd seen on TV and even that had been very little. However, she was as happy that it was nearly race day as her father and Carly Rae were, but it was also bittersweet. She had no idea what was on the other side of the race weekend. Would Carly Rae leave? Did she have a reason to stay? They'd never talked about anything past that race. Even thinking about never seeing her again made her chest ache and her stomach twist into knots. Not to mention the blow from the information her father had dumped on her at the last minute. She was still trying to process all of it. In the back of her mind, she wondered what her mother would've done had she known the winery was sinking and pulling her down with it. Giving up dressage would literally break her heart, but giving up her mother's heritage and childhood home would do the same. Her jaw tightened with anger towards her father for keeping this from her for so long, but it softened when she thought about how he'd taken on the entire burden himself while grieving his wife's sudden death, just so his daughter could grieve without additional pain. Her mother was her rock, and her idol, and her father was her super hero. But, she didn't know how strong he really was until she'd realized what he'd done.

When she felt her eyes start to water with tears, she immediately flipped a switch in her head and sent another text. *It's quiet back there.*

I think Ollie's passed out. He must have run out of questions, Carly Rae answered.

LOL! Poor guy.

You should've ridden back here. There's a trailer behind us, so no reason for your dad to use the rearview mirror, Carly Rae texted. She watched Allison laugh softly and shake her head. *Besides, you think I can't sit next to you in a vehicle for an hour and behave myself?* she added.

It wasn't you I was worried about! Allison replied.

*

All of the horses racing for the weekend were housed in the large stable with three rows of stalls. They were offset so that the horses were not directly across from each other and the walls between them were high enough to not be able to see over. Sir Rigsby neighed a few times when he walked inside. He had enough space to turn around, but it certainly wasn't as roomy as his stall back home. Still, the concrete ground was covered in a nice bed of hay and a bag of alfalfa hung on the door.

"It's not so bad," Carly Rae said, petting his face and neck. "It's not the Four Seasons, but it'll do for the weekend."

"It's funny how you talk to him," Allison said, stepping into the stall with them.

"I know he can't hear me, but he understands me." She pet him a few more times, then let him be. "Where's your father and Ollie?"

"They were 'checking the place out.' Whatever that means."

"Oh, really?" Carly Rae replied, moving closer to her. "I'd like to check you out."

"Don't start something we can't finish," Allison laughed softly as her arms went around Carly Rae's neck.

Carly Rae leaned in slightly, teasing her lower lip with a gentle nip before claiming her mouth in a fervent kiss.

"Well, what do we have here?" a male voice echoed in the stall.

Carly Rae and Allison flew apart like a bomb went off between them. Thankfully, the horse was munching on his snack and hadn't noticed the commotion.

It took a fraction of a second for Carly Rae to realize who was standing at the stall door, staring back at her. "Tibby!" she squealed.

He smiled and opened the door. Carly Rae rushed into his arms.

"Man, I've missed you!" he mumbled, squeezing her just as hard. "This must be the girl who stole your heart," he said, smiling and holding his hand out to Allison when they parted. "George Tibbetts, Jr."

"Allison McKinley," she replied, still feeling slightly nervous.

"Don't worry. Your secret is safe with me." He smiled and winked.

Allison nodded. He looked a lot like his father, whom she'd met in Wyoming, but he was smaller in stature.

"What in the world are you doing here?" Carly Rae asked as they all stepped out of the horse stall.

"I was supposed to be riding this weekend in Santa Anita, but my horse was scratched, so I was able to change my flight to here instead." He smiled brightly. "Surprise!"

"You scared the Hell out of us, by the way." Carly Rae shook her head.

"I second that," Allison mumbled. "Anyway, it's nice to meet you. I've heard a lot about you," she said.

"Likewise." He smiled. "So, you're an Olympic Silver Medalist. What was that like?"

"Surreal at the time. But, looking back on it, that was definitely one of my proudest moments in my career."

"I bet." He nodded. "Winning the triple crown is any jockey's dream, but to me, the Kentucky Derby is my Olympics."

"I'd just like to win tomorrow," Carly Rae muttered, shoving her hands into the front pockets of her jeans.

"Me too," Harris boomed, walking up behind her and putting his hands on the tops of her shoulders. "Harris McKinley," he said, sticking his hand out to Tibby.

"Harris, this is George Tibbetts, Jr., my best friend and the jockey I was telling you about."

"Nice to meet you," Tibby said, returning the shake.

"Are you racing tomorrow, too?" Harris asked.

"Oh, no, sir. I'm just here to support Carly Rae."

"Wonderful," he said, turning his attention to the stall. "How's our boy?"

"Great," Carly Rae replied. "He just ate some alfalfa. I'm sure he'll lie down once we're out of sight. The track will be open in a couple of hours for exercise, but I'd rather let him get used to his surroundings. I'll exercise him in the morning. Our post time is one, so he'll have plenty of time to rest before the race. Plus, the track vet will be coming around to take an initial look at him."

"Sounds good," Harris said. "I'm going to head over to the hotel and get things settled in there. Ollie is staying here. He's getting the lay of the land right now. Let us know if you need anything."

"I'm going to walk around a bit and see if I can't find Ollie," Allison added.

Carly Rae nodded, then watched them both walk away.

"I gather he still doesn't know about the two of you," Tibby said.

"Correct."

"What happens when this is all over?"

"I honestly don't know. My agreement with Harris was to train the horse to race this weekend with the potential to win. Then, I wound up jockeying him as well."

She shrugged. "As far as I know, I pack up and head out when we get back."

"Is that what you want?"

"I don't want to leave her, if that's what you're asking."

"I'm pretty sure she feels the same way."

"Yeah," she sighed. "What about you?"

"You'd be surprised at how many jockeys are gay men, but like her, they hide so deep in the closet, you almost can't find them. Not that I'm looking to date any of them, honestly. Give me a hardworking ranch hand any day of the week. I'm not looking for Brokeback Mountain, just someone who loves horses and the outdoors." He smiled.

"They always say it happens when you least expect it. That shit is true," she muttered, petting Sir Rigsby when he stuck his head out of the opening over the door.

"Is he really hearing impaired?" Tibby asked.

"He's Helen Keller level, just not blind."

"Wow. It's amazing how you've been able to train him. I can't wait to see you both race."

"Thanks," she said, giving him a quick hug. "I still can't get over you being here. Where are you staying tonight?"

"One of the jockeys I know is here riding in a maiden race. I'm splitting the room with him. It was so last minute, I didn't have time to even think about a hotel."

Carly Rae nodded.

"Here comes the vet. I'll leave you to it," he said. "Good luck."

"I'll come find you when I'm done here."

*

Allison stood along the outside rail, staring out at the oval shaped track, just as she'd done when they were there training weeks earlier, except this time felt much different. It was eerily quiet without the sound of hooves pounding the dirt.

"This is my favorite time," Tibby said as he walked up next to her. "The calm before the storm, so to speak."

"You need a bell around your neck or something," she replied, calming her racing heart after being surprised at his presence once again.

He laughed. "Usually, I'm the loud one. When we were kids, Carly Rae was a little eccentric and I was rambunctious. We were misfits together and it made us the best of friends."

"Yeah, I heard about her riding her horse to school."

He guffawed. "Good times."

"You two probably would've made a great couple."

"Our parents sure thought so. I'm pretty sure they were heartbroken." He paused for a second. "I stayed in the closet with my parents after Carly Rae marched out of hers without a care in the world like she was in a lesbian parade minus the rainbow flag. I was more worried my father wouldn't accept me. Even after he welcomed her with open arms, I was still reluctant to tell him."

"What made you change your mind?" she asked.

"I was tired of hiding who I was. I knew I wanted to be a jockey, but I also wanted to be my authentic self, right from the start. It's hard to have your parents support your dreams if they don't really know who you are. To me, it felt fake. Like I was two different people."

"What happened when you told him?"

Tibby smiled. "My mother had suspected all along, so it was fairly easy telling her. My dad was surprised, but he pulled me into a hug and said, 'I don't care who you love, as long as they love you in return.' It felt amazing getting rid of that huge weight, but I was angry with myself for carrying it to begin with. I know everyone's circumstance is different. However, when it's all said and done, it's *your* life to live. Not anyone else's."

Allison pursed her lips as if she was thinking about what to say, but simply nodded her head instead.

"On a lighter note, you made quite the impression back home," he said.

"I did?" She raised a brow.

"Oh, yeah. Word is you two are madly in love and just don't know it yet."

Allison laughed. "They got all of that in less than three days?"

He shrugged and smiled. "Enjoy the quiet. Tomorrow this place will be a circus," he murmured before walking away.

*

Carly Rae removed her belt and slipped her boots off before flopping down on her back in the middle of the bed. Allison walked away from the bathroom, where she was unpacking her toiletries, and climbed up on the bed, straddling her lap. She reached back, pulling her hair loose from the bun it had been in for the last couple of hours and shook it out over her shoulders.

"I like where this is going," Carly Rae whispered.

"Oh, really…." Allison rocked her hips back and forth.

"You set me on fire," Carly Rae muttered, sitting up and wrapping her arms around Allison's waist as their lips met in a sultry kiss. She quickly rolled to the side, putting Allison on her back.

Clothes were soon tossed about, leaving them skin to skin as they continued trading touches and kisses well into the night before falling asleep in each other's arms.

THIRTY-SIX

Carly Rae walked Sir Rigsby out of his stall and stood to the side as the vet started his morning exam. Wearing both the trainer and jockey hats made her job twice as hard. As the trainer, she was the one who made every decision for the horse, and as the jockey, her job was to remain clear-headed and focused. The two were exact opposites of each other.

"Has he been out at all this morning?" the vet asked, checking the numbers on his lip tattoo to identify him.

She nodded. "We took a light jog after he had breakfast."

"Good," he said as he bent down, palpating Sir Rigsby's legs, feeling for heat or swelling in his joints and tissue, as well as pain when his legs were flexed. "No indication of inflammation," he muttered to his assistant who was taking notes. "Any issues with the jog this morning?" he asked, looking at Carly Rae as he stood up.

"No," she replied, shaking her head.

"He's cleared to race," he said, signing the paper.

"Thanks," she replied, but he'd already moved on to the next horse on his list like a robot with programming. Sir Rigsby had also walked away, clearly uninterested in what was happening outside of his stall. She hadn't seen Harris or Allison since they'd arrived at the track together two hours earlier. She began walking towards the barn exit, stopping when she heard a familiar voice. She looked up to see her parents walking with Allison, Harris, and Tibby.

"Look who we found," Harris said.

"More like they found me," Allison laughed softly.

Both of Carly Rae's parents hugged her. She smiled at Allison when their eyes met.

"I'm glad you made it," Carly Rae stated.

"Were you as surprised to see Tibby as I was?"

"Lord yes," her mother said. "He pulled a fast one on us. I haven't seen him in almost a year!"

Tibby laughed.

"Since you're here, let me introduce you to Sir Rigsby. Then, we need to leave him be so he can rest," she said, waving for them to follow her.

Everyone came to a stop outside of stall number ten and peeked inside. Sir Rigsby was standing back away from the door, but he moseyed up to get petted when he saw he had visitors. Everyone took turns petting his face.

"Is he really deaf?" her father asked.

"Yes," Carly Rae replied. "Complete hearing loss in both ears."

"Wow. It's amazing that you can even ride him, much less race him."

"She's always been the horse whisperer," Tibby added.

"Isn't that the truth." Her father smiled.

"Charles and Irene if you're ready, we'll head up to our box. There are two races in front of ours and lunch is being served," Harris said.

Carly Rae gave him an appreciative nod.

"Give those boys Hell, honey!" her mother said, pulling her into a hug.

"I'll do my best." She smiled.

"You've got this, kiddo," her father added, also hugging her.

"I know I don't have to tell you what to do, you ride like your damn hair is on fire…but in my experience, get to the rail early and ride it like you stole it," Tibby said.

Carly Rae grinned and hugged him.

"She's all yours," he said to Allison before walking away to catch up to the group.

"I love your parents," she said, moving closer.

"Why is that?" Carly Rae smiled.

"We were waiting for them, but they saw me first and rushed over, doting on how much they enjoyed having me at their house, right away."

"They definitely like you."

"Yeah, but I thought they were about to out me when they told my father they knew right away that I was a lot more than just the horse owner's daughter, thanks for that by the way, and they're so happy you have me in your life."

Carly Rae laughed. "That's not really outing you, we *are* friends. Plus, they're honestly happy about it because of all the shit I've been through in the past year. And…are we going to go down that road again?"

"Definitely not going down that road. Anyway, my father didn't really catch on. He looked at them oddly for a second, but then he went on and on about you and how lucky he is that you made him an offer he couldn't refuse that day and how you're not just the horse's trainer or jockey, you've become part of the family."

"See, they all sound like parents who love their kids and are happy we aren't deadbeats." She shrugged.

"I agree. You should've seen their reaction when Tibby walked up."

Carly Rae laughed. "I'm sure my mom was ecstatic."

"Something like that," Allison replied, searching her eyes. "I really want to kiss you right now."

"You'll have to wait until it's over. There's no place to sneak off to. And, I need to get to the jockey meeting."

"I guess a hug will suffice," she said, wrapping her arms around Carly Rae in a loose embrace. "Please be careful," she whispered.

"Always." Carly Rae smiled.

*

Everyone was eating lunch and placing their bets for the upcoming races when Allison walked into the box. Her father pointed out the array of food on the buffet tables, but she wasn't interested. Her nerves were frazzled and there was still an hour and a half to go. A glass of wine from the bar sounded much better.

Carly Rae's mother stepped up next to her while the bartender filled her glass with a reserve chardonnay. "Make that two," she added, getting the man's attention. "I'm not much of a drinker, but I'm nervous enough for the both of us."

"She actually seemed fine."

"I meant the *two of us*, dear." She smiled. "If she's uneasy at all, you'll never know it. She buries anxiety somewhere deep and picks it apart until it's gone. She's done it ever since she was a kid."

Allison nodded. "I wish she'd teach me how to do that."

"Me too!"

Allison took a long sip from her glass.

"What do you think?" Harris said, walking up to her when Carly Rae's mother went back to her husband and Tibby.

"Think? About what?"

"Horse racing."

"I don't know yet. I'm waiting to see how the day ends."

He laughed.

"Can we talk…just the two of us?"

"Is it important? The race is about to start."

"Yes," she said, chugging the last of her wine and setting the glass down on the bar.

"Okay," he replied, nodding for her to follow him out of the box. "It's not exactly quiet out here, but we're out of earshot. What's going on?"

"Whether the horse wins or loses, I want you to sell the winery."

"What?"

"I've thought about it enough. My connection to my mother is the UK and all of the time we both spent there, not France, and certainly not a winery I've never been to."

"Are you sure that's what you want to do?"

"It's what she would do."

"Okay." He nodded. "Consider it done."

She gave him a hug before they rejoined the group who seemed to be too busy talking to each other to notice they'd even left.

"I like them," he muttered.

"Who?" she whispered.

"Carly Rae's family."

"Yeah, me too." She smiled.

*

Ollie was outside of Sir Rigsby's stall when Carly Rae returned after the meeting. "Where've you been?" she asked.

"I took my wife on a tour when she arrived."

"Nice."

"I know. She's very impressed. We might not be driving back today." He grinned.

Carly Rae guffawed and shook her head. "Get ready to take Rigs over to the receiving barn. They're about to make the announcement," she added, checking the clock on the wall. The race would be starting in forty-seven minutes. "I'm going to go get changed. I'll meet you in the paddock."

As soon as she walked away, he grabbed the lead attached to Sir Rigsby's race bridle and walked him over to the adjacent barn where the race staff was waiting to get him checked in and assigned a program number. Ollie promptly put on the number 2 armband and carried the saddle towel with the corresponding number as the vet drew blood from Sir Rigsby. Then, he walked him over to the paddock and settled him into stall number 2.

*

Carly Rae checked the mirror. She was wearing white racing jodhpurs with bright green and white checkered silks. The black riding boots were a little tight around her calves, but fit her feet perfectly.

"Are you ready?" one of the jockeys asked as he passed by her.

"As ready as I'll ever be, I guess."

"I'd tell you the first one is always the hardest, but I'd be lying." He smiled. "Good luck out there."

"Yeah, you too," she called before grabbing her helmet. She looked back at herself in the mirror one last time and took a deep breath. Then, she let it out slowly and walked away as the bugle sounded for the call to post.

Ollie was waiting on her when she entered the paddock. They worked together to get Sir Rigsby's saddle on with the number 2 blanket placed perfectly underneath it. When they were finished, she pet the horse's face and handed Ollie the lead. He led him out to the walking ring to be officially displayed to the bettors. Carly Rae joined Harris in the center as Ollie walked the horse around the circle. Then, he gave her a leg up into the saddle and headed back up to the box.

Carly Rae unclipped the lead from the bridle and handed it off to Ollie before cantering Sir Rigsby around to warm him up and get in line for the parade out to the starting gate.

THIRTY-SEVEN

"There she is!" Allison shouted. Her heart raced so fast, she swore she could hear it pounding in her ears. *Win or lose, please keep her safe!*

"I see her. Number two!" Carly Rae's father said.

"Are they at the gate yet?" Harris said, rushing inside the room.

"Just about," Allison answered.

Everyone gathered across the front of the window in anticipation of the start.

*

"Come on, boy," Carly Rae said to herself since he couldn't hear her as she pet his neck. Her nerves had returned, but once she was on his back and settled in the saddle, they'd began to dissipate, leaving her clear headed and focused.

The track staff began ushering the horses into the gate. Sir Rigsby was hesitant at first, but went right in once she pet him. He knew the signals of communication and so far, they were working.

Suddenly, the gate behind them closed. A split second later, the pistol fired and the gate in front of them swung open. Carly Rae jerked the rein, sending Sir Rigsby galloping out. They came out in fourth and were just outside of the horse in third place who was on the rail. Carly Rae held her line as they raced down the straightaway. By the time they entered the clubhouse turn they'd moved up to a tie with second place, but they were on the outside. Sir Rigsby held his line and easily passed the second-place horse on the backstretch. He began closing in on the leader as they entered the far turn. Carly Rae's thighs burned from her squeezing them together harder than ever to keep her crouched position with her butt up out of the saddle.

The leader was only half a horse length ahead when they passed the quarter pole on the far turn. Carly Rae gave him a loose rein, allowing him to run free as the track opened up into the home stretch. She tucked her head down, looking through the very top of her goggles as Sir Rigsby sprinted with all of his might. It felt like slow motion as they began sliding past the lead horse. Carly Rae slapped the reins over and over, urging Sir Rigsby to go faster and faster until the other horse was no longer in sight. By the time they'd crossed the finish line, Sir Rigsby was a full horse and a half ahead. Carly Rae pulled the reins up, slowing him down. Then, she shook her fist in the air and stood up in the stirrups, full of excitement. She quickly sat back down and slowed him to a light jog as other riders came up, congratulating her.

Sir Rigsby had slowed all the way to a walk as they made their way back down the homestretch to the winner's area in the middle of the infield. "We did it, boy!" she said, petting him over and over as they walked.

*

"Oh, no. She's getting squeezed out!" Tibby called, watching through the binoculars.

Allison kept her eyes on the screen. "Come on," she murmured.

Everyone clenched their jaws in suspense as the horses rounded the far turn and headed into the homestretch. Sir Rigsby had moved up, but he was still on the outside.

"Go horse, go!" Harris shouted when the horses hit the straightaway and raced for the finish line.

Everyone was screaming and jumping up and down as Sir Rigsby eased past the leader in what felt like an inch at a time until he was not only clear of him, but way out in front. Suddenly, Sir Rigsby crossed the finish line.

"Holy shit! We won!" Harris yelled, picking Allison up off the ground and spinning her around. "We won! We won!"

"Winner winner!" Tibby cheered.

"That's our girl!" Charles exclaimed, hugging his wife.

"Come on, we have to get trackside!" Harris yelled, ushering them out. "Everyone! Come on!"

*

Carly Rae knew they'd won, but it hadn't truly sunk in until she climbed down from the saddle and was met by all of the officials. Ollie was by her side in an instant and quickly attached the lead to Sir Rigsby's bridle. Photographers snapped pictures while a local equine magazine asked questions for an interview.

"This is crazy," Ollie said.

"No kidding!" she replied, still smiling and answering questions. As soon as the interview was over, Harris appeared with the rest of the group.

"You did it!" he yelled, squeezing through the people who were gathered around taking pictures and waiting to watch the ceremony.

"I told you I would!" she said when he hugged her.

"I know I promised you ten percent of whatever we won today, but if you agree to come to work for me permanently as our trainer and jockey, I'll split all of our winnings fifty-fifty with you from here on out. Of course, you can have all the time you need for barrel racing, which I plan to sponsor, and spend as much time at your family ranch as you want. What do you think?"

Carly Rae stared in disbelief for a minute as her heart pounded like a bass drum in her chest. Was this what she wanted? A thousand thoughts began tearing through her head…until Allison stepped in front of her. As soon as their eyes met, Carly Rae's thoughts calmed completely and her heart began beating wildly for a completely different reason. She mouthed the words: *I love you*.

Allison smiled. "I am so in love with you!" she said loud enough for everyone to hear before closing the distance between them. Her lips met Carly Rae's in a soft, passionate kiss that lasted a handful of seconds. When they parted, Allison moved to her side with their arms still around one another and slowly brought her eyes up.

Harris was staring at both of them with a questioning expression on his face. The crowd around them was mostly silent.

"Does your offer still stand?" Carly Rae asked, still holding his daughter close at her side.

"Of course, it does," he replied with a smile. "We'd all have to be as blind as Sir Rigsby is deaf to not see this happening."

"We agree," Carly Rae's father added with his wife nodding in agreement next to him. Both had huge smiles plastered on their faces.

Carly Rae looked at Allison and smiled before turning back to Harris and holding her hand out. "We have a deal!"

About the Author

Graysen Morgen is the bestselling author of several bestselling lesbian fiction titles. She was born and raised in North Florida with winding rivers and waterways at her back door, and white sandy beaches nearby. She has spent most of her lifetime in the sun and on the water. She enjoys reading, writing, fishing, coaching and watching soccer, snowy vacations, and spending as much time as possible with her wife and their two children.

You can contact Graysen at graysenmorgen@aol.com; like her fan page on Facebook.com/graysenmorgen; follow her on Twitter: @graysenmorgen and Instagram: @graysenmorgen

Other Titles Available From Triplicity Publishing

Outside In by Breanna Hughes. Cali Evans is a survivor. Her life hasn't been easy, but her late father raised her to be smart, tough, and dependent only on herself and her wits. On the eve of her 21st birthday she meets Owen Bray - a beautiful and intriguing young doctor who equally frustrates and captivates Cali. That fateful meeting inspires Cali to make a better life for herself. The next day, hoping to make positive change, Cali hops a bus for the West Coast but never reaches her destination. Instead, she wakes up in an underground bunker with no recollection of how she got there. Upon her arrival, she learns that she's one of just forty survivors of a fast-spreading environmental toxin and that human life outside of the bunker has ceased to exist. Tired of the vague explanations and half-answers coming from the people in charge, Cali takes it upon herself to investigate the real reason why she's there and begins to uncover the sinister truth.

I Love You, Nora Whispered by Kathy L. Salt. Love in the time of horses and polio. England, 1948. Nora Lakes suffers from post polio syndrome and very low self-esteem. When her sister Martha manages to get her a job at Waterhouse Acre Stables, she can hardly believe it. She had never imagined that anyone would have employed her, damaged as she is. She also never imagined she would meet anybody like Katherine. Katherine Waterhouse was born with a silver spoon in her mouth. She has a mean streak and doesn't like people in general. What she does like, is horses. She wants to be a professional rider but growing up in a conservative house where her choices are limited by her sex, Katherine has always been trapped in her role as a woman. Nora and Katherine - two women with very different backgrounds, drawn to each other with an intensity neither of them are prepared for. Do they stand a chance?

Omega Rising by Domina Alexandra. A few months of peace. That was all Bonnie Collins was granted. New trouble has surfaced and go figure, this trouble came with a new pair of claws. When an unknown pack comes to town, Bonnie is forced to make tough decisions that will influence her packs future. Things only get harder when her mate is taken, leaving Bonnie in charge of a pack who still doesn't trust her. With chaos all around, it will be exactly what Bonnie needs to finally embrace what she has become. An Omega Rising. Book 2 of the *Claimed Series*.

Loose Ends by Joan L. Anderson. After her estranged sister is killed when she falls onto the subway tracks in Paris just as a train arrives, Allison goes to Paris to deal with her sister's body and collect her things. But, after talking to the police about the accident and viewing the subway surveillance video, something seems odd about her death. When Allison's hotel room in Paris is broken into with only a few things taken, but not any money or credit cards, she begins to wonder if it really was an accident that killed her sister, or if it was murder. Once Allison returns to Washington, D.C. to handle her sister's affairs, she soon realizes that her sister had been living a secret life and wasn't the person she had always thought she was. As troubling things begin to happen to Allison in D.C., she starts wondering if she will be the next person to die.

Real Love by Graysen Morgen. Leigh Myer is a trauma nurse practitioner who is not happy going through the motions of her daily life. When a friend offers up her mountain cabin for a relaxing vacation, Leigh packs her bags. She's never been to the mountains and certainly never in heavy snow. A chance meeting with a fish and wildlife officer turns her idea of a quiet, relaxing vacation…upside down. Camden Gorely loves her job and loves the mountain she works and lives on even more. She's tired of having flings with vacationers who visit for days or weeks at a time, until she meets the elusive nurse from the city. Can Leigh stop running from her past and allow real love into her heart?

Enticed by Love by Lynn Lawler. Henrietta Bailey is a mysterious woman who has spent her entire life living in the town of Crescent, a sleepy beach community in central coastal California. She loves the beach, the ocean air, and the town itself. Her simple life fulfills her. However, she spends much of her time reminiscing about her long-lost love, a woman who left her devastated. Now, another woman awaits on the horizon; a wise, intelligent, and sexy lady who is sophisticated beyond her years. This woman yearns for her soul mate and lover. Will she be able to win Henrietta's heart, or will Henrietta be fated to live the rest of her days alone?

Love Undercover by Domina Alexandra. Remi Stone never expected to get the opportunity to work undercover for narcotics. But, when the chance arrives, she takes it. With drugs coursing through a high school, Remi has only until the end of the school year to find the suspects responsible. Undercover, Remi plays her role, moving one step further into the drug industry. She never thought she'd be moving one step closer to the woman who would change her life and take hold of her heart. There is just one issue. Remi Stone is undercover as an eighteen year old high school senior. And the woman she can't seem to ignore is her History teacher. There will be a lot of challenges along the way, including one that could cost Remi her life and her heart.

Playing the Game by Graysen Morgen. Randi Rojas is a professional soccer player who seemingly has it all, a successful career, a long-term girlfriend, a loving family, and a great group of friends…until a chance meeting with an attractive woman sends her way offside, and into a whole new game. Berkley Ward lives her life to the extreme, spending her days either in the gym or four-wheeling in the woods, and her nights patrolling the streets as an officer. Affairs with taken women are easy, but after years of playing games, she's finished…until she meets a beautiful woman and a game she can't resist. Both women play a dangerously seductive game of cat and mouse, teetering on the edge of friendship and affair.

Rebel Sweetheart by Sydney Canyon. When a headstrong, country music superstar starts getting threatening letters while on tour, her manager has no other choice but to hire someone to investigate the threats, and keep her safe. Haley Nielsen is as stubborn as it gets. She does things her way, and her way only. The last thing she needs or wants is a babysitter following her every move and controlling everything she does. Shane Crowley isn't your typical private investigator, or bodyguard, for that matter.

She's a former U.S. Deputy Marshal with a lot of experience, and an all or nothing attitude. Tempers flare and the energy burns red hot between the two women as they spend weeks together cooped up on Haley's tour bus, traveling the country. Will they stop resisting each other long enough to see eye to eye? Or will the letter writer make good on his threats?

A Tale of Spiders and Canned Soup by Kathy L. Salt. Living on your own can be hard, but even more so when you're dealing with haphephobia; the death of a twin sister; and a crush on your teacher. Mika is still in contact with her foster family who homes the loves of her life, three young children she would do anything for, when she begins attending University of Aberdeen and meets Pauline, an Australian that teaches Viking history. Neither woman is used to breaking the rules, and their way to each other is a hard one, especially when Mika vows to get custody of the children, whether she is ready to be a parent or not. *A story about growing up. A story about dealing with grief. A story about Mika and Pauline.*

A Night Claimed by Domina Alexandra. Bonnie Collins had plans. And being a werewolf wasn't one of them. Attacked by a rogue who was out to claim her, and facing what she now has no choice of becoming, Bonnie can't let go of her human life as a Paramedic. The last thing Bonnie needs is more challenges. However, Rikki, the Alpha of Mill City will be just that. Finding her to be possessive and ruling, Bonnie begins challenging the Alpha's every breath. Finding out her attack was no accident only makes her more angry at the situation. A group of rogues are out to get her. With no clue why,

Bonnie has no choice but to seek help from the alluring Alpha and her pack, accepting the new world she was forced into.

Stunted by Breanna Hughes. Professional stuntwoman Jessie Knight takes her job very seriously and although she works in the entertainment industry, she has zero desire for fame or notoriety. She also has a very strict no-dating policy when it comes to coworkers. That is, until, she meets famous actress Elliot Chase on the set of her new film. The adrenaline rush of the stunts is nothing compared to the sparks that fly between them. After a passionate night together, a sex tape is leaked that sends Jessie and Elliot's private and professional lives into a spiral. Will the fallout be too much for them to last? Or will they find a way out of the mess together?

Mission Compromised by Graysen Morgen. Natalia Moreno is thrilled when she arrives in Fiji for a relaxing vacation. However, she soon discovers the overwater bungalow she's staying in has been double booked for the entire stay, and the resort is full. Annoyed and frustrated, she has no other choice but to share her hut with a stranger. Christian Garnier is sent to Fiji for what she refers to as a working vacation, until she finds out she has an ornery roommate for the next two weeks who is dead set on making her job twice as hard. Soon, all hell breaks loose and the two women are sent around the world on a wild goose chase.

Stargazing by Kathy L. Salt. Lissa stared open-mouthed at the GIF that played over and over on the screen in front of her. Heat flushed to her face, igniting her skin.

Her heart started pounding in her chest. *Stupid internet, it should really come with a warning label.* She's never been interested in relationships or sex and as the years have gone by she has retreated more and more into her work. Everything changes when she meets Star, a porn actress with a heart of gold and a troubled childhood. *They say that opposites attract, but how much of that is true? What chance do they have when one of them is a virgin and the other one star in pornography?*

I Belong with Her by Domina Alexandra. Tajel Pierce loves the thrill of being a paramedic. Every call she goes on gives her a rush. She makes no time for a personal life. No one can ruin her love for her career. Then there is Arianna Castaldi, who just transferred to her new paramedic position in a whole new state. All she needs is a new start without any distractions. Arianna and Tajel's relationship doesn't start off perfect. Embarrassed of the one night stand Arianna believes she had with Tajel, she wants to pretend they never met and make their relationship strictly business. The only choice they have to keep from strangling each other is to go from denying their feelings to accepting them as they work through intense 911 calls.

Awakened by Fate by Lynn Lawler. Jackie is a woman living life according to her own rules. She's married, but it's the unspoken, open kind. She can have as many female lovers as she likes; she just can't talk about them. After a bizarre encounter turns her world upside down, things slowly begin to change. She finds herself in desperation as she searches for answers. What she discovers is nothing is delivered in a neatly wrapped box. Now that everything has been brought out into the open, she finds she can't run away from her truth anymore. With her new life, comes new responsibilities and a different outcome than what she was expecting. Jackie isn't alone in the story. She meets several new people who help her along her journey.

Nautical Delights by S. L. Gape. Lady Elizabeth Barrington has spent her entire life trying to please her family; constantly opting for a quiet life, she utilises her profession as a doctor to keep out of her families' clutches; bar the annual two-week Caribbean private cruise, where there is simply no budge. Confined to two weeks on board the Iconica super yacht, she intends on keeping her head down and enjoying as much of the holiday as she can, whilst keeping her family at arm's length. Until a crew member catches her eye.

Worlds Apart by S.L. Gape. Hollywood A-lister Heidi Spencer-Brady is everything you'd expect of an Idol. Loved by all, the British Beauty is graceful, talented, humble and so far removed from the 'typical' LA scene. When her husband's infidelity with his new 'leading lady' is leaked, Dawn, Heidi's best friend and manager, goes all out to protect her. She arranges for Heidi to go back to the UK and stay on her cousins farm they had visited as children, much to the disappointment of the animal fearing Heidi.

Castor Valley (Law & Order Series Book 2) by Graysen Morgen. Jessie Henry is torn when she reads about the capture of the Doyle brothers, two young men who were part of her old gang. Unable to let them hang for a crime she's sure they didn't commit, Jessie leaves her wife and the Town of Boone Creek behind, and sets out on a journey back to the one place she thought she'd never see again, *Castor Valley*. Ellie Henry watches the love of her life leave, not knowing if she will ever return. When she gets an odd telegram, nearly a week later, she fears Jessie is in trouble. With no other choice, she goes to the one person who can help her.

Fight to the Top by S. L. Gape. Georgia is a forty year old, single, Area Director from Manchester, UK who is all work and definitely no play. Having no time to socialise or spend time with her family she prides herself on being fit and well-polished. Erika is an Area Director for the same company, but in the United States. Whilst she is concentrating so heavily on the promotion she has been fighting for, she's starting to feel like her life outside of work is falling apart. The two women are exceptionally different, and worlds apart. Both of their lives are turned upside down when their jobs are snatched from under their noses, and they are suddenly faced with being thrown together by their bosses for one last major project...in Texas.

Boone Creek (Law & Order Series book 1) by Graysen Morgen. Jessie Henry is looking for a new life. She's unknown in the town of Boone Creek when she arrives, and wants to keep it that way. When she's offered the job of Town Marshal, she takes it, believing that protecting others and upholding the law is the penance for her past. Ellie Fray is a widowed, shopkeeper. She generally keeps to herself, but the mysterious new Town Marshal both intrigues and infuriates her. She believes the last thing the town needs is someone stirring up trouble with the outlaws who have taken over.

Witness by Joan L. Anderson. Becca and Kate have lived together for eight years, and have always spent their vacation in a tropical paradise, lying on a beach. This year, Becca wanted to try something different: a seven day, 65-mile hike in the beautiful Cascade Mountains of Washington state. Their peaceful vacation turns to horror when they stumble upon a brutal murder taking place in the back country.

Too Soon by S.L. Gape. Brooke is a twenty-nine year old detective from Oxford, who has her life pretty much planned out until her boss and partner of nine years, Maria, tells her their relationship is over. When Brooke finds out the truth, that Maria cheated on her with their best friend Paula, she decides to get her life back on track by getting away for six weeks in Anglesey, North Wales. Chloe, a thirty three year old artist and art director, owns a log cabin on Anglesey where she spends each weekend painting and surfing. After returning from a surf, she stumbles upon the somewhat uptight and enigmatic Brooke.

Never Quit (Never Series book 2) by Graysen Morgen. Two years after stepping away from the action as a Coast Guard Rescue Swimmer to become an instructor, Finley finds herself in charge of the most difficult class of cadets she's ever faced, while also juggling the taxing demands of having a home life with her partner Nicole, and their fifteen year old daughter. Jordy Ross gave up everything, dropping out of college, and leaving her family behind, to join the Coast Guard and become a rescue swimmer cadet. The extreme training tests her fitness level, pushing her mentally and physically further than she's ever been in her life, but it's the aggressive competition between her and another female cadet that proves to be the most challenging.

Never Let Go (Never Series book 1) by Graysen Morgen. For Coast Guard Rescue Swimmer, Finley Morris, life is good. She loves her job, is well respected by her peers, and has been given an opportunity to take her career to the next level. The only thing missing is the love of her life, who walked out, taking their daughter with her, seven years earlier. When Finley gets a call from her ex, saying their teenage daughter is coming to spend the summer with her, she's floored. While spending more time with her daughter, whom she doesn't get to see often, and learning to be a full-time parent, Finley quickly realizes she has not, and will never, let go of what is important.

Pursuit by Joan L. Anderson. Claire is a workaholic attorney who flies to Paris to lick her wounds after being dumped by her girlfriend of seventeen years. On the plane she chats with the young woman sitting next to her, and when they land the woman is inexplicably detained in Customs. Claire is surprised when she later runs into the woman in the city. They agree to meet for breakfast the next morning, but when the woman doesn't show up Claire goes to her hotel and makes a horrifying discovery. She soon finds herself ensnared in a web of intrigue and international terrorism, becoming the target of a high stakes game of cat and mouse through the streets of Paris.

Wrecked by Sydney Canyon. To most people, the *Duchess* is a myth formed by old pirates tales, but to Reid Cavanaugh, a Caribbean island bum and one of the best divers and treasure hunters in the world, it's a real, seventeenth century pirate ship—the holy grail of underwater treasure hunting. Reid uses the same cunning tactics she always has before setting out to find the lost ship. However, she is forced to bring her business partner's daughter along as collateral this time because he doesn't trust her. Neither woman is thrilled, but being cooped up on a small dive boat for days, forces them to get know each other quickly.

Arson by Austen Thorne. Madison Drake is a detective for the Stetson Beach Police Department. The last thing she wants to do is show a new detective the ropes, especially when a fire investigation becomes arson to cover up a murder. Madison butts heads with Tara, her trainee, deals with sarcasm from Nic, her ex-girlfriend who is a patrol officer, and finds calm in the chaos of police work with Jamie, her best friend who is the county medical examiner. Arson is the first of many in a series of novella episodes surrounding the fictional Stetson Beach Police Department and Detective Madison Drake.

Mommies (Bridal Series book 3) **by Graysen Morgen.** Britton and her wife Daphne have been married for a year and a half and are happy with their life, until Britton's mother hounds her to find out why her sister Bridget hasn't decided to have children yet. This prompts Daphne to bring up the big subject of having kids of their own with Britton. Britton hadn't really thought much about having kids, but her love for Daphne makes her see life and their future together in a whole new way when they decide to become mommies.

Rapture & Rogue by Sydney Canyon. Taren Rauley is happy and in a good relationship, until the one person she thought she'd never see again comes back into her life. She struggles to keep the past from colliding with the present as old feelings she thought were dead and gone, begin to haunt her. In college, Gianna Revisi was a mastermind, ring-leading, crime boss. Now, she has a great life and spends her time running Rapture and Rogue, the two establishments she built from the ground up. The last person she ever expects to see walk into one of them, is the girl who walked out on her, breaking her heart five years ago.

Second Chance by Sydney Canyon. After an attack on her convoy, Marine Corps Staff Sergeant, Darien Hollister, must learn to live without her sight. When an experimental procedure allows her to see again, Darien is torn, knowing someone had to die in order for this to happen. She embarks on a journey to personally thank the donor's family, but is too stunned to tell them the truth. Mixed emotions stir inside of her as she slowly gets to the know the people that feel like so much more than strangers to her. When the truth finally comes out, Darien walks away, taking the second chance that she's been given to go back to the only life she's ever known, but she's not the only one with a second chance at life.

Meant to Be by Graysen Morgen. Brandt is about to walk down the aisle with her girlfriend, when an unexpected chain of events turns her world upside down, causing her to question the last three years of her life. A chance encounter sparks a mix of rage and excitement that she has never felt before. Summer is living life and following her dreams, all the while, harboring a huge secret that could ruin her career. She believes that some things are better kept in the dark, until she has her third run-in with a woman she had hoped to never see again, and gives into temptation. Brandt and Summer start believing everything happens for a reason as they learn the true meaning of meant to be.

Coming Home by Graysen Morgen. After tragedy derails TJ Abernathy's life, she packs up her three year old son and heads back to Pennsylvania to live with her grandmother on the family farm. TJ picks back up where she left off eight years earlier, tending to the fruit and nut tree orchard, while learning her grandmother's secret trade. Soon, TJ's high school sweetheart and the same girl who broke her heart, comes back into her life, threatening to steal it away once again. As the weeks turn into months and tragedy strikes again, TJ realizes coming home was the best thing she could've ever done.

Special Assignment by Austen Thorne. Secret Service Agent Parker Meeks has her hands full when she gets her new assignment, protecting a Congressman's teenage daughter, who has had threats made on her life and been whisked away to a Christian boarding school under an alias to finish out her senior year. Parker is fine with the assignment, until she finds out she has to go undercover as a Canon Priest. The last thing Parker expects to find is a beautiful, art history teacher, who is intrigued by her in more ways than one.

Miracle at Christmas by Sydney Canyon. A Modern Twist on the Classic Scrooge Story. Dylan is a power-hungry lawyer who pushed away everything good in her life to become the best defense attorney in the, often winning the worst cases and keeping anyone with enough money out of jail. She's visited on Christmas Eve by her deceased law partner, who threatens her with a life in hell like his own, if she doesn't change her path. During the course of the night, she is taken on a journey through her past, present, and future with three very different spirits.

Bella Vita by Sydney Canyon. Brady is the First Officer of the crew on the Bella Vita, a luxury charter yacht in the Caribbean. She enjoys the laidback island lifestyle, and is accustomed to high profile guests, but when a U.S. Senator charters the yacht as a gift to his beautiful twin daughters who have just graduated from college and a few of their friends, she literally has her hands full.

Brides (Bridal Series book 2) by Graysen Morgen. Britton Prescott is dating the love of her life, Daphne Attwood, after a few tumultuous events that happened to unravel at her sister's wedding reception, seven months earlier. She's happy with the way things are, but immense pressure from her family and friends to take the next step, nearly sends her back to the single life. The idea of a long engagement and simple wedding are thrown out the window, as both families take over, rushing Britton and Daphne to the altar in a matter of weeks.

Cypress Lake by Graysen Morgen. The small town of Cypress Lake is rocked when one murder after another happens. Dani Ricketts, the Chief Deputy for the Cypress Lake Sheriff's Office, realizes the murders are linked. She's surprised when the girl that broke her heart in high school has not only returned home, but she's also Dani's only suspect. Kristen Malone has come back to Cypress Lake to put the past behind her so that she can move on with her life. Seeing Dani Ricketts again throws her off-guard, nearly derailing her plans to finally rid herself and her family of Cypress Lake.

Crashing Waves by Graysen Morgen. After a tragic accident, Pro Surfer, Rory Eden, spends her days hiding in the surf and snowboard manufacturing company that she built from the ground up, while living her life as a shell of the person that she once was. Rory's world is turned upside when a young surfer pursues her, asking for the one thing she can't do. Adler Troy and Dr. Cason Macauley from Graysen Morgen's bestselling novel: *Falling Snow*, make an appearance in this romantic adventure about life, love, and letting go.

Bridesmaid of Honor (Bridal Series book 1) by Graysen Morgen. Britton Prescott's best friend is getting married and she's the maid of honor. As if that isn't enough to deal with, Britton's sister announces she's getting married in the same month and her maid of honor is her best friend Daphne, the same woman who has tormented Britton for years. Britton has to suck it up and play nice, instead of scratching her eyes out, because she and Daphne are in both weddings. Everyone is counting on them to behave like adults.

Falling Snow by Graysen Morgen. Dr. Cason Macauley, a high-speed trauma surgeon from Denver meets Adler Troy, a professional snowboarder and sparks fly. The last thing Cason wants is a relationship and Adler doesn't realize what's right in front of her until it's gone, but will it be too late?

Fate vs. Destiny by Graysen Morgen. Logan Greer devotes her life to investigating plane crashes for the National Transportation Safety Board. Brooke McCabe is an investigator with the Federal Aviation Association who literally flies by the seat of her pants. When Logan gets tangled in head games with both women will she choose fate or destiny?

Just Me by Graysen Morgen. Wild child Ian Wiley has to grow up and take the reins of the hundred year old family business when tragedy strikes. Cassidy Harland is a little surprised that she came within an inch of picking up a gorgeous stranger in a bar and is shocked to find out that stranger is the new head of her company.

Love Loss Revenge by Graysen Morgen. Rian Casey is an FBI Agent working the biggest case of her career and madly in love with her girlfriend. Her world is turned upside when tragedy strikes. Heartbroken, she tries to rebuild her life. When she discovers the truth behind what really happened that awful night she decides justice isn't good enough, and vows revenge on everyone involved.

Natural Instinct by Graysen Morgen. Chandler Scott is a Marine Biologist who keeps her private life private. Corey Joslen is intrigued by Chandler from the moment she meets her. Chandler is forced to finally open her life up to Corey. It backfires in Corey's face and sends her running. Will either woman learn to trust her natural instinct?

Secluded Heart by Graysen Morgen. Chase Leery is an overworked cardiac surgeon with a group of best friends that have an opinion and a reason for everything. When she meets a new artist named Remy Sheridan at her best friend's art gallery she is captivated by the reclusive woman. When Chase finds out why Remy is so sheltered will she put her career on the line to help her or is it too difficult to love someone with a secluded heart?

In Love, at War by Graysen Morgen. Charley Hayes is in the Army Air Force and stationed at Ford Island in Pearl Harbor. She is the commanding officer of her own female-only service squadron and doing the one thing she loves most, repairing airplanes. Life is good for Charley, until the day she finds herself falling in love while fighting for her life as her country is thrown haphazardly into World War II. Can she survive being in love and at war?

Fast Pitch by Graysen Morgen. Graham Cahill is a senior in college and the catcher and captain of the softball team. Despite being an all-star pitcher, Bailey Michaels is young and arrogant. Graham and Bailey are forced to get to know each other off the field in order to learn to work together on the field. Will the extra time pay off or will it drive a nail through the team?

Submerged by Graysen Morgen. Assistant District Attorney Layne Carmichael had no idea that the sexy woman she took home from a local bar for a one night stand would turn out to be someone she would be prosecuting months later. Scooter is a Naval Officer on a submarine who changes women like she changes uniforms. When she is accused of a heinous crime she is shocked to see her latest conquest sitting across from her as the prosecuting attorney.

Vow of Solitude by Austen Thorne. Detective Jordan Denali is in a fight for her life against the ghosts from her past and a Serial Killer taunting her with his every move. She lives a life of solitude and plans to keep it that way. When Callie Marceau, a curious Medical Examiner, decides she wants in on the biggest case of her career, as well as, Jordan's life, Jordan is powerless to stop her.

Igniting Temptation by Sydney Canyon. Mackenzie Trotter is the Head of Pediatrics at the local hospital. Her life takes a rather unexpected turn when she meets a flirtatious, beautiful fire fighter. Both women soon discover it doesn't take much to ignite temptation.

One Night by Sydney Canyon. While on a business trip, Caylen Jarrett spends an amazing night with a beautiful stripper. Months later, she is shocked and confused when that same woman re-enters her life. The fact that this stranger could destroy her career doesn't bother her. C.J. is more terrified of the feelings this woman stirs in her. Could she have fallen in love in one night and not even known it?

Fine by Sydney Canyon. Collin Anderson hides behind a façade, pretending everything is fine. Her workaholic wife and best friend are both oblivious as she goes on an emotional journey, battling a potentially hereditary disease that her mother has been diagnosed with. The only person who knows what is really going on, is Collin's doctor. The same doctor, who is an acquaintance that she's always been attracted to, and who has a partner of her own.

Shadow's Eyes by Sydney Canyon. Tyler McCain is the owner of a large ranch that breeds and sells different types of horses. She isn't exactly thrilled when a Hollywood movie producer shows up wanting to film his latest movie on her property. Reegan Delsol is an up and coming actress who has everything going for her when she lands the lead role in a new film, but there one small problem that could blow the entire picture.

Light Reading: A Collection of Novellas by Sydney Canyon. Four of Sydney Canyon's novellas together in one book, including the bestsellers Shadow's Eyes and One Night.

Visit us at www.tri-pub.com